"Most people will never see this Light in its
physical manifestation because they are out of
touch with this aspect of themselves, but make
no mistake, it burns in every living thing."

—Tuguna the Eldre

scargen: book 2

the dragon within

by

casey caracciolo

illustrated by casey caracciolo

roundstone
PUBLISHING

To ANNORA,

"They say money can't
buy happiness, but
it can buy BOOKS,
and that's close
enough."

9/3/16

ISBN 10: 0692426221
ISBN 13: 978-0692426227

Printed in the U.S.A.
First Edition: September 2015
Edited by Shanna Compton, Joe Hansche,
Christine Carbone, and Casey Caracciolo
Typesetting by Shanna Compton

Visit scargen.com

To my little brother Bobby:

The demons
can't
find you now.

I hope
one day to
walk with
you in the
Spirit Realm.

You are missed.

 contents

the dragon within

prologue
childhood demons

Guangzhou, China—Thirteen years before the return of Grimm

"What we are looking for should be just up ahead," said their masked guide. The man wore a mostly gray, full faced helmet that amplified his voice. The helmet had eyeholes that glowed white and a circular symbol on the forehead. The symbol was blue, circled in a white border with a white icon in the center—an Ancient rune of some sort. The man wore a tactical vest under his black jacket and tactical gloves. He looked like a soldier, but not from any military Marcus had ever encountered.

The group consisted of the Second Marcus Slade, Captain Nevin Cox, Dr. Khalid Farod and his son Gamil, four lava trolls, a squadron of thirty-five Riders, and General Grayden Arkmalis, with the masked stranger guiding them. Marcus did not know what this man had told Arkmalis, but something must have struck the General as important. The young General had not left Grimm Tower since returning from the battle that killed Tollin Grimm, but now willingly followed the strange man into the middle of one of the biggest theaters in the Tech War.

Four days prior, the stranger had shown up at the Tower unannounced, demanding an audience with twelve-year-old Grayden Arkmalis. The boy commander had agreed to the meeting, and now Marcus and the others followed the stranger on the young General's orders.

The helmeted stranger walked ahead of the rest of the Riders with the General at his side. Arkmalis carried the Scythe—Lord Grimm's old weapon—on his back. Marcus noticed the boy's markings had grown up both of his arms since last time he had seen the General.

"This is a bad idea," said Marcus Slade to his captain. "This place is crawling with wartifs."

"Trust me, I know. Do you think I don't know how much this smells like a pile of gorgol shit? We are traipsing around with three squadrons of Riders and four lava trolls through the streets of Guangzhou of all places, and I have little to no intel on why we are in the middle of China to begin with. We're sitting ducks out here," said Captain Nevin Cox. "I'm just following the little shit's orders."

"I understand, Captain."

"He's no leader compared to Grimm. Something about the kid just rubs me the wrong way, sitting around the Tower, wasting all of our time, but . . . orders are orders."

"It's just we don't usually stick our noses into Global Alliance business," said Marcus.

"I'm not so sure that's what we're doing, Marcus. Jakobsen."

"Yes, Captain." Jakobsen now stood at attention next to Cox.

"I want you to take the boys in your squadron and see what intel you can gather on the artif troop movements," said Cox. "Take the doc and his son with you. I wasn't comfortable bringing Gamil in the first place, but Doc insisted—won't go anywhere without him. Whatever shit we're about to step in, can't be anywhere as dangerous as a scouting mission."

"Yes, sir," said Jakobsen. Several aringi dropped down and flew off with one of the three squadrons that had teleported into the district.

"Where are your men flying off to?" asked the stranger.

"I thought it might be a good idea to see what the hell my men are walking into," said Cox.

"I told you to bring three squadrons for a reason, Captain. What we are looking for is very well protected, and those men will be needed."

"I think we will be just fine," interrupted Arkmalis.

"Very well, but you have been warned. This is a task not to be taken lightly."

"I agree," said the General. "You have my assurance that we will be just fine."

The stranger and the General walked up ahead.

"What was I saying?" asked Cox as he turned back towards Slade.

"You were saying you don't think it is GA business we're messing with."

"That's right. I overheard the weird masked man talking with his bodyguards. Apparently we are looking for something Grimm left here. We're supposed to find and retrieve it."

"What is it?" asked Marcus.

"I'm not certain," said the Captain. He leaned in to talk to Marcus in private. "With the energy rating I'm getting from him, he's definitely a fairly versed Necromancer. Grimm must have trusted this man with whatever-we're-looking-for's whereabouts, and Arkmalis probably thinks he can use it—add it to his collection of useless magical shit." Marcus had sensed this man's power as well, but did not want to jump to any conclusions without more information.

"What do you think he meant by *well protected*?"

"I guess we'll find out soon enough."

Marcus sighed. "I don't like that answer."

"That makes two of us."

The men hunkered down on the outskirts of the burning city. Artif corpses stained the abandoned streets. "Where are all the troops?" asked Captain Cox.

"It looks like most of them have been destroyed, but by wh—" Marcus was interrupted by a high pitched scream. The Second looked in the direction of the piercing noise. "It came from the northeast corner of that building." He looked down at his wristcom as his helmet engaged. He looked through the visor and saw the heat signature of something big. "Whatever it is, it's moving."

"What are you seeing?" asked Cox.

"I hate to say it, but it sounds and looks a lot like a demon," said Marcus. "But why would a demon be in the middle of Guangzhou?"

"Most likely protecting whatever we're here to get. Sumner."

"Yes, Captain." One of the younger Riders ran up next to the Captain. His head was shaven. The stubble matched the red in his attempt at a beard.

"Take four men and two trolls and check out that building."

"Yes, sir." The Rider grabbed four others. The five men began weaving through the dead streets towards the burnt out building. The two lava trolls followed slowly as the men entered the complex.

"I don't think that was wise," said the stranger.

"Good thing I didn't ask," replied the Captain.

"You'd be wise to heed my warning, Captain. A High Demon, especially a crag, is not a conjuring to take lightly."

A High Demon? thought Marcus.

"When were you gonna share that little tidbit of info?" asked the Captain.

"It was not pertinent information until now." Marcus heard the noise of laser fire.

"Abort the mission, Sumner," commanded the Second into his wristcom.

No response.

"Sumner, do you copy?"

No response.

"Respond, Sumner. That's an order."

"H-h-he's in here," relied Sumner in a whisper. "I saw him."

"Who?" asked Marcus.

"Nelson's g-g-gone," said Sumner.

"What is happening in there?"

"H-h-h-he devoured h-h-h-him. R-r-right in front of me. Sweens don't look much better, man."

"Who devoured him?"

"His arms are gone, man. N-n-n-no. H-h-he's looking for me," said Sumner.

"Pull yourself together."

"Ahhhhhhhh!" screamed Sumner. The transmission broke off. The interference coincided with an explosion from the south side of the building. Two Riders backed their way out of the smoke. Their escape was abruptly stopped by the demon's quick strike. He tore through the first Rider and then spun to decapitate the second. The beast screamed again, shaking the ground. Bones protruded out of the monster as it stood upright. A bone mask adorned the demon's face. It resembled a skull with two large teeth jutting down its side. It was a crag as the helmeted man had warned.

The two trolls engaged the demon. The demon jumped onto the back of the first lava troll. The other troll sliced at the demon with his stone axe, but the shadowy creature moved at the last second. The axe sunk into the first lava troll's back. Magma sprayed outward from the wound as the rock creature fell to the ground with the weapon stuck in his form. The remaining troll stood defenseless. The demon struck quickly, bisecting the troll.

"Where are you? I can smell your human flesh. Fight me now. For I am Vaw, the Viscerator, High Demon of the Depths, humble servant of Lord Narg. Who dares interfere with my conjuring?"

"Fire!" yelled Captain Cox. The Riders moved on the command, simultaneously brandishing their laser weapons, and began the attack. If the GA did not know they were there before, they did now.

Vaw moved with startling speed. He had decimated the first wave, turning in a flash to destroy ten more men in one fast motion. The smoke trailed behind him as he moved closer to the remaining Riders.

Captain Nevin Cox stood on what remained of an armored vehicle—a casualty of the Tech War. He pulled back his hands and pushed forward. Energy streamed at the High Demon. The attack caught Vaw off guard, hitting him in the left side. The explosion kicked up a black cloud of smoke. The firing ceased as the smoke cleared.

The bone demon grabbed the Captain so fast there was no time for Marcus to react. "That was very impressive, human. You have any more tricks you would like to show me?"

The Captain dangled in the giant beast's grip. The demon closed his hand slowly as Cox screamed. Marcus raised his hand and pulsed electricity in the direction of the demon.

It hit the monster in the back, causing the demon to drop the Captain. Cox's body crumpled onto the street. Marcus intensified the pulse. The High Demon turned and raced at Marcus. Instantly a terrible pain hit Marcus's midsection as he flew across the street into a pile of rubble. Marcus slowly lifted himself up. He knew the demon would be on him soon, and it would be over swiftly.

"Enough, beast!" yelled the young General. "I suppose I will have to deal with you myself."

The demon pivoted to see his challenger. "You? What could a little boy possibly do to stop Vaw, the Viscerator? I will enjoy eating your entr—"

The red energy blew back the demon, cutting off his words and shooting him through the wall of the adjacent building. "Do I have your undivided attention yet, beast?"

The demon lifted himself out of the rubble and tilted his masked head. The blank stare of the mask was mesmerizing and unsettling to Marcus. It did not seem to faze the young General. Arkmalis jumped across the parked aeromobiles in the direction of the crag. The demon spun and unleashed his attack. The boy dashed to the left avoiding the dark energy. Arkmalis planted his feet and pulled the oversized Scythe from his back. He twirled it by its bone handle and slashed in the direction of the demon. The resulting wave hit the monster's left arm, disintegrating the appendage. The creature shrieked in pain. Once the beast ceased his wailing, Marcus heard another cry in the distance. *A girl?*

Marcus heard the girl's cry coming from the building from which the demon had emerged. He rushed into the structure through the makeshift doorway the demon's rampage had created. The stranger stood in the center of the rubble. His jacket had been tossed aside, exposing his tattooed arms. He held the body of a dead woman.

"Where is it? This is where I left it. No, no, it can't be!" yelled the stranger. His eyes were mad with dark energy as he dropped the corpse and turned towards Marcus. The dark marks on his arms began to glow red. Marcus noticed the similarities between this man's distinct markings and the General's. "Where is it?" The man was outwardly upset and frantic.

"I'm not sure what you're talking about. Is it what we are here to find?"

"It is mine. I need it. It is beautiful."

"*What* is beautiful? Listen. I can't help if I don't know what you are talking about."

"The stone, human. My beautiful blue stone!"

Human? thought Marcus. "Maybe it's somewhere around here. I can help—*after* we deal with the crag."

"The boy is dealing with the demon. Finding the stone is the priority." He raised a necklace that was lacking a centerpiece. "The inset is missing. I can no longer feel the stone's power. It must not be here . . . but this is where I left it." The man was now arguing with himself.

Marcus ignored the babbling man. *Where did that scream come from?* To the right of the deranged stranger, a pile of rubble moved slightly.

"They must have found it . . . water-breathing scum," said the stranger. "They must have t-t-t-taken it back. It's over. I'll never f-f-find it again. I-I-I don't know . . . what am I supposed to do?"

Marcus ran and began to clear the rocks from the pile. He had moved three of the bigger pieces of concrete when he saw her face. A small girl lay unconscious under the crumbled cement, maybe five years old. Marcus felt for her pulse. *She's still alive.* He reached down and plucked her from her stone bed. He looked at the stranger, who by now had begun to ramble incoherently. Dark energy encompassed his form. His tattoos glowed brighter.

The remaining roof began to collapse. "I will get you out of here," said Marcus to the girl. The Second ran out of the deteriorating building, cradling her.

Marcus turned to look at the building just as a black, wingless dragon appeared. The flying Aequos flew straight into the building.

"Noooo—" the stranger's voice echoed from the structure. The scream ended abruptly. The dragon flew straight up out of the structure and streaked across the sky. As Marcus stared into the sky, the stranger's helmet smashed to the earth next to him.

"What the—" questioned the Second. *A black Aequos? Did the dragon take what this man was looking for—what we were sent here to get? Or was its attack on the stranger personal?* One thing Marcus knew for certain: dragons are not to be betrayed. The Second assumed the worst for the stranger's fate.

His wristcom began to ring. He looked down and saw that Jakobsen had been trying to contact him, but Marcus ignored it, turning his attention back to the little girl in his arms. Whatever Jakobsen needed would have to wait. "It's going to be all right. You are safe now." He heard Vaw shriek, but it was too late to react.

The demon landed next to him and ripped the girl from his arms. "She is mine, puny mortal," announced the monster, shoving the Second aside. He began to slowly back away from Marcus, the unconscious girl dangling from his right hand.

"You should probably turn around," said Marcus, trying to distract the demon.

"You mortals are amusing. Did you think for one second I was going to fall for that?"

"Suit yourself."

"I'll take care of you, just like I did that boy and his pathetic blade."

"I've never known Marcus to be anything but honest, demon," said the General from behind the beast.

"But I . . . k-k-killed you. There's no way a human could survive." He turned around to see the boy.

"Well, I'm not your typical human." The demon stumbled backwards, and Marcus opened fire. The blasts did little damage, but they were only intended as distraction. The dark creature turned and lurched towards Marcus.

The diversion was all the General needed to press his advantage. He jumped into the air and sliced down through the demon's form, splitting it in two.

"Put the girl down, beast," commanded the General. The split monster turned towards his attacker.

"You cannot destroy me. I am Vaw, the Viscerator. You are just a human boy . . ."

"We shall see about that." The boy's energy discharge shocked the demon, forcing him to drop the girl. Marcus moved to catch her. Soon the High Demon was engulfed in red electricity. His massive form spasmed as the current enveloped him. The dark figure convulsed and contorted, shrieking a deafening bawl.

"Noooooooo!" yelled Vaw as his form disintegrated into a black mist. His bone mask fell to the street.

Marcus's wristcom beeped. This time he answered. "Is anyone there?" The voice came across his wristcom, and the image of Dalco Jakobsen appeared above it.

"What is the problem Jakobsen?"

"We've b-b-been attacked b-b-by a dragon—an Aequos, b-b-but it was black. It came from nowhere, like it knew we were here. The Farod boy and I are the only s-s-s-survivors . . . it happened so f-f-f-fast. The boy is not d-d-doing well. He just watched his father die." Dr. Khalid Farod was dead along with twelve other Riders.

"We haven't fared much better. We have a lot of casualties and several injuries that need attention. Come to our location," said Marcus as he surveyed the battlefield. His eyes stopped on the Captain. In all the commotion, he had forgotten about him. Marcus rushed over to the Captain and delicately put down the girl.

The man was barely alive. He leaned down and grabbed the Captain's hand. "We'll get you back to the Tower, sir. You're going to be fine."

"You're a shitty liar," joked the Captain. "I'm not going anywhere." He choked. "This is just as good a place as any to die."

"It was a pleasure serving under you, Captain."

"Please, call me Nevin, Marcus. This is not the time for formalities."

"It was a pleasure, Nevin."

"The pleasure was all mine, Marcus. The pleasure . . . was . . .

all . . . mi—" The Captain quietly faded. Marcus reached down and shut the Captain's eyelids. He picked up the girl again and turned to look at the General. Arkmalis sheathed the Scythe at his back and knelt.

The boy picked up the demon's mask with both hands. It was all that remained of Vaw. Arkmalis raised it to his face. The mask conformed as he positioned it on his head, glowing for a brief moment. Arkmalis turned towards Marcus. His eyes burned red through the mask's eyeholes. "How does it look?" asked Arkmalis.

"Intimidating," said Marcus without thinking.

"Perfect. Secure the girl. We're getting out of here as soon as Jakobsen lands. Our work here is done."

"But sir, we haven't found anything."

"I said, our work here is done . . . *Captain* Slade." His eyes were different. There was no child behind that mask—only a demon.

the dragon within

1

promoted

"He looks like he's dead," said Nolan Taunt. "We are sure he's not . . . right?" Taunt had arrived to conduct a routine check on the tech that kept General Grayden Arkmalis alive. It had been months since Taunt had seen the General.

"He's not dead. Not yet anyway," answered Captain Marcus Slade. The three Riders stared at the man floating in the dark liquid. "But he probably wishes he were." Tubes and wires dangled from the buoyant, lifeless body. Holoscreens flanked both sides of the tank.

"The damage done to his body has triggered this state," said Gamil Farod as he pointed at one of the holoscreens on the right. "His vitals have been stabilized by the medibots, but he has not been conscious since the battle with the Scargen boy."

It had been six months. The General had not once stirred inside the stasis chamber. Farod was doing his best to revive Arkmalis, but it was starting to seem futile. If it had not been for Tollin Grimm's insistence, Farod would have ceased his attempts a long time ago.

It pained Marcus to think about that day. That was the day that Arkmalis had been defeated—the day Marcus had lost Evangeline.

Marcus quickly dismissed the distracting train of thought. Evangeline was due back from her mission soon, and he was to meet her at the Tower. For what purpose, he was uncertain. Despite her rank as his Second, she refused to communicate directly with Marcus unless absolutely necessary. Lord Grimm had ordered the two of them to meet with him once she returned. Marcus was envious of the time Evangeline had been spending with Grimm. The Captain regretted the rift that had formed between himself and Evangeline. *I wish things were different*, thought Marcus. *I miss her.*

"I do not know what else to do for him," said Farod. "It is up to him at this point."

"If anyone can survive in this situation, it'd be him," said the Captain. He may have had his differences with the General, but Marcus never wanted this—not for the man who had saved his and Evangeline's lives thirteen years ago.

The sound of the door opening roused him from his musing. Evangeline entered the room. Her robotic legs moved as well as her biological ones once had. Farod and Taunt had constructed the appendages for the Second following the battle at the temple in Japan. The fall from her aringi had mangled both of her legs beyond repair. "Can you guys give us the room?"

"Sure, Captain," said Farod. He and Taunt left the medical facility.

She turned her head away from Marcus. This blew her red hair back over her shoulder, exposing the black mark on her neck. The marking was similar to Arkmalis's and the helmeted stranger's tattoos. They were not identical, but the resemblance was apparent.

"That's new."

"Are you trying to talk to me?"

"No, I *am* talking to you."

"Well, stop."

"Don't you think it's time we talked?"

"No, Captain, I do not. I am only here because I was ordered to come get you by Lord Grimm."

"I'm sorry." There was a long silence as both parties endured their mutual loss for words.

"You lied to me when I was the most vulnerable." She was right, and the Captain knew it, but at the time he was doing what he thought best for Evangeline.

"Pria is dead, and there's no changing that, but I did not know that not telling you would lead to this. There is nothing I can say that will bring your aringi back."

"I trusted you, and you betrayed me."

"I am sorry, Evangeline."

"I don't care."

Marcus stood there in shock and silence. He did not know what to say, so he said nothing. His wristcom rang as if on cue. A hologram of Corbin, the imp servant, appeared above his wrist.

" 'ello, Capt'n. Lord Grimm will see you two now."

"We will be there momentarily, Corbin." The Second had already made her way out of the door. *What have I done?*

She doesn't care? Evangeline's words echoed through his mind as Marcus approached the chamber doors. Two large lava trolls occupied separate sides of the entrance. He could already hear the troll's banter.

"It's been chaotic around 'ere lately, 'asn't it? I mean no one's seen duh General in ages, and people are startin' to fink duh Scargen boy killed 'im," said Gibgot, standing to the left of the doorway.

"Don't get me started on Lord Grimm," said Fronik.

" 'ee looks like a bleedin' mummy. Scares duh magma out of me," said Gibgot, looking over at Fronik. "And 'ere I fought 'ee was uvverwise deceased. Who saw dat comin'?"

"Well, I did. It was sort uv obvious wasn't it? I mean lookin' back on it, duh clues were all dere."

"I was too busy finkin' he'd been killed by duh Gauntlet lady from before," said Gibgot, looking perplexed.

"Dat bit was confusin', to be honest," replied Fronik. "Trapped in one uv dose bleedin' stones for fifteen years. No fanks. I would've ravver been dead. I can get a bit claustrophobic, can't I?"

" 'ello, Capt'n. How goes it?" asked Gibgot as he noticed Marcus approaching.

"It goes," said the Captain. He stopped in front of the two lava trolls. He was stalling. The last thing the Captain wanted to do was go to Grimm's chamber. "What are you two doing in here?" asked the Captain. "Aren't you two usually stationed at the main entrance?"

"Commander Suvios promoted us," said Fronik.

"Yeah, we 'av accepted duh prestigious honor uv guardin' Lord Grimm."

"What happened to the other guards?" asked Marcus, somewhat curious.

"Oh, you didn't 'ear? Poor guys. Bofe uv dem got split in bloody two by duh Scargen boy in Japan."

"It's a shame really, bofe were nice enough blokes."

"Especially Bob. I mean what's 'is wife supposed ta do wif duh six lit'l ones muckin' about?" asked Fronik, lowering his head.

"It's always duh nice ones, isn't it?"

"Sad really. What are da odds dey bofe would die?" asked Fronik. "Wrong place, wrong time, I suppose."

"War is not pretty, is it?" asked Gibgot.

"No it is not," said Marcus. "My condolences. Gentlemen." He bowed his head and continued past the two trolls. They returned his bow and continued talking.

"I fink I've got post-traumatic stress disorder meeself," said Gibgot. Fronik started to laugh. "Should you really be laughin' at dat? I 'aven't been right since Japan, 'av I? All dose bloody tree samurai runnin' about, hackin' lava trolls in two wif dose bloody spirit swords. Every time I even see a tree now, I start weepin' a bit. I don't even like to say the word *leave*, in any context. Damn, I just said it."

"Said what?" asked Fronik.

"*Leave* . . . damn, second time. You did dat on purpose."

"You should maybe *leave* the subject alone," said Fronik as he smiled.

"Fronik."

"What, you don't be-*leave* me?"

"Seriously?"

"It will probably make you feel more re-*leaved*."

"Stop messin' about. I'm bein' serious. Dat battle's done me 'ed well in. It's made me bloody mental. Some times I wake up at night because I fink I smell sap."

"You are *bark*-in', mate."

"I just openly admitted as much, and I don't fink my mental hardships should be fodder for your comedic transgressions."

"Do you even know what you just said?"

"No, but it sounded good," said Gibgot as he cocked his brow. "I'm just sayin', it would seem a logical extension of an armed service to have duh proper psychologically learned staff to 'andle such a situation."

"I'm gonna start chargin' ya soon to listen to duh bullocks dat spews forf from dat ravver large mouf uv yours."

"Fair enough, but I want to start when I was a boy den. It all started when me mum . . ." Gibgot's words trailed off as Marcus approached the chamber.

Marcus entered the chamber and moved hastily down the long corridor. Lord Grimm was awaiting the Captain. Marcus was not looking forward to this encounter. The two of them had not spoken since Grimm had returned to the Temple.

When he reached the throne room he saw Lord Grimm speaking with Evangeline. The two of them were looking at a holographic projection of what looked like a schematic of an airship, but not like any airship Marcus had ever seen. There was a comfortability between the two that made him feel uneasy. *He has to be behind her change,* thought Marcus. *But why?*

Grimm put an end to Marcus's pondering. "It's so nice of you to join us, Marcus." Grimm turned towards the Captain as the schematic vanished.

"My Lord," said Marcus. Grimm was dressed in a long, sleek black robe. The hood and several accents on the robe were red. His face was newly bandaged, and he wore long black gloves that covered his forearms. In the left glove was an embedded wristcom. The right glove had an opening on the palm, exposing the black stone. His Scythe was strapped to his back.

"Evangeline and I were just . . . talking. I trust all is well with the General?"

"There has been no change in his condition, my Lord," said the Captain.

"That is good news, Marcus. Good news indeed," said Grimm.

"I don't understand."

"He is alive, Marcus," said Grimm. He walked towards Marcus slowly. "That means there's a chance, and that gives us hope, and hope can do wonders if wielded properly." Grimm stopped walking. "The Scargen boy's power is extraordinary. Weak, mind you, in comparison to my own, but extraordinary nonetheless." His words escaped through the open area of the bandages that wrapped his face. At first, he sounded as overconfident as Arkmalis used to be, but something made Marcus believe that Grimm's assertions were far more calculated. "Enough about the General. Evangeline has just finished debriefing me on her latest mission."

"As I was saying, your friend was correct in his assertions," said the Second. "This could be exactly what we need. It just requires a specific substantial power source."

A mission that I wasn't read in on, thought Marcus.

"Excellent news. I imagined it was not going to be easy to find, but no matter, my dear. I didn't bring you here to talk solely about that." The bandaged man paced to his left. "I have put a rather large bounty on Thomas Scargen."

"For his death?" asked Evangeline.

"No. He is to be brought to me alive." He paused for a few seconds and then smiled. "I now have use for him."

"What possible use could you have for him?" asked Evangeline. "He nearly killed the General."

"I am aware of this fact, Second. But sometimes an appetite for vengeance can cloud rational thoughts. The boy has a unique skill set that could prove most beneficial to our cause."

"Is this our next mission?" asked the Captain.

"No, Marcus. I have someone else in charge of recovering the Scargen boy. I have other plans for you two, but there is a matter I must address before I get to that." Lord Grimm began to pace with his hands behind his back.

I wonder what he's talking about, thought Marcus.

"An army cannot survive long without a leader, much like a body without a head. I hear the murmurs from the Riders and the trolls." He slowly moved towards the Captain. "And in Grayden's absence, I believe a replacement needs to be named for the interim. Mind you this is a temporary arrangement—just until Grayden recovers."

If he recovers, thought Marcus.

"When he is back to full strength, he will take his rightful place as General." That seemed far from a reality. "What we are trying to do will take leadership and a strong will to accomplish." Grimm reached Marcus and put a hand on his shoulder. "I have thought about this for weeks, and, to me, there is only one logical successor to him."

Marcus was trying to focus on the words but all he could think about was her and his mistake. The last thing he could think about now was a promotion.

"I need someone with the strength and will to accomplish any task I set forth. I'd like to introduce the new General of the Grimm Legions . . ." Marcus looked up at the man just as he turned away. Grimm raised his hand towards the Second. "General Evangeline."

2

the dark beast

"Are we sure Mancer Bodes knows what 'ee's talking about? I 'aven't seen anyfing that resembles anyfing man-made," said Malcolm Warwick as he trudged through the jungle. Light orbs illuminated the path.

"He was right about Amara Scornd and the yellow stone," said Yareli Chula. Wiyaloo the Spirit Ghost Warrior walked just behind her, staff in hand.

"And look 'ow dat one almost turned out," replied Malcolm with a wink. " 'ee almost got us all bloody killed, didn't 'ee?"

"Give thy thoughts no tongue, Malcolm. If Mancer Bodes is anything, he is reliable," said Anson Warwick. "He would not have sent us all the way to the Andes Mountains unless it was for a good reason, and I think we both know that finding out as much as possible about the Gauntlet is quite a good reason. Besides, and don't ever tell him I said this, the man is rarely incorrect."

"I suppose you're right, but that isn't getting us any closer to finding duh bloody place, is it? Go find some lost Incan city, but dat's about all we got to go on. It's bloody mental."

"The place we are looking for far predates the Incas," said Anson. "And remember, we are doing this for Thomas."

"For all we know Tommy and dat lit'l samurai of 'is aren't ever coming back to Sirati. Dey're probably out 'avin' duh time uv dere lives somewhere while we traipse around anuvver bleedin' jungle. I didn't 'av to go dis far to walk around aimlessly frough a jungle. I do 'av quite a nice one back 'ome."

"I think you got too much sun today, Malcolm." *He still hasn't told me how he is the only vampire that I've ever seen walk around in sunlight*, thought Yareli. "Ziza has sent Thomas to look for the next stone, and I'm sure that's what he's doing." *I hope that's what he's doing.* It had been six months since she had seen either Thomas or Itsuki. They had left immediately after Thomas recovered from his accelerated training with the High Mancer. Ziza insisted on complete secrecy—no communication unless absolutely necessary. "I'd think you'd be more trusting of Thomas, since he did save your life—all of our lives."

"I know, I know. I didn't mean nuffin' by it. I just miss duh daft git." He lit a cigarette and took a drag. "And I'm just bored mind you. Everyfing 'ere looks the bloody same, and dere are far too many snakes for my liking."

"Well, at least vampires and werewolves can see in the dark," said Yareli.

"Wolves do not have acute vision," said Anson. "But I get your point. Maybe we should make camp for the night. You need to rest more than we do."

"I'm fine. I'd rather keep looking, if it's all the same. We must be close."

"Very well." The wolfman raised his head and began to sniff. "Do you smell that?"

"Somefing's burning," replied Malcolm. "And it's not my cigarette." He smelled the air as well. "I fink it's coming closer to us." The large leaves began to blow above them. Something flashed across the sky. The four companions were suddenly surrounded by flames.

"What was that?" asked Yareli as the trees burned around them.

"I cannot be certain, but if I had to venture a guess, I would say it was a dragon," answered Anson. "A powerful one at that."

"Agreed," said Wiyaloo in his deep monotone voice.

"The better question might be, why is it attacking us? What did we do to piss off a bloody dragon?" asked Malcolm as he moved out of the way of a falling tree.

"I'm not sure. Dragons can be extremely territorial," said Anson. "If we somehow wandered into its territory, that would explain the behavior."

"Then I say we shove off out of its bloody territory before duh bleedin' fing circles back," suggested Malcolm.

"Yes, I concur. Let us make an honorable retreat," said Anson.

"Run!" yelled Yareli as the unseen beast returned, spraying fire across the tree canopy.

The three of them bolted into the jungle, weaving in and out of the trees. Yareli stopped as they entered a clearing. She had no choice—abandoning the cover of the trees would have left them vulnerable. The rest of the company followed suit. Wiyaloo appeared behind Yareli. The group stared across to the opposite tree line.

On the far side of the clearing stood ten large robotic soldiers. They appeared to be humanoid lizards wearing colossal tech suits. The chest regions of several of the suits were opened, exposing the scaly inhabitants. It was hard to discern where the Lizards stopped and the robotics began. Yareli counted ten distinct styles of well-armed machinery. The suits varied in height from five to seven meters—all with oversized hands and feet. The suits' armor and tech were intimidating.

"They do not look remotely friendly," said Yareli.

"Bloody 'ell. What are dey doin' 'ere wif all dat firepower? Duh dragon or whatever dat fing was isn't bloody bad enough?"

"The beast no longer pursues," murmured Wiyaloo.

"Well, dat's good. One less fing and all," said Malcolm. "But what about duh bloody reptiles dat currently block our paf? Do you fink dey wanna play nice?" As he spoke, a laser blast whizzed past his head. "I'll take dat as a resounding no."

"Attack!" hissed the Lizard who appeared to be in charge. All of the creatures' weapons now pointed at the group. The Lizards shut the cockpits located on the chests of the tech suits, preparing for battle. The tech-suited soldiers began to swiftly advance, shaking the ground with their heavy footfalls.

Anson ran out to meet the mechanical soldiers. His shirt ripped down the back as he transformed into wolf form, leaping at the first soldier. The Lizard opened fire. Anson pried one of the armor plates from the soldier's left arm. The Lizard reached over and grabbed Anson with his other hand, plucking the wolf off and throwing him back in the direction of the group. Anson slid to a halt next to his brother who had also engaged one of the Lizards.

"Dat looked like it 'urt, mate," said Malcolm, firing an energy attack at an assaulting Lizard. The vampire turned to look at his brother.

"If I were you, I'd worry about your own fate," said Anson. Just as he said this, a blast spun Malcolm from where he stood, disintegrating his right arm.

"Ahhh!" screamed Malcolm.

"Where is Bartleby?" asked Yareli.

" 'ee said 'ee was gonna find somewhere to . . . ahhh . . . take a bloody nap, and to give 'im a ring when we . . . ahh . . . needed to bloody leave. Dat smarts a bit." Malcolm sprang back up on his feet. His arm began to regenerate. "Dat's a bloody shame, really. I quite liked dis jacket."

"We need to get out of here." Yareli reached back into her seemingly empty quiver. She effortlessly drew and nocked the spirit arrow into her bow. Her powers had grown since she had begun training with Ziza. Together they had learned that she could summon any area's indigenous animal spirits as well as the ones she was familiar with from home. When Thomas did come back, she would be ready.

Yareli loosed the spirit arrow at two of the large robotic soldiers. *Focus*, thought Yareli. The spirit arrow plunged into the advancing Lizards, transforming into a group of spider monkeys. The monkeys erupted in howls and screams as they latched onto the two tech-suited Lizards, tearing at the metallic parts of the soldiers. The two soldiers began haphazardly firing their laser weapons at themselves and one another, attempting to destroy the infestation of monkeys, but hitting each other in the process. "The signal's dead," said Yareli, lifting up her wristcom. "I can't get through to Bartleby."

"Why am I not surprised?" said Anson as he unleashed a volley of orange energy spheres at the smallest of the mechanical soldiers. Several of the blasts hit their target. The right leg of the soldier burst into flames. "We should head for cover."

Wiyaloo appeared above the soldiers and dropped onto one soldier's headpiece. The spirit ghost twirled his staff, pointing it at the chest of the tech suit. White energy flowed through the staff and into the center mass of the Lizard. The suit erupted in sparks and spasmed as the soldier fought to regain control. Wiyaloo reappeared next to Anson. "Agreed." They ran towards the rock formations that circled the clearing.

"I'm not sure we can keep this pace," said Yareli. "We're hurting them, but they just keep getting back u—" A pulse from one of the Lizards struck the ground right below where she was running. "Ahhh!" The impact blew her ten feet in the air. Wiyaloo caught her before she could hit the ground. "I think I broke my leg!" yelled Yareli.

"Agreed," said Wiyaloo. Blue light emanated from Wiyaloo, surrounding the form of the young woman. The energy gathered in the broken leg and then faded.

"You are healed, my lady," said the Spirit Ghost Warrior.

"Thanks," said Yareli as she jumped out of his arms. "Where are Anson and Malc—" Her words were cut off by the sound of weapon systems engaging. She was surrounded by the Lizards.

"Freezzze!" commanded the tallest of the tech soldiers. "There issss no means of esssscape. Continuing to fight would be futile."

"I'm not so sure about that," said a man's voice from behind the soldiers. It did not belong to either Warwick, and Wiyaloo stood next to her. "I would say you're being a bit dramatic." A red energy pulse incapacitated the tall soldier. His tech sparked and the lights of the suit's eyes extinguished. The nine remaining Lizards turned in unison. "That got your attention." Yareli could now see the origin of the voice. It was a Chinese man, about twenty years of age. A fireball churned in his left hand as red energy surrounded him. "So are you going to let the lady go?"

The soldiers simultaneously attacked. The man jumped back and forth dodging their blasts, gradually drawing them away from Yareli and Wiyaloo.

"Come this way," commanded a second unfamiliar male voice. Yareli spun around. A Sea Turtle stood in front of her. In one flipper he held a staff—the other was beckoning. His markings were stunning. His flippers were split into four fingers, and the bottom set were elongated into legs and feet. He looked as though he had walked right out of Sirati. "Follow me. I know what it is you seek." He turned and took off into the jungle. Yareli followed behind him.

He's fast for a Turtle, thought Yareli. "What about the other guy?"

"Garron will be fine. He knows when to fight and he knows when to run. As long as the dark beast doesn't come back."

"What is the dark beast?"

"We have never gotten a good look at it. It only comes out at night, and it moves at astonishing speeds."

"Could it be a dragon?"

"I have never seen one in person, so I cannot be certain."

"Where are my friends?" asked Yareli.

"The wolf and the vampire?"

"Yes."

"They're safe. My brother and sister retrieved them shortly before you were surrounded by the Skinx."

This was a relief to Yareli, but she had more questions. "Those Lizards?"

"Yes, they are the Skinx. They are, like you, looking for the city."

"How do you know what I am looking for?"

"The Ancestors have said as much. Now get ready."

"For what?"

A large rock flipped up in front of them, as if on a hinge. In one motion, the Turtle sheathed his staff into its scabbard on his shelled back and dove head first into the opening.

Yareli fell down the hole before she could stop herself, but she did not free fall. She began sliding down what felt like a water slide. The Turtle rocketed in front of her.

"It's the only way to travel!" he yelled over the splashing water.

The series of slides was ingeniously designed, winding down endlessly into the underground cavern. They turned a corner, and that is when she saw it. *Huacas*, thought Yareli. The city was as enormous as it was old. Purple lights were strewn throughout the subterranean metropolis, illuminating it well enough for her to get a sense of its size.

The ride splashed to an end, emptying into a pool that was lit from below. Yareli lifted herself out of the water. She was exhausted and out of breath. The Turtle was circling around her.

"We're here," said the Turtle.

"This is the lost city of Huacas?" Yareli looked around as she stood in the knee-deep pool. "When Ziza described it to us, he did not do it justice, but I guess seeing something in a book and seeing it for yourself are two very different things."

"You are the first outsider to visit since Garron's arrival almost ten years ago."

"I didn't think an underground city would be so well lit."

"It wouldn't be were it not for the power source."

"And what is that?" asked Yareli as she climbed out of the pool.

"The Gauntlet has powered this city for thousands of years."

"How is that possible?"

"I'd say it's superior engineering. Mind you we are only running on thirty percent power. It's been some years since its last charge. In its heyday it was something to behold."

"It still is," said Yareli. "It's breathtaking."

Wiyaloo suddenly appeared next to her. "Agreed," said the spirit ghost. "There is a strong spiritual presence here."

The city was carved out of the inside of the mountain. The symbols from the Ancient language were everywhere. *This place is narsh*, thought Yareli. She immediately pictured Thomas in her head. *He'd love to be here for this.*

The Turtle swam to the edge of the water and flipped out and onto the bank. He drew his staff from his back. "I'm sure you have questions. Tuguna will answer them when we arrive. Oh, and I almost forgot. My name's Turu."

"It's nice to meet you, Turu. This is Wiyaloo, and I am—"

"Yareli Chula," finished Turu.

His knowledge of her name surprised her. "How did you—"

"The Ancestors."

Yareli was confused. "And who's Tuguna?"

"He is the Ancient One—our master and teacher, The Decipherer and Keeper of Knowledge. He is Tuguna the Eldre."

"Okay. The Eldre is who we are supposed to meet," said Yareli, feeling slightly less confused.

"I am to bring you to him."

"Is that where my friends are?" asked Yareli.

"Yes. Now come. The Eldre awaits. He is eager to discuss the whereabouts of Thomas Scargen."

"Let me guess . . . the Ancestors?"

"You are a quick study, Yareli Chula."

3

tuguna the eldre

Turu led Yareli and Wiyaloo through the streets of Huacas. Throughout the metropolis, waterways paralleled the roads. *I bet Turu normally travels in those*, thought Yareli. She looked around as she walked. She could not believe how immense the underground city was, and that it was crawling with what looked like more Lizards.

"Who are they?" asked Yareli, leery of any Lizard at this point.

"These are not the same creatures that attacked you, if that is what you are worried about. These are the Salamen. They, like us, desire peace and understanding. The Skinx crave nothing but war and thrive on their greed. The Salamen and the Skinx could not be more different."

"Peaceful Lizards?"

"They are actually not Lizards at all," said Turu. "They are Amphibians—very strong swimmers."

"I guess you'd have to be to live here."

"It does help."

They walked up to an enormous building in the city's center. There was a statue of a large human man standing on the crest of a wave. He bore the Gauntlet. Yareli stared at the statue. Although the man did not look like him, it reminded her of Thomas.

"Who's the statue of?" asked Yareli.

"That's is Huacas's founder, Alican Dod. He was a true hero. He made this safe haven for my people and the Salamen."

"If you don't mind me asking, where did all of you come from?"

"When the Gauntlet created this city, there were some unexpected side effects."

"Say no more. Sirati has a similar situation with its indigenous species." They both made their way to the entrance of the building.

"Eventually the men left Huacas, leaving the Turtles, the Salamen, and the Skinx. The Turtles and the Salamen have coexisted here for ages. The same cannot be said about the Skinx. They have never shared the same values and traditions we have. Thousands of Salamen inhabit Huacas, although they prefer to be on the surface as much as they can. It's harder for us to protect them out there though, and that makes them easy targets for the Skinx to capture and enslave."

"No creature deserves to be held in captivity and forced to do anything against their will," said Yareli.

"That is why we have tried our best to nurture this safe haven. We have always done what has to be done to protect the Salamen as well as ourselves."

"How many of your kind are there?"

"Not as many as there used to be, but we make do."

"I'll say. This place is beautiful."

"The Salamen deserve the credit for the upkeep. My people are more the scholarly type as well as Huacas's guardians." The doors opened as they reached the entrance. The Turtle waved his flipper. "After you."

Yareli walked into the pristine building. Water flowed throughout the interior. A smaller Turtle approached Yareli and reached out its flipper, grabbing her hand and tugging.

"Don't mind her. She's never seen a human woman."

"Oh . . . hi there. What's your name?"

"Her name is Yaku," responded a third Turtle in a deep, authoritative voice. He jumped out of a nearby pool of water. He was the tallest of the three. "But you're wasting your breath. She doesn't ever talk."

"Well, she seems to want me to follow her."

"That's about right. She's all about business. I'm Kucha, Turu's and Yaku's older brother. The Eldre wants to see you."

"Well, let's not keep him waiting," said Yareli.

Kucha jumped into the pool and disappeared under the rippling water. Yaku and Turu followed.

"I guess I'm supposed to follow," said Yareli.

"Agreed," said Wiyaloo as he dissipated.

Yareli jumped into the pool. It was deeper than she had initially assumed. *I guess I should've brought a bathing suit.* She looked down into the water and saw where she was meant to swim. She ducked under the water and swam for the hole at the bottom of the pool. When she got closer the current took her. Yareli was no longer in control. She sped along a stone tube that dumped her out into another pool. She swam to the surface of the pool and pulled herself out of the water. She was out of breath.

The room was massive. Huge pillars held up the ceiling. Lights inside carved rock recesses illuminated the cavernous room. Turu, Kucha, and Yaku waited to one side. Yaku reached into her satchel and pulled out a jellyfish. She reached up, offering the specimen to Yareli.

"No thanks," said the young woman. Yaku shrugged her shoulders and chomped down on the jellyfish. She bit it in half and threw the other half to Turu who caught it in his mouth. This made Yaku smile.

"Your friends are over there," said Kucha, extending his flippered hand. She looked across the expanse of the room and saw the Warwicks. She ran over to meet them. Anson and Malcolm were also soaking wet. They stood among large, intricately carved stones that formed a semicircle. The etchings on these structures glowed a faint purple. Just outside this semicircle stood a monolith adorned with Ancient runes.

"Aren't you a sight for sore eyes," said Malcolm as he puffed away on his cigarette.

"Don't smoke in here, Malcolm," said Yareli.

"I told him the same," said Anson as he studied the stones.

"Aw'right, but just because you asked so nicely." The vampire put the cigarette out on the palm of his hand and tucked the butt into his pocket. "What were dose bloody Lizard cyborgs anyway?"

"Those are the Lacertan, the elite forces of the Skinx army," said Kucha. "They are formidable warriors in their own right, but the suits they are wearing are relatively new."

"What do you mean?" asked Yareli.

"Well, they have always used tech, but lately it seems . . . more advanced."

"What are they doing up there?" asked Yareli.

"They've been searching for our city for some time now, but they have not come close as of yet."

"Who is their leader?" asked Malcolm. "The best way to stop a snake is to cut off its bloody 'ed."

"Charming," said Anson, continuing to study the carved stones.

"I fought so," said Malcolm.

"It is hard to say who their leader could be, but the soldiers definitely have a commander."

"How can you be certain?" asked Yareli.

"They are too organized not to, but they will not disturb us down here. We are safe for now."

"Simply marvelous," said Anson as he stared more intently at the carvings in the rocks. He had not been paying full attention to the conversation. "This place is amazing."

"These stones are quite beautiful," said Yareli, touching the markings.

"That they are," said Garron, the man Yareli had seen during the battle. He had come out from behind one of the stones. "The Ancestor Stones are quite stunning works of art. We call them *tuqi*." The man was wearing a tight long sleeve shirt that seemed to be made for swimming. His hair was still wet. "I fell in love with this place long ago, and I have lived here ever since. I can't even imagine what it looked like at full power."

"And who are you?" asked Malcolm.

"He's the one who saved me when we were separated," said Yareli.

"The name's Garron, Garron Dar." He extended his hand to Malcolm who accepted it. He then shook Anson's hand.

When he reached Yareli, he delicately lifted her hand and kissed it. She was taken aback by the gesture, but she did not protest. In fact, she smiled at the man.

Interesting, thought Yareli. "The spiritual forces here are quite remarkable." She took back her hand.

"Agreed," said Wiyaloo as he appeared next to her.

"So what are we doin' 'ere?" asked Malcolm, waking Yareli from her daydreaming.

"I think what my brother here is so eloquently trying to ask is, what is it that we can do for you?" asked Anson. "Mancer Bodes said the message from the Eldre was enigmatic at best, but mentioned Thomas Scargen."

"The Eldre will explain everything," said Kucha. The three Turtles stood side by side.

"And where's 'ee at?" asked the vampire. "It's not like we 'aven't traveled a fair distance to see duh bloody man."

"He is communing with the Ancestors," said Garron. "He will join us shortly. Until then, there is much to show you."

Kucha, Turu, and Yaku moved into the middle of the semicircle. The Turtles' eyes glowed a bluish purple as violet fire sprang forth from the well at the circle's center. The energy began cohering into an image.

"Years ago, these lands were inhabited by an evil force," began Kucha. The image shifted into an army of demons. "Where they had come from was unknown, but wherever they walked, the land dried up and began to wither. The animals that once inhabited these lands became sick, riddled with diseases." The images appeared and dissolved, mirroring the story. "The villagers who had skills to do so confronted this evil with magic, but they were weak and poorly trained. The outcome was terrifying." Images of the conflict reflected in the purple fire. "Many died in the ensuing battle. The humans were divided on what to do next. One group moved far away from these lands, but the others stayed, refusing to let this evil move them from the lands that were their own. No matter what they tried, the evil could not be stopped. They needed help." A silhouette of a man on the horizon appeared. "They found it when Alican Dod arrived."

"The man wore a large stone Gauntlet on his right hand," continued Turu seamlessly, as if he had been telling the story all along. "Alican had learned of the evil from one of the fleeing villagers. He had a plan, and a proposition. He would eradicate the evil these men faced, and in exchange, he would be allowed to build himself a sanctuary. To do this he would need the village's sacred red gem."

"Although some were wary of sacrificing the sacred gem, the villagers had little choice," said Kucha, picking up the story once more. "They agreed to Alican's conditions and handed over the red stone. Once the gem touched his rock hand, the man vanished."

"We've seen dat trick before," said Malcolm, interrupting. Everyone looked at him. Yareli shot a particularly nasty expression in the vampire's direction. "Oh, sorry. Continue wif your fantastic tale."

"Dod returned a few days later noticeably more powerful," said Kucha. "He faced the evil force, and, with the stone hand and his newly amplified power, he vanquished it from these lands forever."

The vampire began to clap. "Dat's a fantastic fairytale, isn't it, but what was really going on?" asked Malcolm.

"The vampire is wiser than he looks," said Garron.

"I don't get called wise very often, so I'll take dat as a compliment."

"Alican Dod was a member of the Council of Mages," said Garron. "They had sent him to find this place. Huacas lies on a spiritual nexus of sorts. It is a convergence point between the Spirit Realm and the Dark Realm. It makes it almost impossible to find our city, and it also makes Huacas a great source of magic—which Dod and the Council would have never found, were it not for the presence of the red stone. The demons made it easier for the Council to reach their real goal—a convenient excuse. The stone is what drew Alican here."

"Alican knew that the evil these villagers perceived as unstoppable, was really just a group of High Demons that had been summoned by a Necromancer, or they somehow had slipped through this crack in the nexus," said Kucha. "He knew with the final stone and a final Augmentor, the demons would be easily defeated, and the people could go back to their lives, and the Council could establish their new headquarters."

"I still don't quite understand how you guys fit in," said Yareli, looking back at the Turtles.

"We were a happy mistake," said Turu. "The Gauntlet created the underground city, but the Council was unaware of the back door."

"Back door?" asked Anson.

"Under us are pools and caverns that connect to currents. These underground rivers connect Huacas with the ocean—hence the happy accident. The Salamen were already here, but some of my kind had been exploring the caverns when it happened."

"This was the Council of Mages headquarters?" asked Yareli.

"Yes. In its heyday, this was the cultural and information center for the world of magic," said Garron. "The Ancient language and all its tomes of knowledge resided here."

"Where are they at now?" asked Anson.

"Some were taken—moved, I suppose. Some were lost to time, but all the information is still here." He raised his flipper and gestured around.

"What?" asked Anson. "You still have all of the material? Where are the books? The manuscripts?"

"It doesn't work like that here, Mr. Warwick. They are all . . . well, I guess the best word is *downloaded* into the place. Only the Eldre can access the information through the Ancestors," said Kucha. "And these *tuqi* are the interface."

"That's not totally true," said Turu as Yaku shook her head no next to him. "We can get to some of it, but most of it is off-limits to us." Yaku nodded her head yes.

"So this place is basically one big magical hard drive?" asked Yareli.

"I guess I never looked at it that way, but yes," said Kucha.

"How did you end up with this responsibility?" asked Yareli.

"The Gauntlet chose our kind to be the Keepers. One Eldre is appointed by the Ancestors."

"So what sort of information are we talking about here?" asked Anson. "Gauntlet history? Augmentation?"

"Yes," said an unfamiliar voice. Yareli turned to face it. An aged Turtle slid across the floor towards the group. This Turtle wore robes. A mark was emblazoned on his forehead. He leaned heavily on a twisted staff.

"Hello, Eldre. I trust you are well," said Kucha.

"I am as well as this old body will let me be, my son. Turu." He nodded. "Little Yaku." She smiled. "Hello everyone. I am Tuguna the Eldre. Welcome to Huacas. I trust you have all introduced yourselves?" The Eldre paused and looked upwards. "Now where was I?"

"You were saying that this place contains the history of the Gauntlet, the augmentation process—"

"To name a few of its secrets, yes, and many more that would be most dangerous in the wrong hands."

"That makes this place extremely valuable," said Yareli.

"I'd say it makes Tuguna the Eldre even more so," replied Anson.

"Precisely who that dark beast and the Skinx are after, no doubt," said Tuguna. "Knowledge, when used correctly, is the most valuable treasure in the world."

"Come, and take choice of all my library, and so beguile thy sorrow," said Anson.

"Well said, Mage Knight Warwick," said Tuguna.

"And you're the key to this whole thing working?" asked Yareli.

"Precisely, my dear."

"And that's why I'm here," said Garron. "To keep the old man safe."

"No offense, but I fink we might know of a place dat's a bit safer," said Malcolm. Garron scowled at the assertion.

"Please, Garron. They mean well. They do not know of your capabilities or your record of service."

"Yes, Eldre."

"But theoretically speaking, what happens if you die?" asked Anson. "All of the information just ceases to exist?"

"No. The Gauntlet is smarter than that. It always has a fail-safe. If I die, the key will be passed down to one of my children—Kucha most likely, as he is the eldest. He has had the most advanced training. I believe he is best suited to pick up the mantle if something were to happen to me." The Eldre looked at Anson. "Now I have a question for you, Mage Knight."

"What is it, Eldre?"

"Where is the Bearer? My message to Mancer Bodes, while cryptic, was explicit in asking for Thomas Scargen to be present. It is imperative that I speak with him. The Ancestors will it. Where is he?"

"He's out looking for the next stone."

"That is a wise course of action, but also why I must talk to him. I must advance his studies if he is ever to assume his full destiny. The Ancestors have a message for him, and only the Eldre can deliver it. It is of the utmost importance."

"Just tell us duh bleedin' message," said Malcolm. "When Thomas pops back into Sirati, we'll tell 'im."

"I'm afraid it's not that easy," said Tuguna. "Even if I could simply tell you, there is another issue."

"What is the issue?" asked Anson.

"As of yet, I do not know what the message is."

"What do you mean?" asked Yareli. "That makes no sense."

"That is just how these things work. If a prophecy is to be made it has to be made directly to the one it concerns. I am sorry there is no wiggle room on this."

"Well, we don't 'av a clue where 'ee is," said Malcolm.

"That is most disappointing."

The Eldre moved to the empty pit in the center of the stone circle. He tapped his staff on the ground, and once more violet fire erupted upward. His eyes turned completely white. The symbol on his forehead also glowed white. He began to move the staff back and forth, chanting to himself. The fire danced above them, developing into four ghostly forms of Sea Turtles. Each ghost was distinct from the next. The spirits moved to the large stones and began to interact with them. The eyes of the other Turtles began to glow as they raised their hands. The Eldre pulled a carved, oblong stone out of the folds in his robe. It was a smaller *tuqi*. Pieces of the carved stone began to shift and move, sliding over each other as they settled into place. The *tuqi* opened. One of the spirits dove towards the opening, merging into it. Yareli could sense that the spirit was old. The rock began to glow the same purple color as the tall stones, and then sealed itself. The other spirits vanished back into the center pit. "It is settled then."

"What's settled?" asked Yareli.

"Garron and I go to Sirati to await the Bearer's return." The Eldre lifted the illuminated stone. "The Ancestors will it."

4

the white wolves of ontinok

Thomas Scargen and Itsuki Katsuo trudged through the blinding snowfall of Northern Ontario. They were both covered in multiple layers of clothing to protect them from the cold, but the bundling also made it easier for Thomas to hide the Gauntlet and Itsuki to hide *Onikira*, his sword. They had left Sirati one year and three months ago. They had yet to find another stone, but the newest lead about Zikrune seemed promising.

Their guide, Mason Greer, led the way, carrying a walking stick. They had been walking for five days, taking only short breaks to eat and rest. They could have opted for other means of transport, but Thomas and Itsuki were trying to keep their expedition quiet. Transportation arrangements always drew suspicion—especially to remote locations. This was one of the many things they had learned since leaving Sirati.

"How much farther?" screamed Thomas over the raucous wind. He looked across at Greer through his goggles.

"We are close," said Greer. He stood as tall as Thomas. Experience had hardened his white-bearded face, but the man did not look old.

Facial hair would be useful in this weather, thought Thomas. He had not shaved in months, but no beard—only a few randomly placed, awkward hairs grew from his chin.

"The bar's just over that ridge," said Greer.

"That's the best news I've heard in a week!" said Thomas. "Itsuki."

"Yes, Thomas." He leaned in to talk quietly. The boy had grown quite a lot in the fifteen months since leaving the Temple of Yokan.

"We're almost at the bar. Now when we get inside, be ready to move on my mark. I know this is supposed to be a friendly meeting, but we should be careful. Greer swears the orange stone is inside, but we've been down this road before."

Greer continued onto the ridge as the two talked.

"I agree," said Itsuki. He tightened the straps of his backpack. Itsuki's pack held supplies, his journal, and Spells, Thomas's magical repository. "We need to exercise caution."

"Are you guys going to keep talking or get your asses up here? There's something you should see."

Thomas and Itsuki climbed to the top of the ridge. Looking down into the clearing they could see the bar. "Here she is—The Oasis," said Greer. "She's not much, but she's the only thing in the area for hundreds of kilometers. The owner's a nice enough fellow. Like I said, he has had that stone for years now. I've seen it with my own two eyes. It's what you're looking for."

"Hopefully he'll be willing to part with it," said Thomas. "It's an old family heirloom. I will pay whatever the man wants to bring it back home with me." Technically he was not lying. The stone had belonged to his mother, and he would pay whatever the man asked.

"Well, I guess we won't know unless we ask," said Greer. "I don't know about you two, but I could use a drink and some hot food."

They made their way down to the bar. Several aeromobiles, cargo transports, and aerocycles, covered in varying layers of snow, were parked in the lot.

"It seems a little crowded," said Itsuki.

"Like I said, only place for kilometers."

"Ladies first, Suke," said Thomas.

"It never gets old to you," said Itsuki as he swung the door open.

The bar had seen better days. The inside was dimly lit, and not terribly inviting. Men were strewn throughout the Oasis, all drinking and chatting. A long bar was at the opposite side of the room.

A woman and an older man tended. She was the only woman in the bar. Mason Greer walked past two groups of men. One of them gave him a smile, and he nodded back. Greer walked straight to the female bartender.

"Jamesmills, neat." He smiled at her, and then turned to Thomas. "What you drinking?"

"Besides this?" asked Thomas as he lifted his goggles off of his face and grabbed the shot of whiskey the bartender had poured for Greer.

Greer smiled and signaled to the bartender for another.

"I assume the little guy's not joining us."

"That would be a safe assumption," said Itsuki as he glared across at the onlookers.

Thomas had noticed how everyone stared at them since the moment they had opened the door. I guess it was not a normal occurrence for a child to be at the Oasis.

Greer raised his glass. "To a long life and to warming up your innards." He clinked his glass against Thomas's and downed the brown elixir. Thomas put his own empty glass on the bar.

"Smooth," choked Thomas. "Now where can we find the owner?"

"Patience, Thomas. Let's kick back for a second. You two grab a table, and I'll fetch us some menus. You're hungry, right?"

"Yes . . . starving, actually," said Thomas.

"If it is not a problem, I would like some tea—jasmine if possible," said Itsuki.

"I'll see what I can do," said Greer. "Can't promise you anything though."

The two companions found a table in the middle of the room. Itsuki was quick to get his pack off of his back. Thomas did the same, careful not to expose the Gauntlet. "That feels so much better," said Thomas as he put his feet up. "If I wasn't so damn hungry, I'd probably pass on the food—all things considered."

"I agree, but circumstances being what they are . . ."

"Sorry, Itsuki. They were fresh out of jasmine tea," said Greer as he returned with two beers and a glass of slightly brown water, but without the menus he had promised.

"Where's the menus?" asked Thomas. "I'm starving."

"I talked with the lovely lady back there, and she says that Sam will be happy to give you a minute to talk with him, but insists that we eat first. I got the rib eye—as rare as they'll make it. Makes my mouth water thinking about it—and I ordered you two burgers, to speed up the proceedings, if that's all right?"

"Sounds perfect," said Thomas.

"That will suffice," said Itsuki. They both had become less picky when it came to diet since leaving Sirati. They ate any food they could find whenever the chance permitted.

"The quicker we get the transaction done the better," said Thomas, starting to feel more comfortable in his surroundings. Truth be told, he was excited at the possibility of finding the orange stone—the Zikrune, the Mind Stone. He was even more excited at the prospect of heading back to Sirati. He missed LINC, his artif. Thomas missed Stella and her purring. He smiled just thinking about it, but he missed her the most. *Yareli*, thought Thomas. *I was an idiot to ever push you away. I'll make it right when I get back.*

"So how long has the rock been in your family?" asked Greer as he plopped down in the seat between the two friends.

"Centuries," replied Thomas. "It was a gift to my great-great-great-great-great-grandmother."

"That thing's old."

"You have no idea," said Thomas.

Itsuki choked on the water, trying not to laugh.

"How long have you been looking for it again?"

"It's been a long time. Almost my whole life."

"It must feel nice that all your hard work is about to pay off—well, that is, if Sam will let you buy it. Knowing Sam, he'll just give it to ya considering the history. Family heirloom missing for hundreds of years—sounds so mysterious."

"Let's just hope we have solved the mystery," said Itsuki.

The whoosh of wind rushed into the bar as the door opened. The sound ceased as quickly as it had started as the tall thin man forced the door closed with his whole body. "It is bloody cold out there," said the stranger in a distinct English accent. The man had dark hair and a pale complexion with subdued features. "A fellow could catch his death, were he not vigilant." He turned and began the process of taking off of his gloves first, tugging on the middle finger and removing each glove with care and placing them on a chair next to him. Just as meticulously, he took off his hat and jacket and stacked them neatly on the same chair. He adjusted the suit jacket that he had kept on, and deliberately made his way to the bar, smiling, nodding, and every once in a while saying, "Hello." There were no verbal responses from the patrons. Their expressions said it all. They looked at this man like he did not belong in their bar.

"Martini. Vodka—the best you have, slightly dirty, three olives," said the new guest. "May I inquire if there are any rooms available for lodging?"

"We don't rent rooms. Do you have any idea where you are?" asked the woman bartender.

"I was under the impression that I had found the Oasis, which I deduced was, in fact, a bar—a cleverly named one at that. In which someone traditionally can order a drink and sometimes stay the evening," said the strange man, with a hint of sarcasm.

She began to make the cocktail as the stranger turned and surveyed the room. His eyes darted from one face to the next, taking in the environment. The patrons now seemed to be fixed on the stranger. Thomas even saw one man sniff in his direction—as if the man smelled funny.

A large man came out of the back carrying three plates. He had a long scar that crossed his right eye. He placed the steak in front of Greer and the burgers in front of Thomas and Itsuki. "Enjoy," said the man. The food looked amazing. It had been so long since Thomas's last real meal. He grabbed the burger and raised it to his mouth.

"You might not want to eat that," said the Englishman at the bar. He lifted his martini up to his mouth and sniffed. "It has, no doubt, been poisoned."

"Poisoned? I mean, granted, the place looks at best sketchy, but poison, really? Who would be trying to kill me in a bar in Canada?"

"Not kill you, Scargen. Kidnap perhaps. I wouldn't be so sure about your food, First Augmentor Katsuo. The bounty is for the Bearer Thomas Scargen, and I believe it is only he who is required to be taken alive."

"Bounty?" asked Itsuki, pushing away the plate.

"It's when a price is put on a person's head. Sometimes with certain caveats, and in this case, the only caveat being that Mr. Scargen here is alive upon delivery. Isn't that right?" The question had been directed at Greer.

"I'm sure I don't know what you're talking about."

"Really? Do you realize your left eye twitches when you're lying? I imagine not. Most people have a tell, but not usually one so telling."

"What is your business here?"

"I am here to ensure the safety of Thomas Scargen and, to a lesser extent, Itsuki Katsuo."

"Well, I assure you, they are fine."

"There it goes again—twitch. I would have to say the situation before us is the exact opposite of fine."

"Please enlighten me on what you mean," said Greer. "And I'll warn you, stranger, if I don't like what I hear, you're going to have a big problem on your hands."

"Yeah, what *are* you talking about?" asked Thomas.

"Idle threats are just that, but I will do my best." He turned to Thomas. "You would be wise to listen to everything I'm about to say." Thomas shook his head. "Where to begin . . . ahhhh I know. The amount of snow covering the vehicles outside is as good a place as any."

"What's that?" asked Thomas.

"Well, the amount of snow atop the vehicles is rather considerable. If one factors in the daily accumulation and the direction of the wind, it suggests that not one of those vehicles has been moved in the last three days. This leads me to believe that no one here has left or arrived for at least that long." The man paused. "Peculiar for a bar that offers no lodging."

That is odd, thought Thomas.

The stranger spun around, talking to the patrons.

"Not one of you has a shred of a Canadian accent—let alone a Northern Ontario one, which leads me to believe that none of you are actually Canadian—which seems a bit off for a bar quaintly nestled in the deep wilderness of Canada."

"Yeah, what's dat all aboot?" asked Thomas with his best Canadian impression.

The Englishman turned back to the bar, extending his right hand. "There is blood splatter behind the bar, and blood under the woman bartender's nails, not uncommon for a rough backwoods bar such as the Oasis, but the blood is dried and has been there for days. If I had to wager, I'd say seventy-four hours to be precise." He pivoted towards the bartender. "And now to the matter of my drink. The dirty martini I ordered is vile at best, but any bartender worth a salt knows that dirty means to add olive juice. There is not one milliliter of olive juice in this cocktail, which leads me to believe that you, my dear, are no bartender."

"You haven't even taken a sip," said the bartender.

"I never touch the stuff when I'm working. It tends to dull the senses. But anyone can detect the smell of olive juice with a simple whiff." He mimed his previous sniff. "Where was I before I was so rudely interrupted? Ahh, yes—the martini, if you can, in fact, call it that. Shall I continue?"

"Please do," said Thomas.

"There are tufts of white fur on every man and woman in this establishment and all over the floor, collecting in various corners and crevices. Couple that with the rather horrid, and might I add, *pungent* stench of wet dog that hangs in the air when I have seen no such animal, and answers start to present themselves." The Englishman paused and placed his horribly made martini back down on the bar. "If this was not enough, the bodies of the actual patrons and staff of the Oasis have been carelessly dragged around back and thrown rather viciously into the dumpster. These facts paint a pretty exact picture of Thomas Scargen and Itsuki Katsuo being led into an ambush of sorts. It also points to the fact that you are not being a hundred percent truthful to these two. Are you, Mr. Greer? You are Mason Greer, are you not? Or should I ask Ms. Ferrence behind the bar, or Mr. Danks over by the fireplace, or Mr. King or Mr. Burke to my right. Should I keep going? Oh, what am I thinking? I should probably just go right to your Alpha, Mr. Janik, who was so kind to bring you the poisoned food, which I would also venture to guess is probably not beef."

Thomas now pushed his plate aside.

"That was most impressive," said Mr. Janik. Mason Greer kept eating his rare steak.

"Or would you be more comfortable if I just referred to you all collectively as the White Wolves of Ontinok?"

"White wolves?" questioned Itsuki.

"I'm starting to think we're not going to get any stone today," said Thomas, grabbing his backpack. "Let alone a cheeseburger."

"No, Thomas, there is no stone here," said the Englishman. "You have been duped as a part of an elaborate ruse in an attempt to incarcerate you."

"Who are you?" asked Thomas. He was completely confused about what was happening.

"I am Loric Bodes—Mancer of the Council of Mages, dear Thomas."

"I thought I had met all of those," said the young man.

"I was hoping we could handle this the easy way, but I should've known from past experiences that never happens. Greer, grab Scargen," interrupted Janik.

"Yes, Alpha," said Greer, suddenly transforming into a werewolf—an all white werewolf. The table flew back, crashing the plates onto the floor. The transformation had caught Thomas off guard. Greer clawed for Thomas, but Itsuki blocked his reach. In one motion, the boy drew *Onikira* and swung the katana. The wolf sidestepped the attack and rolled to his left. The *hitodama* encircled Itsuki as he backed in the direction of Thomas. The blue wisps shot to *Onikira*, spinning around the sword.

"It's always the hard way, but it's way too many credits to pass up. Don't take it personally, kid—strictly business." Janik's shirt ripped off his body as he also transformed into a white werewolf.

Thomas looked around the bar as all of the other patrons followed suit. There were fifteen in total. Some of the wolves now brandished large laser rifles.

"Wow, a whole frickin' pack of them," said Thomas as he jumped back and threw back his sleeves, exposing his Gauntlet-clad arm. Two wolves made a move towards Thomas. "Haaaaaaa!"

Blue light hit the first attacking wolf, destroying the beast's right arm. The wolf howled in agony. The second pounced. Thomas telekinetically caught the wolf in midair and threw the wolf backward into two other wolves.

At Thomas's side, Loric pushed his hand forward in attack. His dark orange energy spheres peppered the white wolves, scattering them. Itsuki thrust his hand forward. The wisps followed his command and shot into the center of the dispersed wolves. These erupted into large flames, blinding the creatures.

"I believe that is our cue," said the Mancer as he pressed his hands together and quickly pulled them away from each other. The brick wall mimicked his movement, splitting down the middle and sliding open—creating a new exit. "Run."

Itsuki grabbed his pack. Thomas lowered his goggles as the three of them rushed out the makeshift door.

"How did you find us?" asked Thomas as they ran through the deep snow.

"It was actually quite easy, once I found out about the bounty. Then it was just a matter of tracking the movements of the world's most highly skilled bounty hunters. Doing that took some time, I must admit. Eventually it became apparent that the White Wolves of Ontinok were the most likely group to ascertain your whereabouts the quickest. I've been following their movements for almost nine months."

"Why were you sent?" asked Itsuki.

"There's someone Thomas must talk to." An energy attack whizzed by Mancer Bodes's head. They were being pursued.

"What is the plan?" asked Itsuki, blocking several blasts with his blade. The wisps flew ahead of him. "We are seriously outnumbered."

"Don't forget that they are all immortal," said Thomas. "And wolves. They're wolves." He heard their howls before he noticed two of the wolves gaining on them to the far left side of the woods. He tracked them through the display in his goggles.

"Whatever you do, just keep running," said Loric.

"That's your plan?" asked Thomas.

"It's no use. They are much faster in the snow than we are," said Itsuki.

"It's not fair," said Thomas. "They're using four legs."

Thomas could now see that the moon was full. *It just keeps getting better.* The wolves on the left had moved in to cut off the three companions. Thomas shot a blast in their direction, but it was hard tracking the white monsters in the falling snow—even with the aid of his goggles. A group of three more wolves advanced on the right. *Who knows where they all are?* thought Thomas. Soon they would be surrounded.

"We need to stop and fight."

"They are not just werewolves, Scargen—most of them are also rather adept Mages. They are the White Wolves of Ontinok."

"You keep saying that like I'm supposed to know what you're talking about."

"They are efficient, practiced bounty hunters," said Loric.

"Well, they're on my nerves at this point." Thomas stopped and turned, planted his feet, and rocketed the Gauntlet forward. "Haaaaaaa!" The stream of energy hit the first werewolf in his shoulder, spinning him off of his feet. Two others took his place. "I guess he was right about running." Thomas turned to retreat, but Mason Greer and Janik, the Alpha, now stood in his way.

"Where'd your friends go?" asked Janik.

"They're around."

"I'm sorry I never got to introduce myself. I'm Samuel Janik. I am the Alpha of this pack."

"You're the big dog then?" Thomas half smiled at the man, proud of his wit.

"That's one way to say it. Tollin Grimm has put a sizable price on you. Like I said earlier, nothing personal."

The wolves had encircled Thomas. He could hear them snarling and howling as they closed in.

"You gotta do what you gotta do, but you won't mind if I don't go quietly."

"I would expect nothing less from the Gauntlet Bearer."

Concentrate . . . focus. He could feel the shift immediately. The Gauntlet glowed slightly yellow and then blue. Thomas moved with incalculable speed. "Haaaaaa!" yelled Thomas, spinning around unleashing the energy blast in a circle. He caught two werewolves off guard, stunning them with the burst. Three more attacked. Thomas spun around kicking the first in his face. The beast flew sideways. Thomas's stone fist connected with the next attacker, shattering the monster's ribcage. The wolf's whimper was the only thing Thomas could hear as he spun around and unleashed another energy blast on the last advancing wolf. The creature flew back, opening a hole for him to move towards. He sped through the gap in the formation, and blazed a trail through the woods. The hologram of Mancer Bodes appeared out of his wristcom.

"Thomas, I need you to adjust your course slightly and run in this direction." The holographic representation displayed the direction he should be traveling directly inside of the goggles. "Itsuki and I are just up ahead." He pushed himself again, but the wolves were still on his heels.

He broke through the tree line. He did not have time to stop. Thomas fell off the cliff, plummeting to nowhere. "Where are you guys?" screamed Thomas into his wristcom as he tried to steady his fall.

He hit the body of the beast without any warning. The impact knocked the wind out of him. Thomas gasped for breath as he heard the familiar voice.

"We are right here, Thomas," said Itsuki.

"Thanks, Suke," said Thomas, trying to catch his breath. "A . . . little . . . late, but thanks anyway."

" 'ello Thomas. Aren't you a sight for sore bloody eyes," said Bartleby Draige.

Thomas found himself flying on the back of the teleport dragon along with the First Augmentor and Mancer Bodes.

"That was close," said Itsuki.

"You're . . . telling . . . me," said Thomas as he turned to look at Loric. His breathing began to stabilize.

"Why did you stop running?" asked Mancer Bodes. "I expressly said, do not stop running. I had heard you were a bit pigheaded—a trait, I must say, I share to a certain extent, but those were extremely simple instructions."

"I'm not sure what happened there. I didn't think we were gonna outrun them, so I thought we could outgun them, but I guess I should've mentioned that to everyone. No harm, no foul, right?"

The Mancer just stared at him sternly.

"Where're we going anyway?" asked Thomas, desperately trying to change the subject.

"Dat would be Sirati, Thomas," said Bartleby. "Dere's so much dat 'as 'appened since you've been gone."

"And when Tuguna the Eldre requests your presence, you listen," said Loric.

"I suppose so," said Thomas. "Wait . . . who?"

5

riddles from the grave

The sky ripped open to reveal the expansive, natural city nestled between two mountains. Thomas could not believe his eyes. He was home. It had been fifteen months since he had last seen Sirati, and with the sun rising, it was even more beautiful than he had remembered.

"Bartleby, take us to your place. Anson is meeting us there," said Loric. "He thought you might want to see an old friend of yours, Thomas. In fact, he insisted. I must admit at first I protested, which is usually a knee-jerk reaction to anything the werewolf says, but seeing as the Eldre is not ready for your audience as of yet, I see no issue with you convening with your artif companion."

"Your place?" questioned the young man. It had taken a second for Loric's words to sink in.

"Like I said, Thomas. A lot 'as changed since you've been gone," said the dragon, gliding towards a Sentry Mage post. After a quick inspection, they were ushered through the force field. Bartleby flew above the large baobab Maktaba and across the jungle canopy that lead to the Grove, making his way towards a series of cliffs that Thomas had never noticed before. Homes were carved out of the cliff face between three massive waterfalls.

The rush of water calmed Thomas as Bartleby made his way to the back of the cliffs. As they approached, Thomas could make out an open hangar that looked like it was still under construction. Some gremlins manned large tech suits. They were using them to build the hangar. Others were controlling several builderbots to aid with the construction.

Bartleby zoomed into the opening and skipped across the hangar floor. Gremlins descended on the dragon from every inch of the hangar as they began the process of taking off Bartleby's armor. "What is all this?" asked Thomas as he jumped off Bartleby. The hangar appeared to be even more advanced than the one in Draige manor.

"Well, Fargus and I got to finkin', if we're really meant ta 'elp, we needed to 'av a base uv operations a bit closer." A black Labrador ran up to the dragon and began licking his face. "And I couldn't stand bein' away from dis guy for too long eiver. Isn't dat right, Webby? Ziza said we could use dis place, and duh lit'l guys started construction straight away."

"Ahem . . ." said the holographic woman, appearing in front of the dragon. "I assure you, Mr. Draige, I helped as well," said ELAIN.

"I know ya did, love," said Bartleby.

"Someone has to keep track of everything when you're away or sleeping, which accounts for approximately 97.432% of your time."

"I suppose you are due a certain amount uv duh credit for us being ahead uv schedule."

"Where is Warwick?" asked Loric of ELAIN, interrupting the conversation.

"He is in the diagnostic center with Fargus Hexelby awaiting Thomas Scargen's arrival," responded the hologram. "Your robotic companion is currently undergoing maintenance."

"LINC!" shouted Thomas. "Which way to the diagnostic center?"

"Follow me, Thomas."

Thomas looked down to see Lenore Bugden. "Lenore, it's great to see you."

"You too. And 'oo's the boy?"

"That's Itsuki Katsuo," said Thomas as he placed his hand on Itsuki's shoulder. "Suke here is one of my best buds, and he happens to also be my First Augmentor."

"Please ta meet ya, Itsuki. Any friend uv Thomas's, an that."
Itsuki bowed his head. "You two must be sweatin' like crazy wif
dose getups on. Take your jackets off at least. I'm startin' to sweat
just lookin' at ya, aren't I?" Thomas and Itsuki removed their jackets.
Another gremlin walked by and collected them. "Aw'right, let's get
goin' den."

"Please, after you Ms. Bugden," said Loric Bodes. "There is much
to discuss."

As they walked through the hallways of Bartleby's new home, Thomas
was stunned at the differences between this place and Draige Manor.
Everything was more modern, but—like most of Sirati—seamlessly
integrated with the natural surroundings. The walkways were also
wider, taller, and a lot less catacomb-like. They reached the door
marked DIAGNOSTIC CENTER, and after the usual security measures,
they entered the room. This room was also bigger than its predecessor. At the center of the room was a headless artif. Thomas surveyed
his surroundings to locate LINC's head. It was directly in front of
Fargus with the back panel open. Anson was discussing something
with Fargus and Ronald Hosselfot, the tech dealer from London.
Hosselfot? What's he doing here? thought Thomas. The three of them
turned to see Thomas and the rest of the crew.

"Anson, we must talk," said Loric.

"Well, it is rather nice to see you too, Loric. It's been months has
it not?" asked Anson.

"That is of no consequence," said Loric. "Grimm has put out a
bounty on Scargen—a rather sizable one at that."

"How sizable?" asked Thomas.

"One million global credits. One of the largest bounties I've
ever seen."

"Whoa . . . all things considered, that's pretty narsh in an odd
way," said Thomas.

"I assure you, Scargen, there is nothing *narsh* about this." Loric turned towards the werewolf. "Do you have any idea what this means?"

"Well, I suppose it means tha—"

"It means that every magic-user on the planet is going to be after him—and some poor souls that do not use magic as well, I would gather. The White Wolves of Ontinok would have had him, if I had not arrived at precisely the right moment."

"They were there?" asked Anson. "Greer?"

"Yes, Mason Greer was there—along with Samuel Janik."

"Janik?"

"Wait you know these werewolves?" asked Thomas.

"Knew them, Thomas—a long, long time ago."

"How did you know them?" Anson turned towards Thomas.

"Samuel Janik is my Alpha," said Anson. "Well, was. He was the one who turned me."

"Whoa . . . I wasn't expecting that."

"Nor was I, at the time."

"But why isn't your fur all white like the rest of them?" asked Thomas.

"There's always one, Thomas. I guess I was the black sheep of the family—quite literally."

"And who's Greer?"

"Greer was a man I called friend at one point in my life—a very low point, mind you. He was also a member of my old pack."

"Is he the Beta?"

"I'm not sure, Thomas. It has been centuries since my pack days, but back then Mason was the Gamma."

"Who was the Beta then?"

"I was, Thomas. As good luck would have it, I was the Beta of the pack."

"Narrrrsh," said the young man.

"Are you two finished? I am aware that social animal ethology and its impact on werewolf hierarchies can be a terribly scintillating topic for discussion, but there are bigger matters at play here."

Thomas nodded in understanding. "Excellent." Loric turned back to Anson. "The High Mancer was displeased when I told him the news. He wants us to meet with the other Mancers and discuss the ramifications of the bounty."

"We will leave shortly, Loric, but there's something I think you're going to want to see first. LINC is no ordinary artif. He is truly one of a kind."

"Very well, but you have my attention for only the next five minutes, and if this exercise becomes exceedingly dull—which I am certain it will—I will leave to talk to Ziza myself."

"Wait . . . you're a Mancer now?" asked Thomas.

"Yes, Thomas. Where are my manners?" Anson awkwardly hugged the young man, then pulled back to look closer at him. "You look . . . tired, quite frankly," said Anson.

"Yeah, you do look a bit off, I'd say, mate. I mean, I only met you once, and all, but yeah, you look a bit worse for wear. Maybe you could use a baf or a breaf mint or seven," said Hosselfot.

"Hi, *Mancer* Warwick . . . what's Hassle-fart doing here?" questioned Thomas.

"I felt like I owed it to you guys after what 'appened at duh Wharf and den wif 'awforne. 'ee didn't deserve dat end, did 'ee? And 'ee was me mate, and all, yeah."

"I still don't trust him," said Thomas to Anson, pretending Hosselfot was not there.

"I swear I've turned over a new leaf, Thomas. Dose Riders did a number on me, bloody near wiped me mind clean. But I still kept quiet, didn't I? Dat traitor Lesinge was duh one dat ratted 'awforne out. I know dat doesn't change anyfing, but dat's why I'm 'ere. I want to 'elp."

"How exactly is he gonna help?" asked Thomas.

"We needed a full-time tech dealer for the work Fargus has been doing, and he's the best in the business," said Anson. "What's gone and what's past help, should be past grief."

"Besides wiffout 'osslefot, bringin' LINC back online would 'av been bloody impossible, an that. Even Bart is fine wif it," said Fargus.

Thomas thought about Anson's and Fargus's words. This man was responsible for saving LINC.

"If Bartleby and you can forgive him, I guess I can," said Thomas. "Welcome to the team."

"I really appreciate dat, Thomas. I'll show you what I can do. You should see what Fargus 'as been gettin' up to. His work has been amazing."

"What work have you been doing?" asked Thomas of the gremlin.

"Well, I've spent months trying to figure out your dad's 'ardware and software, and I 'av to say, at duh end uv duh day, Thomas, I fink I finally did it," said Fargus. "I've been using what I've learned and applying it to uvver applications, an that."

"Like the tech suits in the hangar?"

"Exactly. I learned a lot from puttin' LINC back togevva, but I also found somefin'." The gremlin whistled to himself as he pushed a few buttons on his handheld device. LINC's schematics jumped onto all of the holoscreens. Fargus began to motion with his hands. "I found instructions for upgrades to all uv LINC's major systems. Most uv duh stuff we discussed before you left were included in duh upgrade, along wif some files dat I 'av no idea what dey do. Your old man must 'av put 'im 'ere just in case somefing 'appened to 'im. Quite frankly, it's taken me dis long to be able to implement dem correctly—wif ELAIN's 'elp uv course. I know you've 'erd it before, an that, but your father really was a bloody genius."

Was, thought Thomas. "So, why's his head detached?"

"Like I said, I just finished before you walked in. When I 'erd you'd be returnin', I figured I'd wait for you to do duh honors." The gremlin motioned to the artif's head. "And, well, I'm not really tall enough, am I?"

Thomas picked up his friend's new, shiny head and stared at his lifeless eyes. There were slight differences, but he was definitely still LINC. "Tell me about some of the upgrades." Fargus again motioned with his hands. Thomas looked at the holographic representation of LINC's systems on the display in front of him.

"Weapons upgrades—more powerful, farther range, and more

versatility. I'll show you when 'ee's up and runnin' what I'm talkin' about. Defense systems—shields, cloaking device for more stealf. And like I said, a whole bunch uv subsystem modifications."

"And you don't know what they are for?"

"Not all uv dem. Some uv dem were 'eavily encrypted, but 'ad to be uploaded as a bundle. It was all or nuffin', and I just fought, well, better to 'av some uv duh stuff and den we could learn about duh uvver stuff dat's knockin' about inside uv 'im later. It's done me 'ed in trying to figure it out, to be honest."

"How do you suppose we find out what they do then?"

"I fought we'd turn 'im on and see what 'appens."

"I like it," said Thomas. "Simple, yet elegant. Here goes nothing." He walked closer to his best friend's new body and gently reconnected his head. Thomas stepped back. The artif did not move. Thomas turned to look at the gremlin. "Ummmm, are you sure you did it right?"

"I'm positive, just give it some time, ya know what I mean? Rome wasn't built in a bloody week, was it?"

"Oookay," responded Thomas as he looked back at LINC. The artif's optics flashed for a second then turned off again. "Come on, pal, wake up!"

"I do not have the capability or the need for sleep, Thomas Scargen. Therefore, it would be impossible for me to wake up from anything," said the artif, as if he had never been deactivated. "Furthhhhhh-rr-r-r—r-r-r-mor-r-r-r-r, I-I-I-I c-c-c-cannnnn." LINC's eyes turned red. He brandished his new weapons. "Security protocol Alpha; subsystems upgrade. Password is required. Self-destruct initiating in 20 seconds."

"Twenty seconds?" yelled Thomas. "Do you know the password, Fargus?"

"No, I fought you would, seeing 'ee's your bloody artif."

"I didn't even know he had an upgrade. How would I know the password?"

"I suppose dat's a fair point."

"Fifteen seconds to self-destruct."

"What could the password be?" asked Thomas. "Dad was always so damn secretive about work."

"Think, Scargen. It has to be something you would think of," said Loric. "Your father was far too intelligent to do otherwise."

"Ten seconds to self-destruct."

"Think . . . what would your father use as a password?" questioned Loric. "Something personal, perhaps?"

"Five . . . four . . . three . . ."

Mom, thought Thomas.

"Two . . ."

It has to be Mom, thought Thomas. "Merelda Scargen."

"Password accepted," said LINC as his eyes returned to their normal color. The artif froze as a holographic projection now emanated from his wrist display to float above them all. It was a jumble of symbols and hieroglyphs.

"What is this?" asked Thomas.

"If I had to venture a guess, I would say it is a code," said Loric.

"Someone looks terribly intrigued," said Anson.

"Don't act like you're not," said Loric. "There seems to be characters and symbols from various times and places."

"Can you make out any of the characters?" asked Anson.

"Some, but they seem out of order or place, almost randomly arranged." He pointed up. "These are definitely from Ancient Egypt."

"There are several Japanese characters as well," said Itsuki.

"I would also say there are several Norse runes," said Loric. "And I believe these are Mayan."

"Which ones are yours?" cracked Thomas with a grin. Loric gave him another stern look. "I don't care what you say, that's funny."

"Thomas, how many digs had your father done?" asked Loric.

"Including Egypt . . . I don't know, like seven or so. But four of them were sort of the same dig. Why?"

"I believe there's a pattern. A vague one, but a pattern nonetheless."

"In what way?"

"I'd venture to guess your father's excavations were in Egypt, Japan, somewhere in Central America, and somewhere in Scandinavia, presumably."

"Well, you're almost right. His first several digs were pretty close to home, actually—right outside of Boston. He found several Viking markers."

"That explains the Elder Futhark runes," said Anson. "Not Scandinavia, but close, Loric."

"His second dig was an old Mayan ruin just outside the city of Mérida in Mexico. The diggerbots uncovered a whole new layer of previously unknown temples."

"That covers the Mayan symbology," said Loric. "I am to presume that the next dig was then in Japan."

"Yeah, in Nara," said Thomas. "So, now what?"

"We have to attempt to find order in chaos." Loric paced back and forth, pondering the details. He rested his index finger across his top lip. "Did your father ever send you or bring back anything from these digs—like an artifact or pictures maybe?"

"Dad collected junk from all of his digs," said Thomas. "He would keep one artifact from every excavation. Every once in a while, when he got excited about a find, he would send me pics, but that was a rarity, maybe once a dig."

"Do you still have those pictures, Thomas?" asked Anson.

"I think I have most of them on my wristcom."

"Can you show them to me?" asked Loric. "Whatever this is, it was important enough for your father to hide it within the very thing you treasure the most and to include a self-destruct sequence so it wouldn't fall into the wrong hands. He must have sent you the cipher, being his only heir. You just didn't know he did."

Thomas scrolled through the holographic interface. The first thing he came across was the Egyptian pictures. He opened the file with a wave of his hand. The photos opened in front of them. Loric walked over.

"May I?" asked Mancer Bodes.

"Sure," said Thomas. Loric began moving through the photos studying the details as the symbols continued to float above them.

"Can you find the next set?"

"Yep, here they are." Thomas released the new photos into the collage." Loric continued to silently peruse the images.

"Next?"

"Found them, and the other set," said Thomas. All of the pics from every dig his father and Sigmund had been on floated above them with the symbols.

"There. Look at this one." Loric dragged a picture out from the group. "And this one." He pulled yet another out. "He is pointing at a marking in both of these photos. They are almost identically staged, but one is from Boston, and the other is from Japan. Now, Thomas, eliminate all of the other pictures from these particular digs." The young man complied. "Now, gentlemen, would you help me find the remaining two pictures?" The group began scouring the images, looking for similar photos.

"Found one," said Fargus. " 'ee's doin' the same fing in dis pic from Mexico—pointin' at a bloody stone slab wif junk all over it."

"And I remember the Egyptian pic now," said Thomas, dismissing the other images. Thomas moved the image next to the other three. He had remembered the photograph distinctly. He had stared at it before going to sleep the day he arrived in Sirati. His father was standing next to a stone marker, just like the other pictures, pointing at a hieroglyph.

"So if we highlight the symbols Dr. Scargen is pointing at in each picture, that leaves us with four symbols," said Loric. With a movement of his hand most of the symbols vanished. Four distinct marks now floated above them. "You stated earlier that the order of these digs was Boston, Mexico, Japan, and then Egypt." He arranged the symbols in that order. He pointed to the first symbol. "This is an Elder Futhark rune from the early Norse languages. This symbol is called *sowilo.*

ᛋ

"Looks like an S to me," said Thomas.

"Eventually that is precisely what it becomes, but trust me it's the sowilo," said Loric. "It means *salvation* or *sun* or sometimes *wisdom*. It invites spiritual protection."

"The second figure is an old Mayan symbol," said Anson. "It is called *chum*."

"What's it mean," asked Thomas.

"It means *seated*, or *sit*, or *set*," said Loric.

"So salvation sits?"

"Something like that. It could also mean wisdom is seated, but basically the same."

"This symbol here—"

"This symbol is the kanji for *kata*. It means *shoulders*," said Itsuki.

"Pretty straightforward: salvation or wisdom is seated or sits on the shoulders of . . ."

"The last one is the Egyptian hieroglyph for Bastet—the Egyptian goddess of warfare, daughter of Ra."

"So, salvation sits on the shoulders of war?" asked Thomas. "That doesn't seem like something my dad would agree with."

"Or the sun sets on the shoulders of warfare," said Loric.

"What's that even mean?" asked Thomas.

"I was hoping you would know. It is, in fact, a direct message to you," said Loric. "That much is certain, but I have yet to determine what it means."

"What did you say?" asked Anson.

"I said, I have yet to determine its meaning."

"That's what I thought you said, but it's the first time I've ever heard you say that."

"There is nothing wrong with admitting you do not know something. The problem is admitting that you will not figure it out."

"Okay, so how do we do that?" asked Thomas.

"Research," said Loric as he was already searching through the holograms above his wristcom. "The answer has to be somewhere, and I will find it."

"What about LINC?" asked Thomas.

"I fink 'ee's goin' to be like dat until we solve duh bloody riddle, an that," said Fargus.

"Very well then, have LINC moved to my flat," said Loric.

"Is that necessary?" asked Thomas.

"This will take my complete concentration and faculties, and I work best at my flat."

"What do you hope to accomplish?" asked Anson.

"I will either solve the enigma that has been laid out before me, or l will somehow awaken the sleeping artif."

"So there's nothing I can do here then?" asked Thomas.

"I'd say no."

"Then I have someone I have to talk to," said Thomas. He knew LINC was better, so his mind shifted to Yareli.

"Yes, the Eldre did mean to speak with you," said Anson.

"Well, come get me when he's ready." Thomas moved towards the door of the diagnostic center. He wanted to find Yareli and tell her about everything, but that would have to wait as well. He had a more pressing need.

"Where are you going?" asked Itsuki.

"I have a date with a poison-free burger and a nice cold Warwick Amber."

"But it is only 9:00 AM," said Anson.

"I'm still on Oasis time."

6

the eldre and the bearer

Thomas walked into Warwick's like he had never left. He had missed the sound of the falls. The water had always calmed him. Thomas headed to the bar with his head down. He was tired and hungry. He had been through a lot in a short amount of time. He sat on a barstool and looked up to see the smiling face of Sinclair the Gorilla bartender.

" 'ello, Thomas. I didn't know you were back in town. No one tells me anyfing, do dey?"

"Hi, Sinclair. I just got back about half an hour ago."

"It's nice to see you again."

"You too, Sinclair."

"Are you 'ere to meet Anson? I fink 'ee's over at Bart's new gaff."

"No. I just came from there. I needed some time to think, and I'm starving."

"Well, what you 'avin'?"

"I'll have a pint of Amber and a Malcolm burger."

"How bloody do you want it?"

"Medium rare."

"Comin' right up, Thomas," said Sinclair as he swung across the bar, grabbed a glass with his right foot, and pulled down the tap with his left hand. He set the beer down for it to settle and then topped it off. He typed the order on his wristcom. Thomas looked up at the holovisions. The World Network News channel was on the closest holovision and the volume was high enough to hear it. He put his head back down.

"The House of Alliance met once again to discuss the recent artif troop movements on the outskirts of the Sahara. Leaders from the House are to meet with the Three Primes on Tuesday to discuss the issue in depth. In other news, Scargen Robotics . . ."

Thomas looked up at the holovision. Normally Thomas could not care less about WNN, but the Scargen Robotics graphic was floating next to the anchorman. "Sinclair, can you turn up the volume on this HV."

"Sure fing, Thomas." Sinclair placed the beer in front of the young man, reached down on his wristcom and moved his finger. The volume adjusted on the holovision. "Dis 'as been all over duh news, Thomas. Scargen Robotics has been busy in duh last few monfs."

"Gideon Upshaw has said the new contract will ensure the legacy of Scargen Robotics," said the anchorman. The image shifted to Gideon Upshaw speaking at a press conference. *Dr. Benet is standing next to him*, thought Thomas. Dr. Irene Benet was a colleague and close friend of his father's. She was an excellent robotics engineer in her own right. *At least someone with some brains is still at Scargen Robotics, but she doesn't look happy.* Upshaw smiled and began to speak.

"Together, Ricky Nones and Scargen Robotics will move the world of robotic sports forward," said Upshaw. "Our agreement is exactly the future that Carl Scargen and his son would have wanted for this company."

"What a load of crap," said Thomas. "I can't believe anyone is buying this."

"Dey fink your ol' man and you 'av been dead for over a year. Dey say duh Egyptian dig had collapsed in, buryin' 'im and the excavation team, coupled wif your disappearance shortly afterwards—it's been one uv duh biggest news stories."

"They just covered up the truth of what really happened. This has the Hunters written all over it," said Thomas, then listened as the WNN anchorman continued.

"The agreement will be solidified at Sky Field during the half-time show of the Dallas Cowbots and Green Bay Hackers game, one of robotic football's biggest rivalries," said the anchorman. "This is when the unveiling of the first Scargen sportif prototypes will take place. This deal comes on the heels of the Scargen Robotics announcement earlier this week detailing their new agreement with the Global Alliance—reportedly the largest military contract of its kind. Also as part of the halftime festivities, Upshaw will present the Three Primes with one of Carl Scargen's personally designed Infospheres as a token of their new exclusive relationship. This sphere is one of only two spheres currently in existence—the other is kept under lock and key at Scargen Robotics. Engineers at the world-renowned robotics firm have yet to discern the function of the Infospheres. They were the last project that Dr. Carl Scargen was working on before he left for Egypt. Little to nothing is currently known of their actual capabilities, but speculation is that they could represent a huge shift in artificial intelligence. They are considered priceless, an indicator of the scale and seriousness of this historic agreement. Experts say that this deal could easily net Scargen Robotics hundreds of billions of global credits over the ten-year span of the contract." The screen displayed an image of Gideon Upshaw getting into a stretch aeromobile, with the Hunter's leader Thatcher Wikkaden entering the car immediately after him. "Needless to say, Scargen Robotics stock price has doubled in value so far this week."

"I knew it," said Thomas. "Hunters." He could not believe what he was hearing, but it confirmed the suspicions he had felt in London over a year ago: they were not only using his father's designs for war, but also to hunt and capture magic-users. Gideon Upshaw had taken over the company and had completely compromised the Scargen name.

"Are we alone? That is the question that keeps popping up in Moscow today. Hundreds of eyewitnesses claimed to have seen a UFO flying across the sky. In the past, these sightings have been directly tied to experimental craft or tech projects done by the government . . ." The announcer continued on as Thomas turned to see Malcolm Warwick approaching.

"Why ya look so sad, Tommy? Someone blow up duh Tinman again?" asked Malcolm Warwick as he sat backward on the barstool next to Thomas.

"Malcolm, how are you?" asked Thomas.

"I can't complain, but dat won't stop me from tryin'." The two laughed. "So what's got you so glum, mate?"

"It's nothing."

"Come on, Tommy. I wasn't born yesterday. In fact it's been quite some time since I was born, hasn't it?" Malcolm lit a cigarette and blew the smoke purposely upward. "Why so bothered, mate?"

Thomas smiled. "Well, it seems as if Scargen Robotics is being run by an ass, and the only way to fix that is for me to go back and deal with him, but I can't because that would be suicide—especially knowing that they are working with the Hunters."

"Dat's a tough one, Tommy, but I fink you and I bofe know dat you're doin' duh best wif what cards you've been dealt, mate."

"Thank you, Malcolm."

"Don't mention it. Now, I'm actually 'ere ta bring you to Maktaba. The High Mancer and the Eldre would like to see you now, and I am not takin' no for an answer. I was given a direct order from Ziza. He has called a meeting of the entire Council."

Thomas finished his beer, and transferred the credits he owed to the bar. "Thanks, Sinclair."

"What about your burger?" asked the Gorilla.

"I guess I wasn't meant to eat today."

Thomas followed Malcolm through the expansive library. He could never get over how big or beautiful Maktaba was. Thomas had missed the giant tree, and oddly enough, his studies. He looked up at the books, watching the foliage sort and deliver books from one spot to the next. The sight was interrupted by his stomach rumbling again. "I know. I get it."

"Are you aw'right, Tommy?" asked Malcolm.

"Just starving," said Thomas.

"I know duh feelin', mate."

All Thomas could think about was food. He had not eaten for almost two days and it was starting to unnerve him. They made their way to the tube that climbed upward in the center of the massive tree. The doors opened as they approached, and there in the elevator doorway stood his roommate, Onjamba.

"Hello, Thomas," said the Elephant, holding a serving tray with a monstrous sandwich atop it. "I know you've been out and about for some time, and I figured you might be positively famished when you arrived, so I whipped this up. I know how strong your appetite can be."

"It looks great. What is it?" asked Thomas as he and Malcolm entered the elevator.

"It's four types of cured meats, three cheeses, a subtle pepper aioli, finished off with microgreens and some sliced red onion."

"You have no idea how much I love you right now." The young man took the sandwich and took a huge bite. "It's delicious." He took two more quick bites. "Mmmmm. I missed you so much."

"Are you talking to the food or me?" asked Onjamba.

"Both," said Thomas with a full mouth.

"I missed you too, Thomas," said the Elephant as the doors shut, and the car rocketed upward. "Now, there is much to discuss."

"Like what?"

"Well, for starters the Eldre is here. He has traveled a great distance to personally deliver you a message."

"Narsh," said the young man. "What kind of message?"

"He has not said, but rest assured it should be quite important." The doors opened, and they exited the elevator. Two Cheetahs stood at their usual posts, flanking the tube.

"Good morning, Mortici . . . Chet," said Thomas as he turned towards the Cheetahs and continued to walk backward. The Felids maintained their dutiful poses, ignoring Thomas's greeting. "You guys are doing a phenomenal job. Keep up the good work." He turned back and caught up with Malcolm and the Elephant as they made their way over to the large circular table.

Thomas noticed almost immediately that the old chairs were gone. They had been replaced by new hovering models. *Gremlins*, he thought. His eyes moved to the head of the table—to his mentor. Ziza looked much older than when Thomas left.

"What's wrong with Ziza?" he whispered to Onjamba.

"He has been away from the Gauntlet far longer than he should be."

"What?"

"If he is away from the Gauntlet for long periods of time, it tends to affect him. The union is meant to be permanent, I believe. He has had issues getting around."

"I guess that explains the new chairs?"

"Precisely. We thought it best to replace them all, as not to arouse suspicion. The High Mancer is a great man, but he has problems admitting his limitations. Ziza still refuses to rest as much as he should. With you back, though, Ziza should be his old self in no time."

Thomas nodded in understanding. They all stood to greet him as he approached. An elderly Sea Turtle sat next to the High Mancer. *That must be the Eldre*, thought Thomas. He looked around the table at the faces of the Council: Ziza, Lolani, Neficus, Emfalmay, Itsuki, Anson, Loric, and Malcolm were here, but someone was missing. *Where's Yar?*

The elevator door opened once more, and, as if on cue, out stepped Yareli followed by a young Chinese man. They walked to the table talking back and forth to one another. Yareli laughed. This caught Thomas off guard. *Who's that?* Yareli quickly moved to her seat at the table as the man moved in behind the Eldre. She looked over at Thomas and smiled and waved at him. He smiled back for a little too long.

"We are all finally here," said Ziza as he began pacing with his staff in front of the large circular door to the room that once housed the Gauntlet. "This is the first time the full Council has met in over two years, and with good reason. As some of you already know, Tuguna the Eldre arrived here some nine months ago, awaiting the return of the Bearer." Ziza paused and looked at Thomas. "And our dear Bearer has returned home." Now everyone looked at him. "Where to begin . . . ah, introductions are in order. Thomas Scargen, may I introduce you to Tuguna the Eldre."

The Turtle floated over to him and extended his fingered flipper.

"It is an honor to meet the Bearer. I have been Eldre for many a coming and going of the sun, and you are the first Bearer I have had the pleasure to meet in person. In fact, it has been quite some time since an Eldre and Bearer have met. It is truly an honor."

"The pleasure's all mine, Tuguna . . . or should I call you Eldre?"

"Either will suffice. Now let me introduce you to my Eldre Guard. This is Garron Dar."

The man who had accompanied Yareli walked over and extended his hand.

"This is also an honor for me, Bearer. We are at your service." The man's eyes stared at Thomas and then down to the Gauntlet. "It is simply remarkable."

"Yeah, I guess she's not too bad," said Thomas as he raised his hand and moved his fingers. "A bit of a commitment, but well worth it." The two men laughed.

"Now, down to business," said Ziza. "Mancer Bodes was dispatched to find you when the Eldre arrived here in Sirati some nine months back—a task that proved more difficult than Loric would care to admit. He has also, more recently, brought to my attention the bounty put on your head by Grimm. This business is troublesome, all the more so because he wishes you alive upon delivery. This means he needs you for something, but for what is unclear. I will have to meditate on this further if the answer is to present itself." Ziza's serious expression was replaced with his usual smile. "But that is not why I have called you here today, my boy. New . . . or rather old, information has traveled with the Eldre, and it is most enlightening."

"Like what?" asked Thomas. "You promised you wouldn't hold back anymore."

"And I intend to uphold that promise. That is why you are here. It is time to share some things with you. The Eldre will explain further."

"About what?" asked Thomas. "What things?"

"It is better I show you than tell you, Bearer," said Tuguna as he floated closer to the table. "The Ancestors will it." The Eldre produced a carved stone from under his robe and set it down on the table.

"That thing looks entirely narsh. What's it do?" asked Thomas.

"You are about to find out," said the Eldre. "It is a *tuqi*, an Ancestor Stone." He began to touch the stone, handling it almost like he was typing on a keyboard. His eyes began to glow violet as he chanted to himself. The carvings on the *tuqi* glowed orange. "Let us start with the basics." The lights in the room flickered and then went dark. The energy from the stone and the Eldre was enough to illuminate the room. "The Gauntlet is as old as man and dragon. It has been borne by many men, women, and even other species. At the heart of the Gauntlet's power, lie the Mage stones. You have found your first stone, the Taitokura—the Experience Stone. You have learned that this stone can manipulate time to a degree, enabling you to have faster reflexes and speed. But I understand that you have a very limited knowledge of the other stones and their powers."

"Things got a little crazy here with Malcolm being trapped in the Hive, and then Itsuki and I left shortly after to find the next stone."

"And why did you not enlighten the boy on the other stones, Augmentor?"

"With all due respect, Eldre, that is not my place. I am here to protect and guide the Bearer."

"You did not think that educating him would help to protect him?" asked the Eldre.

"Augmentor's rule number four: 'education of the Bearer will come through his experiences, not from exposition.' That being said, if any information had been pertinent to any task at hand, I would have provided it."

"Itsuki and I agreed not to distract Thomas with too much information on the other stones," said Ziza. "We wanted to focus on the Zikrune. It was the first to appear on our radar, and it was my decision to send them to find it. Itsuki is not the one you should be questioning."

"You guys are talking about me like I'm not here," said Thomas. "I knew the name of the Zikrune and what it was capable of. That was our mission, and I thought we had found the damn thing."

"But you did not," said the Eldre.

"No. Apparently we walked right into a werewolf ambush."

"Sometimes we learn far more from our failures than we do our successes," said Ziza.

"And the path can be more enlightening than the destination," said Mancer Lolani.

"These words are wise, Bearer," said the Eldre. "You should ponder them. And know that my questions are not mere judgment, but fact-finding. I agree with your High Mancer and the Augmentor that too much information may interfere with the Bearer's natural growth, and under normal circumstances your abilities would grow from your experiences, but these are anything but normal circumstances. Things have changed since your departure, and we must adjust course accordingly."

"The Eldre has brought to light information that requires you to understand the bigger picture of how the stones work in unison."

"Ziza and I have agreed that it is time to share with you the knowledge of the Ancients."

"Narsh," said Thomas. "Ancient knowledge."

"Show the Eldre the respect he deserves, Scargen," said Mancer Elgin Neficus.

"Thank you, Elgin, but I can speak for myself," said the Eldre. "He is just excited to learn—a trait I cannot be upset about." The Turtle smiled and looked back at Thomas. "We start with the basics." The light from the *tuqi* glowed brighter. "You may have asked yourself, 'why does everyone have a different color energy?' Yours, for instance, is light blue, is it not?"

"Yes."

"Have you ever wondered why this is?"

"Yeah. Almost every time I use my powers."

"A fair question. Each person has a Light inside of them, Thomas." His flippered hand produced a purplish-blue sphere. "That

Light directly corresponds with each person's strengths. You can tell a lot by a person's Light, and nobody's Light is exactly the same as another's."

"Like a magic fingerprint?" asked Thomas.

"Exactly, my boy. Most people will never see this Light in its physical manifestation because they are out of touch with this aspect of themselves, but make no mistake, it burns in every living thing."

I wonder if LINC has a Light, thought Thomas.

"Each Light brings with it certain abilities," said the Eldre. "Most people, whether they know it or not, sympathize with at least one of these Lights. Others have combinations of different Lights, like yourself, which identify multiple strengths. The stones themselves correlate with these powers."

"Scientifically speaking, one's unique genetic makeup is sympathetic to certain types of particles, and, therefore, resonates more clearly with these specific particles, making them far easier for that person to manipulate," said Loric. "Your Light is a visual reflection of your genome."

"That is one way to put it," said the Eldre.

"So each color is a different power?" asked Thomas.

"Precisely."

"What am I, then?" asked Thomas.

"Ahh, yes. Ziza mentioned your lack of patience." He smiled at the young man. "Your answer will emerge momentarily."

"Narsh," said Thomas.

A yellow stone materialized in front of the Eldre. "The Taitokura—the Experience Stone. This Light allows one to manipulate time to a degree, making the owner faster and seemingly more perceptive. Mages proficient in this skill are called Chronomancers. As stated before, you know of the Taitokura's powers first hand and used chronomancy quite well in your battle with Grayden Arkmalis."

The yellow stone moved aside, replaced with a purple one. "This is the Asar—the Seeing Stone. This stone and its Lightholders are advanced in the art of seeing events before they unfold. This area of expertise is referred to as augurmancy or divination. Mary, the last

Bearer, was an adept Augurmancer." He looked directly at Thomas. "I believe her Light was purple." Thomas grinned proudly at the mention of his mother.

The Asar shifted, and a green stone appeared. "The Turran, better known as the Life Stone."

There goes that theory, thought Thomas. For some time he had assumed that the stone in Ziza's staff was the Turran, but after comparing its distinct shape and size, he realized it could not be. *There's still gotta be a pretty narsh story behind that staff.*

"The abilities associated with this Light are vast, but at the heart of it is the life force. Someone with a green Light can manipulate plants, trees, and even life itself—asking living things to cooperate with them. They are capable of communing with all aspects of nature. They are sometimes referred to as Phytomancers—an area of study your High Mancer knows well."

Sirati makes a whole lot more sense now, thought Thomas.

A red stone hovered in front of Tuguna. "The Ignus or Fire Stone. The red Light signifies control over the element of fire or pyromancy. It is also a stone associated with increased power output. My Eldre guard is a skilled Pyromancer."

"Should I be taking notes?" interrupted Thomas. The Council all glared at him. "Just asking. Wasn't sure if there'd be a test later."

The red stone made room for the appearance of the orange stone.

"The Zikrune—the Mind Stone. Orange Light suggests heightened intelligence and an aptitude for telepathy and telekinesis. These Mages are referred to as Cognomancers."

"Or cogs," said Loric. "That is the common slang term for someone with this particular skill set."

"They shorten everything these days," said the Eldre. The brown stone was next. "The Ektona—also known as the Earth Stone. People adept at utilizing The brown Light are called Terramancers. Terramancy involves manipulating earth, stone, and metal."

Narsh, thought Thomas.

"The early stages of terramancy allows intrinsic understanding of the terra components that make up a system. In short, brown Light correlates with a talent for building things—looking at complex systems and dissecting them in your mind. In this age, you might know them as technics. They have merely embraced the brown terra Light in understanding a system—however, they might not yet know of their deeper terramantic abilities."

That must be how Loric opened up that wall in Ontario, thought Thomas.

"This stone is no longer in play," said the Eldre. "As we all know, it has been tainted by Tollin Grimm." The brown stone disappeared and a blue stone took its place. "Which leaves us with the Medenculus or the Healing Stone. The blue Light indicates a connection with water manipulation—an Aquamancer. Displaying skill in healing oneself and others is a mature trait of aquamancy."

I can manipulate water? thought Thomas.

The seven stones circled above. They all were similar, but each had a distinct shape. "Six stones are needed to fully power the Gauntlet. Without the Ektona, the Medenculus must be found."

Loric stood and began to move to the elevator.

"Where's he going?" asked Thomas.

"The Medenculus is not going to find itself, Scargen, and my unique skill set would be far better employed figuring out the cryptic message your father was good enough to leave you and learning everything I can about the Medenculus and its possible whereabouts." He entered the elevator, turned towards the Council, waved with a smirk, and disappeared down the chute.

"I don't get it," said Thomas. "What's so damn important about the blue stone? Besides the yellow and brown ones, they're all missing, right?"

"The Medenculus has never been found, Thomas," said Ziza. "It was not in the Gauntlet when I carried the Burden. I had the Ektona at my disposal, but with it being transformed the way it has been, it can no longer serve as one of the six stones needed to fully power the Gauntlet. The Medenculus must be found, or the Gauntlet cannot reach its potential."

"It is said to have great power," said Itsuki. "Some think it a myth."

"I assure you, Augmentor, it is no myth," said the Eldre. "The Ancestors know of its existence, but it was concealed eons ago, before the time of the Eldre."

"If it does indeed exist, it is well hidden," said Anson. "The oldest Ancient texts we have here speak of it as something that once existed, but none shed any light on its location."

"So you're saying we need to find a stone that no one's ever seen before, including Ancient spirits?" asked Thomas.

"That is an accurate assessment of the current situation," said Ziza.

"Okay, add it to the list, but I have another question, Eldre," said Thomas.

"By all means, Bearer, ask away," responded the Eldre.

"Why is there no white stone?"

"A fair question, but one with a simple answer."

"And that would be . . ."

"There is a white stone, Thomas. You are wearing it. The Gauntlet *is* the white stone."

"Ohhhhhh," said Thomas.

"White Light is a connection with the Spirit, allowing the person to summon and sometimes even channel the spirits. On rare occasions, this Light will manifest as an adeptness for controlling the wind itself—aeromancy it is sometimes called. I believe Yareli Chula is among those so exceptionally gifted." Thomas looked over at her and smiled. "It is also a strong indicator of someone with the potential to master multiple abilities like yourself, Thomas. Many a powerful, practiced Mage or Necromancer can learn two, three, maybe even four of these abilities and use them in concert—regardless of the color of their Light. The ability to control all of these powers is, indeed, uncommon. It is the first prerequisite for potential Bearers. The Gauntlet does not choose its Bearer haphazardly, and it is more than a mere weapon, Thomas. It is a living thing. It thinks, it breathes, and it will protect you and the stones by any means at its disposal. In the same way it will try to help you find the stones, any way it can—sometimes without you even understanding its messages."

"You're saying the Gauntlet will talk to me?"

"More that it will try to direct you. It can be rather cryptic at times, actually, and it takes time for a Bearer to truly merge with the Gauntlet and understand the connection. You have only just begun this partnership."

"So I've gotta lot of work ahead of me?"

"In a word—yes."

"Is that what you came all this way to tell me?"

"No, my dear boy. The reasons I have come here are twofold. First, we are here to help Ziza escalate your training."

"And what's the second?"

"We have come to deliver a message from the Ancestors."

"Which is?"

"Hard to say."

"In what way?"

"They have not, as of yet, said it."

"So what does that mean?"

"We wait, Thomas. When the time is right, they will deliver the message. One thing is certain: a great evil is coming. Tollin Grimm's power is growing. Even I can sense that. The Ancestors rarely meddle in the affairs of mortals, so rest assured, the message will be of the utmost importance. All of your abilities will be needed if you are to stand a chance of defeating Grimm, and it goes without saying that finding the stones is paramount. In the meantime, we will help expedite your understanding of your current powers and begin to awake some of your still dormant ones."

"You see, Thomas, energy manipulation is you harnessing your inner Light, or what some call spirit, to influence the tiny particles that make up everything," said Ziza. "You are innately adept at this skill, but mastering elemental manipulation can prove most difficult for the uninitiated. It requires communing with the spirits of the elements and guiding the tiny particles within an element itself." The High Mancer paused. "We will start with fire."

Narsh, thought Thomas. "Who's gonna teach me that?" He was excited at the prospect of continuing his training and learning something new.

Garron Dar stepped forward and grabbed Thomas's left hand and shook it. "It would be my honor, Bearer."

"Garron is the most skilled Pyromancer I have ever seen," said the Eldre.

"I also might be the one of the only Pyromancers you have seen in quite some time."

"That may be true. There is much Garron can teach you, Thomas. Your training should begin immediately."

"I agree," said Neficus. "The sooner he starts the better."

There is no way, thought Thomas. "I understand that everyone's excited to get started and all, but, I'm gonna be honest with you: I am completely exhausted. Itsuki too, I'd imagine." The Augmentor nodded his head yes. "Neither one of us has seen a real bed, let alone slept in one for at least two months, and I'm not sure anyone wants to get too close to either of us, because its been even longer since we've had an actual shower." The Augmentor once again nodded. "Not to mention that already today I have trudged through two feet of snow to find a bar in the middle of Canada, almost ate a poison burger, got ambushed by werewolf bounty hunters, then saved by a Mancer I did not know existed. I come back home empty-handed—with a bit of dragonlag, mind you—awaken my artif, only to find a secret message from my dead father. Then I tried to eat an *unpoisoned* burger, but instead I learned that my father's robotics company has been taken over by the Global Alliance. I ran to Maktaba, met the Eldre, who told me everything I need to know about the stones and the Light inside of me—a lot of information and very illuminating."

"Thank you," said the Eldre.

"And now I'm supposed to follow all that up with some fire training? I think it's best for all of us if I meet . . . what's your name again?"

"Garron," said Garron.

"Thank you. If I meet *Garron* in like say twelve hours, so I can get some much needed rest, and then he can teach me to shoot fireballs from my hands. Otherwise I might just fall asleep during training and burn down all of Sirati, and that would not be narsh." Itsuki shook his head no. The Council was quiet for a few seconds.

"High Mancer, the Bearer's attitude is unacceptable," said Neficus. "When I was training, we never got breaks, let alone time set aside for rest."

"But you were also trained by a Necromancer," said Anson. "And if I'm not mistaken, she almost killed you."

"*Almost* killed me, and this has only made me stronger," said Neficus.

"We do things differently here, and you know that, Elgin," said Ziza. "If Thomas knows he is tired then we should respect that."

"Weary with toil, I hasten thee to thy bed, the dear repose for limbs with travel tired," said Anson.

"Give him the time to reenergize his Light," said Lolani. The pudgy woman smiled. "It is more beautiful when it is full."

"It is settled then," said Ziza. "The second phase of your training will begin tonight, Thomas. Garron will meet you here at midnight. Is that agreeable, Eldre?"

"I trust the wisdom of the Council," said Tuguna.

"Does this decision suit you, Garron?"

"Yes, High Mancer. That will give me enough time to plan."

"Good. Then be here at midnight, Thomas. Until then, I advise you get some rest, and possibly a shower," said Ziza, winking at Thomas. "That goes for you too, Itsuki."

"Yes, High Mancer," said Itsuki, pulling Spells from his pack. Flora shot down and grabbed the book out of the clutches of the First Augmentor and promptly shot back up from where she came.

"That sounds like a great plan," said Thomas. "I like it so much better than that first plan."

"You will need your full faculties if you are to master pyromancy," said Ziza. "Great responsibility comes with the study of this ability."

"Say no more. If I learned anything, it's to sleep when you tell me to—even though, technically, this time it was my idea . . . and now I'm rambling again . . . so I'll be headin' out." Thomas got out of his seat and began to walk to the elevator. He saw Yareli and stopped. All of a sudden, he did not feel so tired. "Hey, Yar. Before I go to bed, can we talk? It's been a while, and we have a lot to catch up on."

"Of course, Thomas," said Yareli.

"Can we go somewhere a bit more private?"

"Okay," said Yareli. "Lead the way."

long overdue

Thomas began walking towards the natural balcony that lead to Ziza's study. Yareli followed. He had never told anyone that his mother was Mary, except Ziza and Itsuki. He had not had time. Before he knew it, he was off looking for the next stone. It had all been a blur to Thomas. One minute he was training with Ziza, the next he was following a new lead on the next stone. He never told Yareli how he felt, and he never told her about his mother. Today he would do both.

They reached the opening in the branches that overlooked Sirati. It was as private as it was gorgeous and easily the best view in Sirati. He turned slowly towards her. He had not seen Yareli in a year and three months, but now when she was so close, he felt so far away. How could he tell her that he loved her? He did not know what to say. Thomas still felt strongly about not putting her in harm's way, but he could not shake his feelings. She beat him to it. Her embrace caught him by surprise. He had forgotten how fast she was—and how warm. She pulled back from the hug.

"I wasn't sure when you were coming back. Mancer Bodes said it might take some time to retrieve you."

"Am I the only one that didn't know there was another Mancer?" asked Thomas.

"Probably," said Yareli. "He was away looking for the first stone when you had arrived. Loric is good at solving mysteries—the best actually. He's a professional finder of things. It was his information that led us to the Hive and the Taitokura."

"Narsh . . . sort of. That place still gives me the creeps."

"Yeah, I still have nightmares myself."

Wiyaloo appeared behind her. Thomas had missed them both. After all, they were a team. *If you want one, you have to take them both*, he thought.

"Hello, Thomas Scargen," said Wiyaloo. "It is good to feel your spirit once more."

"Agreed," said Thomas as he winked at the spirit ghost.

"Stop teasing him, Thomas," said Yareli.

"Come on. The big fox knows I'm joking with him."

"Agreed," said Wiyaloo as he winked back at Thomas.

"There are so many things to talk about," said Yareli.

"I know . . . there is a ton of stuff I want to tell you as well."

"Did you get to see LINC yet?" asked Yareli.

"That's a long story. He's back up and running, but now there's another issue."

"What's that?"

"It seems like my dad left an embedded code inside LINC, which we were almost able to solve, mostly because of Mancer Bodes."

"That sounds about right."

"But when the code was deciphered, what was left made no sense."

"What did it say?"

"Salvation or wisdom is seated on the shoulders of Bastet, who's the goddess of war from Egyptian mythology or it might be about the sun setting on the shoulder's of war."

"Sounds like you've been busy already."

"Yeah, I just needed to get out of there. I was so hungry and tired, and I wasn't helping things anyway."

"Somehow I doubt that's true," said Yareli. The two of them shared an awkward silence. Yareli broke the quiet. "So what was it you wanted to tell me?"

What do I want to tell you? I want to tell you that I haven't felt right since leaving you. That I dream about you almost every night, and that it's a miracle that Itsuki is still my friend after listening to me talk about you nonstop for fifteen months, thought Thomas. "Just a few things I've been thinking about."

"Like what?"

"Well, I missed you." The words had just fallen out.

"I missed you too, Thomas. We both did."

"Good . . . I mean, not good, but I'm glad you felt the same way." He was sweating—his face, his chest, even his rock hand seemed to be clammy. "There's more."

"Okay, what else?"

"Well, when I was out there looking for the stone, I began to think about life more. There was a lot of down time, and Itsuki isn't the best conversationalist—"

"What are you trying to say, Thomas?" asked Yareli as she moved a strand of hair back behind her ear.

This is it. You just have to say it. Let it out. Put it out there and everything will work out fine. "Well, it's just that I wanted to tell you that . . . What I mean to say is that, I'm pretty sure that I l—"

Yareli's wristcom interrupted Thomas's declaration. "Do you mind if I answer this?"

"N-n-no, not at all," said Thomas. A hologram of Garron appeared above her wristcom.

"What's up, Garron?" asked Yareli.

"Are you busy?"

"I'm just trying to catch up with Thomas. Why? What's going on?"

"I need help finding a suitable place for my training session later with the Bearer."

I wish he'd stop calling me that, thought Thomas.

"And I thought I could pick your brain, seeing as you have a vast knowledge of Sirati and its surrounding regions. One needs to be careful when wielding fire, and I don't have an awful lot of time to figure it out."

"I could see that," said Yareli. "But I'm talking to Thomas right now."

"You should go, Yar," said Thomas. "We will have plenty of time to catch up. I wouldn't want my training to be subpar. Besides, I should be sleeping anyway." *What is wrong with you? You are such a wuss.*

"Oh, okay, sure. I guess I am free to talk, Garron," said Yareli. "I'll see you in a bit." The hologram dissipated as she began to move back towards the Council's chamber. "Well, I guess I'll see you later, Thomas."

"Yeah, see ya later."

Yareli began to walk away, but she turned back. "What were you gonna say earlier—before Garron interrupted?"

"Nothing, Yar. It was nothing."

"Okay. See ya."

Thomas waved with a fake smile and turned away. *I'm such an idiot. Why didn't I tell her?* Yareli disappeared through the entrance back to Maktaba.

"Man, I'll never understand human relationships," said Emkoo as the Lion dropped from the branch above and walked towards Thomas.

"W-w-what are you talking about?" asked Thomas.

"Come on. It's pretty obvious you like her," said Emkoo. "And welcome back."

"How did you—"

"Animal instincts, I suppose," said Emkoo. "I do not envy you."

"That makes two of us," said Thomas.

Thomas walked up to the circular door. The treehouse had almost instantly felt like home when he had first come to Sirati, but he had been away for some time now. Onjamba opened the door.

"Hello, flatmate."

"Hi, Onjamba." Thomas walked in and threw his pack down on

the sofa. He could not believe it. There were even more plants strewn about the place. "I love the new plants."

"Best to have a hobby, I suppose. I think someone is trying to say hi." Thomas felt the cat rub up against his left leg and meow loudly.

"Hello, Stella. I missed you too." He picked her up and cradled her in his arms as she purred vibrations. "You are such a little monster." Thomas petted her under the metal pendant on her collar. The cat batted at him once she had had enough. He put her down on the ground.

"Will Itsuki be joining us?" asked Onjamba.

"I'd assume so. He doesn't like to be too far away for too long. One of his rules."

"I will make sure his bedroom is ready." Onjamba picked up Thomas's pack with his trunk. "And you, my boy, should go rest your eyelids." He placed the pack on one of the hooks next to the door.

"Good night, Onjamba."

"Good night, Thomas . . . and I must say, it's great to see you around once again."

"It's great to be seen."

The Elephant chuckled as he exited the room. "I suppose it would be, wouldn't it?"

Thomas made his way up the staircase to the landing and the door to his bedroom. He entered the bedroom, looking at all his old stuff. It comforted him, but it also made him sad. None of it really mattered anymore. He did not need any of it, but it reminded him of simpler times—before his life was dedicated to finding stones to power a magical Gauntlet that only he could wield. And then he saw it—the chanunpa. Yareli had given to him what he had thought was a peace pipe for his seventeenth birthday before everything changed.

"I really need to get some sleep, Stella," said Thomas as the cat entered his bedroom. "I'm gettin' all sentimental."

He thought of the information he was given earlier about the stones—specifically finding the Medenculus. He also pondered the riddle his father had left inside the hibernating artif. He flopped onto the bed and pried off his boots and lay flat on his back. He did not realize just how tired he had been. He had not had a proper night's sleep in months. His bed felt good. Stella hopped up next to him and nuzzled his side and assumed her sleep position. "I don't suppose you know where the blue stone is?" asked Thomas of the cat. The Gauntlet twinged as Stella started to purr. "I didn't think soooooo." He yawned and closed his eyes. Thomas quickly fell asleep to the sound of purring.

the old dragon and the sea

The gilled man slithered in the darkness on the outskirts of the underwater city, near one of its three main entrances. Viewed from out there, the city was astonishing. Tiers of tall buildings were situated inside of an immense force field that held back the water. The sleekly designed structures were connected by large tube-like swimming passageways. The inhabitants used these waterways for travel between levels and across the vast city. Outside the force field, smaller towns built from the sea floor encircled the main city. These areas were inhabited by the water-breathing denizens.

"Are you sure it's here?" asked the man.

"For the last time, I'm certain," said the hologram of a black dragon. The dragon had a distinctly English accent. "It is in the center of the city, so you will have to do this with precision and stealth. No one must notice you."

"I know. We've been over this a million times: no interference from the Atlanteans."

"They will not be expecting this. Because of their relative anonymity, they have lived in peace for millennia, but be warned—I cannot stress this enough—they do not like outsiders."

"I know, I know. Hence the disguise. I'm pretty convincing—if I do say so myself."

"You *look* like an Atlantean. Now, make sure you *act* like one."

"Whatever that means."

"I'm simply suggesting that you blend in until the time comes to make your move. Once you're done, we will rendezvous at the agreed coordinates."

"Of course."

"Now switch me to audio in your earb, and initialize the recon orb." The man moved a few keys on the holographic display. A small orb released into the water. If you did not know it was there, you would not see it. "Okay, it's time."

"Here goes nothing."

The man swam towards the entrance to the massive city. One thing was certain: he could swim like an Atlantean. He moved effortlessly through the ocean, gliding through the murky waters. Two crustacean-like beings stood guard, one on each side of the gateway. Both creatures held two-pronged bidents that glowed blue.

"Do not look at the guards. They have extremely acute senses, and will detect any inconsistencies if you draw attention to yourself."

"What are those things?"

"They are the Kra—one of the two humanoid species in Atlantis."

"And I am a Mer?"

"Correct. Now concentrate."

He continued closer to the entrance. Several Atlantean residents swam in and out of the force field gate. He swam through the opening. The Kra guards did not budge. His disguise had worked. Once through, he landed on his webbed feet. The sensation of going from the underwater towns into the artificial air of the city was jarring. He adjusted his breathing and took a deep breath as he stood in the main thoroughfare of the incredible city.

"Now the hard part," said the dragon through the earb. "You have to make your way to the center of the city. See the building in front of you to your right?"

"Yes."

"Move to it." The man moved as fast as he could without drawing attention to himself.

"Now what?"

"Enter the swim tube to your right." He walked through another force field and found himself once again swimming. This time there were two distinct currents—one going upward and one going downward. "Swim downward to level three of the city. It should be clearly marked."

He made his way down to level three as fast as he could, then exited. "Done."

"Good. Now access your wristcom. I uploaded a program that, when in close proximity, should be able to detect certain energy signatures. Do you see it?"

"Yes."

"Activate it." The man did as the dragon ordered, and a three-dimensional screen appeared on his Atlantean version of a wristcom. "You are looking for something giving off a considerable amount of energy."

"How much energy are we talking about?"

"Enough to run the entire city."

"That narrows it down . . . found it." The energy signature was immense and easily located by the program.

"Good. Now move towards it, but be careful. There is bound to be more security the closer you get."

He looked down at his wristcom to see what direction he was supposed to proceed. He quickly gathered the data and began to move. The entrance he had arrived by was located close to where he needed to be. The energy signature emanated from a large building—the largest on the level. "I found it. It's in the center of the building directly in front of me." The place was surrounded by Atlantean guards—Mers. These guards wore different attire. "There does seem to be a tad more security here," said the disguised man.

"I see that," said the dragon through his earb. "I surveyed the perimeter with the recon orb. There is a maintenance door with minimal security towards the back of the building. It could be the easiest way in. I will leave the orb there so you can move to its location."

"You've done this before, huh?"

"A few times."

"Okay. Moving there now." The man casually walked around the perimeter of the building through the busy streets of the city, making his way to the poorly protected door. Two guards flanked the entrance. He knelt down behind several cargo pods.

"You think you can handle them?"

"Please, really? There's only two of them. Have a little faith."

"Atlanteans are a very physically strong race of people is all I'm saying, mate."

"I'll remember that after I kick their finned asses. Besides, none of that matters when you're not playing fair." The man shot out two distinctly different orbs from his wristcom. They whizzed towards the two Atlantean guards. When they got close enough to their targets, they simultaneously struck both guards in the bases of their necks, shocking the Atlanteans until they dropped. "See, like I said. No problem. Stunner orbs work every time."

"Stop congratulating yourself and hide the bodies. And don't forget to swap bloody outfits with one of them."

"Good call."

"Like I said, not my first time."

The man tucked the guards' bodies behind the cargo pods. He switched clothing with the guard that was closest to his build and commandeered his weapon and then entered the building.

The interior walls were covered with glowing blue lights. He walked down the hallway as much like a guard as possible, looking for his next turn. He moved down the next hallway to the elevator that led to his target. He passed several guards, none of whom paid him any attention. "According to the energy signature, the signal is coming from the top floor of this building," said the dragon. "You're a-a-a-almost there."

"What was that?"

"Inter-r-r-r-ference. F-f-f-from h-h-here on out, y-y-y—" The voice in the earb abruptly ended.

"I guess I'm on my own." He entered the elevator and pressed what he determined was the corresponding key to the top floor.

Once he arrived at his floor, the door automatically slid open.

Two Kra guards stood at attention, flanking the doors. He walked past them as if nothing were wrong. He moved along the corridor. There were thousands of tubes moving blue energy from one place to another, and several engineers attending to the various terminals, channeling the energy to different parts of the city. Still others were harnessing the energy into intricate stone carvings that floated in front of them. As each of the stones absorbed the energy, its carvings glowed blue.

He continued through the facility in the direction his wristcom had mapped out, being careful not to look out of place. He turned the last corner, and there it was at the center of a grid of glowing blue tubes—the Medenculus, the blue stone. "Remarkable." One of the engineers looked up at him and mumbled something in Atlantean. He had forgotten to engage the translator, and he had just spoken English. He immediately turned the translator on.

"What was that, guard?" said the engineer.

"I was just saying how remarkable this all still is to me."

"Yes, yes, all well and good, but why did you say it in a surface-walker's tongue?"

"They fascinate me. I've been trying to practice speaking their language as much as I can."

"Practice of any of the surfacewalkers' ways is expressly forbidden by order of the Senate," said the engineer. "An Atlantean would know that."

"I . . . forgot?"

"Guards, arrest this man!" shouted the engineer. Several Kra guards rushed over and tackled the man. He had come so far only to be thwarted at the last second.

"Enough!" shouted the disguised man. His strength knocked the guards backward, and he began to transform. His body enlarged as his mouth extended into a snout. A black Aequos stood where the Atlantean impostor had been just moments before. The dragon moved quickly towards the stone, flying directly at it as the remaining guards engaged him with their staffs. He grabbed the stone, prying it from its harness. Energy coursed through his wingless form. He turned and unleashed a firestorm down on the guards with his newly enhanced power. The guards dispersed as the lights flickered and then faded. Darkness was an advantage to the dragon.

He moved across the room to a large set of windows and burst through them, out of the building. Glass rained down on the Atlanteans below. The force of the dragon's maneuver threw him into the adjacent building. The roof of that structure began to collapse as he oriented himself. He launched himself from the crumbling structure towards the swim tubes.

The dragon quickly moved to the passage tube on level three and shot upward through the water, back to the upper level by which he had entered the city. He burst through the force field and on to the thoroughfare. Atlanteans and various sea creatures shot in several directions as they dove to avoid the dragon. Blue beams of energy fired down upon him as he made his way to the exit.

The black Aequos burst through the final force field and moved upward to the surface. The two guards gave chase, firing at the dragon, hitting him once in his back left leg. He pushed himself harder, breaking the water's surface. A teleportal formed immediately above the water, and into it the dragon disappeared.

The Aequos surged out of the other side of the tear—blue stone in his talons. The dragon buzzed over the city of Cairo, out of sight of the aeromobile traffic that moved along below him. Once through the city, he sped for the large pyramid in the distance.

He slowed his pace and moved towards the base of the structure. Energy still rippled around his body as he landed.

"Did you secure the artifact?" asked the Dracavea as he walked out from around the other side of the pyramid.

"Yes." The Aequos held the stone out in his claw. His eyes glowed blue. "Why did we meet here, of all places?"

"The Ancient magic that permeates this place hides any power signature the stone would give off. I don't need any overzealous Mage interfering with my plans. Now, hand it over." The Aequos stared at the blue stone, mesmerized by its power. "I said, hand it over."

"No." The Aequos pulled the stone into his chest and growled.

"What was that, boy? I don't care who you are. You don't say no to Larson Ragnor. Hand over the stone."

The Aequos powered himself down. The energy that had encircled him dissipated. He shook his head back and forth. "S-s-s-sorry. I don't know what came over me." He handed the stone to Larson. The massive Dracavea closed his talons on the stone.

"Finally. The Medenculus is back in the claws of dragons. Now we begin."

Thomas shot up out of his sleep. He exhaled hard as he relaxed back onto his palms. "Larson Ragnor?" Stella tilted her head as she yawned, exposing her pointy teeth. "That was a weird dream." *Or was it a dream?* His pondering was interrupted by the rapping on his balcony door. "Doesn't anyone use the front door anymore?" It was dark out now, and all he could make out was a silhouette on the balcony. "Who is it?"

"Itsuki."

"One second." Thomas got out of his bed and opened the door. "Hey." Thomas's hand was rubbing the top of his head. "Onjamba should have your room ready by now."

"I know. I arrived shortly after you did and did as the High Mancer suggested."

"Then why are you here on my balcony?"

"I heard you screaming."

"Well, I was having a dream—if you can call them that anymore."

"Another premonition?"

"I'm not sure. It felt real like the dream about my Dad, but it was stranger than that dream."

"In what way?"

"This one definitely took place a while ago—at least sixteen years or so."

"How can you be so sure?"

"Well, besides the older-model aeromobiles I saw . . . the dragon flew over Cairo."

"That's odd. That city was buried along with Ancient Egypt when your mother trapped Grimm."

"Exactly. I think you-know-who is trying to tell me something." He raised the Gauntlet. "I'm just not sure what. One thing I know, though: the Medenculus is extremely powerful, and if my dream's correct, Larson Ragnor has it."

9

loric's flat

"Are you sure we should be disturbing him? He seems to have enough on his plate," said Itsuki. The two had set off into the jungle shortly after Thomas's quick shower.

"Do you have a better plan, Suke?" asked Thomas as they approached the stone structure on the outskirts of Sirati. The wisps were already at the circular door. "He might be the only person who could find this information remotely useful."

"You have a point. This is where he lives?"

"That's the info I got from Sirati's database," said Thomas.

"It's gloomier than I would have thought."

"What happened to not judging books by their cover?" He smiled at Itsuki as the wisps circled above the Augmentor's head. Thomas could hear an instrument playing as they approached the door. "All right, here goes." He knocked on the door twice. The music abruptly stopped and almost simultaneously the door opened. Loric Bodes stood in the entryway, holding an odd looking musical instrument.

"What do you want?" asked Loric. He wore a lab coat and protective goggles rested on his head.

"Can we come in?"

"Oh, yes. Do come in. I wasn't expecting you so soon." Loric stepped aside to let them in. "Please resist the urge to touch anything."

The first thing Thomas noticed was the abundance of books—all meticulously placed and categorized, the only exceptions being the five books that were open and levitating around Loric. Thomas noticed one of the books was opened to a picture of a woman with the head of a cat.

"What's she all about?" asked Thomas.

"That is Bastet, the goddess of warfare from your father's puzzle. I was studying the mythology to see if it would further my understanding of your father's clues or the goddess of warfare herself."

"Did it work?" asked Thomas.

"I am afraid not, but I have not given up hope as of yet."

Thomas turned his head. Along the back wall were twenty-three holovisions—all on different channels, all with the volume up. Loric walked across the room and placed the instrument into its case. He began dabbling with his wristcom as he proceeded to walk over to a blank area on the rear wall. As he approached he lifted his hands, raising a section of the stone wall, creating a doorway. Loric walked through. Thomas and Itsuki followed.

"Now that was pretty narsh," said Thomas. "You're a Terramancer."

"Amongst other things, Scargen. Nothing seems to slip past you."

"Come on. I just learned they were even a thing like twelve hours ago."

The back room was laid out like a lab. Holoscreens floated around the room containing data and graphs and charts. To the right were several carved stones that resembled the one the Eldre had shown them, the *tuqi*. To the left was the still silent LINC. Thomas studied the quiet artif from afar. He turned towards the Mancer and looked across at the *tuqi*. One of the carved stones floated in front of Loric, who was staring at it.

"What's that all about?"

"I am in the middle of an experiment of sorts."

"What sort of experiment?" asked Thomas. "And where did you get these stones?"

"I made them—with the help of the Eldre of course. It has taken me months to perfect this one in particular."

"Just like that? You made all of these?"

"Yes. If you have not put two and two together, I am also a technic like your father. I use my problem-solving skills to figure things out. Your father used them to create amazing machines. But I too dabble in building things from time to time."

"What does the stone do?" asked Itsuki.

"Good question. These *tuqi,* or stones as you so quaintly refer to them, depending on the carvings, can store different forms of energy—not unlike batteries." He took the *tuqi* in his hands. "The real-world implications are staggering. I was about to see how much energy it could contain before you two so politely barged in."

"But you were playing music," said Thomas. Loric levitated the *tuqi* across the room and placed the stone on a pedestal. He moved directly across from the carved stone and lowered his goggles. He motioned for Thomas and Itsuki to get behind him.

"I am fully capable of doing multiple tasks concurrently, and if you must know, the music helps me process my intolerable cerebration."

"Cerebration?" asked Thomas.

"The astounding number of thoughts that rush through my mind at any given time."

"It was beautiful, by the way, Mancer Bodes," said Itsuki. "Sounds like you have been playing for years."

"Thank you, Itsuki. I wrote that particular piece, as it were, and I *have* been playing for quite some time." Without warning Loric threw his hands forward and dark orange energy flew at the *tuqi.* The stone absorbed the blast, containing every bit of the pulse. Loric powered down. The carvings on the stone glowed orange. "Simply amazing." He walked over and picked up the *tuqi.* "But I expect complimenting my musical prowess is not why you have come to my home at such a late hour. Which one will it be?"

"What do you mean?" asked Thomas.

"You've come either to deliver news about your father's puzzle, or the Medenculus. Have you not?"

"How did you know?"

"Well, I imagine you would not disturb me at this hour, precisely one hour before your pyromantic training is to commence, unless it was of the utmost importance, and seeing that the only two subjects that are important to *me* at this time are your father's puzzle and the Medenculus, it stands to reason that one or the other would be motivation for your otherwise delightful late-night intrusion."

"You talk very fast," said Thomas.

"Time is an important commodity when trying to find things." He turned the carved stone over as he examined it. "So out with it, Scargen."

"I had a dream about the Medenculus," said Thomas.

"And when you say *dream*, you mean a premonition—a seeing of events," said Loric. "I heard from a reliable source that this phenomenon happens to you from time to time."

"Well, until this one, it had been only one other time."

"And?"

"And what?"

"And what happened in said premonition."

"I saw a black Aequos dragon disguised as an Atlantean swimming through an underwater city, which I'm assuming was the lost city of Atlantis, and at the end, he stole the blue stone and delivered it to another dragon—a Dracavea. And I'm pretty sure it was Larson Ragnor."

"The Draige-family tormentor?"

"That's him, but that's not all. This vision was from a long time ago."

"How old?"

"I'd say from the tech they were using, twenty years or so, but definitely over sixteen years."

"How can you be so certain?"

"Their meeting place for the handoff was Cairo."

"Interesting. I must admit, I had hit a dead end of sorts on this subject."

"That's not all. Once the dragon touched the Medenculus, he seemed to change."

"Please be more specific."

"He seemed obsessed with it."

"Which dragon?"

"The Aequos."

"What facts do you have of this obsession?"

"He was retrieving the stone for Ragnor, but when it came time to hand it over, the Aequos, at first, refused. When Ragnor threatened him, he gave up the stone."

"And this temporary refusal is the sole fact upon which you are basing your presumption?"

"No. The Medenculus seemed to be powering the entire city, and when he grabbed the stone, there was a power surge. Afterwards the dragon looked different—acted different."

"Many people when brought into close proximity with the stones, experience adverse reactions. Some people cannot control themselves around such power."

"Amara Scornd?" asked Itsuki.

"Precisely. Not the first and certainly not the last. But your information may prove most useful. It's not much, mind you, but I've done more with less. It's at least better than the dead end at which I arrived. It gives me a proper starting point. I will contact the Council of Dragons."

"I was under the impression that that was a no-no for humans."

"I am friends with Aldrich Baldemar, the Head Dragon, and he owes me quite a few favors. I have found many an item for the Council. One thing seems certain."

"What's that?"

"At one time or another, the stone was in Atlantis. If the stone was, in fact, powering Atlantis, I would not be surprised if these Atlanteans might come looking for it. I may be able to use this information as well." Loric turned and walked across the room. "Now, the other matter."

"What other matter?" asked Thomas.

"Your father's riddle, if we can call it that. I detest riddles. I was at a dead end with the Medenculus, but I have made progress with the other matter."

"You solved the riddle?"

"I have not solved it, but I have found a few interesting tidbits that you should see." He approached the hibernating artif and held out the carved stone. The stone's energy erupted and fired at LINC. Before the blast could hit the artif, a shielding device activated and deflected the assault.

"What are you doing?" shouted Thomas.

"Demonstrating two of my findings at once."

"Which are?"

"One: the stone can release the energy it has stored. Two: your father programmed the artif to defend itself even when in a dormant state."

"So?"

"Sooo . . . whatever information that is contained in your artificial companion is extremely important, hence the upgrade. Which brings me to my next point. I did some digging into your father's financial records and some startling information began to reveal itself."

"Like?"

"Well, for starters your father's obsession with archaeology was more than just a hobby."

"What makes you say that?"

"Your father has spent millions of credits over the last fifteen years—across several digs."

Millions? thought Thomas. "I though the money for those digs came from grants."

"Well, you thought incorrectly."

"So when you say millions you mean?"

"Thirty-seven million to be precise. Most of the credits were tied to creating the diggerbots—a marvelous invention, mind you."

"He loved going on digs."

"One does not spend that many credits on a mere hobby. Your father was looking for something, and I think he found it."

"Found what?"

"That is still unclear, but rest assured, I will figure it out." He gestured from his wristcom and several holographic documents floated in front of them. "He went on a series of digs outside of Boston in the span of three months—the Norse digs. A rather quick turnaround for archaeology—suggesting that he did not, in fact, find what he was looking for and abandoned these sites quite quickly. But look here. This dig is the longest before Egypt, and he sunk approximately twelve million credits into it."

"That was when he was in Mexico. He spent six years on that dig. It was the first time he relied solely on the Diggers for excavating. He seemed happy after that one."

"He never finished the dig."

"What do you mean?"

"He abandoned this dig, like the others, and with haste moved on to Nara."

"He didn't abandon the Mayan dig. He ended up donating what he found to the Penn Museum in Philadelphia. I went to the opening."

"I did not say the dig was never completed, but that your father didn't finish it. Those artifacts were found well after Dr. Scargen had shifted his interests to Nara, and after he sunk several million credits into another new venture."

"What new venture?"

"That's the mystery. The credits were transferred to a company called Carbone Industries, but when I tried to follow the trail, I found nothing."

"What do you mean, nothing?"

"The company does not exist—at least not under that name. The money simply disappeared."

"What's all this mean?"

"My best hypothesis, if I had to wager, is that he found something in Mexico, but he wasn't done. He abandoned ship and directed his attention to Japan, from which he withdrew rather quickly, presumably because he did not find what he was looking for their either."

"How do you know?"

"Egypt. If he had found everything he was after in Mexico or in Japan, then why would he keep up his clever ruse of being an archaeologist."

"He wouldn't."

"No, he would not. The great Dr. Carl Scargen then moves on to Egypt and again, he spends millions of credits to dig deep and meticulously. He was looking for something particular."

"What are you trying to say?"

"Despite contrary appearances, which I believe Dr. Scargen carefully designed to disguise his success, I think he did, in fact, find something, perhaps an artifact of sorts—maybe several, across these collective digs."

"What kind of artifacts?"

"That is hard to say with any certainty, but one thing *is* certain."

"What is that?"

"I believe whatever your father was after . . ." Loric pointed towards LINC. "It is most assuredly hidden inside of your artif."

10

the goblin hole

M arcus looked out over the railing into the massive lava pit, taking the last drag of his cigarette. He took a swig from the bottle of Voracek and tossed the butt into the abyss. He had resumed his smoking habit two days after hearing about Evangeline's promotion. It had been six months since the announcement, and he had not been right the whole time. He did not particularly like the taste of cigarettes, but anything was better than the taste he had in his mouth after hearing the news. It was not as if he were jealous or mad. He knew she would make a fine general, but not like this. He walked to the bar with the inexpensive bottle of vodka. He took a slug as he sat down between Nolan Taunt, his new Second, and Brett Jurdik—two of his best Riders.

"Ahh, the good stuff," said Taunt, looking around. "That actually might be the good stuff here."

"Why did you want to meet here?" asked Marcus. He had been wondering about it for the last ten minutes. "Of all the places in the Tower, why did you want to meet in the Goblin Hole?"

"Atmosphere," said Taunt as something rat-like scurried past his leg.

"It's not the cleanest bar in the Tower, but it's certainly the loudest," said Jurdik.

"Which makes it the best place to discuss such things," said Taunt.

"What did you bring me down here to discuss?"

"It's been months since I've seen you, Captain," said Taunt. "The General keeps me busy with all these new design upgrades and whatnot, but it's not the same. And a lot of crazy shit is going on."

"Like what?" asked the Captain.

"Well, for starters, I've been training to develop more of my terramantic skills."

"I didn't know you were a Terramancer," said Marcus.

"Yeah, I just thought you were a straight up technic," said Jurdik.

"Me too until I accidentally tore open a wall while trying to build something for the General. Scared the shit out of me."

"Terramancy is a rare skill," said Marcus. "You should be proud."

"I'm just starting to get the hang of it. I can't do metal yet, but from what I hear, that's advanced stuff anyways."

"What kind of something are they building?" asked Marcus, refocusing the conversation.

"That's just it, they never told me, but they are building something massive. They have been for months. My team converted some of the lower levels near the base of the volcano into a hangar, but no one seems to know what the hangar is for."

I think I might know, thought Marcus, remembering the schematic of the airship he had seen months earlier—the day she got promoted.

"Grimm is overseeing the project himself—Project Dred, I believe it's called. Apparently he's outsourced to the Skinx. I mean, they are good with tech, but why leave your best guy on the bench. It's just insulting."

What are those two up to?

"She's got me running three squads, doing all of this extra training," said Jurdik. "She also had me working on my telekinesis—like I need the practice." His glass slid over to him, and he took a sip. "She even made me train her precious General's Guard in underwater tactics. Then, after I've done a solid two months of aquatic training with those uptight assholes, she dismisses me. She said she was finished with me—like we didn't even know each other."

"I'm sure she had her reasons, Jurdik," said Marcus.

"It seems like straight bullshit to me," said Jurdik. "It seems like busywork to keep us out of the way. Training for training sake. It's like we're being phased out or something, and that just pisses me off. I should be out in the field—not wasting away in this tower. What I wouldn't give for a real mission."

"For once I agree with the cog. It's like she's holding what happened between the two of you against us."

"Maybe she's just doing a better job than Arkmalis," said Marcus. "Did you ever consider that?" The Captain took another drink from the bottle. "I've had my hands full as well, with the influx of men and the new tech we're integrating into the ranks, but change was long overdue. Arkmalis sat on his ass for years, waiting for Grimm."

"We all know that's true," said Taunt. "Arkmalis wasn't the best General, but at least you knew what you were getting with him, and if he did something, he did it with confidence."

"His overconfidence was his undoing. She seems determined not to make the same mistake. The General has a plan, and we will wait here and keep training until we get our orders," said the Captain as he drank from the bottle.

"You call that training, Captain?" Taunt pointed at the bottle. "Your liver will be ready at least. You have to pull yourself together. You're supposed to be our Capt—"

"I *am* your Captain, Second."

"I know, and I'll follow you to the Depths and back," said Taunt. "But I also know that deep down, in that awkward place, where you don't let anyone in, you're thinking the same damn thing. She's changed, Captain, and there's no sign of it going back to the way it was. You look in her eyes now, and her humanity is gone—just like Arkmalis." A Rider leaned over from the barstool next to Taunt.

"Are you boys goin' on about duh General?" asked the Rider at the next table. His name was Herman Porf. He sat with the rest of his squadron. "Has us trainin' day in and out. It's bloody mental it is." He leaned in closer. " 'av you seen dat tattoo uv 'ers lately? It's like it's bloody grown or somefin'. I fought Arkmalis was bad, but turns out duh devil ya know, an that . . . and 'er relationship wif duh Master is a bit suspect, isn't it?" The men with him laughed.

"What did you say?" asked Marcus slowly, looking up at the man.

"No disrespect, Capt'n. It's just she's spendin' an awful lot of time wif Lord Grimm, is all I'm sayin'—behind closed doors and whatnot. Makes duh mind start to wonder, don't it?"

"Maybe they're . . . you know," said the man to the left of Porf. He was the leader of the squadron, Rider James Neal. A smirk rolled across Neal's scarred face.

"Enough!" shouted Marcus. "You are talking about the General of the Grimm Legions and the Legions' namesake. You would do well to keep your thoughts to yourself."

"And who's going to make me, old man?" James Neal stood and looked at Marcus. "You?"

He was the biggest Rider any of them had ever seen. Marcus remained seated, drinking from his bottle of vodka. The Second and Jurdik started to stand.

"Sit your asses back down. That's an order," said Marcus under his breath.

"Yes, sir," said Taunt as the two Riders sat back down.

"Oh, I forgot. You two were close. My apologies," mocked Neal. "Maybe you want to cry some more about it."

Marcus said nothing.

"The way I see it, we're about due for a new captain. Ain't that right, boys? The old one's looking a bit sad and tired." His squadron laughed in agreement as the massive Rider smiled and looked around. "In fact, I'd say this model's gotten pretty unreliable and slow, and we should just scrap him. Wouldn't get much in trade-in value anyway."

Marcus remained quite.

"Maybe make room for some new blood. Who wants some new blood?" Neal's squadron again laughed.

The Captain moved faster than Neal expected, catching him square in the chest with his energy blade. There was a distinct gurgling sound as Marcus slightly twisted the blade. The man began to spit blood as he struggled to breathe.

"There ya go, Jimmy. There's plenty of room now for some new blood." The Captain extinguished the blade as the man's corpse fell to the ground. Captain Slade's eyes went blank as he held out his hand. The electricity caught the five Riders off guard. Marcus continued the assault until all that was left were the charred remains of Neal's men. Marcus powered down. He looked out and around the Goblin Hole. Marcus pulled out a new cigarette and put it in his mouth. He leaned over and pressed it into the charred corpse of Herman Porf, puffing until the cigarette was lit. The Captain took a deeper drag and blew out the smoke. "Anyone else looking for some new blood?"

The remaining Riders went back to eating like nothing had happened. Newts appeared and wasted no time in clearing away the bodies.

"I didn't think so," said Marcus. He turned towards the goblin bartender. "I got their check and a few extra credits for your troubles." Marcus hit a few buttons on his embedded wristcom. He slid his hand across the holographic display, transferring the credits. "It's been nice catching up," said Marcus to Jurdik and Taunt.

The Captain moved towards the exit. He walked down the corridor that lead outside. Marcus could not shake the feeling that he was being followed. He turned around and saw them immediately. Two Riders followed from a distance. Years of tracking made it easy to spot them. They were members of the General's Guard. He walked like he did not notice them.

Once he reached the exit he quickly moved to the right. As the two guards emerged from the doorway, Marcus grabbed one and pressed the energy blade against his neck. "I guess someone else wants to have a go."

"Please, please, Captain. That is not why we followed you," said the guard with the blade pinned against his throat.

Marcus extinguished the blade and pushed the man towards the other guard, a woman. She had short blonde hair and midnight blue eyes. He recognized the man immediately from his distinctly red hair: Rider Harl Vance. He must have been promoted by the General.

He was one of the older Riders—midthirties. She was younger. From the looks of her she was in her late twenties.

"State your business," said the Captain. "And do it quickly."

"We have a message from the General," said Vance. "She wishes to speak to you about an urgent matter."

"She urges that discretion should be used in such matters, and to tell no one at this time of your meeting," said the female guard.

"Not even your Rider friends Taunt and Jurdik," said Vance.

"What is this about?"

"That is not our place to say," said the female guard.

"Whose place is it?"

"General Evangeline will be expecting you in her chambers within the half hour," said Vance. The two guards turned and walked away as fast as they had come.

What is she up to? wondered the Captain.

11

playing with fire

"How much farther?" asked Thomas. "I feel like we have been walking for hours."

"That's because we have," said Itsuki as he used *Onikira* to chop at the vegetation blocking the path. The *hitodama* danced around the trio. The wisps added to the light that emanated from the two floating fire spheres Garron was maintaining as he walked.

"From the coordinates Yareli gave me, it should be just up ahead, over that ridge," said Garron Dar, studying the holomap as he trudged through the thick, dark foliage.

"She's not usually wrong," said Thomas.

"I've noticed that," said Garron. The three of them were blazing a trail through the dense web of the jungle. Itsuki stopped and turned around. The blue wisps continued up the ridge.

"How will we know when we are there?" asked Itsuki.

"Trust me, Augmentor, you will know," said Garron.

"And what exactly does that mean?" asked Thomas.

"You will see shortly. From Yareli's description, it should be hard to miss. But I have to say the conversation was odd."

"In what way?" asked Thomas.

"It took forever to get the location out of her—like it was some sort of secret or something. When she started to talk about it, it was like she caught herself and tried to change the conversation." Garron stopped and turned back towards Thomas. "And after telling me, she said I should not discuss it with anyone else on the Council."

"That *is* odd," said Thomas.

"I thought so too, but from the way she explained the place, it's exactly what we need to start your training."

"I guess that's all that matters then." *What is she hiding?* thought Thomas. "Let's see what all the fuss is about."

The three Mages walked up to the summit as Itsuki sheathed *Onikira*. They looked down into the massive crater.

At the center of the crater was an enormous lake of fire and magma. Small islands of volcanic rock dotted the lake. Surrounding the lake were several smaller fire pits. These pools sporadically sprayed lava into the sky. Acrid fumes wafted off the bubbling pools. Several burnt, gnarled trees were trapped between these pools. Monstrous dark rocks surrounded the area. Thomas jumped down into the crater. Garron and Itsuki followed.

"What happened here?" asked Garron.

"What could have caused this much destruction?" asked Itsuki.

"I think I know," said Thomas as he raised the Gauntlet and waved.

"You did this?" asked Garron.

"No, Gare I meant the Gauntlet—the big rock glove on my right hand. I'm not the only one who's worn it, you know?"

"Sorry, Bearer. I meant no disrespect."

"I know you didn't. And please just call me Thomas."

"I apologize, Thomas."

"Apology accepted. What I meant was that it has that *Gauntlety* feel to it. It's like it's telling me it did this. Just not on my watch."

"But if you didn't do this, who did?" asked Garron.

"I'll have to get back to you on that one, but it's a short list of suspects." *Consisting of my mother and my mentor—neither of which are very comforting thoughts.*

Itsuki knelt down and felt the scorched earth. The *hitodama* circled his hand. He closed his eyes. "I can sense much anger here." He looked across the landscape. Itsuki's head stopped turning when he found it, and the blue wisps shot in the direction of his gaze. Thomas saw what Itsuki was looking at. An obelisk jutted out in front of the largest fire lake. The *hitodama* examined the stone structure.

"What's that?" asked Thomas.

"There is only one way to find out," said Itsuki as he launched himself after the *hitodama*.

Thomas looked at Garron, and they simultaneously took off after Itsuki. By the time they reached the First Augmentor, he had redrawn his sword and was in a guarded stance.

"What is it, Suke?" asked Thomas.

"There is a strong presence here." He held out his hand. "It is hard to say for certain what it could be. The anger is palpable, and it culminates in this lake. This appears to be a Spirit Marker."

"What's a Spirit Marker?"

"They are placed in areas of spiritual convergence," said Garron.

"That's a little creepy." Thomas stared at the obelisk. The stone sign had more of the Ancient glyphs that adorned the interior of the Gauntlet. The Glophitis was at the top, just like the one at the Temple of Yokan. This, Thomas knew, confirmed his fears. The Gauntlet had created this place. "Any idea what this means?"

"The first glyph is the Glophitis," said Itsuki.

"Which roughly means *Gauntlet*," said Garron. "But over the millennia it has become the sigil for the Council of Mages."

"That's the only one I know . . . wait, you know the Ancient language too?" asked Thomas.

"I've been in the employ of the Eldre for quite some time, Thomas. I've spent the last ten years learning the ways of the Gauntlet. Knowledge of the Ancient language is necessary."

"I suppose so." Thomas looked at both of them. "So what's the rest say?"

"The Fires of Sorrow," said Itsuki and Garron almost simultaneously.

"Okay, this place just jumped a few notches on the creep factor scale," said Thomas.

"The Spirit Marker must have been placed by someone on the Council as a warning," said Itsuki. "The energy I am feeling is tremendous. It is riddled with anger and pain."

Thomas could feel it too and something inside of him wanted him to touch the obelisk, but he fought the urge.

"This place will do nicely, then," said Garron. "Anger will be needed."

"I don't follow," said Thomas still staring at the stone structure.

"Controlled anger is a Pyromancer's weapon," said Garron. "*Controlled* being the key word. Your anger, if dealt with constructively, can be channeled into a positive force. If left to fester and grow . . . well this is what can happen." He swept his arm across the view of the valley. "First we need to harness some of these emotions. Then we will regulate the energy that comes from them and release it."

"It seems like a fine line between control and completely losing it."

"It is, Thomas, but that is why we are here."

"But what about the presence I felt?" asked Itsuki.

"We will stay wary, but there is no better place to begin this training."

"I will keep watch." Itsuki backed away with *Onikira* at his side.

"Very well, Augmentor," said Garron.

"I will be ready if I am needed," said Itsuki as he walked away.

"The Augmentor is cautious."

"He's always worried about things," said Thomas. "It's sort of his job."

"He is obviously good at what he does."

"I don't have another Augmentor to compare him to . . . well, yet anyway. But Suke is the real deal." Thomas looked out over the lake. "So how do we start?"

"Follow my lead," said Garron as he leapt onto one of the islands in the lake of fire. Thomas did the same.

"What now?"

"First we start with our breath. Our breath will be our best tool to temper and focus the anger."

"But I'm not angry."

"Come, Thomas. There must be something that upsets you. Some sort of regret or past experience."

Dad, thought the young man. His face bunched up with anger.

"You have found something."

"You could say that," said Thomas, forcing himself to remember the circumstances of his father's untimely demise.

"Good. We will use anger to summon the fire."

"Are you sure this is safe?"

"The anger is in there already. You might as well put it to good use, and do something constructive with it. Fire is not just a source of destruction. It is also a giver of life. A rebirth occurs in one after the fire has been released."

"Okay . . . I think I get it."

"Let's begin. Breathe inward and outward. The magma in the lake is like the anger churning inside of you. The pressure builds until the lava can no longer be tempered, and then—an eruption." Garron inhaled deeply. On his outward breath, a flame grew from the palm of his right hand, as if his exhalation had inflated it. He began to toss it in the air. It moved across his fingers and around his arm. The flame returned to his hand as he closed it. "Your turn, Thomas."

Thomas closed his eyes and began to breathe with intention.

"What is this thing that has you so angry? Think about it. Dwell on it." Thomas did as Garron said. He began to replay the events at the Temple of Yokan in his head. A burning sensation entered his body.

"Feel the burn start in the stomach. The fire has a rhythm to it, just like your breathing. Stoke the fire with your breath. Make your body a furnace, and when you are ready push the fire from your stomach through your chest and out into your hand."

Thomas could feel the burning and the more he thought about his father the hotter his body became. He opened the palm of the Gauntlet and pushed upward. An inferno shot from his hand, powerful but brief.

Thomas fell backward as Garron jumped out of the way of the blaze. "They warned me you were an advanced learner."

"Yeah . . . sorry about that."

"You sure you've never done this before?"

"Positive."

"It is a great start, Thomas, but you need to remember that no matter how in control we think we are, fire has a natural unpredictability about it that we need to respect."

"Unpredictable . . . lesson learned."

"Let's try it again, but this time, try to contain your anger, and then let it go."

Thomas closed his eyes again and began the process anew. He pushed outward to his palm and there it was. A flame danced on the Gauntlet's open surface. It was larger than the one Garron had shown him, but it was still being controlled by Thomas.

"Try moving it around."

Thomas threw it in the air and caught it in his other hand. "This is pretty freakin' narsh, Garron."

"I think so as well, but you have to focus. Now try extinguishing the flame."

"Why would I want to do that? We're just getting started." Thomas enlarged the size of the ball and stopped it above the Gauntlet's palm.

"Thomas, I think that's enough," said Garron.

"Come on, just a little more." Thomas pushed his energy level. Fire shot out of several of the pits surrounding the lake as the fireball doubled in size.

Itsuki ran over to the pool with *Onikira* at his side. "Thomas, stop!" he yelled, but it was too late.

"What's up, Suke?" The young man turned towards the Augmentor. Spirits began to appear above the surrounding pits, moving like fire. They glowed orange, with white auras surrounding them.

"It seems your power spike has stirred these fire spirits."

"Are they dangerous?"

"I sense no threat from them. They are creatures of the Light. Protectors of sorts."

"I guess they came for the show." Thomas lifted the ball of fire on his palm. "Who am I to disappoint them? Haaaaaaa!" Thomas pushed his power level again, rhythmically breathing. The burning sensation began to grow once more, but something was wrong. Thomas could not control the anger raging in his body. It was not just his anger anymore. It was the anger that had created the Fires of Sorrow. The burning coursed through him, gathering inside the Gauntlet. Thomas could not temper the emotions. He knew what was about to happen, but he was powerless to stop it. He reached down and focused the blast straight into the fire lake. The energy was ferocious.

The island Garron and Thomas stood on began to crumble apart. Thomas ceased his torrent and fell down onto the rock island. His body was smoking. Garron picked up the Bearer and jumped to the bank of the fire lake. He placed Thomas down on his feet next to the obelisk.

"What just happened?" asked Thomas, grabbing his head. "Once second I was fine, and the next thing I knew, all the anger in this place was inside of me . . . well, more like in *here*." He raised the Gauntlet.

"I am not certain, Thomas," said Itsuki.

"I think they might be," said Thomas as he stared up at the spirits that had been circling above the lake.

The fire spirits ceased their movement above the pits, turning back towards the lake as the elongated form of a beast surfaced from the center of the fire. It looked similar to the demon Thomas had fought in the elephant graveyard. It too had a bone mask and a long tail, but this monster was covered in flames. "Who has dared enter my domain?" The beast looked directly at Thomas and Garron. "State your business or begone."

"What is that?" asked Thomas.

"It appears to be a louhi—a fire demon—demoness in this case," said Itsuki. "The real question is, what is she doing here?"

"Really? That's your only question? Is there a place she should be?"

"They are said to be protectors of the darkness," said Garron.

"Enough, mortals," said the louhi. "State your business or leave this territory. This will be your last warning."

"I'm not sure I like your attitude, lady demon," said Thomas.

She moved quickly, spraying a wall of flame down at the three Mages. They dispersed, avoiding the blaze. The louhi lifted herself out of the fire lake onto one of the islands. She raised her head into the sky and let out a shrieking cry. She bounded her way towards them across the islands of the lake.

"What's the plan?" asked Itsuki.

"I got this," said Thomas, throwing the Gauntlet forward. Blue energy flowed at the beast, hitting her left shoulder. The demoness was sent spinning and landed in the fire lake.

"That was easy," said Thomas.

"You know—"

"Yes, I know it's going to emerge from the lake once more to attack," said Thomas, cutting off Itsuki's words. "I was just trying to be positive." As if on cue, the louhi jumped from the lake and landed in front of Thomas. "Let me save you some time, Lucy, or whatever your name is."

"Thomas, I wouldn't do that," said Garron.

"I am the Gauntlet Bearer. Have you heard of me before? Demons are no match for me."

"Well, to be fair, she is far more powerful than the one you fought, Thomas," said Itsuki.

"Wait . . .what?" He turned towards Itsuki. "What do you mean?"

"Let me show you," said the louhi as she flung an energy attack at Thomas, knocking him backwards. Thomas landed, grinding to a halt far from his companions. Garron and Itsuki fought the demoness in his absence, but the towering monster seemed unaffected. Out of nowhere, a green light blurred past Thomas.

Ziza? thought Thomas.

Ziza moved with incalculable speed. He reached the demoness and twirled his staff and slammed it into the ground. A pair of dead trees ripped up from the earth like two hands, grabbing the fiery beast and halting her advance.

"Now, Neficus!" screamed Ziza.

Neficus appeared from behind the monster, chanting incantations. He unloaded a black energy attack that wrapped around the beast and began to pull the monster back towards the lake. Thomas got back to his feet and moved to help.

"Now you, Lolani," said Ziza.

Lolani zipped in front of the monster and began moving her hands around. Her essence began to glow white as the fire spirits rushed at the demoness.

The spirits are helping, thought Thomas as they enveloped the demoness and began to push her down into the lake. The louhi peeled off the spirits off one by one, but they persisted. Ziza twirled his staff once more and green energy poured out towards the beast. Once the energy hit the creature it stopped struggling.

"Thomas!" yelled Ziza. "Get to the Spirit Marker!" Thomas rushed to the obelisk. The old man continued his instructions as green energy encircled his frail form. "Once the beast is back beneath the fire's surface, I need you to place the palm of the Gauntlet on the top symbol!"

"The Glophitis?"

"Very good, my boy! Who taught you that?"

"Oddly enough, it was you! Well, the younger you inside the Gauntlet!"

"I am a good teacher!" The louhi sank down into the lake of fire. "Now, Thomas!"

Thomas placed the Gauntlet on top of the Glophitis. Energy drained into the stone from the Gauntlet, turning the glyphs the same blue as the Gauntlet. Another spirit rose from the Spirit Marker. This one had a more distinctive humanoid form than the others Lolani controlled. He was definitely male and horribly overweight, if spirits can be such. He wore a formal jacket with spectacles resting on his upturned nose. His eyes were half opened.

"Name?" asked the spirit.

"Thomas Scargen."

"Why have you summoned me?"

"I didn't summon—well, I mean, maybe I did."

"Your hand is in the Gauntlet that has activated the Spirit Marker, is it not?"

"Yes."

"Well, then you have summoned me."

"I don't really have time for semantics right this second."

"I will ask again. What is it you need, Bearer?" asked the Spirit.

"I need to trap that demon thing back down in the fire lake place."

"Very well," said the spirit as it vanished back into the rock.

Thomas could instantly feel the obelisk draining his energy, but he now understood what needed to be done. The Gauntlet was communicating with the stone. At that moment he knew who had created the crater. The torment and pain that enveloped him earlier belonged to the High Mancer. Thomas now knew that for certain: the obelisk had revealed as much to him. "Haaaaaa!" said Thomas, energizing the Spirit Marker. A pulse wave shot out from the obelisk across the fire lake, covering its surface in a flash of light.

Ziza ceased his energy output. Lolani and Neficus did the same. The spirits emerged from the lake and vanished back into the pits from which they had come. The connection between the Spirit Marker and the Gauntlet broke off, and Thomas stepped back. He looked at the Gauntlet's palm as the Glophitis disappeared.

"What just happened?" asked Thomas.

"You trapped the demoness back into the Fires of Sorrow," said Ziza.

"Yeah, I got that much from the obelisk." He leaned in closer to Ziza. "The Spirit Marker divulged a few things."

Ziza's head sank a bit as he once again leaned on the staff. "It is a long story, my boy. One I promise I will tell you some day when I am ready."

"I understand, High Mancer. And I'm sorry I lost control."

"I believe this time it is I who owe the apology. Without my anger, this never would have happened." Thomas looked at Ziza.

"Can I ask you another question?"

"Yes, my boy. You can always ask me questions."

"Did it ever stop hurting?"

"Not yet, my boy. Not yet."

12

demonology 101

Thomas was weary after his training session. He had grasped the concept of pyromancy quickly, but he could not shake the feeling of Ziza's anger and sadness. He walked back to Maktaba by himself. Thomas did not know what had happened the day the High Mancer created the Fires of Sorrow, but he had a good guess it had something to do with Ziza's best friend killing his fiancée. Another thing was certain after the training; he needed to resume his studies, and Spells was in Maktaba.

He made his way up in the elevator. The guards were at their usual posts when Thomas walked into the Council's chamber and touched the Council's table as he slid past. Thomas stepped out onto the branch that connected to Ziza's study. Emfalmay's son Emkoo was on guard.

"Hey, Emkoo," said Thomas.

"Hey, Thomas. Will I be seeing you in the morning for perimeter duty?"

"Yes, you will. I'm not as conditioned as I was before leaving." The two of them laughed. "Where's your dad?"

"My father went to find Ziza, but Mancer Warwick is up there."

"Anson? Narsh. Well, I guess I can get some studying done. Thanks, Emkoo. I'll see you in the morning."

"Will you be joining us for breakfast?"

"No, I'm not too keen on raw meat that early in the morning." He jumped up to the landing and into the study.

"The good time of day to you, sir," said Anson when he saw Thomas.

"Hey, Anson." The werewolf was sitting behind a desk and had several volumes open at once, one on the table while three others floated in front of him. He seemed to be researching something. "I guess you're playing the part of Ziza tonight?"

"Yes, Thomas. Your lesson has already been assigned."

"Narsh. I wonder what it is?"

"I'm not sure, Thomas. The High Mancer did not tell me."

"What are you up to?"

"I'm trying to decipher your father's riddle, and I have to be honest with you, I have gotten nowhere. This is the short and the long of it."

"If it makes you feel any better, Mancer Bodes hasn't made much progress on the riddle itself, but he's found some things about my dad that are kind of odd."

"You speak of your father's expenses for his hobby. Bodes has kept me in the loop as it were. We used to be a team, the two of us, for a while anyway. A damn fine one, I would say—back in London. Well, it seems like ages ago."

"Yeah? What exactly happened between you two?"

"The band that seems to tie their friendship together will be the very strangler of their amity."

"Huh?"

"There was a falling out of sorts—a difference of opinion, if you will. The man cares far too much for the game, and not enough for the players in it. Something I learned the hard way."

"He isn't the easiest guy to get along with."

"No, no he is not . . . and never has been, but there is good in him. He just forgets that from time to time."

"I can believe that."

Flora extended a vine towards Thomas, offering him *Scargen's Repository of Magic*. She then reached out to Anson with another book he must have requested.

"Good. You have found it. Thank you, Flora. In fact, Thomas, I have also been researching Atlantis and its inhabitants for most of the day, based on your conversation with Loric. I was not sure we had this particular volume." Anson looked up at Thomas. "It seems we both have studying to do."

"Fair enough," said Thomas as he walked to his usual nook and sat down. He placed the book on the table. Spells sprung open.

"Hey, Thomas. How have you been?"

"Better now that I'm back home. You?"

"Myself, I loved being out in the world after being shelved for so long. I consider it a great *chapter* in my life, and you really showed such *character* out there."

"And now that you're back in Maktaba?" asked Thomas.

"Keeping busy. I've been *booked* since we got back, but I think I'm coming down with something."

"What do you think it is?"

"I can't get a good *read* on it, Thomas, but I think I might need my *appendix* removed."

Thomas groaned. "You never cease to amaze me, Spells. That was the worst one yet."

"They can't all be *happy endings.*" Spells flipped into the air and opened in front of Thomas. "Okay back to business. Today's topic—demonology."

"Narsh. Better late than never, I suppose," said Thomas. He moved over as Spells settled on the table. Thomas focused on the heading.

DEMONOLOGY
Understanding the Classified Inhabitants of the Dark Realm

"Sounds promising," said Thomas. He continued to read.

The Depths, or Dark Realm, is a parallel universe wherein darkness thrives. There are countless types of inhabitants of the Depths. Several have been catalogued, but due to rampant interspecies breeding, classifying all of the diverse inhabitants of the Dark Realm is difficult. The following is an attempt to simplify the species diversity within the Dark Realm.

NONDEMON CONJURINGS

EERAH: dark, tar-like beings that do the bidding of their conjuror. A threatening force when in groups, they have the ability to combine with other Eerah, forming larger versions of themselves. An advanced Necromancer can wield the *Eerah*, using the dark creatures' malleable forms as a fierce weapon. The *Eerah*'s resilience is directly corollary to their conjuror's power and skill.

IMPS: diminutive creatures with goat-like legs and a spiked tail. Most imps display a basic knowledge of magic. This coupled with their intense anxiety, make them perfect underlings and are commonly used as servants in Earth Realm.

GORGOL: Massive four-legged creatures that roam the Wastelands of the Depths. They normally hunt in packs, but some have become loners. They are formidable creatures, especially in packs.

NIR WORMS: Large worm creatures that devour earth and rock. They are extremely poisonous and can shoot electrical current from their tails. They inhabit the Dark Desert in the Wastelands.

DEMONS

JINN: Medium-sized, shapeshifting demons that can assume the forms of animals or humans. Because of this skill, they are used mostly by conjurors for spying. Unlike most demons, a jinn cannot be bound to a master because of their advanced intelligence. They are usually physically weaker than other demons, but become stronger with age. A jinn that has achieved the ranking of High Demon can prove most difficult to control and/or defeat. In its original form, a jinn has wings and hindquarters similar to a goat's. They are capable of flight and teleportation over great distances. Some develop the skill of spirit tracking in their later years. This ability allows jinn to hunt down victims after contact with a personal item. The bone-like appendage, that extends from a jinn's wrist, can inject its prey with a poison that incapacitates the victim.

LURCHON: Smaller-sized demons that can latch onto the spirit of another creature using a protruding trunk-like appendage, taking control of the host. A conjurer can then control the host through suggestion via the lurchon. These demons are weak magically and frail and can be easily manipulated by a seasoned conjuror. A lurchon can remain latched onto its victim for long periods of time, often going unnoticed.

MARD: Nightmarish demons that feed off of fear. They secrete a toxin that can cause hallucinations in humans, exacerbating the fear response. The demons turn this fear into energy. Mard come in many different forms, the most common being spider-like. They are easily controllable demons.

THUL: Sea demons of the Depths. These huge tentacled monsters have been conjured into the waters of Earth Realm. They are massive creatures that cause havoc and damage when unleashed. These demons are extremely strong, but lack the intelligence of most demonic species.

CRAG: Also referred to as bone demons or death demons. They are thought to be the original demonic dwellers of the Dark Realm. They are dark, sinister winged creatures with a predilection for self-gratification. Distinguished by their distinct bone masks and the bones that protrude from different parts of their bodies, no two crag have identical bone markings. Crag are hard to control when fully mature, even when bound to a conjuror. These demons use speed, along with dark energy manipulation, to attack their opponents.

Crag are capable of flight, using their retractable wings that sprout from their backs. They also display the ability to use their protruding bones as weapons. Crag can bind with organic (and sometimes inorganic) forms. These beasts are highly intelligent and should never be trusted.

Thomas thought about the High Demon he had defeated a little over a year ago the day he accepted the Burden. *Mephist was a crag . . . or is a crag.* Thomas continued to read. There were several more examples of demons, but his eyes darted to the next section heading.

ELEMENTAL DEMONS

This should be interesting.

These are demons that are trapped for long periods in Earth Realm. This time on Earth has twisted them, merging them with their environment, causing further mutations. These mutations have resulted in numerous varieties of elemental demons, and make them masters of camouflage. Elemental demons are not always combative, making them a more peaceful sort of demon, but do not confuse this for weakness. Elemental demons can achieve higher ranking than most Dark Realm demons, but after long periods in Earth Realm they prefer to be left undisturbed, migrating to and inhabiting areas of convergence of the three Realms, and often become protective of their territory.

EXAMPLES OF ELEMENTAL DEMONS

NIKAR (WATER DEMON): The appearance of water demons can vary, taking on properties of various sea creatures. For example, a nikar may have tentacles, fins, tails, or even coral growing on it. They have the ability to breathe underwater. Nikar have been referenced in literature since the dawn of man's seafaring ventures.

LOUHI (FIRE DEMON): Louhi appear to be made of fire and smoke. The louhi is one of the most dangerous of all elementals, but is seen least often due to its need for proximity to fire. They feed on anger and hate and will respond to this type of energy.

MOKA (EARTH DEMON): Moka can be made of stone, sand, lava, earth itself, or any combination thereof. Moka can be found in all manner of environments.

YODI (FOREST DEMON): Yodi are made up of trees or other vegetation, depending on their habitat. These demons can become fiercely protective of the inhabitants of their territory.
Moka and yodi are closely related, and are the most commonly seen elementals in Earth Realm.

TROLLS

Though not exactly demons themselves, trolls are distant cousins of elemental demons, and their appearances are similarly tied to their environment. Trolls originated as the inadvertent offspring of an elemental spirit and demon communion. Now large populations of trolls populate various habitats across Earth Realm, ranging from the desert to the forest to the sea, taking on the physical characteristics of the elements around them. This makes these creatures masters of camouflage. Unlike demons, trolls are not necessarily mischievous creatures. They tend to be quite peaceful when not manipulated or coerced by humans.

Thomas paged through various drawings of the types of creatures and their known anatomy, until he came upon the next topic heading.

DEMON REPRODUCTION & LIFE EXPECTANCY

Demons procreate with physical intercourse, but lay eggs. Newly hatched demonlings achieve a larval stage in the first few years, then go through a pupal stage before assuming their final forms.

Few immature demons reach final form, however, due to the pro-pensity for hunger in all demons, which frequently results in filial cannibalism.

Demons cannot be killed in Earth Realm, but they can be forced back into the Dark Realm if vanquished. This process can take months or even years to be completed, depending on the degree of power used in their expulsion from Earth Realm. It is rumored that a demon can be destroyed and killed within the Dark Realm—a notion reported by other demons.

But why are some High Demons and others not? wondered Thomas. The pages turned and stopped on a new heading.

DEMON RANKING

Most demon ranking is believed to be in accordance with age and experience. It is also believed that certain types of demons are more predisposed to achieving higher positions in the hierarchy faster than others. Crag demons achieve High Demon status the fastest, but some elementals can have power ratings that surpass even that of High Demons. Demons intrinsically know their own ranking within social groups. However, like all social groups, ranking is tested frequently from the lowest of levels to the highest, making social groups impossible to track and record.

"That pretty much *covers* it," said Spells.

"Do the puns ever stop?"

"Why? Can't you *bear* it anymore?" asked Spells.

"Stop, really," said Thomas as the two laughed.

"I guess it's about time to *close the book* on today's lesson," said Spells.

Emfalmay entered the room, partially supporting Ziza, who also leaned on his staff. The High Mancer looked drained.

"What's wrong?" asked Thomas.

"It is nothing, my boy," said Ziza. "Just a bit too much sun, I suppose."

"Nothing? You completely overexerted yourself today," said Emfalmay.

"Stop being so dramatic, Emfalmay," said Ziza. "I am perfectly fine. I just need to get some rest, and I will be good as new."

Thomas remembered what Onjamba had said about being away from the Gauntlet for long periods of time. He placed the Gauntlet on the High Mancer's shoulder. Ziza stood up a little straighter, leaning only on the staff for support.

"It seems that it is past my bedtime." The old man made his way behind the curtain that separated the study from his bedroom. "Goodnight, everyone."

"Goodnight, High Mancer," said Thomas.

"For being a High Mancer, he is a very stubborn human," said Emfalmay. The Lion exited the study.

Thomas turned towards Anson. "I think you should call it a night too. Come back to this with fresh eyes in the morning."

"Care keeps his watch in every old man's eye, and where care lodges, sleep will never lie."

"Yeah, I'm an insomniac sometimes myself. Not usually while I'm training though. But I don't feel like going home just yet. I'm still buzzing from connecting with that Spirit Marker."

"Warwick's then?"

"It's like you were reading my freakin' mind," said Thomas. "Wait, can you do that?"

"I'll never tell." He smiled at Thomas.

"I could use a beer or three," said Thomas.

"I would give all of my fame for a pot of ale," said Anson.

"Good thing you're not that famous." The two shared a laugh. Thomas looked over at Anson. "But in all seriousness, do you have any more of that whiskey?"

"Now that is indeed a silly question."

13

general attraction

Captain Marcus Slade approached the large doors. A holo screen was mounted above the entrance. As he approached, an image of Corbin, the imp servant, floated above the console. "What can I do for you, Capt'n?" asked the holographic image of Corbin.

"I would say letting me in . . . might be a good start."

"Dat does seem to make sense, doesn't it?" A small door at the bottom of the door swung open. Corbin's head popped out. "Sorry about dat, Capt'n, but we are still tryin' to work out duh bugs. I myself 'av never trusted technology in general. Go wif your gut, is what I always say." Corbin drew his head back in, but popped out again shortly. "One second, Capt'n." Corbin popped his head back in again. A loud sound interrupted the silence as the large doors swung outward. Corbin stood where the shadows parted. The imp turned and began to waddle down the corridor.

Marcus walked into the familiar chamber, surprised to see how much had changed. The darkness had been balanced with sparse lighting. The lewd taste of the last General had been replaced by impressive rows of the General's Guard. An absurd amount of tech covered the walls of the room. The transformation was astounding. *Now this is a war room*, thought Marcus.

" 'ello Capt'n. It's good to see ya," said Corbin, pulling Marcus from his pondering. They began to walk with one another down the corridor.

"Hey," said Marcus.

"How've you been?"

"Fine I guess," said Marcus. He was lying, but there was no need to inform the imp of how he actually felt. "You?"

"As good as any subservient, diminutive, demon dat can be summoned at duh drop uvva 'at can be, I suppose."

"Good," said Marcus, not actually listening to the response. The Captain began to look around.

"I see ya noticed all uv duh changes around duh ol' place."

"The General I'm guessing."

"Good guess. Yeah, she finks we were a bit behind duh times. I guess I agree, but like I said, I'm a bit ol' fashioned meeself. I'll tell you one fing, dough: she treats me betta den Arkmalis evva did, but dat doesn't set the bar too 'igh, does it?"

"I suppose not," said Marcus.

"She's a good one, Capt'n. She gets it. Don't get me wrong, she's a bit mad at times, but you 'av to be a bit mad to do her job on a daily basis, don't ya?"

"And Lord Grimm?"

" 'ee's a different story entirely. 'ee's completely mental, but just as smart. Dat one's always finkin' about fings. You can just see it in 'im. 'ee might be barkin', Capt'n, but 'ee's sharp as a bloody tack dat one."

"The two do tend to come as a package."

"I suppose you're right, Capt'n. I suppose you're right. Well, it's been nice chattin' wif ya, but I'm afraid all good fings, an that." The two had reached the end of the corridor and now entered the main chamber.

"You as well, Corbin." He turned to look forward and saw her almost instantly. Even in his inebriated state, he could recognize her silhouette.

"Your Grace, Captain Marcus Slade," said Corbin. The imp turned and scurried off.

"Captain Slade, there is much to discuss," said the General. Marcus looked at her.

"You could say that," said Marcus, stumbling a bit to his left. She was wearing a sleeveless uniform, and he could now see what the Rider had spoken of at the Goblin Hole: her left shoulder and whole left arm were now covered in dark tattooed glyphs. "So how's it feel to be General?" The question just popped out.

"Clear the room," said the General. Corbin, the General's Guard and the rest of the personnel left the chamber.

"I'm sorry. Really . . . I'm sorry." He did not know what to say, and said the first thing that popped in his mind. "Nice tattoos."

"I think so." She looked directly at him. "And I have earned every last one of them."

"And how did you do that?"

"Captain, I did not ask you here to discuss my tattoos."

"Sorry . . . my bad. I just thought we were doing an almost passable job at faking being almost cordial to each other."

"You look like shit, Marcus. And you come in here talking about my appearance. I chose the tattooing."

"Well, I chose to look like shit. Sooooo . . . there's that."

"By binge drinking and smoking again? Really, Marcus? You haven't smoked in twelve years."

"You noticed? I'm flattered."

"I could smell it on you when you walked in, and you're barely able to stand."

"Well, maybe if I had time to shower before your minions cornered me."

"Right after your secret talk with Taunt and Jurdik."

"It wasn't a secret talk."

"You were in the Goblin Hole. There are plenty of nicer places for Riders to drink."

"All right, granted, that doesn't look great, but I hadn't seen the guys in a while, and we wanted to try something new."

"Come now, Captain. You know I'm not an idiot. Taunt is heading up our renovations and Jurdik has proven an excellent trainer to my Guard, but their loyalties will always lie with you. They obviously had something they wanted to discuss."

"They were telling me what a great job you're doing as General."

"My spies say otherwise."

"Then why did you even ask?"

"Was it necessary to destroy half of a squadron, Marcus?"

"That was an accident."

"You accidentally stabbed a man and electrocuted five others?"

"Yep," said Marcus, smiling. "And can I just say that you've got a lot of nerve, talking about secrets."

"My secrets are secrets because I have been ordered to keep them as such."

"That's convenient."

"What is it you want?"

"I want you to stop punishing the others for what I did. Taunt and Jurdik are good Riders—some of the best."

"I'm not punishing anyone, Captain. I am trying to get this army back into shape. Arkmalis was a lazy General, but I suppose you dealt with that yourself. Trust me when I say, despite our past transgressions, I am doing what is best for this army. I am responsible for getting the Grimm Legions ready for the largest undertaking it has ever seen, and I will do that any way I see fit."

"What sort of undertaking?"

"All in due time, Captain. I am currently worried about your ability to perform your duties."

"You picked an odd time to start worrying."

"When did the self-pity start, Marcus? Because I have to say, it's not doing anything for you."

"Well, someone I once called friend became a general and turned her back on me."

"Is that what this all about—a promotion?"

"I think we both know that *that* is not what this is about."

"Are you referring to my fall?"

"Yes, among other things." Marcus looked her directly in the eyes. "Or are we pretending that didn't happen now?"

"It was never about Pria, Marcus. It was about you lying to me. I trusted you, and you betrayed that trust." She closed her eyes for a second and slowly reopened them. "But that part of me is gone now . . . buried in the past, and that's where it will stay. Besides, Lord Grimm has shown me many things." She moved her wrist slightly, and an orange fireball appeared above it. Her eyes were trained on the energy sphere. "I always knew I had a knack for certain things, but I did not know necromancy was one of them." She slightly moved her fingers and the flame turned a far darker orange. Her eyes widened as the sphere grew exponentially in size. "See, Captain, the power that flows through me: it has always been there. Lord Grimm has shown me as much."

Marcus grabbed her wrist, and the energy sphere dissipated.

"Is that where the tattoos came from?" asked Marcus.

"Your obsession with my tattoos is remarkable," said Evangeline as she ripped her hand away from his. She turned her back to him. Her hair flipped around, revealing more of the dark glyphs. "And if you must know, each one signifies a new milestone in my training." He reached out and put his hand on her shoulder.

"It's just in all the years I've known you, you never once mentioned any interest in ever wanting a tattoo."

The General turned around quickly. "I have already told you. I am not that same little girl you found in that rubble all those years ago."

He stepped closer. "You don't think I know that? You haven't been that little girl for quite some time."

"You are quite perceptive, even when you are half in-the-bag and reeking like an ashtray." She crossed her arms in front of her.

"Flattery will get you nowhere, General."

"The Captain can still make a joke. Well, I guess my worrying was for nothing." He pulled her in closer. She gasped, but not unpleasantly.

"There's something else that might worry you."

"And what's that?" whispered the General, slightly tilting her head.

"I just wanted to tell you th—" His words were interrupted by the noise of a door sliding open. There was a compartment he had not noticed before, set towards the back of the chamber.

"Ahh, Captain, how good of you to meet with us on such short notice." The wrapped silhouette of Grimm emerged from the opening. He made his way over to where the two had just separated. "I trust Evangeline has debriefed you."

"I was just getting to that, Lord Grimm."

"Very well, then. If you do not mind, my dear, I will take it from here."

"Of course, my Lord." Evangeline bowed and walked down the corridor.

Grimm motioned for the Captain to follow him. Marcus moved as fast as he could manage in his inebriated state. They crossed into the room from which Grimm had appeared.

The room was expansive and adorned with various artifacts and oddities. These were juxtaposed with several holoscreens, displaying various artif schematics and tech. An elevated platform rose from the floor against the back wall, which was made entirely of glass. The large window looked out at the lava pit and down into the many structures and living quarters of the Grimm Legions. An elevator shaft stood in the center of Grimm's inner chamber. Grimm climbed the stairs to the platform. Marcus followed. Tollin Grimm looked out the immense window.

"See them, Marcus? All of these cogs in the greater machine. Each individual cog has no idea that without it, the machine stops. But with a tiny bit of grease, the cogs move along and do their parts." He turned and looked at the Captain. "You are not one of these cogs—are you, Marcus? You will always want to see how it all works. It's a commendable attribute, but one that can lead to misery and disappointment. Trust me. I suffer from the same affliction." He turned towards Marcus. "What would you say if I offered to show you part of the big picture?"

"I would say that I would be interested."

"We have been busy, Marcus—the General and I—in the last few months, and from the looks of things, so have you."

"Sorry, my Lord. I did not realize that I would be meeting with you. I would have straightened myself up had I known."

"Marcus, I do not put too much stock in appearances. It is actions that interest me. I need a man of action—not appearances . . . one I can trust." Grimm smiled at Marcus. "Evangeline has assured me that man is you, Marcus. Are you up for the task, Captain?"

"Yes, my Lord. I will do whatever it is you ask of me."

"Good. That is what I wanted to hear. I need you to locate an object for me. And once you have located it, I need you to retrieve it. You will have whatever you need at your disposal, within reason . . . but discretion will be needed. Take only the Riders you trust. General Arkmalis's life may depend on it."

Arkmalis? thought Marcus. "Understood, my Lord."

"Let's start at the beginning then, shall we?" The man leaned forward. " How familiar are you with the lost city of Atlantis?"

14

it comes in waves

Tuguna sped through the river with ease. Thomas swam next to him. At first it had been difficult for Thomas to keep up, but he had been swimming the river with the Eldre in the afternoons, and the practice had helped tremendously. The Eldre had said it was the start of his aquamantic training. They had not done anything but swim, but Thomas was not about to question the Turtle. Besides, he was still busy with his pyromantic training. He had continued to meet with Garron after his swimming exercises to work on his pyromantic skills. The Fires of Sorrow were off limits, so they had moved their training to the elephant graveyard where Thomas had defeated Mephist and accepted the Gauntlet. This schedule had continued for three weeks, and Thomas had slowly begun to embrace his new training regimen. He began to feel at home again in Sirati.

There was only one thing that he had yet to do. He still had not told Yareli about his mother or how he felt. That would change today. He would call her after his swim with the Eldre. He would first tell her the truth about Merelda Scargen, and then he would tell Yareli how he felt about her.

The water rushed across his skin. Thomas felt at home in the water: he always had. His father used to take him to the shore every summer. He would spend hours in the ocean, riding waves into the surf. He felt at peace there. He had been meant to go back last summer before all of this happened. His father was going to take a break from his dig and spend a week with Thomas. That all seemed so long ago. Tuguna circled around and stopped in front of Thomas.

"Stop thinking about the past, Bearer. You need to focus on the now. Like this river you have to go with the flow. Let it go, my boy. Feel the river's current all around you."

"Sorry, Eldre. My mind started to drift."

"It's okay, Thomas. As long as you just keep moving forward, it is nearly impossible for you to be pulled under."

"There's just some things that I need to deal with."

"Understood. So let's deal with them." The Eldre placed his flippered hands at his sides and rose out of the water atop a wave that kept moving next to Thomas.

"Narsh," said Thomas.

"We can learn a lot from the river."

"O-o-okay."

"Water is forgiving. It makes its own path at times, and follows others' at other times. When water is presented with an obstacle, it adapts, changes, and flows. Over time it can accomplish amazing things. If something gets in the water's way, what does it do?"

"It goes around it?"

"Precisely, or through it, or it carries the obstacle along with it. But eventually the things it's carrying along, drift away, and get caught along the banks, as the river continues on."

"I'm sorry. I'm a little confused. What exactly is your point here?"

"Be more like the river, Thomas. "

Be more like the river? thought Thomas. *Could it be that simple?* He laid back and stopped swimming. Thomas floated on the top of the river as it carried him along. He tensed up for a second—the sound of the river was all he could hear. His body relaxed and began to become one with the water. All of his thoughts, worries, and concerns washed away. He felt like he did when he rode the waves as a kid, and it felt incredible.

"Now, I think you're ready to begin."

"And it only took three weeks . . ." The two of them laughed.

"Follow me, Bearer."

Tuguna's wave accelerated and took off down a tributary that Thomas had not noticed before. Thomas sat up in the water and began to swim again. They turned the bend in the new tributary and the Eldre disappeared in front of Thomas.

"Uh oh," said Thomas as he went over the falls. "Ahhhhh!" He hit the water hard, but not hard enough to hurt. Thomas was submerged in seconds. The whole thing was exhilarating. He pushed up through the surface of the water. The Eldre sat on the wave right next to him, laughing hard.

"You should have seen your face when you went over the falls." The Turtle rolled onto his shell.

Thomas spit out water. "I'm glad you're laughing. Next time, how about a little heads-up."

"That would have defeated the purpose of the lesson."

"Which is?"

"Always be ready, Thomas. Water can be as unpredictable as fire."

"Yeah, but it's a little more forgiving if you fall into a pool of it."

Thomas looked around for the first time. This place was beautiful. It was a pool that was fed by three separate waterfalls. At the center of the pool was an island of rounded rock formations similar to the ones around the waterfalls above. Tuguna's wave made its way towards the mound. The wave lifted him up, and he jumped onto the formation. Thomas swam towards the rocks as well. When he reached it he pulled himself out of the water and climbed up to where the Eldre rested.

"So what now?" asked Thomas.

"We begin." The Turtle lifted his flipper and a stream of water shot into the air. He began to circle his flippered hands, and the water rushed into a sphere, churning clockwise in front of the Eldre.

"How are you doing that?"

"The same way everything else works that you have learned, Thomas. I simply asked the water to cooperate."

"Narsh," said the Bearer as he looked on stunned.

"Now you try it," said the Eldre, lifting his hand.

The water sphere came flying over to Thomas, but before he could attempt to control it, the water splashed onto his head.

"That was a good try, Thomas."

"Thanks. I am obviously a skilled Aquamancer."

"I would say so," laughed the Eldre. "Now let's try that again." He lifted a water sphere out of the water. "The water wants to crash back down into the river, but you simply help it to churn in a different direction. You need to feel the push and pull of the liquid. Use your hands and arms to guide its flow." Thomas listened intently. He began to feel the water's movement in Tuguna's hands, and without thinking he received the water sphere from the Eldre.

"Narsh," whispered Thomas.

"Narsh indeed, my boy."

"Now what do I do with it?"

"That is a great question, Thomas. Maybe you should ask the water what it wants to do."

This statement confused Thomas. The water splashed onto the rock and slowly crept back into the river.

"And how exactly does one do that?"

"You have to listen to it. It has to be a symbiotic relationship."

Listen to the water, thought Thomas. He closed his eyes and opened his ears. The rushing noise of the falls was coupled with the subtler, nuanced rippling of the pool below. Thomas could feel the water, churning and rolling. Energy began to radiate around him. His eyes began to burn as he lifted his hands.

"Good, my boy. Now, feel the push and pull of the water and its strength and lift the water upwards."

Thomas circled his hands as he felt the water sphere rise out of the pool. The ball grew larger and larger as Thomas moved his hands.

"Thomas," said the Eldre. "You may want to open your eyes." At his insistence the young man did just that.

The water sphere was enormous. Most of the water in the pool was gone, enveloped in Thomas's handiwork. *I-I-It's too much . . . I can't control it.* He did not know what to do, and, without thinking, he inadvertently moved his hands, throwing the large sphere of water towards the opposite bank.

"Thomas, no!" yelled Tuguna, but it was too late.

The water hit the side of the pool with tremendous pressure, creating a massive wave. The wave crashed into a copse of trees along the embankment. Animals retreated from their perches and moved deeper into the jungle. The pool was half full now and slowly rising once more from the falls.

"Come on, my boy. I'm afraid the lesson is over for now. We must assess the damage."

The two jumped into the pool and swam to the shore where the wave had crashed. Fish flopped on the bank. The Eldre began to telekinetically throw them back into the pool. Thomas looked down as he helped the Eldre.

A baby baboon lay motionless in the middle of the last few floundering fish. The Eldre took care of the remaining fish and leaned down, pressing his earhole against the monkey's chest.

"We must act quickly, Thomas." The Turtle scooped up the baby monkey. "Time is dwindling for this one's spirit."

"This is all my fault," said the young man.

"Blame is not helping this creature. Everyone makes mistakes, Thomas. They are what makes us alive. It is how you learn and adjust from mistakes that defines you."

Tuguna moved into the center of the copse and placed the monkey on the ground. The Turtle began to move his arms in circles. Energy surrounded the Eldre. Ghost-like forms began to rise out of the water. They glowed a bright blue and were surrounded by white auras. One by one they flew over to the monkey.

They must be water spirits, thought Thomas. "Can they help?"

"Yes, but we need one more thing." The Eldre walked over to the first tree he saw, touched the bark, and closed his glowing eyes. "The trees have agreed."

A cold wind whipped through the treetops, chilling Thomas. The spirits flew from the trees and into the form of the Turtle, turning his Light blue. Tuguna raised his flippers and placed them on the motionless body of the tiny monkey. The energy from Tuguna flowed into the small creature. The monkey's eyes shot open as power flowed through him. It was then that Thomas noticed the leaves and looked up. It was hauntingly beautiful. As the leaves fell to the jungle floor, the trees that surrounded them began slowly turning gray. Thomas looked back down just in time to see the monkey spring back to life in the center of the circle of now dead trees.

"They sacrificed themselves for this monkey," said Thomas.

"They were old trees, Thomas. Sometimes the old must give way for the new. They agreed that the transfer was wise." The monkey sat up, ran up the arm of the Eldre, and jumped into Thomas's hands.

"How is this possible?"

"It is another aspect of aquamancy and blue Light in general. Spirits are attuned to healing. I believe Wiyaloo is an adept healer, if I can remember correctly."

"Yes he's great at it."

"Water spirits are the finest healers, but it always has a cost, Thomas. Reviving one spirit, must extinguish another. It is the way of things."

Thomas thought about what the Eldre had said. "If only I had thought before I acted, these trees wouldn't have had to die."

"These trees were already dying, Thomas—the second they were planted, actually. And what did I tell you before?"

"Be more like the river?"

"Precisely. Let it go, my boy. The trees agreed to the exchange for the greater good."

An adult baboon had poked through the brush. The baby baboon jumped off Thomas and ran up the back of the adult. The adult baboon started at Thomas and then at the Eldre. She bowed her head slightly and then took off into the jungle.

"Have others had these problems?"

"Others?"

"Other Bearers. Have they had problems with aquamancy?"

"Most of the past Bearers have shied away from it, and a blue Light Bearer is rare indeed. In fact, Alican Dod, the founder of my home, was the only other Gauntlet Bearer that I know of who was proficient with aquamancy and possessed a blue Light. He was strong but abrasive, from what the records tell, but he was a great Bearer. There's no denying that. He faced down a very strong Necromancer, himself." The Turtle looked at Thomas. "You should meet with him next time you are inside." The Eldre placed his flippered hand on the Gauntlet. "He might be able to teach you a thing or two about aquamancy that I cannot." The Eldre looked around at the dead trees and earth and then back at Thomas. "They are not all great, you know? The Bearers I mean. For some, it is too much."

"Do you think that's the case with me?"

"No, my boy. Not even close. You have the makings of a great Aquamancer. Control is the issue, and this will come with training."

"It's just everything else has come so easy to me. I mean, I was almost too good at pyromancy."

"Aquamancy is most difficult. And you will find, Bearer, that most things that are worth doing rarely come easily. I believe in you, and so do all of your friends and fellow members of the Council. I do not think so many wise people could be wrong." The Eldre smiled at Thomas.

"Well, maybe not Mancer Neficus."

"Yeah, he seems a bit off, but immensely skilled in the dark ways." Tuguna smiled. "Warrior Mage Chula's confidence in you—that alone makes up for him tenfold."

Thomas thought about Yareli and how little he had seen of her since being home. This was something he needed to rectify. "Thank you, Eldre."

"You are most welcome, my boy." The Eldre again laughed. "I will see you soon." The Turtle walked over to the edge and jumped into the pool.

"Are you not coming back with me?" asked Thomas.

"No, not just yet. I think I'll stay here for a bit. This place is beautiful, and I want to enjoy it. I do not have many of these days left in me you know."

Thomas wanted to say something, but fell silent. "O-o-okay. I guess I'll see ya later."

The Eldre waved his flippered hand as he submerged.

Thomas began to walk back to Sirati. He had enough of the water for one day. Besides, a proper conversation with Yareli was long overdue. Thomas lifted his wristcom. "Computer, call Yareli."

15

about a girl

They were to meet at the monument, the installation that had been erected in honor of Mary, the Gauntlet Bearer. *The last time I was here, I didn't know this was all for you, Mom*, thought Thomas. He walked slowly to the entrance. Thomas poked his head in and looked around the grounds of the monument. He saw Yareli, sitting on the bench they had sat on together on just over a year ago. She had kissed him there. Thomas would tell her about Merelda Scargen first. Mary was Yareli's hero—her role model. It was unfair of him to keep Mary's true identity from her, and he knew that. He just hoped that she would understand, considering the circumstances.

He entered the manicured grounds around the monument. He could not believe how beautiful she looked. He was mesmerized. *Why did I ever think I was going to be able to let her go?* thought Thomas. He walked up to her and Yareli stood. She was smiling and Thomas was too.

"I feel like I haven't seen you in days," said Yareli.

"Twenty-one days, to be exact," said the young man. "But who's counting?"

"So what's up? You sounded almost frantic when you called. I rushed over as fast as I could."

"I've been meaning to talk to you since the first day I was back, but we got interrupted that day, and I have been focusing on training so much . . . well, I just haven't had the time, but there's something I have to tell you, and I hope you understand that I didn't mean to keep it from you."

"What is it, Thomas? It can't be that bad. I mean, we're good friends.

"Great friends," said Thomas.

"Great friends. I couldn't stay mad at you if I wanted to."

"Well . . . I've been thinking a lot about my life before coming here, and how it used to be." Thomas paused. "I had friends and my dad was always there for me, but I never felt like . . . like . . ."

"You fit in," said Yareli.

"Yes, exactly, but more than that. I never felt like I belonged where I was. I didn't realize it then, but now, looking back, it's so obvious. It's just, I loved my dad, but he was gone a lot and I never had a best friend, well, besides LINC." He looked her in the eyes. "What I'm trying to say is that I finally feel like I have a family now and that I fit in, and you have a lot to do with that." He smiled, but the grin slowly faded. "But that's not exactly why I asked you here. It's not easy to talk about, and I think I just wanted it for myself for a while, and after the battle with Arkmalis and then leaving with Itsuki to find the next stone—"

"Spit it out already."

"Mary was my mom." There was a long silence. "My mother's name is Merelda, and my dad had always called her Mary. My mom was . . . well, sort of is . . . the last Gauntlet Bearer."

"W-w-what do you mean? I don't understand."

"My mom was the one who trapped Grimm in the stone and died doing so—the one who this monument is dedicated to. The woman who sacrificed her life for all of us."

"How do you know that for certain?"

"She told me."

"H-h-how is that even possible?"

"She's inside the Gauntlet."

"Did you get too much sun today, Thomas? Maybe Ziza is pushing you too hard. You should probably sit down."

"No, Yar. I'm telling the truth. Her spirit is inside here." He raised the Gauntlet. "Along with the spirits of every other Bearer in history. It's like a Bearer reunion inside of this thing."

"When did you find this out?"

"During the battle with Arkmalis, when I was hibernating after the augment. I woke up and a young Ziza took me to see her."

"Wait, a young Ziza?"

"Yeah, apparently the Gauntlet takes an impression of you from the moment you wore the Gauntlet."

"So let me get this straight. You have known about this for over a year and you didn't tell me?"

"I wanted to, but everything got so complicated after the battle. I wasn't myself for a while. I had just found out that Grimm had killed both of my parents."

"Who else knows?"

"I think only Ziza and Itsuki."

"I don't know what to say."

"Are you mad at me?"

"No . . . disappointed more than anything. Your mother is who I have looked up to—who I have modeled myself after, and you knew that, but that's not why I'm disappointed. I'm disappointed because you didn't feel compelled to share something like this with me after all we've been through. I am here to help, Thomas, and if I don't have all of the facts, how can I do that?"

"You're right, Yar. I just had so many things swimming around my head, and I didn't want to just unload them on you."

"It makes me feel like you don't care about how I feel or care about me at all," said Yareli. Thomas gently grabbed her arm.

"Well, you know that's not true."

"How do I know that, Thomas?" She ripped her arm out of his hand. "You took off on your own grand adventure and left me here."

"I didn't want to, Ziz—"

"Ziza only wanted you two to go, I know. I was so worried when you were gone. But I guess I just thought that you cared more about me than you obviously do."

"That's not fair. I do care about you. In fact there is another reason I asked you to meet me here."

"And why is that?"

"Well . . . I'm pretty sure that I l—"

"Hey, Yareli." The man's words cut off Thomas's. He turned around to see Garron walking towards Yareli. "I figured when I couldn't find you, you would be here."

When he reached her, Garron bent down and kissed her, and she kissed back. That second felt like hours.

No. What have I done? thought Thomas. The two pulled back from one another, but Garron left his arm around her.

"I'm sorry, Thomas. What were you saying?" asked Yareli.

"Who knows? Honestly, I can't ree . . . member." *I love you. I love you so much it hurts.*

"You said that there was another reason you asked me here—and then you stopped when Garron walked up."

Garron . . . how did I not see this coming? "I was saying that I am pretty sure that I . . . like being the Bearer. Yeah. It's entirely narsh."

"Oh . . ." Yareli looked at Garron and then back at Thomas. "Thomas here was just telling me about going inside of the Gauntlet, weren't ya? And how his mother was the last one before h—"

"To bear the Burden. Yes. I know this."

"Wait, you told Garron too?"

"No, Yar, I swear I didn't."

"The Ancestors told the Eldre this, and he informed me. It was not Thomas." Garron paused and looked at Yareli and then over to Thomas. "Are you two all right? Should I come back later? I didn't mean to interrupt."

"No, Garron. We're done here," said Thomas. *I can't believe this is happening.* He began to walk away and he turned around. "I guess I wasn't the only one with a secret."

"No. I guess you weren't," said Yareli, holding hands with Garron.

"We still on for training later, Thomas?" said Garron.

"No. I've trained enough for one day."

"Okay. Then tomorrow."

"Sure, Garron. I'll see you tomorrow." Thomas began the longest walk he had ever undertaken. Tears began to stream down his cheeks before he had left the grounds. *How could I be so stupid?*

16

momma's boy

"I can't believe she has a boyfriend," said Thomas as he moved to attack. There were four of them total, inside the Ludus, the training facility within the Gauntlet. The Ludus offered the ability to pick location and environmental factors of any type for the purpose of training simulations. Today they had opted for the mountainous terrain of Wulingyuan, China at sunset—a favorite of Ziza's. Hundreds of sandstone structures, covered with lush foliage, jutted upwards while mist clung to their bases. The scenery was breathtaking, but Thomas's mind was elsewhere. He needed to blow off some steam, and this was the best way he knew how. Thomas was fighting three other Bearers at once. Through this exercise, his mother had hoped to teach him how to deal with multiple enemies.

"You have to calm down, Thomas," said Merelda Scargen. "You were gone for over a year. Did you expect her to wait forever? I'm not sure you should be upset with Yareli. Now, please, can we focus on your training?"

"I know. I'm not mad at Yareli, Mom. I'm mad at myself. I should've never left." He parried the energy output from Ziza, who had unleashed an attack from the right, several meters above Thomas. Thomas quickly formed a shield to deflect Ziza's attack. "We completely failed our mission and almost died in the process."

"There is always knowledge in experience," said young Ziza as he jumped across to the nearest structure.

"You mentioned earlier about learning from failure, but I'm having a hard time seeing what it is I should've learned." Thomas turned and fired several energy spheres in Ziza's direction.

"The time you spent away was invaluable"—Ziza dodged the first sphere—"for you to grow and learn more about yourself"—he dodged the second one—"as well as the Taitokura." He kicked the final sphere back at Thomas. "You may not have found the Zikrune, but you found something far more powerful."

"And what exactly is that?"

"A friendship with your First Augmentor."

Thomas paused and looked down. "I guess I didn't look at it like that," said Thomas as the third attacker struck him from the side with a powerful pulse, knocking Thomas against a stone wall and onto the ground.

"You need to cease lamenting over the girl and concentrate, Thomas, or you are never going to be prepared to face the Necromancer Grimm," said the third attacker—Alican Dod, the Bearer the Eldre had suggested Thomas contact. The man stood tall with a muscular build. His square jaw was clean-shaven, and his black hair was well manicured.

He's right, you idiot. Concentrate, thought Thomas.

Thomas quickly got back to his feet and scaled the rock structure next to him. "That's better, Thomas. Always try to seek the high ground, especially when outnumbered," said his mother. "It gives you a better vantage point."

"But be mindful of getting yourself trapped," said Ziza as he appeared behind Thomas. Thomas ran in the opposite direction.

"There is also nothing wrong with a strategic retreat," said Merelda.

"Yeah, but where's the sport in that," said Alican as he rushed Thomas from the opposite side. Thomas moved right at Alican and pushed his hands forward. The energy hit Alican square in the chest, knocking him down the side of the mountain. The bear of a man stood up and shook his head. "You purposely did that . . . well done, Bearer. There still may be hope for you yet."

"Always go after the strongest one first," said Thomas.

"But you may have miscalculated who that was," said Merelda who had moved in behind Thomas. The young man turned around to see his mother holding an energy sphere. "And in doing so, you have let yourself be surrounded." He turned to see that both Ziza and Alican were moving in on opposite sides. He was caught in the middle of the three former Bearers.

"Uh oh," said Thomas as the purple wave knocked him backwards. Thomas was caught by some foliage that Ziza adeptly controlled. It wrapped around him and held him tight. He was then hit by a gush of water from Alican. Thomas was trapped and soaking wet. He opened his eyes to see the three former Bearers looking up at him.

"That was a bit disappointing, Son," said Merelda.

"I think the young man's thoughts dwell on other things," said Ziza as he released his phytomantic hold. Thomas dropped to the ground. "I know the feeling all too well."

"Why did you summon me here if you were not going to take this seriously?" asked Alican.

"The Eldre mentioned how strong you were and said I could learn a thing or two from you—especially when it comes to aquamancy. I'm supposed to be good at it, because of my Light, but I'm having some control issues, and . . . I just got some bad news right before coming in here."

"This Eldre seems wiser than the one who sat on the Council in my time. That one would prattle incessantly about the Ancient Ones and their perpetual prophecies. It is a wonder I ever got anything done. I apologize for the waterlogging. You were just distracting me with all the talk of the female you desire." Alican reached down and grabbed Thomas's hand and effortlessly lifted him back to his feet. "If you want help learning aquamancy, I will gladly teach you. I myself, regret never getting the chance to wield the Gauntlet with the augmented Medenculus. I could have been even more astounding than I already was."

"How were you doing that, anyway?" asked Thomas.

"Of what do you speak?" asked Alican.

"Pulling water out of thin air," said Thomas. "The Eldre didn't get that far."

"Why not?" asked Merelda.

"Let's just say the lesson was inadvertently cut short and another impromptu lesson took precedence," said Thomas.

"That is understandable," said Alican. "Was he instructing you on how to produce ice shields or offensive frost weapons, or maybe water whips?"

"Wait, what?" asked Thomas. "You can do that?"

"I can do that." Alican waved his hand in a circular motion and an ice shield formed in front of him. He flicked out his other hand and a water tendril extended from the hand.

"Narsh. Can you show me how to do that?"

"Yes, I suppose . . . you just . . . I do not know. I have not pondered on it for centuries." Alican looked like he was thinking hard. "You ask the water particles in the air to collect and focus. The rest is like manipulating existing water, pulling it together."

"Which I'm not so good at either apparently."

"These things can take time to learn," said Ziza. "Especially manifesting the water from the surrounding atmosphere."

"Not for me. I did it quite easily," said Alican. Thomas lowered his head. "I am just giving you a hard time, Thomas. It took me years to master these skills—even longer to use them in conjunction with one another."

"Aquamancy is widely considered the hardest skill set to master," said Ziza. "Most Mages simply do not have the focus or patience."

"The African is correct," said Alican. "Look, Thomas, I am sure you will master the skill in time, and I'll help you all I can, but first . . . let us discuss the female," said Alican.

"I thought you said you didn't want to?"

"Not while we were in combat. That is absurd. But now that we have ceased our engagement, I am prepared to listen and offer guidance. I am quite skilled in the romantic arts as well."

"Okay. So there's this girl."

"What is the female's name?"

"Yareli."

"What's the issue you face?"

"I sort of . . . well . . . fell in love with her last year, and she started dating a guy while I was away looking for the stones."

"Well, explain your situation to her."

What if I did just that? thought Thomas. "It's not that simple."

"It actually is that simple. You walk right up to this female and describe your longings."

"What happened to you not wanting to put her in harm's way?" asked Merelda.

"I thought about that a lot when I was gone, and the truth is she's already in harm's way, Mom. She actually brought harm's way to my doorstep."

"I just do not think it is wise to interfere with Yareli's new relationship," said Ziza. "It is a consequence of your own inaction."

"I agree. You could end up pushing her away for good," said Merelda. "Is it worth losing her friendship as well?"

"I guess you have a point . . ." said Thomas.

"Come now, Thomas," said Alican. "Who are you going to seek advice from . . . the dramatically inexperienced Bearer? Or maybe the vengeful Bearer who lost the burden over a personal vendetta?"

"Careful, Alican. She's my mother, and he's my mentor."

"I was attempting to bring humor into the conversation, but in all seriousness I wielded the Gauntlet for over a thousand years, and I have had more than my share of dalliances. Women are attracted to power. I am highly perceptive when it comes to female wants and desires. They require a man who knows what he desires and is not afraid to obtain it. Stand up for yourself, Thomas. If you wait too long, you will end up only ever being her friend."

"But if you don't let her current relationship run its course, you might end up with nothing," said Merelda. "Yareli needs some space on this." She moved over and put her hand on his shoulder.

"I'm more confused now than I was before."

"Females are always confusing," said Alican. "Would you like to practice aquamancy?" asked Alican. "It might help distract your thoughts."

"I would love to, but I gotta get back to the outside world. I have a lot to think about." He grabbed his right arm where the Gauntlet usually resided. "And I'm starting to itch without it."

"I know the feeling all too well," said Ziza.

They all nodded in agreement. Thomas kissed his mother and shook Ziza's hand. He turned towards Alican and before he could extend his hand the large man lifted and bear hugged him. Alican placed the young man back on the ground.

"The offer is always open, Thomas," said Alican. "I can assist you in becoming almost as skilled as I in the art of aquamancy."

"I appreciate the vote of confidence," said Thomas. Alican leaned in closer and began to whisper.

"I am fairly certain your mother is correct in her assumptions," said Alican. "Give the female the time she requires." Thomas started to feel himself getting pulled back to reality. "Sometimes it is difficult for people to find what they are looking for, even when it is dangling right in front of them."

Darkness . . .

He opened his eyes slowly and looked down at the Gauntlet. He always checked to make sure it was there when he came back from inside. Stella jumped up onto his chest and lay down on top of him, staring at Thomas. She meowed.

"You little monster. What are you doing? You know I want to get up so you're just gonna sit there."

She extended her paw towards his shoulder like she was hugging him. The Scargen logo medallion that resided on her collar hung in front of him. He stared at the medallion.

It hit him like one of Arkmalis's punches. "You did it, little monster. I can't believe it. Alican was right. It is sometimes hard to find what you are looking for even when it's dangling in front of your face." He grabbed the medallion on the collar and disconnected it.

"Who's Alican?" asked Itsuki.

Thomas jumped up and Stella scratched him for the trouble.

"Owww, but it' okay. I'm not even mad at you, you beautiful furball." He rubbed the scratch on his chest. "And what are you doing here, Suke? It's bad enough when LINC does it. How did you get in here?"

"Ninjutsu, remember? I am trained in the ways of the shinobi," said Itsuki. "And as far as why, it is my job to protect you, especially when you are inside." He pointed to the Gauntlet. "Why are you grinning?"

"Because wisdom sits on the shoulders of Bastet."

"The riddle?"

"Yep, and I figured it out. Well, with Stella's help of course."

"Meow," said the cat.

"What does it mean?"

"It was so obvious. I mean even down to the first rune. I told Loric it was an S."

"I am having a hard time following you."

Thomas played with the medallion in his hand.

"Salvation or wisdom sits on the shoulders of Bastet," said Thomas. "But we were concentrating on the wrong aspect of the goddess Bastet. It wasn't about warfare. This is the key to solving the riddle. Wisdom . . . this medallion"—Thomas held up the cat's ornament—"clearly marked with an S, sits on the shoulders of the cat headed goddess, or in this case the head of a cat that thinks she's a goddess."

"Meow," said Stella.

"That's right. You're my little cat goddess," said Thomas.

"Very clever, but now what do we do?"

"We put the key in its hole."

17

deserted

They had flown in above the sandstorm, but at this point they could not see where they were going. The aringi could not take the stinging sand any longer and still stay in flight. The Riders had detached from the beasts in midair, leaving the creatures to circle above in the desert night. They would have to walk the rest of the way. They were protected by their armor and the force field visors on their helmets, but it was still impossible to see more than a few feet in front of themselves.

Marcus knew getting inside the dragon city would be no easy task. Once inside, there was no telling what could happen. He needed the right Riders. The Captain opted for Taunt the Second and Rider Brett Jurdik first. Gamil Farod remained with Arkmalis back at the Tower. *He's needed there, and his hatred of dragons would be hard to hide, especially from Oramus,* thought Marcus. The Captain had added three of the General's Guard to his team at the insistence of General Evangeline.

The first Rider's name was Katar Kist. She was the other Rider who had followed him from the Goblin Hole. Rider Kist was top of her class in tactics and hand-to-hand combat. She was also a fairly accomplished Mage. Her specialty was aquamancy. This skill was a rarity. *She might prove useful in the coming days,* thought Marcus. She had discovered this power as a child while at the beach. Kist had accidentally manipulated a wave and inadvertently drowned her sister. She was only eight years old. *It's not a fair world*, thought Marcus. She left home as soon as she was capable and searched for others like herself. Her search led her to General Evangeline. The General had hand-picked Rider Kist nine months earlier, and Kist advanced rapidly through the ranks.

Rider Harl Vance was a recruit of Marcus's. He had been in the Tower for some time. Marcus had found this man a home with the Riders, and now he was in the General's Guard. Vance had a knack for killing things which made him a handful at times. Rumor had it that when he was just a boy, he would kill small animals for sport, using only his mind. When he grew up and realized his magical potential, he became even more dangerous. He was a loose cannon, but incredibly effective and oddly loyal. He respected the chain of command. Vance would do anything for Marcus as long as it did not conflict with the General's orders. The Captain needed a new Cognomancer, and he had gotten a good one in Vance.

The third was a last minute addition. Marcus felt he needed to even out the squadron in case they needed to break off from each other. Alan Jett was a bit overweight for a Rider, but he had proven himself early as a natural on the aringi. This was Jett's first real-world mission.

Marcus and this team of Riders intended to find the exact coordinates for Atlantis—easier said than done. Orac the Seer had been no help. The information they sought was not accessible through divination. Marcus had consulted him, but the closest the Seer had gotten was showing Corbin and the Captain an obscured view of the ocean floor. Orac's powers did not extend into Atlantis. The Captain switched to Plan B: Oramus Nizam.

Oramus was a Fimus, a desert dragon. He was the Master of Syn, a small underground city in the middle of nowhere. Few outside of the dragon world knew of Syn's existence, and fewer knew of its location, but Marcus was an exception. He had acquired the coordinates years ago from Oramus Nizam himself, after befriending the dragon over a game of *Jadoon*. The dragon loved the magical game and was quite capable at it, but he envied Marcus's skill level. The Captain had played *Jadoon* from an early age and was a superior opponent. That first night they met, Oramus underestimated him, losing quite a few credits to the Captain in a one-on-one match. But the dragon was known for seizing hold when opportunity arose. The rest of the evening Oramus bet heavily against all opponents who faced Marcus, earning himself millions in credits. As a token of gratitude, Oramus offered the Captain a marker for his services—an IOU of sorts, redeemable at a future time.

Oramus dealt in a highly specialized commodity—data, and his memory was impressive. If you needed information on any thing, place, or person, Oramus would have the relevant data, and if he did not, he would get it. He had spies everywhere. And for the right price, this information would be shared. It had been several years since Marcus had last seen the dragon, but the invitation was always open, even if he was now the Captain of the Aringi Riders. Still, Lord Grimm was not someone dragons of any kind would purposely help. His previous experiments were known throughout the world of dragons.

"Why couldn't we just call ahead?" asked Jurdik.

"That is not how he works," said the Captain. "It's not that simple."

"There is a reason it is so difficult to get to," said the Second into his helmet. Taunt looked down at a holomap floating above his forearm armor. "And besides, we're almost there."

"I don't see anything," said Vance.

"Yeah, alls I see is sand," said Jett.

"That's because you're not looking in the right direction," said Taunt.

"And which direction would that be?" asked Kist.

"Down." Taunt pulled up the holoscreen showing the vast catacombs that lay below. "These tunnels are enormous, Captain."

"They have to fit dragons, Taunt."

"Fair enough." The Captain signaled and everyone fanned out. Taunt kept looking at his display. "That's odd."

"What is it?" asked Marcus.

"Well, these are the dragon-made tunnels." Taunt pointed at the holoscreen. "But I have no idea what these are." As Taunt said this, the sandstorm quieted.

"We need to find that entrance as soon as possible," said Marcus, remembering the warning that Oramus had given him years ago.

"What's wrong, Capt—" Jurdik's question was cut off by a shrieking noise the enormous worm made when it pierced the sand.

"Nir worms!" screamed Marcus, barely avoiding the second worm's lunge from below. The worms were the size of aerotrains. One of them was bad enough, but now there were two tracking them.

"What is a nir worm, sir?" asked Jett.

"*They* are nir worms, Jett. Now, everyone, arm your Taunters and engage." Marcus turned as the laser weapon in his forearm armor charged and fired. He caught the first worm under its gigantic circular mouth. The segmented monster screamed, but it did not retreat. It jumped back down into the sand, but reemerged quickly behind Marcus. Taunt and Jurdik were attacking the second beast along with Kist. Vance and Jett fell in to help the Captain.

"Try to keep them above ground, and stay away from their tails," commanded Marcus. "They are charged with electrical current. And whatever you do, don't let them bite you. They are extremely poisonous, and you will be dead in seconds."

"That's good to know!" said Taunt as he slimly avoided the striking tail of the second worm. "Safety first!"

"Vance, Jett, get its attention."

The two Riders began firing at the worm's underbelly. The nir turned towards the two Riders, leaving Marcus free to enact his plan. The Captain leapt above the worm's thrashing head and landed on its back. He held on as tight as he could while the monster tried to throw him off. Marcus energized his blade and stabbed deep into the back of the nir's neck. The beast moaned in pain, but continued to writhe back and forth.

Tough son of a bitch, thought the Captain. "Let's hope this works." Marcus took both of his hands and placed them on both sides of the monster's head. The Captain's eyes burned with energy as the yellow electricity left his hands and entered the worm's head. The nir worm was instantly killed. Momentum carried the worm's lifeless body forward for a few more seconds before coming to its final rest. Marcus jumped down and ran to help the others.

All of the Riders turned their attention to the second creature. Noticing this, the beast decided retreat was its best course of action and burrowed straight down into the ground. The Riders looked around for any signs of the nir, but the desert was silent.

"I guess that takes care of that," said Rider Jett as the second worm rose up once again from the desert floor, biting down on the torso of the young Rider. In two gulps Jett was gone.

Jurdik moved swiftly and grabbed the beast with his telekinesis, holding him in place. The worm was stuck in midair.

"Fire!" yelled Marcus.

The nir stood no chance. The blasts erupted on both sides of the flailing, defenseless monster. Jett had been its last victim. The tattered, fried body of the nir fell into the sand.

"That was fun," said Vance.

"I feel sick," said Kist.

"Show a little respect, Vance," said Marcus. "One of ours just died." It never got any easier losing a Rider.

"Sorry, Captain," said Vance as he looked down. "My apologies."

"Let's take a moment to gather ourselves," said Marcus.

"That was crazy," said Taunt.

"I've never seen anything like that," said Jurdik.

"I wish I could say the same," said Marcus. "Nir worms are nasty creatures. We were lucky to only lose one."

Everyone was quiet. The Second's wristcom interrupted the stillness.

"What is it, Second?" asked Marcus.

"We are close," said Taunt. He moved to the far left. The Second was pointing down, walking slowly. "And the entrance should be right . . . about . . . here." Taunt's eyes glowed a light brown as he moved his hands. The sand began to move to each side, exposing a large circular stone tablet. An insignia was carved into the stone. Taunt powered down. "I guess I can scratch sand off the list."

"What do you think it means?" asked Vance.

"I'm not sure, but I'd be willing to bet it's the city's sigil," said Marcus.

"How do we get in?" asked Kist.

"Like this," said Taunt. The Second moved his hands in the air as though he was opening the large seal with them. The sigil stone opened from the center, and an expansive capsule emerged from the sand. Its size could easily hold a few dragons. Sand rained down from both sides of the tube, uncovering a door with a holoscreen on the right hand.

"I guess we go in," said Jurdik. The team moved towards the door on the tube. The sand in front of the structure moved upwards.

"I'm not doing that," said Taunt.

The sand began to take shape, solidifying into sandstone, forming a massive sand troll. The troll was easily ten meters tall and held a scimitar energy weapon in its left hand. Its sunken eyes glowed yellow in its elongated head. Its right arm hung to the ground.

"State your business," said the sand troll in a masculine voice.

"Security?" asked Marcus.

"I'd imagine," said the Second.

"We're here to see Oramus," said Marcus.

"No one sees Master Nizam without prior authorization."

"Oramus and I go way back, and we'd like to get inside before these worm's friends come looking for us." The troll stood there with no expression on his face. "I'm sorry. I didn't catch your name."

"That's because I did not throw it to you, and I don't care if you babysat the Master when he was a dragonling. No one gets by me without the prior written or verbal consent of the Master himself. No consent, no entry."

"Tell him Captain Marcus Slade of the Grimm Legions is here seeking information. That should spark his interest."

"I am afraid that *that*, although intriguing—I must admit—does not fulfill the criteria laid out for clearance. You need prior written or verbal authorization." The holoscreen sprang to life. A holographic projection of a medium sized demon emerged—a jinn, the demons that Oramus used for much of his spying. Their skills in mimicry and camouflage made jinn perfect for this job.

"Who opened the gate, Sabul?" asked the demon on the holo-screen. "I am busy, you know."

"These men did after killing two of the Master's pet worms."

"Pet worms?" whispered Taunt.

"Great," said the jinn. "That's all we need."

"They are seeking clearance without documentation or prior authorization and are claiming to be friends with Master Nizam."

"We both know that's impossible. The Master does not have friends."

"I would say *business associate* would better define my dealings with your Master," said Marcus.

"What sort of business?"

"The sort where I give him a load of credits for useful information," said Marcus with a smile through his visor. "And he owes me a marker." The jinn disappeared and then immediately reappeared.

"Clearance is granted, Sabul," said the jinn. "Initiate entrance protocol, and make sure you send out some of the guys to clean up that mess."

"Initializing entrance protocol. Security clearance password 7, 3, 2, 5, 4, Omega, 3, 2, 5, 4, 7, 1, 9, 8, 2, 3, 0, 1, 5, 6, 2, 9, 8, 8, 8, 7, 6, 5, 5, 5, 5, 5, 5, 5, 5, 5, 5, 5, 5, 5, 5, 5, 3." The door unlocked. The entryway revealed itself inside the large, plain gray tube.

"How do you remember that password?" asked Taunt.

"What else do I have to do?" replied the sand troll. He placed his scimitar on his back and moved into the tube. "Everyone in."

The Riders followed the towering sand troll into the tube. The door shut behind them. They were in complete darkness. A holo-screen appeared in front of them, lighting the inside of the tube. Marcus extinguished his visor. The other Riders followed his lead. The sand troll began punching keys on the controls.

"You should probably stabilize yourself," said Sabul. "It can be a little jarring the first time."

That was all the warning that was given before the tube rocketed downward. If not for his training on the aringi, Marcus would have vomited on the spot, and from the looks of the other Riders, they were just as close. The car came to an abrupt halt.

"Are we there?" asked Marcus.

"Not quite," answered the sand troll, hitting more keys on the panel.

The car took off sideways. Marcus stumbled backwards and caught himself. The car was hurtling underneath the desert sands. Just as fast as it started it stopped again.

"We have arrived at our destination."

The door slid open. Marcus stepped from the car, following the sand troll.

"Someone will be here shortly to escort you." The sand troll stepped back into the tube. "Welcome to Syn." The doors slid shut.

Marcus turned and looked around.

The underground city was immense. Everything was oversized. Dragons walked through the streets of Syn as others flew overhead. The moving lines resembled aeromobile traffic. Marcus was taken aback by how big everything was, but more so at how modern it was. All the buildings looked as if they were carved out of the sandstone, but they were also covered in tech. "I wasn't expecting this," said the Captain.

"I'd say it's safe to say that none of us were," said Rider Kist.

A red dragon flew down and landed in front of the Riders. The Incendias lowered his head. "Welcome to Syn, Captain Slade. My name is Mikus Chard. I am the city's treasurer. I will be taking you to see Master Nizam."

"What is all of this?" asked Jurdik.

"This, Rider Jurdik, is one of the great underground dragon cities," said Mikus.

"I thought that was just a children's fairy tale," said Vance.

"No, Rider Vance, but it almost became just that, until Master Nizam came along."

"I was under the impression that it was a small city," said Marcus.

"Syn is the smallest of the dragon cities. The richest one, mind you, but the smallest."

"How many are there?" asked the Second, still taking in the scenery. "And how do you know all of our names?"

"I imagine they have been compiling dossiers on each one of us the second we stepped into the transport tube," said Marcus.

"I see you are familiar with what we do here," said Mikus. "As far as how many dragon cities there are, there are seven."

"According to the stories, there are twelve dragon cities," said Vance.

"There *were* twelve. Seven still operate. We are what you would call the black sheep of the group." Mikus paused for a second. "I never understood the predilection for white sheep, though. Trust me, they both taste the same when eaten whole." The dragon smiled. "As far as knowing your names, that is our business—to know things. It is a lucrative commodity, data, when used correctly."

"That is why we have come," said Marcus. "We seek information that only your Master can find."

"I assure you, if he does not possess it now, he will acquire it for you by any means necessary."

"It will just cost us, I'd imagine," said the Second.

"Like I said, an exceptionally lucrative commodity, indeed."

18

syn city

Marcus found the flight through the city to be astonishing. Lights were everywhere. The city was an odd combination of old dragon architecture and the most modern tech. Marcus, Taunt, and Jurdik flew on the back of Mikus while the other two flew on the back of a female Dracavea named Gor Yan. Gor seemed to be Mikus's equal, judging by the way the two communicated with one another. She had not said much after Mikus's initial conversation with her.

"We're here," said Mikus, landing in front of a stone building.

Intricately carved depictions of all the dragon races covered the columns that held up the structure. A statue of Oramus stood in front. It was a flattering depiction of the Fimus. The building jutted out from the cavern's wall. It looked like a king must live inside, but Marcus knew better. Oramus was not royalty, at least not by birthright. But he may have been the closest the dragon world had seen in centuries.

"This place is unbelievable," said the Second.

"Wait until you see the inside," said Gor as she walked past the Riders. They approached the doors, where two sand trolls stood at attention, holding energy scimitars. The dragon continued without hesitation as the trolls opened the doors for her.

Gor had been right, the view on the inside was unbelievable.

Holoscreens were everywhere. Images filled the room from every news outlet in the world, in addition to numerous security feeds from around the globe. Hundreds of jinn and dragons were pouring through this information and material, looking for the next tidbit that would net credits. The jinn fielded the wrist communications, morphing from person to person, assuming whatever identity was useful in each instance. Artifs raced above their heads, correlating and filing the data. It was a remarkable industry, all terribly illegal, but remarkable just the same. "Welcome to the Farm, Riders," said Gor. "This is where all the magic happens. Thousands of workers sorting through terabytes of data in seconds, all with one purpose—information. But this is not what you are here for, is it?"

"No, it is not," said the Captain. "My request is for Oramus himself."

"As I imagined. He is expecting us in his chambers."

"Let's not keep him waiting," said Marcus as they followed Gor through the Farm. A new set of doors opened in front of them. The hustle and bustle of the previous room was replaced with a riotous display of artwork in the next. Paintings littered the walls and thousands of sculptures were cleverly placed in the long hallway. "I know Oramus well enough to know that these weren't his idea. He'd think these were a waste of money."

"Yes, but he also knows that keeping up appearances is a must in this industry," said Mikus. "Wouldn't you agree, Gor?"

"I would say that this place needed a feminine touch and that's exactly what it got. You cannot believe what this place looked like before. The richest dragon in all of Syn and he was sitting in his own filth."

"Not literally of course," added Mikus. "But Gor's point is a valid one. The four of us make a formidable team."

"Four?"

"Gor and I, and Oramus and his . . . brother. We all bring different skill sets to the table."

"That's an understatement," said Gor as they approached the last set of doors. A female dragon was answering holocalls behind a large floating platform.

"The Master's prices are final. I'm sorry, there can be no negotiating terms . . . Hold please," she said, turning towards the group. "The Master will see you now." She went right back to answering calls. "Hello again, Mr. Parson. I'm afraid he is busy at the moment. Can I relay a message?"

The doors were opened from the inside. The dragons entered first, followed by the Riders. The room was immense and circular. There were four doors equidistant from each other. In front of these doors stood dragon guards—all Dracavea. Three floating chairs were situated in the middle of the room, but only one was occupied.

Mikus and Gor took their places in their floating chairs on each side of the already inhabited chair. A plump, yellow dragon sat at the head of the arrangement. He was flanked by two young female dragons. He wore a tailored shirt and had several necklaces hanging under his quadruple chin. The Fimus drank from a large chalice.

"Hello, Oramus," said Marcus. "You haven't changed a bit."

"Well, well, well, if it isn't Captain Marcus Slade. How long has it been, my friend? Fifteen years?"

"Closer to twenty actually, but math was never your strong suit."

"This is a correct statement. The only counting I like to do is after a good transaction, if you know what I am saying, my friend?"

"Like I said, you haven't changed a bit."

"Yes, but you have. There is something different about you. I can't quite put my talon on it." He contemplated the thought for a second. "But where are my manners. Would any of you like a drink? Or maybe some dragonweed. We have the finest quality in the world here. Only the best for my honored guests."

Marcus looked around. Taunt had his hand raised, but the look that the Captain gave him made him lower it.

"We are fine, Oramus. Thank you for your hospitality."

"Suit yourself," said the yellow dragon as he grabbed the pipe piece attached to his chair and inhaled. The smoke from his exhalation circled above the Riders. "I still cannot believe you gave up *Jadoon*. You were the best, the best. It hasn't been the same without you. You made me so much money." Oramus smiled. "I've had to resort to betting on batilloc matches—batilloc matches. Why did you ever quit?"

"Life's not a game, Oramus. Sooner or later, the game becomes you."

"Ah, he fancies himself a philosopher of sorts, but I suppose you have a point. It is a young man's game, and neither of us would ever be confused for young these days." He chuckled and drank from the chalice. "Anyway, to what do I owe the pleasure after all of these years?"

"Well, I thought it was probably time to call in my marker."

"I see. Ladies can you excuse us?"

"Sure, Master O," said one of the young female dragons as she walked out with the other.

"Now where were we?"

"I am in need of information."

"You have come to the right place, but I am not sure if I can help you, my friend. You see, your boss is a killer of dragons, and, no offense to you, but I do not do business with such scum."

"None taken. I am aware of my Master's transgressions. That behavior is in the past. I can assure you of that."

"Can you now? And I suppose that should be enough. Do you know what you're asking of me?"

"I am asking you to honor your word."

"And what of the abominations that currently fly around in the desert sky—the aringi I believe they are called? They are living proof of your Master's meddlings—playing God, of all things."

"I am not asking this for him, I am asking it for me."

"I do not believe that is totally true, but a marker is a marker, and Tollin Grimm could make an excellent ally . . . but give me one good reason why I should betray my own kind and help you."

"The only reason you've ever needed—credits."

Oramus laughed and took a sip from his goblet. "Very well, my friend. I will do it."

"Are you sure, Master?" asked Gor. "This Necromancer is a powerful ally yes, but an unpredictable one as well."

"A rather rich one too, do not forget. As always, Gor, your counsel is wise, but I made a promise to this man, and I am a dragon of honor if nothing else—a greedy dragon of honor."

"Yes, Master, I understand," said Gor.

Oramus floated closer to Marcus. "What is it you need?"

"I need to know the location of the lost world of Atlantis."

Mikus and Gor turned towards Marcus.

"Are you sure it even exists?" asked Mikus. "I mean besides in bedtime stories?"

"Lord Grimm is not someone who wastes time with fairy tales and what ifs," said Marcus as he turned towards Mikus. "If he says Atlantis exists, it does."

"It is only a legend. There is no such city," said Gor.

"We have thought that before," said Oramus as he lifted his goblet and drank. "In our industry, assumption is our worst enemy. Fact is our only salvation, and there is only one way to know for certain."

"And how's that?" asked Marcus.

"My brother." Oramus looked down at his oversized wristcom. "Baramus, can you come in here? We have a question that needs answering."

"Not now. I'm almost finished the last level of *Gargantua*. Can't it wait?"

"I am afraid it cannot, my brother. This is more important than getting the high score in some silly hologame."

"You have no idea what you are talking about. You are, by far, the worst older brother ever. I hate you sometimes. You know that? Mother did too. She told me on her deathbed."

"Baramus that is enough. Get in here immediately."

"Yes, your grace," said Baramus with a heaping dose of sarcasm.

The door to the left of Marcus slid open. Smoke drifted out of the opening followed by a fourth floating chair. This chair was different than the other three. An even more obese, yellow dragon lay sprawled in the center of the chair surrounded by tech. He was eating a dragon sized sandwich. Stains covered his button-up shirt. He wore an eyepiece on his right eye. Several holoscreens that were attached to the chair relayed information to the Fimus. The chair settled into the opening on the floor. "What is it, Oramus? I'd like to get this over with as quickly as possible. I have a game to finish, along with thousands of networks to oversee. So what is it you need, Brother?"

"This gentleman here would like to know the location of the city of Atlantis," said Oramus. "And we cannot even agree if it exists. Can you help us?"

"Give me a second." The obese dragon stared at the holoscreens as he moved data with his talons.

"So you're saying it might exist?" asked the Second.

"I'm not saying anything without the relevant information in my claws," said Baramus. His eyes began to glow brownish yellow as his talons moved with speed and precision across multiple holoscreens. His chair pivoted with his movements while his hands blurred from the speed of his gesturing. He seemed to be in a trance. "Hmmm."

"Can you not find it?" asked Marcus.

"If an imp farts in the Depths, I smell it before he does. Okay. I have written many extensive algorithms that would blow your tiny human minds. I am so good at my job, I . . ."

"Baramus, can you just give them the information they are looking for?" interrupted Oramus.

"Yeah, sure, Brother. Okay . . ." Baramus rifled through information, stopping every so often on an image or a story. "That's not it . . . that's definitely not it . . ." He turned in his chair to another holoscreen. "Promising, but still not quite it . . ." He again began to blur his movements. "Ahhhhh." The dragon slowed down. He moved his talon across the holoscreen he now faced. "Wait . . . this looks like something."

"What is it?" asked Marcus.

"I'm afraid I cannot find the location of the city."

"So you are saying it does not exist?" asked Gor.

"No. I am saying that I can't find the location of the fabled city. There is no solid evidence on the whole of *Interface*." He stopped and took a hit from his pipe and slowly blew out the vapor. "But I'm pretty sure this guy can." A hologram of a man appeared in front of them.

"Who's he?"

"His name is . . ." Baramus stared intently at the screens while he flicked through the information. "Vedd Delphin. His name is Vedd Delphin."

"Who's he, and what does he have to do with Atlantis?" asked Marcus.

"I believe he's an Atlantean. That answers both questions."

"How could you possibly know that this man is an Atlantean?" asked Oramus.

"A fine question indeed. I can prove he's an Atlantean right now." The hologram zoomed into his neck. "Look on both sides of his neck. There are definitely two sets of gills, indicating that this man is most likely capable of breathing underwater."

"Impressive, but that doesn't prove he's from Atlantis," said Marcus.

"No, but it definitely distinguishes him from any humanoid species that exists on the known Earth, but there's more. The way he is dressed. He's dressed in what looks like an underwater suit of some sort. When I cross reference the make and model of the suit from visual markers, there is no known manufacturer of this particular outfit—in the entire world. Again, pointing to a foreign or possibly alien design. His physiology is congruent with every account ever documented on the inhabitants of Atlantis. Even if most of these descriptions are fictitious, this man obviously is not. In most of the images I retrieved you cannot see his gills, but in the most recent ones that I found he seems to be taking fewer precautions."

"So you basically searched several world image databases looking for a man with gills?" asked Taunt.

"Or woman. I also searched through cached security feeds from across the globe . . . look, you make it sound way easier than it was. Do you know how many hours it took me to write the code just for that to be possible? This is next-level shit were talking about here. Trillions of lines streaming in milliseconds. This doesn't write itself—well, it sort of does, but I wrote that program too."

"Impressive," said Taunt.

"Thank you. At least someone appreciates the work I do." Baramus scowled at Gor and Mikus.

"But how did you get his name?" asked Taunt.

"Once I found the gills, I then searched his likeness through every known GA database and crossed referenced it with some unknown ones. I also scanned every profile on every social media outlet available . . . and there were several matches, but after facial and logistical comparisons, it was obvious that they were all the same person, just using various pseudonyms."

"Why did you settle on one?" asked Marcus.

"Vedd Delphin was his first alias, which, based on worldwide user patterns, usually means that this is his original name. If I was guessing, I'd say that Vedd here is a spy for the Atlanteans, or at least a hired hand."

"But how do you know for certain he's from Atlantis?" asked Taunt.

"Besides the amount of seafood this guy consumes in a given week? You should see his credit expenditures. It's like all this guy eats, and at the weirdest hours."

"Yeah, maybe something a bit more concrete that connects him to Atlantis."

"That was the easy part. Once I knew his alias, I hacked his wristcom and did a log search on his whereabouts for the last two years."

"All in that short period of time we watched you?" asked Marcus.

"I know, right? Pretty impressive. What did you think I've been doing the whole time you are talking to me? But I haven't even gotten to the most impressive part. The locations in the log are pretty normal, until you look at three separate occasions when he seemingly vanished, but instantly reappeared on the other side of the world in the middle of the damn ocean. Each time, the signal went dead again, and I'm not talking for a few minutes. I'm talking a couple weeks at a time. Once he disappeared for four months. All three times, his wristcom's reactivated in the very spot that he disappeared."

"Meaning?" asked Marcus.

"He's going somewhere where a wristcom would do him no good—a place mind you that's in the middle of the damn ocean, a few hundred miles off the southern coast of Greece, always within the same 80- to 160-kilometer radius."

"That's a big area to search," said the Captain.

"Yes, but not if you have him," said Baramus.

"Who?" asked Mikus.

"The Atlantean in question—Vedd Delphin. He could lead you straight to Atlantis," said Baramus. "Assuming that is where he's been going. But I have never heard of any other underwater city."

"I have to admit, with that much evidence, it seems you have proven the existence of the city," said Gor. "But what of the Atlantean?"

"Yes, where can we find him?" asked Marcus.

"That's the only problem. He seems to have dropped off the grid. His last known coordinates are from three days ago."

"That is not as big a problem as you might suggest," said Oramus. "Remember; tech is essential for our operation, but it is not our only means."

"Oh, you're talking about them." Baramus pointed back in the direction of the Farm.

"Come now, Baramus, our family was in the business of information distribution long before the advance of computers and satellites and such."

"Yeah, but we weren't as good at it as we are now," said Baramus.

"That may be, but sometimes the old ways still work best," said Oramus.

"They are just so . . . I don't know," said Baramus.

"Reliable and efficient?" said Oramus.

"*Gross* was the word I was searching for," said Baramus. "And a little creepy."

"What they lack in social graces, they make up for tenfold in their results." Oramus turned to Marcus. "Now let's find you an Atlantean."

Oramus floated over to his original position and began to chant to himself. Candles all over the room sprang to life as a circle began to glow under the dragon. The yellow dragon continued to chant as his eyes turned black. There was a flash in front of the glowing circle. When the smoke cleared, there knelt a jinn.

The demon was shorter in stature than a crag, but by no means tiny. It was the size of a tall man. It had small horns and a set of wings. A loincloth covered the expected region of its smoke-colored body, so Marcus assumed it to be male. The jinn was hunched over and its legs were reminiscent of a goat's.

Marcus had never worked with jinn. They were known to be highly intelligent, but also conniving and manipulative. These qualities made them perfect for spying but not so perfect for trusting. The Grimm Legions relied on lesser conjurings for the most part. Sometimes exceptions were made, but usually restricted those exceptions to demons that could be bound. A jinn had no such limitations, making them disliked by most other demons. They had free will, but understood their place. A jinn, once summoned, could perform the task asked of him if he so chose or be sent back to the Depths. Most picked the former. Oramus's family over centuries had nurtured a relationship with these entities and knew how to treat them in order to circumvent most of the loopholes in the somewhat tricky proceedings.

The jinn stood. Oramus was the first to speak.

"Mukt, so good to see you once more, old man."

"And I you, Master Kizam. It 'as been quite some time since I 'av been called 'ere before you. I was beginning to fink dat you 'ad forgotten about me or 'ad upgraded to a newer model."

"You are the best at what you do, but unfortunately your expertise is not always needed." He pointed to Baramus, who cautiously waved back.

"By expertise do you mean my advanced maturity?"

"Your age is often an asset, and I believe it will be thus again, my friend."

"To what do I owe duh pleasure?"

"We are looking for the lost city of Atlantis."

"Dere's a reason it is called a lost city."

"So you have heard of it?"

"Oh yes, many years back, mind you, but 'erd of it I 'av. I was summoned dere once, a long bloody time ago. But it's no use dough. Finding duh city is virtually impossible. It moves, you know? Shifts from time to time."

Like Sirati, thought Marcus. "That will make it most difficult."

"Like I said, damn near impossible—especially wiffout an Atlantean, and dey tend to be a slippery lot."

"And that is why I have summoned you, Mukt. We have found one such man, and we need your help tracking him."

"Why didn't you say so? Which form should I assume?" The jinn switched from his current form into a huge spider. "No, too scary and just a bit conspicuous." He turned into a small squirrel. "No, too small and weak—cute dough." He transformed into a polka-dotted alligator. "Too confusing." He continued changing forms, one to the next, dismissing them as they came. His shape finally settled into that of a human woman. "Men are all so easily duped by a beautiful woman, especially Atlantean men. How much time do I 'av?"

"We'd like this done as soon as possible," said the Captain.

"What information do I 'av to go on?" asked the jinn.

"A name and his prior location as of three days ago," said Oramus.

"Dis should be easy den. Okay, give it to me."

"His name is Vedd Delphin. His last known coordinates place him midlevel in New Amsterdam," said Baramus.

"He's in the States?" asked Marcus.

"Seems so," said Baramus. "Let's just hope he's still there."

"Don't worry your pretty little 'ed about it. You lot sit tight 'ere. I'll 'av Mr. Delphin collected as soon as demonly possible. Ta ta." The jinn vanished in a whorl of smoke.

"Can he be trusted?" asked Marcus.

"I trust him with my life, my friend," said Oramus. "And there are few I'd include in that group. He will not disappoint you. You have my word, Marcus."

"And that is all I need."

"That is great news," said Oramus.

"That means we can talk about payment for services rendered," said Mikus.

"My favorite part," said Oramus as he once again drank from his goblet.

19

the missing linc

Thomas pounded on the door. "Wake up, Mancer Bodes."

Itsuki stood next to him, wisps circling his head. It was early in the morning, but what Thomas had found could not wait. "I've figured it out—my dad's riddle."

Loric answered the door before his sentence was completed.

"Go on. Out with it." The man stood in the doorway with only a towel wrapped around his waist.

"Are you going to let us in?" asked Thomas.

"Very well." He opened the door all the way and motioned them to enter. As Loric turned, Thomas noticed something he had not before. On Mancer Bodes's right shoulder blade there was a simplified, black tattoo of a tiger's head in profile.

I wonder what that means, thought Thomas. He was so preoccupied with the marking that he almost ran into the woman. She looked exhausted as she headed towards the door.

"Thank you, Mancer Bodes," said the woman. Thomas could not place how he knew her.

"The pleasure was all mine, Beatrice. I trust I will see you later at Maktaba?"

That is where Thomas had seen her before. She was one of the scholars and teachers at Maktaba. Beatrice Trent was her full name.

"That *is* where I work," said Beatrice. Mancer Bodes smiled at her as she waved and exited.

Loric wasted no time. "What have you discovered? It had better be substantial to warrant the speedy end to my consultation with Beatrice."

"Consultation?"

"Nothing more. I assure you. Our consultations often help to untangle the web that infests my mind from time to time."

"She looked pretty flustered."

"Consulting with me can prove most difficult at times, but it did bear fruit."

"I bet."

"Beatrice brought to my attention something that Anson had found that I connected with a bit of information that I had uncovered about your father, but that is of little matter compared to the information that you have yet to share with me."

Thomas had almost forgotten. "I solved the riddle."

"You have said as much, but I am still waiting to hear this hypothetical solution."

Thomas produced the medallion from his pocket. "You were right when you said the message was meant for me to figure out." He held it up. "Wisdom sits on the shoulders of Bastet. We believed that the emphasis was on her being a goddess of war, but the actual emphasis was on her being the cat goddess." Thomas paused for a second. "Wisdom sits on the shoulders of the cat goddess, or, in this case, the cat who acts and is treated like a goddess. This is the medallion that was on the collar of my cat, Stella. I never gave it a second thought before because it was just the Scargen logo."

"Genius. It was literally an S. You were right from the beginning. Although I suppose if I knew that you were the owner of a feline, I too might have come to a similar conclusion. The irony. Me of all people should have seen the overt signs of feline ownership." Loric held his chin between his thumb and pointer finger. "And am I to suppose that said medallion is a key of sorts?"

"That's what I was hoping. I'm just not exactly sure what it is a key to."

"That is where my expertise can be of use." Loric snatched the medallion out of Thomas's hand and walked back towards the lab area of his apartment. "If my original hypothesis is correct that Dr. Carl Scargen is in fact hiding something inside of your artif companion, then it would stand to reason that this is a key to unlock the sleeping artif."

He walked up to LINC and placed the circular medallion over the identical Scargen robotics symbol on the artif's chest. The medallion glowed a faint blue color as the two logos connected. LINC's optics fluttered as the key began to unlock whatever lay hidden inside of the artif. LINC lifted his arm and a life-sized holographic representation of Thomas's father appeared in front of them. Beyond the simple movements the artif performed, he still seemed lifeless.

"Hello, Tom," said Dr. Carl Scargen. "If you are watching this, then I am most likely dead."

Thomas squinted at the reality of this hologram's words.

"I knew you were smart enough to figure this out, or at least smart enough to surround yourself with people smart enough to figure this out." His father chuckled and so did Thomas. "There is much to tell you. Miraculous things to tell you even, but first, your immediate action is needed. An upgrade was either time dispersed or initiated externally to begin this chain of events. As you may already know, LINC is more than a mere companion artif. He is also a protector. I believe there are people that may come looking for you one day. I believe this was your mother's fear as well."

He knew? thought Thomas.

"I know you never came to terms with her leaving us, but I assure you it wasn't as selfish an act as you might have previously thought. I will explain what I mean soon, but first I need you to look up an old friend of mine. He holds the next step to the puzzle. I have placed a locator beacon on a second medallion that he will have in his possession. He does not know what it is he has, but knows of its importance and that it is meant for your eyes only. I had to hide the second medallion with someone I trusted in case something happened to you as well. The man's name is Cayde Galeos. He is an old friend who I can absolutely trust to keep my secret, in the same way he's trusted me to keep his."

"That name is familiar," said Loric.

"Find Cayde and retrieve the second medallion. It is of the utmost importance. The information contained in the pendant will change the world, Tom. LINC will reactivate after this message is completed. It may take a few seconds for him to initialize his new systems, but you're going to need him. He alone contains the coordinates to the second medallion. Take the original medallion with you as well. It will be needed again. I know this is a lot to ask of you, Tom, but I know you can do it. You were destined for great things, and I love you, Tom. There's one more thing. It is important that you listen to Cayde's story before engaging the second medallion. It should help fill in some of the holes I've left." The message ended.

"That was pretty vague," said Thomas.

"Purposely so, I'd imagine, to assure that this information would never fall into the wrong hands," said Loric. "And I think I remember where I saw one Cayde Galeos's name before." He ran to the closest holoscreen. "There was a book your father downloaded on his second dig." He gestured with his finger moving data backwards and forwards. "Ahh, here it is." The cover of the book enlarged in front of him. "*Atlantis Lost* by Cayde Galeos."

"I know that book. Dad had a copy of that in his lab at home too. He was kind of obsessed with lost cities."

"I think there might have been a bit more to it than that."

"Look at some of these designs," said Thomas. "They look almost Scargenesque."

"There is somewhat of a shared design aesthetic, yes," said Loric. "I think this was more than a mere work of fiction."

"Are you saying what I think you're saying?"

"I'd say Cayde Galeos has definitely just become a person of extraordinary interest in this mystery."

"Hello, Thomas Scargen. I have missed you," said the unforgettable voice of LINC. Thomas ran over and hugged the artif. He broke himself free and gently removed the medallion from LINC. "The coordinates have been placed in my navcom. Destination—New Amsterdam, USA."

"Going back to the States," said Thomas.

"I suppose I should put some pants on," said Loric.

"That's probably a good idea," said Thomas.

20

upgrades

Thomas, Itsuki, LINC, and Mancer Bodes arrived at Bartleby's lair soon after leaving Loric's. They were welcomed as usual by the gremlins and an unusually large breakfast. This did not please Loric, who wanted to make his way to New Amsterdam as quickly as possible. But Bartleby had not eaten since the night before. He had been asleep, and asking a dragon to work on an empty stomach is futile.

Truth be told, Thomas was hungry as well. He also wanted to speak to Bartleby in private regarding his Atlantis dream. He needed to tell his friend about the possible connection to Larson Ragnor.

Thomas approached the dragon shortly after finishing off his generous helping of banana pancakes and three glasses of Gloop. "Hey, Bart. Can I talk to you for a second?"

"Sure, Thomas. I suppose I can let duh little buggers wait a few more minutes to start suitin' me up. What's up, Thomas? Everyfing aw'right?"

"Yeah. I mean as good as can be expected. I'm excited to see what's waiting for us in New Amsterdam, but that's not why I wanted to talk."

"Out wif it already."

"So, I had this dream a while back that I wanted to discuss with you before we left. I haven't seen you since, and I thought you should know—"

"Know what Thomas? What exactly was dis dream about?"

"It was about a black Aequos who had shapeshifted into an Atlantean."

"Dat makes sense. Most Aequos have some level of shapeshiftin' abilities. I always found it a bit odd myself, but to each dere own."

"That wasn't the part I wanted to discuss with you. The black Aequos stole the blue stone from Atlantis."

" 'av you been drinkin' bloody whiskey wif Anson again?"

"No . . . yes, but that's not the point."

"I must admit, I'm strugglin' to find a point myself, Thomas."

"When he stole the stone, he escaped and delivered the goods to another dragon. The other dragon is who I wanted to tell you about."

"What's so special about dis uvver dragon?"

"The other dragon was Larson Ragnor."

Bartleby's mouth hung open for a few seconds.

"And you are sure about dis?"

"Yes."

"And when you say dream, you mean it was more den a dream?"

"Yes, like the one I had about my dad the night we met. Only this one seemed to take place in the past. Like I was seeing someone else's memories."

"I'm glad you said somefing, Thomas," said Bartleby.

"I just figured you should know. That stone in the hands of Larson Ragnor could be trouble."

"But if you're right about when it 'appened, duh stone might not even be wif 'im anymore. I find dragons are always misplacing priceless gems, aren't dey? In seems to be one uv our flaws."

"It's just . . . if it isn't relevant, then why now? Why would I be seeing this now? The Gauntlet is trying to tell me something. I just don't know what it is."

"Well, I might be able to help wif identifying duh uvver dragon, duh black Aequos."

"In what way?"

"I fink I know 'oo it could be."

"Who?"

"Well, Larson's wife was an Aequos, wasn't she? And Larson is 'imself a Dracavea."

"And?"

"I just fink dat maybe dere's a connection between dose two facts."

"Which is?"

"It sounds like the black Aequos could be Larson's son. I never found out what happened to duh two eggs after Mum and Dad 'ad left dem wif duh Dragon Council."

"I thought Larson didn't know about his wife's eggs."

"Dat could be true, but dat was a long time ago, Thomas. A lot of fings can 'appen in dat amount uv time . . . and 'av, come to fink about it."

"It does make sense. But where's the stone?"

"Dat I know I don't know," said Bartleby. "But Larson or dis new dragon might. We find dem, we might find duh bleedin' stone." Bartleby looked down the hallway towards the hangar. "But we 'av uvver fings to worry about right now, don't we, Thomas?" said the dragon. "I'm not tryin' to cut you short or anyfing. It's just I'm due to get my new suit fitted today, and I got to get goin' or Mancer Bodes will go mental." Bartleby's new systems needed to be implemented and a diagnostic was being performed by Fargus on the newly awakened artif—both needed to be accomplished before their departure.

"I understand. One mystery at a time."

"Fank you, dough. I appreciate you coming to me wif dis. We'll deal wif your father's past first, mate, and den maybe mine. If Larson is involved, I'm going to need all uv dese new bloody gadgets." The dragon began to move down the hallway towards the hangar. "I'll see you in a bit, Thomas."

Thomas walked into the hangar. Gremlins covered Bartleby, trying to get him ready for departure. Talya chatted with Bartleby while drinking a massive mug of coffee. Loric had insisted that they keep the field trip to find Cayde Galeos to themselves. The only person they were bringing into the fold besides Fargus, Bartleby, and Talya was Anson. Anson had been involved since the beginning. Fargus and Bartleby were needed for transportation, and Talya just happened to be in the lair. Thomas wanted to include Yareli, but he still felt betrayed, even though he knew he had no reason. *It'll just be awkward*, thought Thomas. His father's secret might appear to have nothing to do with the Council, but something told Thomas that there was a connection somewhere. His father would not have spent that much time and credits on nothing.

Anson had joined them after breakfast. Thomas walked over to Loric and the werewolf while they spoke to one another.

"From my research, I can safely say that Atlantis does, in fact, exist," said Anson.

"Hello, Thomas. I'm glad you are here for Warwick's story. Anson found several Ancient texts that reference a power source that ran the whole of Atlantis. This was also the case in Cayde Galeos's novel *Atlantis Lost*—which on second perusal, reads more like nonfiction. We believe that the power source has to be one of the stones," said Loric.

"More precisely, the Medenculus," said Anson. "Which seems to give further credence to the notion that your dream was not a dream at all."

"It was a seeing of events—a premonition or, in this particular case, a look into the past—at a specific moment in time," said Itsuki who had just joined them.

"And if we take your premonition to be fact, then we have to deal with the possibility that Larson Ragnor still has the stone," said Loric.

"But I think Bartleby's assessment might be right, though," said Thomas.

"And what was that?" asked Anson.

"The events I saw took place years ago. A lot of things can happen in that amount of time. What if Larson doesn't have it anymore?"

"One must concede the plausibility of that hypothetical outcome given the amount of time since the heist," said Loric. "That being said, these dragons are our only solid lead. If Larson or this other dragon do not have the blue stone, they might know who does." Loric looked over at Anson.

"About the new dragon . . ." began Thomas.

"I am afraid the Dragon Council was little help with the identity of the black Aequos, Scargen. A pity actually."

"Well, Bart might have a theory on that too. He thinks it could be Larson Ragnor's son."

"Perhaps. Aldrich Baldemar suggested the same, based on the late Ilyana Ragnor's race. It would stand to reason that her and Ragnor's offspring could be, in fact, a black Aequos. But there is no credible evidence that suggests that Ragnor and his offspring ever knew each other, let alone colluded with each other. I'm afraid we may be grasping at straws, as it were. It may be worth a look when we get back, but now we must invest our attention to the current matter."

"Dad's puzzle."

"Yes. And remember, this is only a fact finding mission," said Loric. "Stealth is, as always, of the utmost importance. We must not be seen nor heard. The fewer people who know about this, the better."

"There is no telling what secrets your father is hiding," said Anson.

"That is precisely why I think that the Council need not be involved at this juncture," said Loric. "Your father seemed adamant about this information not falling into the wrong hands—whatever this information is."

"But shouldn't we inform, Ziza?" asked Thomas.

"There is no reason to wake the old man for mere conjecture," said Loric. "And besides, I am a grown man and I do not require permission to act."

"I agree that there is no reason to bring the entire Council in on this until there is something a bit more substantial to talk about. This should be something that two Mancers, an Augmentor, and a Bearer should be able to handle," said Anson.

"Are you agreeing with me, werewolf?" asked Loric. "I think that is a first in quite some time." Anson smirked at him with an eyebrow raised. Loric smiled back and turned towards Fargus. "How much longer until he is ready?"

"Well, dat's just it, isn't it?" said Fargus as he looked down at his handheld device. "We are in duh middle of implementin' a lot of new systems and tech into Bart's arsenal. We should 'av 'im up and running in about twenty minutes or so. I must admit, dough, I'm more worried about LINC muckin' about wiffout duh proper tests being run."

"Your concern is warranted and noted, but the artif is essential to the undertaking of this mission, and we do not have the luxury of time in this matter," said Loric.

"I'm just sayin', what if 'ee goes mental again and starts doin' crazy fings, an that?"

"This is why I agreed to the diagnostic before departure. I, too, harbor similar concerns. It is also why you are accompanying us on said mission."

"Dat makes sense, I suppose. And dis way I can keep an eye out on 'ow well Bart's new upgrades work as well. Between the new armor, functionality, and the new weapon's systems, it should be bleedin' interestin'—to say duh least."

"I have the utmost confidence in your work, Mr. Hexelby," said Loric. "And the artif?" Loric leaned in as he raised his closed hand up to his chin.

"LINC's new systems appear to be fully functional," concluded Fargus, pulling his tiny hand out of LINC's control panel, as the opening on the artif's back slid shut. "As soon as duh uvvers are done suiting up Bart, we can get goin'."

The artif sprang back to life.

"I assure you, Thomas Scargen, that my systems are running at the highest functionality levels possible. My fully integrated artificial intelligence has no rival in the field of robotics. And—"

"I know, LINC. We're just being careful."

"That is a logical course of action, considering my track record in combat."

"Don't be so hard on yourself, LINC."

"My composition has in no way become more rigid."

"I just meant that Dad could not possibly have known what you were going to face." *I think anyway.*

"Dr. Carl Scargen seems to have rectified any shortcomings my tactical and defensive systems capabilities might have had in the past with my current upgrade."

Thomas, LINC, Anson, Itsuki, and Loric made their way over to where the gremlins were fitting Bartleby. The dragon's new armor was amazing. Fargus's skills coupled with Hosselfot's tech had made this all possible.

" 'ello, gentlemen. We are almost ready 'ere, and wif duh couple uv minutes we 'av left, let me go frough some uv duh features of Bartleby's new armor," said Ronald Hosselfot.

"You sound like a bleedin' used aeromobile salesman," said Bartleby. "Just get on wiffit."

"Okay, okay. You 'erd duh impatient dragon." The holographic display leapt from Hosselfot's wristcom. "As you can see 'ere, duh main change 'as been to duh weight and functionality of duh dragon's armor and artificial wing. Duh initial procedure was quite impressive for duh time, but tech 'as come a long way since den, 'asn't it? Uvver upgrades 'av also been done specifically to combat duh main fret as we see it. Using duh tech dat I was able to procure for a small markup, combined wif duh skills of Fargus and 'is gremlins, 'ere, we were able to do a complete overhaul uv Bart's systems."

"None uv dis would be possible wiffout duh fings I've learned from looking inside LINC, 'ere." Fargus looked at Thomas. "Your father was a bleedin' genius, an that."

"Thank you, Fargus. That means a lot."

"And wiffout duh 'elp uv me main crew, an that. Dey are bleeding amazin' as well. Bloody geniuses demselves.

Three gremlins popped their heads over the side of the dragon. One of them was Lenore Bugden.

" 'ello, Thomas. 'ow 'av ya been?"

"Good, Lenore, and you?"

"Just grand. Dis is all terribly excitin', isn't it?"

"Yes it is. Who are your friends?" Thomas looked at the two male gremlins.

"Dis one 'ere is Valv Tinger," said Lenore pointing to the first gremlin on Thomas's left.

" 'ello," said Valv.

"Aiken Gloop," said Lenore pointing to the next gremlin. He was a bit fatter than Valv.

" 'ello, Mr. Scargen," said Aiken Gloop. Thomas recognized the last name immediately.

"Gloop, aye?"

"Mr. Scargen," said Lenore, giving him a look. Lenore had asked him not to tell anyone about what she had told him about the wariness of the Gloop family when they had first met.

Thomas diverted. "I trust we've brought some Gloop with us?"

"Four cases," said Fargus. "Dat should be enuff." A fourth gremlin now appeared to the right of Aiken Gloop, holding a small device similar to Fargus's.

"And Torc Barwin, lead engineer," said Lenore pointing to the new gremlin. He was taller than the others and thinner.

"Pleasure," said Torc as he turned towards Fargus. "I fink 'ee's just about ready, Mr. Hexelby."

"Good, then can we get on with it?" asked Loric. "You were saying, Mr. Hosselfot."

Hosselfot moved a few symbols with his hands and schematics of Bartleby's new weapons systems appeared on the holoscreen. "Laser cannons have been mounted on duh rear uv duh dragon for obvious reasons and also on duh cybernetic wing. We have also installed electronet missiles for capturing and incapacitating aringi in midflight. Duh riders of duh dragon will also have a bit more room to travel on my armored friend 'ere. Frow in a more secure shield and a fully functional cloaking device and dere you 'av it: duh all-new Bartleby Draige, Warrior Dragon. Everyone aboard."

"A cloaking device?" asked Thomas as he jumped up onto Bart's new cockpit-type saddle.

"You didn't think we were going to fly a dragon into the middle of the largest city in the world without some camouflage, did you?" asked Loric as he positioned himself in front of Thomas on the dragon. Itsuki sat behind Thomas and Anson moved in behind Itsuki, facing backwards.

"I guess I hadn't thought of it like that," said Thomas.

"New Amsterdam will be crawling with BLUEs and security drones," said Anson.

"Yeah, Thomas. New business calls for new tech," said Bartleby. "I was never intended to be doing anyfing so militaryesque or 'awforne would have seen to dis 'imself. I mostly did transport jobs and the like, as you know."

"I guess we all need to be more prepared these days," said Thomas.

"Speaking of which," said Fargus as he appeared on top of the dragon's head, facing the other passengers. "I got somefing for ya, Thomas. I made a bit uv an upgrade for you, as well." He threw the item at Thomas. Thomas caught the band. It looked similar to a wristcom but had no display.

"I understand if you don't like it, but I figured it could make it easier on you when you're out in public. To not draw attention to yourself with dat massive Gauntlet, an that."

"What does it do, exactly?"

"It fools duh Gauntlet."

"In what way?"

"You had told me about the first time you went to change after getting duh Gauntlet, and it got duh wheel in me 'ed turnin', an that. And I fought, well what if dere was a way to make it fink dere was like a situation dat required duh same size change, but for a longer period uv time? I believe if you go to slip it on, the Gauntlet will act like it does wif a shirt, but den duh band locks onto your wrist, keepin' duh Gauntlet normal hand-sized instead of massive. Ya know what I mean?"

"I think I do, but then the Gauntlet is useless."

"Only while duh band is on. It can be removed instantly by voice or just by tappin' dat button on duh left. Dere is also a small laser canon inside uv it, for dose times you don't need the whole magic Gauntlet fing. Gives it an added purpose, an that."

"What do you call it?"

"I call it Sheath, on account uv it's like duh sheath for your weapon."

"That is brilliant, Mr. Hexelby," said Loric. "And it is also well timed. The only thing more conspicuous than a three-ton dragon walking about in New Amsterdam would be a teenager with a over-sized magical artifact dangling from his forearm."

"I suppose when you're right you're right," said Thomas. "Here goes nothing."

Thomas started to put the Sheath on, and the Gauntlet collapsed. The Sheath settled on his forearm and extended up the back of his stone hand, locking around his thumb. He turned the arm over. The Gauntlet seemed to be fine. He could feel it become dormant, but it did not affect him too badly. For the first time in over a year, he almost looked normal. "Wow, thank you, Fargus."

"It was just an idea, an that. If you don't like it, I can work on it some more."

"No, Fargus. It's perfect. I love it." Thomas hit the button on the left and the Sheath slipped off and levitated in front of him. The Sheath came to rest in his left hand as the Gauntlet returned to its usual size. He replaced the Sheath onto his forearm. "Just checking."

"Should we go now, or are there other gifts that need exchanging?" asked Loric.

"Just one," said Talya as she walked over to Bartleby and kissed him. "Stay out of trouble, Barty."

"I'll do me best, sweetie," said Bartleby with a wink.

"What am I going to do without you?"

"You'll be too busy to even notice I'm gone wif duh gremlins, 'ere, fittin' you for your armor, an that."

"If you say so," said Talya as she backed away. "Love you."

"I love you too, hun. See ya soon."

Bartleby waddled his way out the hangar door and into the sky above Sirati, bearing his passengers. After clearing a checkpoint, he ripped open a teleportal and sped through the tear. LINC followed.

21
levelheaded

The sky ripped open over New Amsterdam, though from an outsider's standpoint it might have looked as if nothing had happened. The cloaked artif and his dragon-borne cohort poured through the slice in space. The city was beautiful in its scale and engineering. Multiple tiers, with multiple skylines. The seven main levels formed a sphere that sat right on top of the water. The city at night was breathtaking. Even in the downpour, it was a sight to behold.

New York City had flooded decades ago, and New Amsterdam rose from its drowning streets. This new city was built from the bones of the old. The top five levels had retained the same names as the old boroughs. Level 1, Manhattan; Level 2, Brooklyn; Level 3, Queens; Level 4, Bronx; Level 5, Staten. The sixth was named Aen. And Level 7 was called Falrin. Each of these main levels also had various sublevels, making up thousands of different neighborhoods and districts.

Bartleby buzzed the Statue of Liberty. It had been placed on Manhattan Level, atop the tallest building as a symbol of America's freedom and resilience. However, things had changed in the United States over the years. Personal freedoms gave way to security. People's fears were used to manipulate and control them. Corporations slowly took over the government, and the distribution of wealth ceased.

This was more apparent in New Amsterdam than any other city. The rich got richer, but the poor just kept dropping down levels in New Amsterdam.

"The signal is resonating from district 1573, one of the lower sublevels of Falrin," said LINC. "There are transport corridors connecting the sublevels that we can intercept once we reach Brooklyn Level."

"I am afraid that Bartleby is not going to be able to come the whole way," said Loric.

"Why can't we just fly down there?" asked Thomas.

"That would garner the attention of every Hunter or sentry artif in New Amsterdam," said Loric. "A dragon, even cloaked, is bound to set off a sensor or two. Our safest bet is through the center of New Amsterdam, even if Bartleby is conspicuous for that part of the trip."

"I will show you the most efficient way of getting there," said LINC as he flew down one of the transport corridors.

"Den 'ere we go," said Bartleby as he rose into the air and went straight down into the same transport corridor. Fargus had made sure that Bartleby could track the artif's movements through his navcom, and Thomas could do the same through his goggles. LINC was going extremely fast, weaving in and out of cargo ships and aeromobiles. Bartleby followed, being careful not to give them away.

"You need to switch corridors after the next exit," said LINC.

"Will do," said Bartleby. The dragon followed the artif at a safe distance. LINC's size made it easier for him to weave in and out of the other vehicles. The artif banked right down another corridor, and then went downwards into an intersecting corridor.

The artif and the dragon continued down through the maze of corridors at ridiculous speeds until they reached Aen Level. Aen was the sixth level of New Amsterdam, the last level that was not partially submerged and where they would be leaving Bartleby. Security between Aen Level and Falrin Level was traditionally intense. Scans were routinely done on all levels, but more so on Falrin Level. They could not simply fly down the transport corridors. They would be certainly caught in a scan.

The dragon landed in a small clearing inside a park. LINC landed there as well. The artif decloaked, and the others came into sight as they disembarked from the dragon's still-cloaked form.

"I'll stay put around 'ere until needed. Maybe take a nap on one of dem buildings."

"Okay, Bartleby," said Loric.

The motley group walked towards the nearest building lead by Mancer Bodes.

"What now?" asked Thomas, raising his goggles. "What's the plan?"

"How *do* we intend to continue down to Falrin Level?" asked Itsuki.

"Leave that up to me," said Loric.

"This does not look like the best neighborhood," said Thomas.

"It isn't, Scargen. That is precisely why we are here. Now where is my Urchin? "

"I wish I understood what he was talking about," said Thomas to Anson.

"You get used to it," said Anson.

"Really?" asked Thomas.

"No, not really," said Anson. "Though this be madness, yet there is method in 't."

"He's late. That is not like Snigwig. He is usually very prompt."

"Wait, we're meeting someone here?"

"Yes, a friend, or more like a colleague. It is hard to explain."

"Try me."

"Yes," said Itsuki. "I would also like to know more about these Urchins."

"The Urchins, as I refer to them, are my underground network of people, mostly vagrants, that are my eyes on the street." He pointed at Mancer Warwick. "It started back in London when Anson and I worked together and it has grown exponentially since. I supply the Urchins with tech and a modest stipend, and in return, they give me valuable information that one cannot necessarily ascertain from a wristcom or artif. No offense, LINC."

"None taken. Your assertion has not been proven truthful as of yet, so no offense could be felt, even if I were capable of such things."

"They will supply us with the kind of data we will need to progress down to Falrin."

"But they're still homeless even though you pay them?"

"Some of them by choice, Thomas. I actually have a solid track record of turning some of these people's lives around. Many stay on afterwards. Over the years the Urchins have become rather irreplaceable, although most are not technically homeless anymore. Some move on and become full-time hackers of various metropolitan areas, allowing us access to places we would otherwise not be able to enter. We've expanded the system into almost every major city across the globe."

"How do you communicate with them?" asked Thomas.

"Coded messages displaced over several social media outlets."

"It appears tech still plays a vital role," said Itsuki.

"Ah, yes. It does serve its purpose," said Loric, putting his hand on LINC's shoulder. Loric's wristcom rang. He looked down to see the message. "It seems he is waiting inside that building."

Thomas looked over at the structure that Loric had pointed at. It was more than a building. It was a support for the city, descending from Staten above, through Aen Level and presumably down into Falrin. This had to be the way they were getting down to the next level. *This is starting to make a bit more sense*, he thought.

"Are we sure we can trust this guy?"

"Snigwig's reliable, Thomas," said Anson. "At least he used to be."

"I was talking about Loric," cracked Thomas as he followed Anson towards the structure.

"Love all, trust a few, do harm to none," said Anson.

"Why do I find the last one so difficult?"

They had made their way to the building. Loric had already entered.

"You should probably cloak again LINC," said Anson. "These people are not used to artifs of your caliber. It will be a dead giveaway that we're not from around here."

"Understood, Mancer Anson Warwick," said LINC as he disappeared.

Thomas entered the large structure and saw Loric waiting for them. Loric walked towards them with intent.

"Follow behind me and do not say a word," said Loric.

"But—"

"Not a word."

The building looked deserted, but Thomas knew better. There were camera orbs everywhere, watching the groups every movement.

"We have precisely forty-three seconds to move into the next room. The Urchins are currently controlling the security orbs. Snigwig is on the fifth floor. Room 537."

They opted for the stairs, moving swiftly up the five flights.

"Open that door when I give the go signal . . . go!" They moved into the hallway. "Move down the corridor. The room should be on the right side."

They made their way to room 537. Thomas tried the door.

"It's locked," said Thomas.

"To some, maybe," said Loric as the attachment left his wristcom.

Anson stepped in his way, interrupting. Seconds later, the door slid open.

"You taught me that much," he said, smiling at Loric.

"You haven't forgotten everything then," said Loric.

They all entered the room and shut the door behind them. The dark room appeared empty at first, except for the holoscreen in front of them. An image appeared above it of a young black man who could pass for homeless.

"Hello, Loric," said the hologram.

"Hello Snigwig, I was expecting you in the flesh."

"Sorry for the inconvenience, but I do not make it down that far very often. This is safer for all of us. We now have the building under our complete control."

"And this connection?"

"Untraceable and being rerouted through several thousand pathways. Even if they knew we were here, they still couldn't find us."

"Do you have the other asset that I had requested?"

"Yes. I am transferring the location data now. You should have it."

"It seems like everything is in order, except one minor detail.'"

"Which one is that?"

"How do we make our way down to Falrin?"

"Like this." The lights in the room came on. They were standing at the far end of a warehouse sized room. In the center of the room was a large round beam that pierced through the heart of the building.

"The structure?"

"Yes. That's a support that stretches from Manhattan Level down into the ocean's floor."

"We can travel down this support?"

"Not exactly. I know that you are all Mages, so I assumed that a long, controlled fall was not out of the realm of possibilities. Humans could never use these shafts to jump between levels so they are largely unmonitored. It will provide an effective way to enter Falrin. I'm opening up the access panel near the base of the structure. The support is not due for a scanning for another six minutes. That should give you just enough time to get down into Falrin Level."

The warning signal began to sound as the bottom of the building opened up, revealing the fall that they were about to attempt.

"Thank you, Snigwig. The credits have been transferred to your account, and as usual your work has been exemplary."

"The pleasure was all mine. Good luck down there. You're going to need it." The display went blank.

"After you," said Loric to Thomas as he grinned.

"Here goes nothing," said Thomas as he lowered his goggles, and without hesitation, jumped.

The air rushed on every side of him. He could hear nothing except the sound of winds whipping across his open ears. He squinted his eyes as the floor of the structure swiftly began to come into focus. He braced himself and pushed downward with his feet, landing perfectly, shattering the concrete where he landed. Anson, Loric, and Itsuki followed suit. LINC decloaked in front of them as he hovered down.

"We better get out of here. We just made a ton of noise," said Thomas as they moved out of the room and out of the building. Thomas could not believe the stark differences in just the last two levels.

Falrin was partially submerged, and if not for the pollution and dilapidated buildings, it would be breathtaking. Many of this levels structures were the backbone for the city of New Amsterdam, but few legitimate corporations existed on Falrin Level. This level had been taken over long ago by the poor and those not wanting to be found. Organized crime thrived on these streets. On Falrin Level, the poor of New Amsterdam lived in the shadow of the great sphere.

Thomas raised his goggles as he stared at the other structures that extended down from the upper level. He looked over at his artif companion. "Which direction is the signal, LINC?"

"It is coming from the northeast quadrant of the city, along the ocean. I have pinpointed the location. It is 25 minutes away on foot."

"Good thing we will not be on foot," said Loric playing on his wristcom as they walked out of the building.

Thomas was so preoccupied with his new surroundings that he almost did not see the two aerocycles settling in front of them.

"Aerocyles are the only way to get around Falrin," said Loric as he turned towards the Bearer. "Anson will go with me, and Itsuki can ride with you, Scargen."

Loric took off in the same direction as LINC. Thomas lowered his goggles and followed the Mancer. LINC was once again cloaked, but Thomas could still see him through the specs' display. Thomas accelerated in front of Loric, taking the lead. The aeroways were packed with mostly aerocycles and aeroscooters, moving this way and that. Thomas could see vendors selling food and drink from their small floating stands. Most of the people seemed happy, even though they obviously had little.

"Thomas Scargen, I have settled on the destination. The second key must be in that building there." LINC slowed down and decloaked.

They were on the outskirts, and the building was sitting in the water. LINC landed and so did the aerocycles a block from the building. Thomas got off of his cycle and moved down the alley, following LINC. LINC settled in front of a small door around the back of the structure.

"What now?" asked Thomas.

"I say we knock," said Loric. "If Cayde Galeos is here, I imagine he is expecting you. What reason would he have to not let you in?"

"I like it." Thomas moved over towards the door. He leaned over and knocked three times. The sound echoed through the alleyway. And then silence again. "I am here to see Mr. Cayde Galeos."

"Who are you?" said a loud female voice from inside the door.

"Tell him Thomas Scargen is here to see him." When the little old Chinese woman opened the door it startled Thomas. *I wasn't expecting that.*

"Quickly, follow me," said the small woman. "And wipe your feet."

"I'm sorry. We must have the wrong place," said Loric. "We are looking for Cayde Galeos."

"If you'd keep your mouth shut and follow me, I imagine you'll see him shortly."

"Very well then. On you go," said Loric. The five companions entered the room behind the Chinese woman. It was a shop of sorts, or had been at some point. The shelves contained more dust than merchandise.

"Okay let's move it. I don't have all day. Go on through there." The elderly woman pointed at a doorway at the back of the shop.

Loric turned towards Anson. "She's lovely."

"Mend your speech a little lest you should mar your fortunes," said Anson.

"Are you ever going to stop doing that?" asked Loric as they walked.

"It is actually sound advice that maybe you should think about heeding," said Anson.

"Your unabashed devotion to the Bard's words, while lovely, is really quite annoying," said Loric.

"And once again, the annoyer becomes the annoyee," said Anson.

"Well, at least that's your own line," said Loric.

"I can see now why you two don't work together anymore," said Thomas. The two looked at each other.

"Do you two want to keep yapping your mouth, or do you want to find Galeos?" asked the woman.

"We want to find Galeos," said Thomas.

"Then shut up and follow," said the woman.

"She kind of reminds me of my mom," said Itsuki.

"I can see that," said Thomas. "Well, minus the floating and being dead thing." Itsuki nodded in agreement as they entered the room. It was a small storage room that shared the same lack of products as the store. "What now?"

"We go down," said the woman, hitting a button on her wristcom. The door slid shut behind them as the whole room began to move downwards.

"I didn't see that coming," said Thomas.

"A secret elevator masquerading as an old storage room," said Loric. "Who knows what other surprises are in store for us?"

"The probability of that outcome was exceedingly low, according to my calculations," said LINC.

"Augmentor Rule number twelve: Always be ready for anything at anytime," said Itsuki.

"Is there a place I can see all of these rules written down?" asked Thomas. Itsuki looked up at the Bearer, crossed his arms, and rolled his eyes. The storage room stopped, and the back wall rose up.

"This just got a tad more interesting, wouldn't you say Warwick?" asked Loric.

Anson nodded in agreement. "Fortune brings in some boats that are not steer'd."

"Now you're just doing it to annoy me," responded Loric.

"Come on," said the small woman. They left the storage room behind and entered the next room.

Thomas could not believe what he was seeing. They were underwater. The whole outer wall was glass. The view was astounding. He began to look around. The room was actually a long open hallway with pools every twenty or so feet tempered by force fields. *There's something so odd about this place*, thought Thomas. *But familiar.* The architecture seemed foreign, almost alien, but the design was completely Scargen.

"My father designed this place."

"I miss your dad. He was a friend," said the Chinese woman. "He and Cayde were close." She looked at Thomas with sincere eyes. "I'm so sorry for your loss."

"How'd you know?"

"It's been all over the news, but also because you wouldn't be here otherwise." She stopped and turned around. "This place was a gift from your father to suit its unique inhabitants."

Before he could ask the obvious question, two men sprang forth from two of the pools in the hallway. Their momentum carried them into the air. They landed on the floor of the hall, water beading off of their skin and suits, both holding energy spears. The one on the right was considerably older than the other. He appeared to be in his midforties, while the second man seemed in his late twenties. The older man had dark hair and a beard that etched the curve of his chin. From the wrinkles on his face, Thomas could tell that in his life this man had smiled more than frowned. There was a foreign mark on the suit clinging tightly to his athletic form. It reminded Thomas of a wetsuit, but not like any wetsuit he had ever seen. *Why aren't they wearing tanks or flippers?* thought Thomas. The two men, at first, appeared human, but at a second glance it dawned on him, Thomas could see the obvious difference. Gills marked both of the men's necks, and their feet were elongated and webbed. Their skin was not just pale, but slightly tinted a grayish blue. Thomas had seen this before in his dream.

"Atlanteans!"

pupil

Corbin watched from the corner. He had been present for all of these training sessions, but they did not get easier to watch. If anything, witnessing them was proving more difficult. This had been going on for months. There were only three of them in this room on one of the training floors—the General, Lord Grimm, and himself—besides the demon that Evangeline had conjured. She was becoming proficient in this skill.

From what Corbin could tell he was merely a midlevel entity—a crag. The demon was in a crouched position, awaiting instructions. The imp was disgusted by the manifestation, but that did not deter his appetite. Corbin was doing what he did best, eating, when the General woke him from his daydreaming. The dark sphere shot close to Corbin and nearly consumed the imp. He choked on his sandwich.

Grimm was situated behind Evangeline. "Again," said Grimm. Evangeline had been at it for a couple hours, manipulating energy.

"Yes, my Lord." She held her hands apart in front of herself. Orange energy began to form between her hands. The color slowly grew darker. Grimm slithered to the other side of her.

"Good, good. Feel the particles and bend them to your will." Her eyes glowed more intensely now. "Now force them to move. Make them bow to your power. They do not have a choice. The particles are not your friends. They are your slaves, and you their master."

Evangeline began to shake. The energy that swirled in her hands had become black.

"Now use this energy," said Grimm.

"Demon, attack me!" commanded Evangeline.

"Yes, my master," said the crag as it pounced at the General.

Evangeline pulled her arms apart and the black energy split in two. She swung her arm forward as the dark energy flew out like a whip and wrapped around the attacking demon. He pulled his arms apart, but before he could break free she lassoed him with the second dark whip. She pulled the demon towards her and lifted the crag above the ground.

"That will be enough for today. You have a big day coming up tomorrow."

The energy dissipated and the demon dropped to the ground. "Cease your attack," said Evangeline. The demon went back to his crouched position. Evangeline dropped her arms.

Grimm plucked her right arm before it fell to her side. "Now, your reward," he said, placing his finger on her wrist.

She winced in pain. The black energy flowed through her veins and began to attach to the already established tattoo, expanding the marking up her forearm and causing it to glow. Evangeline screamed out in pain. She grabbed her arm and collapsed to the ground.

"Get up!"

"Yes, my Lord."

She got up as fast as she had fallen. Lord Grimm placed his hand on her shoulder and the other one stroked her hair.

"There, there, my child. Pain is an essential part of power. Remember that. One can feed the other. Now, a bit of business before the final part of today's lesson."

"What is it, Lord Grimm?"

"Will the Dred be ready for departure?"

"Of course, my Lord. Everything is going as planned."

"It is only a matter of time then—as long as the Captain does not fail me."

"Marcus will get what you have asked of him," said Evangeline.

"You have great respect for this man, my dear. Make sure that does not interfere with our plans."

"It won't, my Lord."

"Very good, my child." He ripped open the air with his Scythe. "Come. We are almost finished for today. There is but one thing left to show you."

"Where are we going?" asked the General.

"Let's call it a field trip."

She followed him through the tear. Corbin cautiously followed.

"Bring the demon."

"Follow, demon!" shouted Evangeline.

"Yes, my master," said the demon. He shot through the tear as well.

They appeared in the center of a busy aerotrain station in Tokyo, Japan. There were thousands of people milling about, waiting, in their own ways, for their respective trains. The four of them looked completely out of place in the station, and people started to notice. Six securtifs descended upon them.

"Please put down the weapon and back away," said the artif on the right.

Tollin Grimm looked at the artifs, raised his hand with his palm open. When he closed it, the body's of the securtifs collapsed into themselves. The lights on the artifs went out and they dropped to the ground. Grimm continued as if nothing had happened. People began to run back and forth to avoid the two Necromancers and their Dark Realm conjurings.

"A war is about to start, my child, and I am not sure you are quite ready as of yet."

"I am ready, my Lord."

"That is good to hear, but words mean little without action." Lord Grimm turned towards the crowd. "Look at them run, my child. They fear us . . . as well they should. They are just like the particles. They are easily controlled once you bend them to your will."

He twirled the Scythe in his hand and cut through the air. A dark wave was sent into the middle of the crowd. An explosion followed shortly after. The attack instantly killed hundreds of people.

Evangeline watched the massacre. Her face did not change at first, but, slowly, she began to smile.

Corbin cringed behind the General, as imps tend to do in these situations. *I can't believe she is just standing 'ere watching dis. She 'as lost it, and 'ee's more mental den I fought.*

Lord Grimm held up his hand with the stone embedded in it. The fleeing spirits were sucked into the Necromancer's hand. The power surged through him as he laughed aloud. His eyes burned with the dark energy as he closed his eyes and powered down. "Now it's your turn, Evangeline."

General Evangeline's eyes began to glow orange, and slowly transitioned to a deep, dark color. She turned towards the dispersing crowd, pulled her hands back. Screams rang out from the epicenter of the blast. Hundreds were dead, but thousands were injured. Evangeline began to move her hands forward, but Grimm put his Scythe in her way. He began to laugh.

"No need, my child. I was just seeing if you would. Save your energy for Atlantis. You will need it."

"Yes, my Lord."

"That's why we conjured the crag. He will take care of our dirty work. Mustn't waste our resources."

"Yes, my Lord. Demon." She motioned with her hand, and the demon pounced into the retreating crowd.

23

an old friend

"You're both . . . Atlanteans," said Thomas as he stared at the two men.

"Well spotted, Thomas," said the older man on the left. He spoke with an accent that Thomas could not specifically place, but it definitely sounded Mediterranean.

"I figured Atlanteans would look less human," said Loric.

"You would not be saying that if you had the pleasure to meet a Kra warrior," said the man.

"Those're the lobster-looking guys, right?" asked Thomas.

"How do you know this?" asked the man.

"Long story," said Thomas.

"The good ones always are," said the man.

"Your book speaks of these creatures," said Loric. "I am beginning to think that this supposed work of fiction, is anything but invented. Is this true Mr. Galeos? You are him, are you not?"

"I am Cayde Galeos, and yes, my book is more fact than fiction." He looked back at Thomas. "The books were your father's idea. He thought of writing as the perfect job for someone who was trying to be inconspicuous." He pointed to the gills. "The publisher loved the concept and how real it all seemed." The two Atlanteans laughed.

"My dad was friends with an Atlantean . . . narsh." Thomas extended his hand. "I'm Thomas Scargen, which . . . you already know apparently. This is Itsuki Katsuo, Loric Bodes, and Anson Warwick."

The men all nodded to each other. Cayde walked right over to the artif.

"And this beautiful piece of engineering must be LINC," said Cayde. "Amazing . . . simply astounding. He is even more remarkable in person."

"I too agree with your assessment of my core functionality being more apparent when in closer visual proximity," said LINC. "And that I exude a certain design aesthetic that is pleasing to the human eye."

Cayde turned around and looked at Thomas. "I'm sure you already know this, but it bears repeating," said the Atlantean. "Your father was a genius."

"I might have heard that a few times before, maybe even once already today, come to think of it."

"His death is a great loss for all of us—Atlantean and surface-walker alike."

Cayde turned around as he remembered the other Atlantean. "Oh, I am a forgetful fool. Where are my manners? I am so sorry, my dear. This here is Vedd Delphin, my partner . . . not that we are exclusive or anything."

Cayde walked over and caressed the man's face, then turned back to his guests. Vedd also nodded at the others. He was blond with no facial hair, but just as fit as Cayde.

"I will remember that next time I am back in Atlantis," said Vedd. The two chuckled.

"You know I love you," said Galeos as he turned back towards the group. "But an Atlantean sovereign has to keep his options open."

"Sovereign?" asked Loric, looking around perplexedly.

"You know, the king. I thought the entourage for a Gauntlet Bearer would be slightly more intelligent than this."

"We are not simply his entourage, as you so casually put it. I am Loric Bodes, Mancer on the Council of Mages, and this here is Mancer Anson Warwick, also a member of the Council. And he is Itsuki Katsuo, the Bearer's First Augmentor, and Shogun of the Temple of Yokan."

"Please, I mean no disrespect Mancer Bodes, Mancer Warwick, Itsuki Katsuo. My sense of humor sometimes betrays me. It can get lost in the translation. It is an honor to host members of the Council of Mages. I apologize if I insulted you."

"Apology accepted . . . how'd you know I was the Bearer?" asked Thomas.

"The same way, I suspect, you knew I was an Atlantean—observation." He walked closer to Thomas and slowly lifted his right arm, keenly looking at the Sheath that Fargus had created. "Although the device masking it is clever, it does not hide the overt power of the Gauntlet," said Cayde. "I too was an engineer like your father." He let go of Thomas's hand. "We shared a lot of interests actually, besides taking things apart and seeing what makes them tick."

He walked over to the glass wall and stared out the window into the ocean, towards the faint shape of a sunken ship that rested on the old streets of New York City. "We both shared a love of ancient things, but the thing we had most in common, was a love of family and friends." He turned back and began to walk in the direction of Thomas. "He spoke of you all the time, and your mother, well, she was the world to him . . ." He turned away once more. "Some interests, however, we did not share."

"Like what?" asked Thomas. He was curious and honestly just wanted to learn more about his father.

Cayde looked back at Thomas, and his smile squinted his eyes as he slowly shook his head from side to side.

"Your father did not share my affinity for combat." He twirled the spear in his hands. "A sovereign must have strength as well as smarts, if he is to lead properly." He looked at Thomas. "But differences can help a friendship grow as much as similarities."

"What is the sovereign of Atlantis doing in the bowels of New Amsterdam?" asked Loric, interrupting Cayde.

"That is a story for later, perhaps. I believe there is another more pressing tale to tell. One, Thomas Scargen, I promised your father I would tell you one day, and that day is upon us."

"He did mention that in his last message," said Thomas. "That's one of two reasons we came here."

"And the other?"

"To retrieve something my father left for me—a medallion."

"Ah, yes. In due time. The two are connected, I believe. First, the story. This tale your father thought to be just a nice piece of fiction the first time he heard it, but I assure you, where I come from, this is not mere conjecture. This is our history—our origin."

"I could a tale unfold whose lightest word, would harrow up thy soul, freeze thy young blood, make thy two eyes like stars start from their spheres, make thy knotted and combined locks to part and each particular hair to stand an end like quills upon the fretful porpentine," said Anson.

"I could not have said it better myself, friend," said Cayde. "But first let us retire to my sitting room and indulge ourselves with culinary delights and spirited libations."

"Does that mean food and drinks?" asked Thomas.

"Yes, my boy, it does indeed. A good tale is always best told with a good drink," said Cayde.

"Good. I'm thirsty and starving," said Thomas.

"You are always starving," said Itsuki.

"Doesn't mean it's less true," said Thomas.

"I do not think it wise to delay the purpose of this visit any longer," said Loric.

"Patience, my new friend—a Mage of your power should understand its value. I think even someone as learned as you will find purpose and wisdom in the telling of this particular story. Madame Ling, will you be so kind to prepare the sitting room before you leave."

"Of course, Sovereign Galeos," said the old Chinese woman.

"I will see you later, my sovereign," said Vedd. "I have matters to attend to elsewhere before returning to Atlantis. I am overdue." He leaned over and kissed Cayde on the cheek. "I long for the day when this is a thing of the past."

"I too, my dear, but we both know you must return to Atlantis or things will appear off. You cannot be away for too long. You know this. I want nothing more than for you to stay here with me, but we know that is selfish and we do not have that luxury as of yet."

"Yes, of course, my dear. My emotions get the best of me at times. As always, the sovereign is wise." The two men kissed once more.

Vedd turned to the others. "It is an honor to have met one of the fabled Bearers and members of the Council. I hope you enjoy the tale. It is a marvelous one." He jumped into one of the wells as fast as he had come up through it.

"Come now. Follow me," said Cayde. He walked down the hallway towards the large doorway. Various weapons from different eras adorned the walls, along with diverse artifacts and works of art.

"You have an impressive collection, I must say," said Loric.

"I have been . . . collecting for a long time. The art and relics are from me gallivanting around the world when I was a bit younger." He pointed to the small armory that took up most of the wall. "Most of these are the weapons of my opponents over the years—simple trinkets to remember them by. Still others I have searched for over the many days of my life."

"Fascinating," said Loric. "And here I thought you were just another spoiled sovereign."

"We must have bloody noses and crack'd crowns," said Anson.

"I've had my share of both in the arena," said Galeos. "But this story is not about me." He looked directly at Thomas. "I made a promise to your father all of those years ago, and an Atlantean never goes back on his word."

As the group approached, the doors opened automatically. The sitting room was a cylinder that descended deeper into the dark water. A spiral staircase surrounded it on the outside. The walls were made entirely of glass. It was as close to living underwater as Thomas had ever felt. There were separate lofts and sitting areas that broke off from the main cylinder, each with a force field doorway leading to the outside waters. They proceeded to the bottom of the staircase.

At the bottom was another pool contained by a force field, in the center of which stood a comfortable-looking circular couch covered in pillows. This room led to another tunnel that seemed to connect back to the original structure.

"Please sit, everyone." Artifs began to fly down the cylinder with trays of food and refreshments. "Make yourself comfortable."

Everyone sat down and began to take food from the trays and drinks from the bottender.

"First, I would like everyone to raise their glass." They all followed the man's wishes. "To Carl Scargen, a friend, a father, and a genius. Earth misses you and is a sadder place without your wit and smile. *Graveomas.*" Cayde raised his glass to his lips and when he brought it down, it was empty. "There is nothing like a good Atlantean ale."

The toast had caught Thomas by surprise. Here was a close friend of his father's he had never met. How many more people were there out there that Thomas's father had affected that he would never meet?

"What does *graveomas* mean?" asked Thomas.

"It is a toast to the dead from the living. It is almost like 'see you soon, my friend,' if there were a direct translation."

"Narsh . . ."

"To the business at hand," said Cayde as he placed his empty drink on one of the floating trays. His eyes glowed blue as he lifted his hands above the water.

Thomas listened intently as he sipped his ale. *This is going to be so entirely narsh.* He bit into one of the many tasty morsels that Madame Ling had provided.

The pool began to bubble and pop. The water rose up out of the well and the shape of a boy began to materialize. The form then transformed into a three-dimensional representation of the boy walking in a wooded area.

"Now . . . I will tell you the tale of Og of Enzal," said Cayde, "the First Gauntlet Bearer."

24

og of enzal

Long ago, many years after the firestorm, before man was the dominant species on Earth Realm, there lived Og. Og was a boy, at least at first, but he was different than the others.

Og had three siblings—Oash, the oldest brother; Gayan, his only sister, the youngest of the four; and Narg, the youngest boy. The four of them could do things that the no other children could. Oash could control water, and he was an excellent swimmer. He also had an uncanny ability to heal. Gayan was an adept horticulturist, controlling vegetation. She could make anything grow in the barrenest of landscapes. But Narg and Og were even more distinct: they could do all of these things and more.

The people of the village hardly paid them any attention until Narg accidentally caught one of the houses on fire. Using their gifts, Oash, Gayan, and Og put out the fire immediately, but it was too late. The village had witnessed their abilities, and for that, they were shunned.

They left their tribe and wandered out into the dark, foreboding world. Eventually the four came upon a new village on a mountainside, known as Enzal. The men in the village lived in the shadow of Drook. Drook was the dragon kingdom situated on the adjacent mountain. Dragons did not mingle in the affairs of Men but were their equals in wisdom and sense. This did not stop the men from being afraid of the dragons. If anything, it frightened them more.

Among the people of this village, were three who could accomplish feats similar to Og and his siblings. There was Pyre, Denk, and Lyth. Each one had their own unique ability. Pyre could create fire from seemingly nowhere and she could manipulate it. Denk had high intelligence, and he could move things without touching them, and knew things that you had not spoken aloud. And Lyth had a tremendous ability for figuring things out, and an affinity for building creations to be marveled at. Stone was his preferred medium, but he was skilled in all materials, and could manipulate them at will.

Since Lyth and Og shared this passion for invention, they became friends instantly. The two boys were inseparable. Narg did not like this. Og was, after all, his older brother and his best friend.

Years passed, and with time, came wisdom. The townspeople and the dragons began to peacefully coexist. Og had grown into a special man, garnering the trust of the dragons with the help of this siblings and friends—the Mages, as they were now known. Because of this new found alliance, he became the village leader. The dragon leaders and village elders, including the seven Mages, formed the first Council. Og helped the dragons develop their natural gift for teleportation, and in turn, the dragons allowed the Mages to ride atop them—traveling great distances in seconds. A symbiotic relationship was born.

With Og as its leader, the town attracted more people with special abilities. The first to come was Kala from the south. He was fast. Time seemed to stop for him. Then came Astra from the Far East. She could see things before they happened—her visions were usually cryptic but always true. The Mages now numbered nine.

Dragons and Men lived in peace on the mountain for years. Through Og and Lyth came ingenuity. The dragons also shared this need for invention and craftsmanship. Their stoneworkers and smiths were the greatest in Earth Realm. Together, they made all manner of tools, weapons, and contraptions with the help of the dragon forge. The most extraordinary of these objects were the Seven Artifacts.

The Artifacts had been Og's idea. Og believed that if the Mages could enhance their abilities, they could help the city of Enzal that much more. It had taken some time and quite a few missteps along the way, but in the end, the Seven Artifacts were born through the ingenuity of the dragons and the magic of the Mages. Each Artifact was forged to enhance the specific ability of its wielder: the Hammer for Lyth, the Trident for Oash, the Axe for Pyre, the Eye for Astra, the Sword for Kala, the Stave for Denk. But none of these tools were as special as the seventh Artifact, for Gayan, the Scythe. It was beautiful as well as elegant. The long blade was made from dragon steel and fired in the hottest dragon forge in Drook, the handle carved from the strongest materials known to dragon and man. It was created to help with the harvest, and help it did. The tool, coupled with Gayan's power, soon transformed the mountainside with crops and foliage. Trees and vegetation sprang out of the Earth. Life was abundant.

Neither Og nor Narg had been given an Artifact, since they had no single skill to augment. Both of the brothers were skilled in all of the others' abilities.

Over time, the Mages used these Artifacts to make Enzal the finest city of Earth Realm. Decades passed. Enzal prospered. All was well with the ways of human and dragon, until the morning Astra called for a meeting of the Council.

She had seen a vision within the Eye that foretold of a Darkness descending upon the cities of Drook and Enzal. This Darkness consumed everything in its path, leaving nothing but sadness in its wake. In her vision, the Seven Artifacts the Mages wielded were no match for the Darkness.

The Council debated. Astra's visions were never wrong. The Darkness was coming and something had to be done, but what?

Denk was the one who first thought of the idea of the Mage stones. The dragon stonecutters were the finest in Earth Realm. What if their skills along with the concentrated powers of Og and the other Mages' special abilities, could somehow create special stones with which to amplify the Artifacts' effectiveness? With such enhanced power, the Mages would stand a chance against the Darkness.

The Mages began the process of harnessing their powers into the dragon stones. It was decided that Og and Narg could not take part in this process because of their lack of specific focus. Og was certain the process would be unstable if he and Narg were to try it.

This exclusion made Narg feel inferior to his fellow Mages. His sense of inferiority lead to anger, and his anger clouded his judgment. He stole one of the dragon stones and ran deep into the forests of Garswoog. Deciding he would try to possess one of the stones like his brethren, he found a clearing and began his experiment. He placed the stone on the ground, focused his powers and then released his energy. The stone radiated with multiple colors of light that twisted and combined into a black energy that infused the stone. Narg was excited. Og had said it could not be done—that the stones could not hold all of the powers at once.

But Narg's elation was premature.

The stone began to jump from its resting place, levitating in front of Narg. Smoke poured from the stone as it tried to contain the energy within, but it was not to be. The dragon stone exploded into black, putrid smoke. Narg cowered beneath the explosion. Og's assertion had been correct.

When the cloud dissipated, Narg saw the opening before him. He was curious and walked towards the split in the air and began to pull both sides apart as he looked inside the gash in space.

He could not believe what he was seeing. It was a different world. Dark creatures roamed the marred landscape and shadow-like beings blanketed the skies. To him, it seemed amazing. He had discovered a new world, and although foreign, it seemed oddly familiar to Narg.

But then he saw it: the Darkness that Astra had foretold was moving towards the tear.

Narg jumped back. His instincts told him to run, but it was too late. The Darkness poured out of the rip and blanketed Narg. He could not breathe. The acrid smoke filled his lungs, and just when he felt he was going to suffocate and die, the smoke rose and churned above him. It spoke in a deep, sadistic tone, but only said one word.

"*Tok-ah*," said the Darkness.

The cloud swirled into the sky blacking out the sun, spilling ominously towards Enzal.

Narg stood up. He was unharmed physically, but something inside him was different—changed forever. He had to warn the others, but there was no time. *Tok-ah* was on its way.

Meanwhile, the Mages had all successfully charged their dragon stones with their essences, but at a cost. By focusing and directing their powers in conjunction with Og's, the Mages forfeited their human bodies, assuming forms more befitting their strengths. They all still looked partially human, but their Lights now shone as well. Og knew he was somehow responsible for these mutations. His powers had mixed with that of the others to create the distinct stones, and in doing so, had released their inner spirits. Their Light had been exposed and could never be dimmed again.

Oash became living water, flowing from one spot to the next, and then collecting again in an almost-human liquid form. Gayan still looked quite human, although a tad greener. She was covered in moving vines, and where she walked, flowers bloomed and foliage sprung forth. Pyre was covered in dancing flames. Kala had become moving sand, but like Oash he could collect himself into a human-like form. Lyth had become stone and much larger than his old self. Denk was still mostly human, but he now levitated a foot above the ground surrounded by orange energy. When he spoke his mouth no longer moved, but you could hear his words in your head. Astra erupted into violet light, resembling a ghost of sorts.

The Mages did not have much time to adjust to their new forms. *Tok-ah* had already reached the city. Og, with the help of the dragons, augmented the Seven Artifacts with their new power sources. His knowledge of all their powers and the Artifacts he had helped create, made him the only one capable of these augments. The Mages assembled. The Sword was augmented with the Taitokura, the yellow stone; the Scythe with the Turran, the green stone, the Axe with the Ignus, the red stone; the Trident with the Medenculus, the blue stone; the Eye with the Asar, the purple stone; the Stave with the Zikrune, the orange stone; and the Hammer with the Ektona, the brown stone.

Og mounted his dragon counterpart, Skath, and they all set out to meet the Darkness, but where was Narg? He was still nowhere to be found. His fellow Mages were worried and feared the worst, but there was no time to waste. *Tok-ah* had come.

The first day was devastating. Many men and dragons perished in the Darkness. The dragons had sent in their greatest warriors, but *Tok-ah* decimated their ranks. The men did not fair any better, losing thousands.

The Mages' arrival changed everything. In their new forms with their newly augmented Artifacts, the Mages were unstoppable. On day three Narg had made his way back to join the battle, rallying the men, and the tide had begun to turn. The battle was waged for days, but in the end, the Mages, using their augmented powers in unison, were able to destroy *Tok-ah*. Enzal and Drook had paid the price, however. The cities had been all but destroyed.

But like the woods after a great fire, Enzal and Drook grew back bigger and stronger. Most of the Mages had moved on to live with the dragons in Drook, except the four siblings. The people of Enzal had been happy about the result of the battle, but the new embodiments of the Mages scared some, an unforeseen side effect of the mutations. Og remained in the city as their leader and leader of the Council. Gayan moved into the forest of Garswoog where she felt most at home, and Oash went to the sea, building his own city with the help of his brother, Og. Several of the men from Enzal, looking for a new start after the War of the Darkness, followed him.

Narg had also opted to stay in Enzal, but he no longer attended the Council meetings. He had become reclusive. Narg had never told the others that he had released *Tok-ah*. In his mind, the others had ostracized him, especially Og. Og had excluded him from the process that had altered the Mages. With Og's help, Narg was certain he too could have reached his ultimate potential, but Og had denied him that opportunity. Narg saw this as an act of betrayal. Narg's jealousy of the Mages' new forms led to anger. He was determined to find a way to enhance his powers without Og or the other Mages, and he had an idea how he would accomplish this feat.

Narg returned to the forest of Garswoog, and to the tear in the clearing, hoping to explore the Dark Realm he had discovered.

Tok-ah had found power in this foul world and Narg would do the same. He began to search the Dark Realm looking for this source of *Tok-ah*'s energy, staying there longer with every consecutive trip.

His frequent visits slowly twisted his mind, and he began to befriend the dark inhabitants of this realm. They seemed to bend to his will, and he was even able to summon them while in Earth Realm. A darkness now stirred in Narg that unlocked a different kind of power inside of him. Time in the Dark Realm had jaded the forgotten brother and made him cruel. This cruelty led to madness, and this madness changed his abilities—extinguishing his Light.

It was then that Narg realized that his great power had transformed, just like the powers of the other Mages. The Dark Realm energized him with the same Darkness that *Tok-ah* had imbued in him all those years ago. He would show the Council who was stronger. He would bring his beloved Dark Realm into Earth Realm, but he needed a distraction.

Narg went to the men of Enzal and told them that Astra had foreseen a war coming to their city. He suggested that the dragons were not content in their own kingdom, and that they would attack Enzal the next day. The men, twisted by fear and coerced through Narg's deviousness, attacked the dragon's nesting area—destroying hundreds of eggs and dragonlings in the process.

Retaliation was swift. The dragons attacked the mountainside. Og was caught off guard. His people stood no chance without his help. Og went out to face the dragons, not to fight, but to talk. That's when Narg attacked, blindsiding his older brother. Now that he had accepted the Darkness, Narg's power was superior to Og's, who would have been destroyed had Gayan not intervened.

She whirled the Scythe through the air, sending a green energy wave at her brother's attacker. The dark Mage knocked the attack aside. She was not aware of who the creature was, until it was too late. She froze when she realized it was her other brother.

That was all the time Narg needed. He was on her before she could react and pried the Scythe away from her. Narg picked up the weapon and rolled it in his hands. Og moved quickly, grabbing the Scythe. The brothers struggled, but Narg's power was too much for Og. Narg won the Artifact, but not before Og had removed its green stone. Narg raised the weapon in the air as the dark energy infused the Scythe, twisting it and changing the strongest of all of the Artifacts into a weapon of darkness.

The other Mages arrived. They could not believe what they saw. Narg stood wielding the dark Scythe. Both the man and the Artifact were now distorted, dark versions of their prior forms.

Narg made the first move, firing a black pulse at Oash, knocking his watery form backwards as he tried to deflect the attack with the Trident. His body splashed against the ground.

The other Mages attacked simultaneously, except for Pyre. She had stepped in the way of the Mages. She explained that Narg was just sick, and that there had to be another way. He was one of them. The power of the Scythe was quick and sliced through her midsection, tainting the bright red flames. The Axe fell to the ground as the once-bright Pyre was extinguished in a dark cloud of smoke. The smoke gathered itself into a new embodiment of Pyre, but she was different. She was no longer covered in flames. She was living gray smoke, and she belonged to Narg now.

The remaining Mages attacked Narg, as he stood inside his dark shield. None of their powers seemed to work. Lyth lifted the earth under Narg, tripping the dark Mage. Lyth rushed in close to attack Narg with the Hammer. Narg recovered, spinning around the Scythe, severing Lyth's right hand, which held the Hammer. The disconnected arm flew down to the feet of Og as he watched his best friend slowly change into dark, molten stone—his eyes soulless. Lava poured from where the arm had been severed and cooled into a new one. Lyth now belonged to Narg as well.

Og secured Lyth's fallen appendage and the Hammer, along with Pyre's Axe, while the remaining Mages occupied Narg and his new minions. Og had no choice but to call for a retreat. He had just lost two of his companions, and they could not afford to lose anyone else. They retreated to Drook.

What was left of the Council convened, but it was too late for the city of Enzal. Narg had taken it over in a few short hours, leaving pain and misery in his wake. Og was unsure of what to do next. Narg's power seemed unstoppable, and with two new dark Mages, and the Scythe, the odds did not look good.

Then inspiration struck Og in the darkest of moments. He would need to create a new Artifact—one that could handle more than one stone at a time, or maybe even all of them. All seven stones would be placed inside this Artifact creating the ultimate weapon against Narg.

Og told the Council of his idea, and they agreed. Some voiced concerns that so much energy could destroy the bearer of this Artifact, but there was no other way. He would need something tough, and reliable, but already mostly constructed. There was no time to start from scratch. He looked at all of the Artifacts. Not one of them could withstand the power of all of the stones. He stared at the Hammer—Lyth's Hammer still cradled in his friends cold stone hand, and in that second it occurred to Og that with a little bit of help from the others, he knew exactly what weapon to construct—a gauntlet.

He would fashion it from the forearm and hand of Lyth. Lyth had been his best friend, so it seemed fitting they could still work together in this way. With his powers, Og began to transform the hand, creating an opening on the back that could accept the stones when it was ready for augmentation. Og would be the Bearer. He was the only Mage that could wield the energies that were contained in each of the Mage stones. The others gathered around and, with Og and the Mages' collective Lights, they forged the Gauntlet.

The original Augmentors were the dragons. Their knowledge of the stones made them the perfect candidates. Seven were chosen to carry out the process. Once the new Artifact was ready, the dragons carried the Mage stones to Og and placed them into the Gauntlet one at a time. Og fell unconscious.

When he woke from his two-day hibernation, the collected powers of all of the Mages now coursed through his mortal frame. The augments took time to be completed, but now that they were done, Og's power was intense. The other Mages grabbed their stoneless Artifacts and joined Og as they set out to put an end to the tyranny of Narg. The dragons came as well, and in the end so did the men of Enzal.

The power of the Gauntlet was overt. The new Artifact was effective, but also unstable. Og had never controlled such power before and the energy expenditure took its toll. Narg's power was too great for the other Mages. Og feared that their fates would mirror those of Pyre and Lyth. He marched out to meet Narg, and in the end, Og faced Narg alone—brother to brother. Their powers were almost even, except Og had the power of good on his side. Even in the darkest moments, light will shine where you let it.

"If it is darkness you seek, brother. So be it."

With his last bit of energy, using the collected powers of all the stones, Og ripped open the portal to the Dark Realm, and forever banished Narg to the Depths.

Exhausted and weak, Og spoke to his people one last time. He told them that the Mage stones' collective powers were too much for a single Bearer. He tasked Oash with hiding the blue stone—the most powerful of the Mage stones. Og had energized the stone and placed instructions inside of it to help with this task. He told the others that the remaining stones would be dispersed across Earth Realm until a new Bearer emerged. The Gauntlet would be a weapon for the worthy and a tool against evil, but it would never hold all seven stones again.

Og's dying body fell to the Earth where it was caught by the others. The Gauntlet rocketed into the air, glowing white, and the stones separated from the empty rock husk and streaked across the morning sky in seven different directions. The blue stone shot straight down into Oash's watery hands. The Gauntlet fell to the Earth. The Mages were silent.

They buried Og's body on that original hill in the middle of the city of Enzal. A statue was erected. Silence was observed by the survivors in its presence.

The Gauntlet was hidden in Drook and looked after by the remaining Council until another suitable Bearer was to be found.

Oash took the Medenculus and augmented the Trident once again. With the instructions and the power with which his brother had charged the stone with, he moved his city, Atlantis, and its inhabitants to the deepest darkest parts of the ocean, never settling on one location for too long. The power of the Gauntlet that Og had transferred into the blue stone forever changed the men of Atlantis and the city itself.

25

father knows best

"So that's why it's called the lost city of Atlantis," said Thomas.

"It should, in fact, be called the hidden city of Atlantis," said Cayde. "We have known where we are the whole time." Cayde smiled.

"I have heard a similar tale before, but more of a fairy tale growing up—a child's bedtime story, a poem actually, if memory serves," said Loric.

"I too know the poem," said Anson. "I think I remember it."

"Of course you do," said Loric.

"I would love to hear it, if you don't mind," said Cayde.

"And it begins," said Loric.

Anson cleared his throat:

> *"Four siblings born, each with a gift*
> *Outcast from home and set adrift*
> *In Drook the dragons ruled on high*
> *While in Enzal valley, the Men did lie*
> *Safe haven made with time and care*
> *To keep all children with powers rare*
> *All stayed that way through many of ages*
> *With help from the Council of dragons and Mages*

Until upon Earth Realm, Darkness then fell
And a plan was forged by Og of Enzal
The stones were created to win the day
Narg's Light was lost in the brutal foray
Young brother was scorned and left to rot
Inside Dark Realm, all but forgot
His vengeance would indeed have won
If not for Og and men's Kingdom
The Gauntlet built from sacrifice
Would not by its mighty self suffice
The Mages' stones augmented the hand
And vanquished Narg from Earth Realm land"

"Well done, Mancer Warwick," said Cayde. "You must have studied acting. Your elocution is stupendous."

"Please, Your Majesty, do not get him started," said Loric as Anson glared at him.

"It is a nice poem, mind you, but of all of the tales of the origins of the Gauntlet, I would have never picked that one to be the truth," said Anson.

"Like all children's fairy tales, there is truth behind these words," said Itsuki. "A similar tale was told by my ancestors. Although, some of the names were different, and everyone spoke in Japanese."

"There is no data to verify the validity of said tale anywhere on *Interface*," chimed in LINC.

"Am I the only one that thought the story was entirely narsh, and for the record, I've never heard it before . . . or that poem."

"You really have to start reading more," said Anson.

"Yeah, in my spare time," said Thomas.

"Is there any proof of this fantastical origin story?" asked Loric as he turned back towards Cayde.

"Well, yes, but first things first. I have fulfilled half of my promise to Thomas's father. Let us deal with the other half. I must admit,

I, myself, am dying to know what is on the infodisc as well, and it might shed some light on your inquiry, Mancer Bodes."

The Atlantean whistled and a creature splashed out of the well in the center of the room. The creature perched on the edge of the well, looking around. It was reptilian in appearance, but it acted much like a dog, running directly at Cayde once it recognized its master. Around its neck bounced the second medallion. "Come here, Elvis."

"Elvis?" asked Anson.

"Is he not a famous Earth king from the past?" asked Cayde as he rubbed the animal's head.

"Well . . . sort of . . . it's kinda hard to explain," said Thomas. "Either way, it's a narsh name for a pet."

"Narsh?" asked Cayde.

"It means cool, awesome, extraordinary, stupendous, amazing, astonishing," said Loric. "Scargen uses the term ad nauseam."

"Oh," said Cayde. "Elvis is . . . pretty narsh." Cayde winked at the Bearer.

Thomas could not help but laugh. His father would listen to the King sometimes when he worked at home. "He is a frol. They are a mostly docile species . . . mostly." Cayde petted Elvis under the chin. He grabbed the medallion and unattached it from the creature. "Here is the second part of my promise, Thomas." He handed the medallion to the young man.

Thomas took a deep breath. "Come here, LINC." The artif moved over to the Bearer. "Here goes nothing."

Thomas lifted the medallion on top of the Scargen Robotics logo that resided on the artif's chest. There was a flash of energy and the hologram of his father appeared once again.

"Hello, Son. I'm recording this and sending this encrypted message from the dig in Egypt. This is the fifth message update that I have downloaded into LINC over the time that you've had him. By now you have met Cayde Galeos. If you do not already, you should trust him. He is a friend. As close as Sig, and that should tell you something." He paused. "I guess there's no easy way to start this." He awkwardly smiled. "I'm dead. I'm sorry, Tom. I wish we could have had more time together, but there is so much to tell you.

"Look, Tom, there are some things that you need to know about your mother. I hope you're sitting. Your mom was a Mage, which means she could perform magic. I know what you're thinking, but please just keep listening. I never put two and two together until years after she left, but it all makes sense now." The hologram paused. "Your mother talked a lot in her sleep. She would talk about saving the world, and bearing a gauntlet, defeating a Grimm, powerful magic, and Necromancers, and I used to think it was all rubbish. I started to think there was something wrong with her. She would wake up some nights covered in sweat, telling me about these dreams. I'm sure you're sitting there thinking the same thing I did at the time, but I assure you, Tom, it's all quite real. The man who is rarely wrong was just that. Believe it or not, your mother was a Mage. I had seen your mother do unexplainable things in the past, but I just chalked them up to me being overworked and exhausted. I remember one time she reached out for her coffee mug on a particularly tough morning with you, and it was over a foot away, but it zoomed right into her hand. She hadn't even realized what she had done, and like I said, I was out of it a lot right after you were born, between running the company and waking up with you in the wee hours of the morning."

He knew? thought Thomas.

"Cayde Galeos came to me after leaving Atlantis. He said he had experienced a vision. I thought the guy was nuts to be honest, until he showed me his gills, and then proceeded to create an energy sphere out of thin air. I was mesmerized and astonished. My whole life I had missed something that now seems so obvious. Men are capable of amazing things. Of course at first I was taken aback, but everything started to make a lot more sense. Cayde started by explaining that he knew that the time would soon come for the next Bearer and that this Bearer would need the Medenculus, the stone that fuels his old city. He had recovered it after it had fallen into the wrong hands. Cayde knew one day that someone would come for it. He also knew that that someone was a Scargen, and he wanted to help. His own people had shunned him for this belief and his vision.

"I assumed it was your mother he was talking about after piecing it together, and as you know we did not leave on the greatest of terms. I figured that I would use everything at my disposal to find her and the stones. When I told Cayde that I thought it was Merelda, he hesitated. In Cayde's vision he saw the Gauntlet rise up from a woman's hand into the air. When he described her, it was obvious the woman that he spoke of was your mother. She had died saving the world, but Cayde was not here for her. Then it hit me: You were the Scargen he was talking about. You are the next Bearer of the Gauntlet.

"I learned as much as I could about the magical world. Which is harder than you think."

I totally understand that, thought Thomas.

"Cayde helped obviously, and it didn't hurt having my skill base. It made it far easier to find materials through *Interface*. See, Tom, I am what they call a technic. It means I can figure things out fast and am adept at building things, like the artifs."

"He did know he was a technic," said Thomas.

"I also started studying archaeology shortly after realizing what had actually happened to your mother and hearing the story that Cayde has just told you. The least I could do was to use my abilities to help find the stones for you and the rest of the inhabitants of this crazy rock twirling through space that we call Earth.

"I never told you, well, because you weren't ready to know yet, Tom. I was going to wait until after you graduated. You did graduate, I hope."

Thomas smiled.

"I wanted you to enjoy your childhood. You seemed like you had some more growing up to do before I could lay this all on you, but I just want you to know that I did all of this for you. The long nights, the even longer trips abroad—it was all for you." He paused and laughed. "I never told Sig. He believed in so many conspiracy theories already. There was no reason to tell him another one that actually is true.

"Cayde assured me that looking for the blue stone was futile at this early stage and that the Atlanteans had it very well guarded, but that there were other stones out there that he would help me find. I started Carbone Industries as a shell corporation to fund some of the things we were doing behind the scenes. I also had sacked away a good deal of money for you in case things got out of hand. Apparently the GA frowns on the use of magic.

"I had created a machine based on the design of the one Cayde had used to retrieve the Medenculus and with Cayde's help we reversed engineered a machine that could help in finding all of the stones. We called it the Artificial Intelligence Recovery System or AIRS for short, but its code name was the Infosphere project.

"When we traced what we thought was the power signature of one of the stones it lead us to the Norse dig in New England. That is why I created the Diggers. We needed to handle these digs with precision, but we had to keep the digs on the smallest scale possible as far as manpower was concerned. More eyes, more problems.

"But when we traced the power signature it did not lead us to a stone. It lead us to something quite different and unexpected. We had found the Axe, Tom. It was nestled in with several other stores of weapons, but there was no denying the language on the hilt and the blade. It was the Ancient language. Any doubts I had had on the validity of Cayde's story completely disappeared that day. During this dig, Cayde and I worked on AIRS, tweaking it. We soon realized that the Axe could help us find the red stone. We could use the energy signature that the Axe emitted to find the stone that used to be embedded in it.

"We found the Ignus, the red stone, in Mexico, outside the city of Mérida. AIRS led us to Mérida, but once we were there, the Axe made finding the stone that much easier. The closer we got to the area we needed to be in the more the weapon glowed. It took a while to uncover it, but when we did it was a sight to behold.

"We used AIRS once more and it pointed to Nara, Japan. This was a false reading, we believe. Or it could have been a Mage stone, but it was not there when we arrived. We looked for weeks, but found nothing. We packed up and moved to the next energy signature the AIRS had picked up—Egypt.

"We knew we were going to need some help with this one, and that's why I approached the GA for more funding. I'm sure there is something here, but I can't say for certain that it is one of the stones, but I believe we are finally digging in the right direction. If you are listening to this, I guess something went horribly wrong."

You can say that again, thought Thomas.

"That is of no matter anymore. Now, I need you to retrieve the Infospheres that are inside Scargen Robotics. This should be easy for you, considering you are in charge now and have the master codes for all Scargen Robotics facilities. After you secure the spheres, you need to seek out a man named Ziza Bebami—a name from another one of your mothers midnight ramblings, but so far they've all panned out."

"Man, he did not see this coming." Thomas raised the sheathed Gauntlet. "Well, I guess he sort of did."

"The Infospheres cannot fall into the wrong hands, Tom. That is why they are the priority. Gideon Upshaw cannot be trusted. I let him believe he was pulling the strings so I could use the GA's money to help fund the digs, but I wouldn't put it past him to have had something to do with my death or to have tried to take over the company. I also realize that could make securing the Infospheres that much more difficult. One of the spheres resides in my office, and the other is in the high-security vault. At least, that's where they *were*. There are beacons attached to both spheres. The information is currently being downloaded into LINC and your wristcom along with any security overrides that may be needed while inside Scargen Robotics."

Thomas remembered the football game and the announcement of the token gesture that was to be done at halftime: Gideon Upshaw was scheduled to give the Global Alliance one of the spheres as a symbol of continued cooperation. *Sounds more like a hostile takeover*, thought Thomas. This game was to take place the following day in Dallas. The other sphere, as far as Thomas knew, was still situated within Scargen Robotics headquarters.

"Those Infospheres contain terabytes of information, concerning all of the ideas and projects I had been working on before and during this Egypt trip. But there is more to them than that. The first sphere is the Artificial Intelligence Recovery System. This device could prove vital for you in finding the rest of the stones. However, the machine is not foolproof. A versed Mage—or worse yet, a Necromancer—can shield the stones' energy signatures fairly easily. The same masking effect can happen in locations of great power. It is one of the reasons that pinpointing the stone in Egypt is proving rather difficult. That being said, this device should still give you an advantage that no other Bearer has ever had."

"Narsh," said Thomas under his breath.

"And, Tom, this is a one-of-a-kind device. I have made it so it will interact with LINC's hardware and only that. This is not the kind of item you want being cloned, so I reprogrammed it specifically to integrate with LINC's new upgrades. He will know what to do with it when the time comes."

"Of course I will," said LINC.

Thomas looked at the artif and put his finger on his lips. Thomas's father continued.

"The second Infosphere is of even more importance and should be your first priority." A holographic image of the sphere appeared and slowly opened. "It contains the red stone, the Ignus." The stone floated in front of the Mages. "It is my final gift to you."

Thomas stared at the holographic projection of the Ignus.

"Goodbye, my son. I love you, and I believe in you. The world is in good hands. I always knew you were destined to do something amazing. Your mother would've been so proud." The holographic projection of Carl Scargen paused as the man Thomas had called Dad wiped away a tear. He looked up and a smile spread out from the center of his mouth. "And remember, Tom, like I always told you, even in the tough times, just keep smiling, no matter what."

The hologram disappeared. Thomas's eyes swelled with tears. Half of sadness, and half of joy. His father had known of his destiny, of his mother, and had been working so hard to give his son the advantages he needed. Thomas felt an overwhelming sense of comfort inside of him—a connection to his father that he had never felt before. He had gotten his goodbye.

"What happened to the Medenculus that you needed to track it down?" Thomas asked Cayde, thinking about the dream he had had before and what his father had said.

"It was stolen from Atlantis."

"An Aequos?" asked Thomas. He knew full well that his dream had been the truth.

"Yes . . . but . . . how do you know this?"

"Same way I knew about the lobster men. I had a premonition, but after the fact. Does that even makes sense? It was like I was seeing someone else's memories."

"Yes, it is a well-known skill among certain Mages—very rare mind you. This particular dragon I have been looking for for decades, but still have not found him."

"Because of the stone?"

"No we retrieved the stone. It again powers Atlantis."

"Then why?"

"You are very inquisitive. Just like Carl." The Atlantean's face changed. His demeanor had switched from jovial to extremely serious. "This dragon killed my wife and my daughter while stealing the Medenculus."

"You had a wife?" asked Thomas.

"Yes, at one time I did," said Cayde. "You sound surprised."

"Well, I just thought because of Vedd—"

"Atlanteans do not have the same hang-ups that surfacewalkers have with sexuality. You do not choose who you love." Cayde looked out into the water once more. "The dragon collided into the royal palace, destroying the supports that held up the structure. The building collapsed on my wife and daughter while they played together in the courtyard.

"I promised myself, if I were ever to find this beast, I would kill this dragon with my own hands. Onica was only nine years old when it happened, and my wife, Galene . . . she was the smartest and most beautiful creature on the Earth—top to bottom. They both deserved better." He looked away out into the ocean with his hands behind his back. "One day, I will find this dragon, and I will kill him, and not quickly."

"I'm s-s-s-orry," said Thomas. "I know how you feel." Thomas thought of his mother and father. The Gauntlet twinged.

"Thank you. That means a lot coming from a Scargen," said Cayde as he turned back to the group.

"What happened to the stone?" asked Thomas.

"We were finally able to find the stone after some most difficult hurdles. It was in China, hidden in a necklace belonging to the mother of a small child. One of my men surprised the mother. He acted without orders, killing her. As soon as she died he materialized. Her child was being protected by a monster—a High Demon."

"They seem to pop up in the worst places," said Thomas.

"Summoned more like it," said Loric. "The demon was no coincidence. He was protecting something."

"The demon only wanted the girl. He wanted nothing to do with the Medenculus. I always thought this strange. When I tried to help the girl, the beast attacked. I was lucky to escape with my life that day. And if not for Vedd, I might not have. He had saved my life, but I always felt bad for the girl. At the time, I thought it a tragic ending to an otherwise successful mission, but I did not know the consequences of my time away from Atlantis."

"What do you mean?" asked Thomas.

"This is how Jusip Tad usurped my power and exiled the Sovereign of Atlantis. His men were among mine when we attempted to retrieve the stone. We were looking for the stone for years, but I did not realize what had been happening at home while I was away. This man, Jusip Tad, he is a horrible man. He saw an opportunity, and he took it. He used fear and propaganda to control my people. He lied to them as well. The Medenculus had energized the city enough to run on half power for some time, even without the stone. But when it was returned, he kept Atlantis on half power purposely."

"Why would he do something like that?" asked Loric.

"Jusip began trying to weaponize the stone. He needed to run tests and experiments, and this meant the stone couldn't always be activated. He had planned to throw me into prison, marking me a traitor to my own people. I'd always said that the stone would one day have to leave Atlantis, and he used this well-known belief against me. I had said many times publicly that I had seen things that suggested that the Medenculus would be needed by a new Bearer, but like your father at first, most Atlanteans do not believe the tale of Og. Tad used that doubt against me, to sway support his way. He was not believed by all, but by the right people."

"What made you so sure that it was true?" asked Thomas.

"You have had these visions before, right?"

"Yes. I just told you about the dragon."

"Did you ever truly doubt their validity?"

"No, I guess not, once I got over the implausibility of the whole thing."

"That is why I believe. Plus it did not hurt that I had definitive proof."

"Really, like what?"

"I will show you on the next part of the tour."

"Why didn't you use this mysterious proof, whatever it may be, to show you were not insane or, in fact, a traitor?" asked Loric.

"It was too late. The years away finding the Medenculus gave rise to the Atlantean military, which Tad controlled. He had also slowly dismantled the Atlantean Senate one bribe at a time. We were always a peaceful people, living in quiet anonymity, but after that day everything changed. Atlantis was militarized."

"How did you escape?" asked Thomas.

"Vedd is a resourceful man, and on my orders, had begun to evacuate my belongings long before the balance of power had swayed completely to Jusip Tad. I heard the rumblings and asked him to do this, strictly as a precaution. I never could have foreseen the betrayal that would happen to me that day I returned, and afterward. Key members of the Senate had been compromised. Greedy for more power, they did not realize how far Jusip Tad's plans spread. And like I said before, I had been collecting trophies for quite some time. When I knew these things were safe, I escaped to the Top World where I have been ever since. Jusip had the Medenculus, but I had something he did not. I had the knowledge of the sovereign, and I knew Atlantis like the back of my webbed hand. Evading his forces was easy."

"And what about Vedd?"

"He still travels back and forth to the city, gathering information. He lives there most of the time, actually. I thought it best for one of us to keep ties with the city. Vedd was part of the security force before the incident with the Aequos, so he knows how and where to find the city at any given time as well as how to enter it. This will one day come in handy, but what I told your father was true. Attacking Atlantis would be a hefty task, even for the Council of Mages. When the time comes, we will be here to help you, but Carl's assertion that the Ignus should be your priority is wise advice."

"Especially since one of the Infospheres is going to be given to the Global Alliance at the Dallas Cowbots stadium during halftime tomorrow," said Thomas. "And we have no way of knowing which sphere has what in it."

"The Global Alliance is the last organization we want with that sort of power," said Itsuki.

"The Augmentor is correct," said Loric. "If memory serves, I read when researching your father that this event will coincide with the debut of the new line of Scargen sportifs. That does not give us much time to prepare. We need to get back to Maktaba. There is much to discuss with the Council."

"I know it is a rarity, but I tend to agree with Loric," said Anson.

"We can't leave yet. The tour's not over," insisted Thomas. "And I don't know about you guys, but I would also like to know what happened to the Axe."

"I will show you." Cayde gestured to indicate they should move along the corridor that connected back to the main building.

26

artifacts of life

They walked down the new corridor. Thomas felt excited. Twenty minutes ago he had not known of such an Artifact and now he was going to see it with his own eyes. He did not know what to expect.

"Your father entrusted me with keeping this weapon until it was needed," said Cayde. "He thought it wise to keep the Ignus and the Axe separate—a position that I share. If the two were joined once more and fell into the wrong hands, the consequences could be Earth-shattering."

"It would be an easy feat for one versed in augmentation," said Itsuki.

Cayde Galeos, the Sovereign of Atlantis walked ahead of them with his hands clasped behind him. Lights in the dark hallway lit as he walked close to them. Several sentry artifs flanked a set of gray sliding doors at the end of the hall.

"Your father donated a great deal of money and time so we could complete construction of this structure. I contributed what I could, but I am far from a bestselling author. Part of the deal was that your father never knew where I hid it. The results speak for themselves."

"This is truly remarkable work, Your Majesty," said Loric. "But would be no match for an advanced Mage or Necromancer."

"This may be true, but secrecy is our number one asset," said Cayde. "And you have not seen everything yet."

When they reached the artif guards, the robots armed their weapons.

"Name and nature of business?" demanded the artif on the right.

"Cayde Galeos, Sovereign of Atlantis. I am here to service the security panels."

Beams scanned the body of Cayde Galeos, culminating on the insignia on his chest. The insignia glowed yellow and then faded.

"Voice recognition certified. Facial and ocular scans are a match. Access Key found and initiated," said the artif. The two artifs disarmed and moved aside. "Access granted, Sovereign Galeos." The two doors slid apart.

"Please, after you," said Cayde with one hand behind his back and the other gesturing the others into the newly opened chamber.

The room was amazing. Sentry drones zipped above their heads. Holoscreens and tech were seamlessly integrated into the chamber. Several stasis fields surrounded the perimeter of the chamber with two of them in the center.

"You had asked me before why I believed in the tale of Og, the First Bearer, when no one else did. Here is my proof," said Cayde as he pointed at one of the stasis fields in the center of the room.

They moved in closer and Thomas could see it. It was the Trident, but it had been destroyed. Its pieces floated in the field.

"This is the Trident of Oash. It has been passed down from one sovereign to the next. It is the royal family's biggest secret. My predecessors thought it necessary to keep the tale for themselves. They thought that if people knew the truth it could compromise Atlantis's integrity. My predecessors could have never seen that the attack would come from within."

"What happened to it?" asked Thomas.

"It is said that the power of the Gauntlet-charged Medenculus, which created the underwater city and evolved us into what we are now, was too much for the Trident. It was destroyed during the transformation. A noble end to a noble weapon."

"Narsh," said Thomas. The Gauntlet twinged when Thomas put it onto the stasis shield.

"I would have used this to sway the opinion of the Atlanteans, but once I returned with the Medenculus, I realized it was too late. My destiny lay elsewhere. Which brings me to your earlier request. Follow me." He walked again smoothly with his hands behind his back. He led Thomas around the first circular field to the next one, and there it was.

The Axe was floating in the center of the stasis field. Thomas stared at the weapon. It was stunning. The Ancient runes covered the ornate weapon. The Gauntlet twinged again. That was proof enough for Thomas that these were legitimate. Cayde walked over to the holoscreen and moved some icons around.

"Stasis field disengaged," said the computer.

The Axe flew into Cayde's grasp. He spun the weapon in his hands and presented it to the group.

"Remarkable," said Loric.

"Simply marvelous," said Anson.

"Utterly narsh," said Thomas.

He grabbed the handle of the Axe as energy circled the weapon and Thomas's hand. He stared at the weapon as he slowly twisted his wrist. The sound from his wristcom interrupted the proceedings. Thomas handed the weapon back to Cayde. He looked down to see who was calling. It was Fargus. Thomas answered and a holographic Fargus appeared above his wrist.

"Thomas . . . we 'av a bit uv trouble 'ere. What I mean to say is, we've been found out and it's not pretty, mate. There's like loads uv bleedin' artifs and collectorbots knockin' about, and they're following us down the transport hubs, an that."

"Where are you guys now?" asked Thomas.

"We 'av just made it down to Falrin Level, I believe, but we need some bloody 'elp and quick, mate. Bartleby's shields are about to fail, and duh bloody cloakin' device is knackered. It's well done in, innit? Just malfunctionin'—bugs an that, I imagine. To be honest, I told everyone it weren't ready for field tests an that, didn't I? But no one listens to the bloody gremling. I'm just the one dat's implemented duh bloody systems, an that. I mean you'd trust duh bloody baker if 'ee told ya duh bleedin' cake wasn't finished. Ya know what I mean?"

"Quit your moanin', Fargus," said Bartleby. His voice came over the wristcom. "I need you to bloody focus."

"I'm not moanin'. I'm not really sure I can take much more uv dis abuse, to be honest. He's a miserable bastard when 'ee's fightin'. Anyway we would 'av just teleported out, an that, but we couldn't just leave you lot down there. So we are on our way to you now, but could ya maybe meet us 'alfway? It's gettin' a bit dodgy, innit?"

"We're on our way, Fargus," said Thomas as the image of the gremlin faded. "We have to get going, Cayde."

The Atlantean let go of the Axe as it floated back into its position and the stasis field reengaged.

"And what is to be the fate of the Axe?" asked Loric.

"For the time being it is to stay here with me," said Cayde.

"And why, pray tell, is that?" asked Loric.

"The Axe technically belongs to me," said Cayde.

"But what if it is needed?" asked Anson.

"What is the phrase you surfacewalkers use? We will cross that bridge when we come to it," said Cayde. "My job is to protect it until that day arrives."

"I do not feel completely comfortable with that assessment," said Loric.

I advise that you leave the weapon with me, said Cayde without moving his lips. The voice was only in Thomas's head.

How are you doing that? asked Thomas.

I have created a telepathic link between us.

Narsh.

We are the only two connected. You need to trust me on this, Thomas. Your father did. It is safer here than with you at this juncture. I have successfully hidden this weapon for over ten years, but rest assured, I will relinquish the weapon when the time is right. You have a lot to do in a short period of time. Let me worry about this for now.

"The Axe should stay here," said Thomas. "That was my father's plan."

"According to my navigation systems, the dragon is heading to our current coordinates," said LINC.

"We may want to evacuate this structure before the dragon leads the Global Alliance right to this place," said Anson. "The Atlantean may be our best option for handling this weapon for now."

"It does seem to be the only plausible option currently," said Loric. "The Axe will remain here . . . for now."

"We all agree then," said Thomas. "Thank you, Sovereign Galeos. It's been totally narsh. It's been great to meet such a good friend of my father's."

"Please, Thomas, call me Cayde. The pleasure was all mine. I hope one day we will be friends."

"I think I would like that," said the young man. He then turned to the others. "Now let's go save that dragon's ass."

the blues

They had said their hasty goodbyes to Cayde Galeos. Something told Thomas that this was not the last time he would see Cayde, and the Atlantean had all but assured that. They had reached their aerocycles and were racing through Falrin Level to rendezvous with Bartleby. LINC was ahead of them cloaked. Thomas was tracking the artif through his goggles' systems. They were moving at incredible speeds in an effort to reach the dragon as fast as possible. *I hope Bart's all right*, thought Thomas.

The young man's notion was interrupted by the sirens. Two police artifs pulled out from behind a structure and began chasing the two aerocycles. They were predominantly white with touches of dark blue. Blue and red lights accompanied the sirens. These originated from the shoulders of the artifs. They were bulky humanoid artifs.

Copbots . . . figures. "We have some BLUEs on our tail."

"As if I did not deduce as much after hearing the sirens. We do not have time for this," said Loric. "We will have to deal with them while we make our way to Bartleby. This was supposed to be a stealth mission."

"You need to calm down," said Thomas. "There's only two of th—" As the words left his mouth five other police artifs dropped in behind the initial two along with two squad ships and three collectorbots. "Never mind. I'm gonna shut up."

"What are BLUEs?" asked Itsuki.

"Binary Linked Urban Enforcement," said Thomas. "Basically they're copbots, police artifs, but these don't look like they're in the business of protecting or serving."

"Pull the aerocycles over. You are in violation of thirty-seven city and transportation ordinances. Failure to comply will result in further action."

"Anson, can you distract them?" asked Loric.

"LINC could do it," said Thomas.

"He's currently busy directing us to Bartleby's location," said Loric. "The artif is connected into the dragon's navcom, calculating Bartleby's ever-changing trajectory."

"What about the artifs?" asked Thomas. "They're just doing what they are programmed to do."

"Which if you have already forgotten, also includes the collection and detention of magic-users, which all of us are, Scargen," said Loric. "I do not like this any more than you, but we have little choice in the matter. These artifs lack higher faculties and therefore cannot be reasoned with. They are programmed to kill and are not self-aware like LINC."

"The arms are fair, when the intent of bearing them is just," said the werewolf as he unloaded a volley of bright orange spheres at the pursuing artifs. "It is unfortunately the nature of war, Thomas."

The BLUEs dispersed to avoid the attack, but two of Anson's spheres found their targets. One hit a squad ship, which veered directly into one of the collectorbots. The collectorbot batted the ship aside and continued to pursue. The other orb hit one of the flying artifs whose siren made an odd noise before the artif caught fire and plummeted towards the ground.

Thomas was conflicted. On one side he understood that they had no choice but to defend themselves, but it still felt wrong. His father had taught him to respect life, no matter what form that life took. It was the same humanity that kept him from killing Arkmalis and that had plagued him after the death of Nicolas Gorter. In the end, there was no real choice. Anson was right. It is the nature of war, and that is what they were fighting—a war. He would do what he had to defend his friends. There was a bigger picture here, and personal feelings aside, he would have to engage the enemy.

"How long till we rendezvous with Bart?" asked Thomas.

"Approximately 23.5 seconds," said LINC. "His situation is considerably worse than our current predicament."

"What exactly does that mean?" asked Loric.

"He has approximately 21 police artifs following him, along with a squadron of 15 fully armed collectorbots."

"How do you know that?" asked Thomas.

"I have hacked into the city's mainframe and can track the movements of the police and also see the surveillance footage from the city's extensive security network."

"This is going to be interesting," said Itsuki.

"If you have not noticed, Augmentor, it already is," said Loric as he veered his aerocycle to avoid a series of blasts from the trailing BLUEs.

Thomas saw the magnificent beast as he dropped out of one of the transport hubs. Bartleby was moving fast and the city's entire force seemed to be on his tail. The dragon's shield deflected the artif's onslaught.

"We have a dragon incoming," said Thomas. "Concentrate your fire on the group of BLUEs that is directly behind him," said Thomas. They would be crossing paths momentarily.

Anson, Itsuki, and LINC all opened fire on the line of artifs, destroying seven of the pursuers. Bartleby unloaded his fiery breath as he passed the group. Fargus fired two of the electronet missiles at the same time, harnessing two BLUEs. The rest were engulfed in Bartleby's flames.

"Come not between the dragon and his wrath," said Anson.

"You can say that again," said Thomas. "Well done, Bart."

"Fanks, mate," said Bartleby across Thomas's wristcom. "Fargus also nailed a few uv dem blokes as well. You guys should be good now, but I'm still in a bit uvva pickle. I'm gonna circle back underneaf uv you guys."

"Itsuki, I want you to take the wheel."

"Where are you going?"

"Bart and Fargus need a little help," said the Bearer as he leapt from the aerocycle and down towards Bartleby Draige. Thomas landed on the saddle of the dragon. Fargus turned around. "Miss me?"

"You are a sight for bloody sore eyes, mate," said Fargus. As he said the words, six of the collectorbots descended on the dragon.

Thomas wasted no time. He pushed the button on the underside of the Sheath and it collapsed into a small piece, which he slipped into his pocket. He concentrated and focused his power on the first artif. The collectorbot was consumed by light blue energy. Thomas then moved his arm steadily from one artif to the next, destroying the large robots as they attacked the dragon.

"Six more down," said Thomas.

"Look behind you," said Itsuki out of Thomas's wristcom.

Thomas turned around. Two more squads of BLUEs filed in behind him as the two aerocycles and LINC were engaging the left-over BLUEs and collectorbots.

"We've slowed dem down, an that, but dey just keep bleedin' comin'."

"I got a plan," said Thomas. "LINC, can you pull up that schematic of the city and cross-reference our current location with utility corridors or sewer systems."

"Completed."

"Now eliminate ones that cannot fit a dragon."

"Completed, a city this size and scale requires massive utility corridors. This did not significantly change the results."

"Can you send that info to everyone's wristcom and Bart's navcom?"

"I already have."

"I love you."

"If I had the capacity or inclination for such trivialities as love, I am sure the sentiment would be mutual."

"You have a way with words, my friend."

"Bart, see that opening around the second structure on your right?"

"Yes."

"When you turn around that corner head straight for it as fast as you can."

"But it's not bloody open, is it?"

"Have you forgotten that you are a teleport dragon?"

"You are a genius, mate."

"Give it all you got, Bart."

"O-o-okay, Thomas, but what about the collectorbots on my tail?"

"Leave them to me, Bartleby," said Loric.

The dragon raced out in front of the artifs. It took everything Thomas had to hold on. The collectorbots still kept up with the dragon.

Loric turned the aerocycle towards Bartleby. He sat up on the aerocycle and moved his free hand. Part of the wall of the building Bartleby flew next to began to crumble. Huge chunks dropped off of the structure and fell onto the chasing collectorbots. The BLUEs slowed to avoid the collapsing building.

"Nice shot, Loric," said Thomas. Bartleby turned the corner of the second structure and flew towards the closed corridor.

"Now teleport, but just into the corridor."

" 'ere goes nuffin'," said Bartleby as the familiar sound of ripping pierced the sky above Falrin Level. The dragon disappeared and reappeared inside of the corridor. He slowed down and came to a clumsy stop. Bartleby, Fargus, and Thomas were now safe within the corridor. LINC, Anson, Loric, and Itsuki were still outside.

"Any landing you can walk away from. Right, Bart?" said Thomas.

"Dat's right, Thomas."

"Now let's figure out where we are exactly." The maintenance lights had engaged and from the looks of it, they were inside a sewage pipe. Thomas sniffed the air to confirm that was exactly where they were.

"That was brilliant, Thomas," said Anson. His image appeared above the wristcom. "I trust you three are all right?"

"Yes, Anson. Bart's a little dinged up, but overall we're fine."

"I can't say the same for meeself," said the gremlin. "Next time I'm leggin' it. Dat was proper mental, that. What if, Bart would 'av been off by a centimeter. You need to fink about these sorts uv fings before ya go an do somefing like dat, don't ya? We could 'av all died. Den what?" Fargus collected himself. He pulled out the handheld device he always kept on him and began to scan Bartleby. "I'm sorry. I'm 'avin' a bit of a moan, a rant. I just got a bit scared, an that. Dis 'ole 'ero fing is a bit taxin' on me bloody 'art, innit? I mean at duh end uv duh day, is it wurf it?"

"I totally understand, Fargus, but the alternative wasn't looking great either. There were a lot of police to deal with out there. Speaking of which, how's it looking now, Suke?" asked Thomas into his wristcom.

"The remaining artifs have scattered, some still pursue, but they seemed confused by the disappearing dragon," said Itsuki.

"That should make it easy to ditch the BLUEs and use the schematics to find the nearest entrance to this corridor so you can rendezvous with us."

"I will be there shortly," said Itsuki.

"Good. See you guys soon," said Thomas.

"I must admit, it was a well executed plan," said Loric. "We will be there shortly."

Thomas heard a loud splash next to him that startled him. Thomas jumped back, pointing the Gauntlet in the direction of the sound.

"My analysis of your plan also has concluded that it was well conceived," said LINC as he uncloaked next to Thomas. "Your problem solving abilities are improving." Thomas lowered the Gauntlet.

"You have to give someone more warning before doing that, buddy," said Thomas. "I didn't even know you were inside the corridor yet."

"But you had said to find the nearest corridor and to find each other using the schematics and that is precisely what I did."

"I did say that," said Thomas. He heard the aerocycles echoing as they approached from the opposite direction.

"Sounds like da gangs all 'ere," said Bartleby. "Good. We can find a bloody way out of 'ere and get back 'ome. Dis place smells like shit."

"Not like it, mate," said Fargus, using the handheld to diagnose the dragon. The gremlin had been working hard on Bartleby's systems since they had landed in the corridor, and the dragon's tech, while not a hundred percent, was still quite functional. "Well, it seems dat you can still teleport, an that. Dat's all dat bloody matt—"

An explosion interrupted the gremlin, originating from the far end of the corridor. A single aerocycle flew out of the vast tube and stopped in front of them. Itsuki was the only one on it.

"Thomas, they are on their way," said Itsuki as he jumped off of the cycle.

"Loric and Anson?"

"No, I mean yes, but not just th—"

Loric Bodes and Anson Warwick came running out of the tunnel and posted up on both sides of the corridor. Blasts came flying down out of the darkness.

"Take cover!" shouted Loric. The two Mancers returned fire.

"So much for my plan," said Thomas as he moved up against the wall. "The BLUEs have found us that quickly?"

"They are not BLUEs, Thomas," said Itsuki as the wisps flew down into the darkness.

"Then what are they shooting at?"

The wisps lit up the sewage tube, exposing the creatures galloping on the sides of the walls at an inhuman speed. "The White Wolves of Ontinok."

28

the spirit of jinn

"I can't believe I can't find dis bloody twonk," said the jinn as he stared down into the apartment. " 'ee was ere just a few bleedin' minutes ago. I can still smell 'is aquatic stench. Reminds me uv salty seaweed, it does."

Mukt had tracked Vedd Delphin back to his apartment on Manhattan Level in New Amsterdam, but the Atlantean was nowhere to be found. No one had answered the door.

"I guess dere's only one fing to be done den." Mukt casually elbowed the window. The glass broke to the floor. "Oops."

He could have teleported into the apartment, but there was no fun in that. The jinn slithered into the pristine apartment. The place was empty. It looked like a place to eat and sleep. There was no art on the wall, and the walls were painted a neutral color. There was only a minimal amount of furniture. Mukt needed to find something personal. That could prove difficult here.

They usually at least have a few bleedin' pictures lying around the flat, thought the jinn. Mukt moved to the refrigerator. *Teleportation is a nasty business, and makes me a wee bit peckish*, thought the jinn as he reached into the refrigerator. Mukt grabbed a whole fish and took a bite out of the side of the scaled treat. He looked around at the sparsely decorated flat. "Where does 'ee stash 'is personal belongings?" Mukt chewed on the raw fish. "I fink I know."

Mukt made his way to the only bedroom. He slowly opened the door. If there was anything personal, it had to be in there. Centuries of spying had taught him that. He saw it as soon as he entered the room. The aura was unmistakable. There was plenty of spirit residue for what he needed. The object was simple—a bauble really—a simple statue that must have meant a lot to Vedd Delphin. His spirit was all over it.

Mukt leaned down and picked up the statue. He closed his eyes and ingested the spiritual residue. He saw them in a flash. Vedd and another Atlantean. This man was important to Delphin and Atlantis. He had given Delphin this statue. It was a medal of sorts for exemplary duty. Mukt put the statue down. Mukt was an adept spirit tracker, and he had gotten what he needed from the object. "Aw'right. Duh rest should be quite simple now, shouldn't it?" The jinn disappeared.

Mukt reappeared somewhere on Falrin Level. " 'ee's gotta be around 'ere somewhere, don't 'ee?" The jinn sniffed the air. He hung in the sky above the shabby bustle of the level. He smiled when he picked up Delphin's trail and darted in its direction.

The jinn could move at exceptional speeds and could also teleport, but teleportation was not effective when tracking a spirit. Mukt veered out of the way. He was almost hit by two aerocycles racing by followed by a squad of police artifs.

I 'ate robots, thought Mukt.

He made his way down to the street level, but something seemed odd. The scent was coming from underneath the street. He made his way down into the water and promptly changed forms, becoming a bluefish. He began to swim towards the scent.

Once he had caught up with the scent, he saw the hangar. The large structure was situated under Falrin Level, with two aeroships parked inside. There was a small Chinese woman on the platform and a tall, thin man dressed in what looked like a wetsuit. It was Vedd Delphin. Mukt could smell his spirit, and it was pungent.

Mukt made his way out of the water, creeping closer to his prey, quietly transforming into a spider. He had done this hundreds of times, and one thing he knew was that there should be no loose ends. He would listen to what was happening before making his move.

"Are you sure nobody followed you, Mr. Delphin?" asked the Chinese woman.

"I've been doing this for years. I'm pretty sure I know how to cover my tracks," said Delphin.

"Some tracks cannot be covered," said the woman.

If she only knew, thought Mukt.

"Well, if you know a bloodhound that can sniff underwater, I'd like to see him . . . well besides Elvis."

Elvis? questioned the jinn.

"Okay, okay. I just worry sometimes. I'm an old lady you know."

"We both know that's not entirely true, Ms. Ling."

The Chinese woman smiled as she ran to the edge and dove into the water. She appeared frail at first glance, but this maneuver looked graceful and practiced.

"What do we 'av 'ere?" asked Mukt under his breath. The woman remained submerged for quite some time. The demon was patient, but she had been under the water for a full two minutes. Mukt thought about making his move, and then it happened.

A pale blue Aequos ripped up through the water and into the hangar. Water dripped from the beast as it settled in front of Delphin. She might look remarkably different, but Mukt could tell the dragon was the Chinese woman, shifted into her natural state.

Good form, that. Now I know how 'ee's makin' duh trip, thought Mukt.

"Let's go. I'm one busy dragon. I've gotta drop you off and be back in time to cook dinner for the sovereign."

Good, thought Mukt. *I just 'av to bide my time den. Dere's no bloody reason to engage a dragon if you don't need to.*

"Are you ready, then?" asked the Aequos.

"As ready as I ever am to go back there," said Delphin.

"Cheer up. Sooner or later you two will be together. You will see."

"I suppose you're right, Ms. Ling." Delphin jumped onto the back of the dragon.

Mukt had to work quickly. He flew down from his perch and landed on the Delphin's shoulder. The Atlantean noticed nothing. The dragon dove into the water, then accelerating as it effortlessly moved through the water. The current quickly became too much for the demon. Mukt flew from his perch.

The demon had to act fast. He shifted his form into a great white shark and pursued the dragon.

The Aequos moved swiftly through the sea. The dragon opened a teleportal in the water and raced through it. Mukt followed in her wake, barely making it through the opened gate.

When they appeared on the other side of the teleportal they were still in the ocean, just somewhere different—somewhere bluer—somewhere much cleaner than New Amsterdam. One thing was certain, it would be easier to track the dragon in the clear water.

The dragon swam for a few seconds more and then turned. Mukt, in his shark form, swam past the dragon, acting as natural as possible. The Atlantean swam off of the Aequos. The two exchanged goodbyes and the dragon departed as quickly as it came. The Atlantean began to swim in the opposite direction.

Mukt shifted into a squid. The squid matched the Atlanteans pace and began to gain ground. Delphin did not seem to notice. Mukt was on him in seconds, wrapping all ten tentacles around Delphin. The Atlantean struggled to get away, but Mukt held fast. The jinn transformed back into his normal state and placed his hand on Delphin's neck, shooting poison into the Atlantean's bloodstream. The toxin was designed to incapacitate the prey, not kill him. Delphin still fought back, but time was on Mukt's side. Gripping his victim, he teleported out of the water and onto the nearest beach. Mukt threw the Atlantean to one side and immediately doubled over breathing erratically. The Atlantean struggled to stand. Delphin held a hand to the spot on his neck where Mukt had stung him.

"Yeah, hi. Cheers, mate. I . . . just . . . needed a second . . . to catch me . . . bref." The jinn breathed in heavily. "I didn't . . . sign . . . up . . . for dis, you cheeky bastard. You're . . . one . . . slippery fish." The jinn began to laugh as the air flooded back into his body.

"What have you done to me?" asked Delphin as he stood up.

"Dat would be duh toxin dat I just injected into your neck."

"W-w-hy?"

"Conserve your energy, please, Mr. Delphin. You might even consider sitting down, mate. It won't be long now. I wouldn't want you to 'urt yourself. As to your question, why would I do dat? Well, I've been following you now for about an hour or so. It weren't easy eiver. I have to tell you, for me . . . it was a personal worst time for collectin' someone I was after, but fun is fun."

"W-w-what's going on?"

"You've gone bloody mental, you 'av. I 'av to bring you back, don't I? Me master would start whingin' away if I didn't. An I 'ate when 'ee moans. It does me 'ed well in, that. Aw'right, fish boy. On ya go. We 'ad a laugh, some adventure, and dare I say a bit of romance, but it's time to be shootin'. My master wants to see you . . . well, actually some associates of his really want to see you and ask some questions uv ya. Dey've paid top credits, dey av, even called in a bloody marker. Now dat should make you feel special."

"Who are you?"

"If you must know, duh name's Mukt, Mr. Delphin, and I'm afraid we're on a bit uvva tight schedule, so I will ask you to keep duh uvverwise tedious inquiries to a bloody minimum."

"I don't feel so good."

"And seeing as you don't seem to be grasping what is 'appening at the moment, I suppose I'm just going to have to fill you in. I 'av just injected you wif a toxin that when once administered would knock out a bloody mature blue whale. All I really need to do is wait for duh bloody aforementioned toxin to knock you out and den take you safely back to me master. Duh conversation is just me bein' me cordial self and tryin' to pass duh time, I suppose."

Delphin's eyes began to flutter. Mukt teleported behind Delphin and tried to grab his body as it fell to the sand.

"Nighty night."

Vedd Delphin was unconscious. Mukt reached down and scooped up the Atlantean.

"A bit 'eavier den you look, mate. I fink maybe you need to lose a few pounds. Almost frew me bloody back out, didn't I? I know just duh place for you. We 'av some uv duh best facilities in duh world. We'll 'av you good as new in no time, mate. Trust me, Mr. Delphin. We will be dere shortly."

Mukt blinked from the white beach, holding Vedd Delphin.

cat's out of the bag

"They must have been tracking us," said Loric. "It all makes perfect sense. They would not have been able to use the tracker in Sirati, but as soon as we left . . ."

"A family reunion I was not ready for," said Anson.

"How do you think I feel, Anson?" asked Samuel Janik, the Alpha of the White Wolves. He stood in werewolf form at the entrance of the sewer system. He wore tactical gear. "Of all the sewer systems, in all the metropolitan areas, in the known universe, you happen to be in this one."

"Fair point, Sam," said Anson. "I trust you are well?"

"As well as can be expected for a seven-hundred-year-old wolf. You?"

"Well, besides the current predicament we find our selves in, quite nice actually."

"History aside, mate, we have to be takin' the Scargen boy off of your hands. You understand. It's just business. 1,000,000 global credits is nothin' to scoff at."

"Well, I'm afraid that will not be happening, even if you have us severely outnumbered."

The other wolves began to fill into the tube.

"If you hand him over now, Anson, I will let everyone else go. I promise you this. I will even let your traitor ass go. You have my word as your Alpha."

"Grant I may never prove so fond, to trust man on his oath or bond," said Anson.

"I swear it's always the hard way. Just once I would love if people could recognize their surroundings and make an educated decision based on the facts presented. It would make my job so much easier. Greer!"

"Yes, Alpha."

"Bring me the Scargen boy—alive. I don't care what you do with the rest . . . but leave Warwick for me."

"As you wish," said Greer. The werewolf looked over at Anson. "You're on the wrong side of this, Anson."

"That remains to be seen, Mason," said Anson.

"I don't think you understand what you're up against," said Thomas.

"Let me give it a shot," said Greer. "One werewolf, a boy samurai, an artif, a dragon, a gremlin—"

"Gremling," said Fargus.

"And a yet-to-be-defined shapeshifter of sorts," said Greer.

"Well, that's where you're wrong, Greer. The only shapeshifter over here is Mancer Warwick," said Thomas.

"This nose might not be able to tell what type of shifter he is, but I know a shifter when I smell one," said Greer. "I had my suspicions at the Oasis, but now I'm certain. Your Mancer Bodes is a shifter, which should make this a little more interesting. Attack!"

"What's wolfman talking about?" shouted Thomas, noticing the werewolves pouring into the chamber.

"I believe Mancer Bodes has not been completely forthright about the extent of his powers," said Itsuki as he drew *Onikira*.

"I must say, that is one way to put it," said Loric. He started sweating profusely. He looked back at Thomas. His eyes had changed. The white parts of his eyes had become orange and were glowing. "I can usually mask my ability, but in extremely stressful situations it can become exceedingly difficult to do so." Loric darted at two werewolves that made a run for the group, running on the side of the wall. He leapt into the air and before he hit the ground his body had transformed into its new hulking form: half man, half tiger. Loric had the posture of a man, but the features of a tiger. He was massive and strong. His claw stopped the first wolf in his tracks. Loric roared as he threw this wolf into the next advancing werewolf.

"He is a weretiger, Thomas. The mystery has been solved," said Itsuki.

"Weretiger?" Thomas noticed Loric's clothes had adjusted to the transformation when they certainly should have torn. Loric moved with the precision and grace of a tiger. His coloring was beautiful. The orange-brown colors of his coat reminded Thomas of the Mancer's Light.

"Let's do this!" shouted Loric.

The weretiger pushed his paws forward as energy poured at the advancing werewolves. Their laser rifles disintegrated in their hands. The wolves themselves lost limbs here and there.

"That explains the tiger tattoo!" yelled Thomas, extending the Gauntlet. "Haaaaaaaaa!" Light blue energy flowed out halting the attack of three more wolves. "And why Anson and him go at each other like cats and dogs!"

Bartleby wasted no time entering the fray. He unleashed flames down on the haired horde. The smell of burnt fur and flesh now added to the aroma of the sewer systems.

Laser blasts erupted from the wolves. LINC stepped in front of them and formed a shield.

"Thomas Scargen is in danger. Evasive maneuvers are required."

The artif's hands transformed into laser cannons and began to return fire alongside Bartleby. Anson had transformed and engaged Janik. The two fought with a similar style and were perfectly matched.

Loric was vicious in his new form, tearing through werewolves with his claws while firing energy attacks on others. The werewolves dropped but regenerated in his wake. The whole thing seemed futile. Loric retreated back to the line LINC had established.

"These bleedin' wolves are getting on my bloody nerves," snarled Loric.

"We need to run," said Thomas.

"But I want to fight," said Loric, clenching his teeth.

"Someone's a tad more aggressive in tiger form," said Thomas.

"No," said Loric as he smiled. "I'm just enjoying myself."

"O-o-okay," said Thomas. "LINC, find me an exit."

"The nearest exit is approximately 164 meters directly behind us, Thomas Scargen."

"That's plenty of room for Bart to teleport. You are a genius, LINC," said Thomas. In all of the fighting and chaos, he had forgotten that simple fact. They were going to leave the same way they had come in. "Everyone, get to Bart," said Thomas.

Itsuki deflected a few blasts as he mounted the dragon. Thomas made his way to Bartleby.

"Come on, Mancer Bodes. Snap out of it."

The tigerman raised his hands and placed them on his temples as he transformed back into human form.

"I suppose a retreat is in order," said Loric, hopping onto Bartleby as the dragon continued to hold the wolves at bay with his fire. "LINC, grab Anson when I give the signal."

"Affirmative, Thomas Scargen. Retrieve Anson Warwick."

Bartleby again pushed the fire from his mouth, but this time, Thomas controlled the fire, forming it into a sphere. His pyromantic training was on full display as he wielded the flames.

"Haaaaaaaaa!" screamed Thomas.

He hurled the fireball directly at Samuel Janik. The werewolf did not see the attack coming. The impact separated the Alpha from the Beta. Anson began to run towards the group.

"Now, LINC!" yelled Thomas.

The artif swooped down and raised Anson off the ground.

"Turnaround, Bart, and do exactly what you did to get into here, but don't stop at New Amsterdam. LINC, I need you to follow us as fast as possible."

"Aw'right, mate. 'ere we go."

The dragon barreled at the closed corridor door as fast as he could. LINC banked towards the door as well.

"I will be reaching you in approximately 34.7 milliseconds."

The teleportal ripped open in front of the dragon as the wolves rushed along the walls. Bartleby launched himself into flight. The dragon and then the artif both flew through the portal.

30

mind the gap

They had been waiting for quite some time inside Oramus's chambers for the return of the jinn before the demon had reappeared in front of the host of Riders and dragons. This time he was not alone. He held a seemingly lifeless Atlantean. The jinn had completed his mission and returned to the dragon city of Syn with his prey.

"Master Oramus, 'ere's your Atlantean." The jinn placed the unconscious man in front of the dragon.

"Is he still alive, my friend?" asked the dragon.

"Oh yeah, 'ee's just a bit on duh sleepy side." He raised his hand.

Oramus shook his head in understanding as he drew from his pipe. The dragon reached over and grabbed his half-full goblet and poured it onto the Atlantean. Vedd Delphin choked on the liquid and fell onto his side breathing hard. Marcus could see the gills on the man's neck opening and shutting.

"Mr. Vedd Delphin, how are you?" asked Oramus.

"I'm doing just grand. Thanks for asking," said Delphin as he stood. He spat to his right.

"I bet you're wondering what you are doing here," said Oramus.

"That was only the first of a long line of questions, but yeah now that you mention it, I am intrigued."

"My associate here, Captain Marcus Slade, has a few questions and possibly a couple of requests." Oramus drew once more from the pipe. "He assures me that if you cooperate, you will be promptly released back where we found you. Is this true, Marcus?"

"I have no need for you after I get what I want. You will be free to go, but if and only if you answer some questions about Atlantis."

"I'm not sure I know what you are talking about."

"An Atlantean should know where their own city is located Mr. Delphin."

"What makes you think I'm an Atlantean?"

"First of all, I do not *think* you are an Atlantean. I am certain you are. It will save all of us time if you stop pretending that you are not," said Marcus. "And are those not gills on the sides of your neck?"

"Let's say I am an Atlantean. That doesn't mean I know where Atlantis is currently located."

"See. Now we are getting somewhere." Marcus smiled. "The jinn was right about the city moving."

"And I have no way of knowing where it has moved to."

"Come now, Mr. Delphin, I find that very hard to believe. If there is one person who should know where it would be, it would be an Atlantean."

"I will not betray my home."

"I have no time for this, Mr. Delphin. Either answer my questions or we will get the answers our way, and trust me, our way is not pretty."

"I will not betray the true Sovereign of Atlantis."

"In the end, you don't really have a choice," said Marcus. I will get the information I seek one way or another."

"I have told you all you will hear this day on the subject of Atlantis."

"So confident in your convictions," said Marcus. "Very well. Vance."

"Yes, Captain."

"Strip his mind."

"It will be my pleasure, sir."

The thin man walked directly at Vedd Delphin. The Atlantean seemed to be held in space. He could not move.

"Let me go."

"I have hold of you now, Atlantean," said Vance as he stopped in front of Delphin. Without touching him Vance forced Delphin to kneel. "That's better. So this is going to hurt tremendously, and I'm quite sure your brain will never be the same."

Marcus knew Vance was getting a kick out of every second of the proceedings, but the Captain needed the information, and Vedd Delphin was the only person who had it. Marcus had a mission, and he would complete that mission no matter the casualties.

Vance placed his right hand on the Atlantean's head. He leaned over and put his mouth next to Delphin's right ear. "I just want you to know that I won't be gentle."

Energy poured from the man's hand into the skull of Delphin. The Atlantean struggled to maintain his composure, but soon began to convulse. Vance's pupils disappeared. He slowly turned his head to one side.

"Where is the city of Atlantis located?"

"I will not betray the true sovereign of Atlantis," said Delphin.

"We will see about that." The energy jumped from his hand and the Atlantean twitched even more violently. "I will ask you again. Where is Atlantis located?"

"I-I-I-I w-w-w-w-will NOT betray the true sovereign of Atlantis!"

"I'm afraid that is a foregone conclusion at this point."

"Ahhhhh!" yelled the Atlantean. "I-I-I w-w-il-l-l n-not betray the true sovereign of Atlant—"

"But I'm afraid you already have," said Vance.

The output ceased for one second. The Atlantean crumpled to the ground.

"I'm sure Cayde Galeos would be quite disappointed in your lack of mental fortitude."

"How did you . . . I said nothing," said Delphin.

"I never remember saying I needed you too." Vance lifted Delphin off the ground using telekinesis and increased the energy output once more. "Last chance to cooperate."

"Ahhhhhhh!" screamed Delphin, then fell silent.

"Good. I didn't want you too anyway."

The body of Vedd Delphin fell to the floor.

"You weren't supposed to kill him," said Taunt.

"He's not dead—yet anyway."

"Report," said Marcus.

"I know where Atlantis is currently located, but we will need him alive if we are to get inside."

"Very well, Vance. Excellent work—albeit a tad sloppy." Marcus looked down at the Atlantean.

"Thank you, Captain." Vance paused for a second. "There's something else I found inside the Atlantean. Something slipped out while I was probing for Atlantis."

"Out with it."

"There's a weapon. A very old, powerful weapon."

"What sort of weapon?" asked Marcus.

"An axe."

31

the council convenes

They had been waiting patiently in Ziza's study. An emergency meeting of the Mancers had been called, and the Eldre brought in to consult. Thomas could tell that the High Mancer was less than thrilled by the actions of the group, but fortunately, Ziza's displeasure was overshadowed by the news of the Infospheres and the Ignus.

The Mancers were discussing what the next step would be in obtaining the Infospheres. They had to simultaneously extract one sphere from Scargen Robotics and secure the other during the halftime show in Dallas. The timing was crucial—it would be the only way to ensure success in securing both spheres.

Itsuki was asleep where Thomas usually studied. LINC was recharging, but Thomas could not sleep. He was too excited about everything he had learned from Cayde Galeos. The idea of a second stone was invigorating, and the fact that his father had known about his mother and him, even before Thomas himself did, was, among other things, unexpected. He had also learned the origins of the Gauntlet and the Mage stones. It was a lot to take in, but he had gotten to say goodbye to his father, and now, even in death, his father was helping him. The only thing that troubled him was Yareli. He felt guilty for not including her, but he still did not know how he was going to face her.

Loric walked into the room.

"The Council is assembling now," said Loric.

Itsuki squirmed around for a few seconds and then woke up. LINC fired on.

"Electric sheep, indeed," said the artif as his optics fluttered.

Itsuki left first, yawning. LINC followed closely behind. Thomas started to make his way to the door, but stopped. He looked over at Mancer Bodes. He had to know more about Loric's latest surprise.

"A weretiger?" asked Thomas. "You didn't think that was pertinent information that we should all know?"

"I assure you, Scargen, that was not the case."

"Then what exactly was the case?"

"I am . . . embarrassed by that side of me—if you must know," said Loric as he looked away. "I do not like when it happens. If it were up to me, I would never transform into that hideous beast again. But . . . sometimes it is needed, and sometimes I have no choice. The beast takes over." He looked back over at Thomas. "I do not feel in control when that is happening, and I think you know that I hate not being in control."

"But . . . how?"

"My particular abilities are not unlike Anson's, but with a small caveat. My ailment is not transmitted from a like creature through biting or other such methods. No. My particular transformations are a result of a family curse, if you will—not to suggest that there are not others like me, because there are." Loric looked down. "The first time it happened I was fifteen. My father was a Mage, and he had already started training me, but at the time, he did not know of my mother's family secret. We lived in Lontica when it first happened. We had moved from England when I was twelve years old."

"I've never heard of Lontica."

"Not many besides magic-users have. Not to say that you are a not a magic-user, but you were not until recently. Lontica is the Ice City."

"Ice City . . . narsh. Where is it?"

"Lontica resides far below the ice of Antarctica."

"How is that possible? It's way too cold for anyone to live there."

"The climate is regulated with magic. I would postulate that the Gauntlet was responsible for its creation and continued existence. It is home to many a Mage and Necromancer alike."

"Another freakin' magic city?"

"Yes, Scargen. You sound rather surprised. Did you think Sirati to be the only one?"

"Well, that and Atlantis, but yeah, sort of . . . yeah." The thought of another magical city was overwhelming to say the least.

"Well, it is not. You have much to still learn of the magical world."

"Yeah, I'm starting to see that. I think Anson might be right about me spending some more time in Maktaba reading."

"I suppose it could not hurt. Sirati, mind you, is far more peaceful and serene, but Lontica will always be home. However, England is a close second." He smiled. "Lontica is where I first heard the rumblings about the Taitokura and Amara Scornd's newfound power, which led directly to you securing your first augment."

"Narsh."

"It is a marvelous city in its own right. But I'm afraid its current leaders are ignorant and misguided."

"In what way?" asked Thomas.

"They believe the Council of Mages to be an antiquated notion. They have never recognized Ziza as the High Mancer, and are oblivious to the threat that Grimm poses to the whole of Earth. Furthermore, they act as if you do not exist. It is terribly frustrating and the main reason I stepped down from my post."

"What post?"

"I was a thriving member of their parliament for quite some time. Ziza attempted to reason with them about the threat posed by Tollin Grimm, but he was met with opposition."

"How long ago was this?"

"This was before your mother accepted the Burden. I knew Ziza to be anything but a fool. I resigned from my post, left my home once again, and joined the Council here in Sirati."

"I'm sorry, Mancer Bodes. I know what it feels like to have to leave your home. Maybe one day we'll go there together and show them how antiquated the Council is and just how real I am."

"I'd like that, Scargen," said Loric. "You continuously surprise me. Now where were we?"

"You were telling me why you turn into a hulking tigerman."

"Ahh, yes. My mother's family was from India, hailing from Odisha, before coming to England and then subsequently Lontica. The weretiger curse had always plagued her side of the family, as far back as her family had recorded such things. The story goes that one of my ancestors had killed a Bengal Tiger for sport, but did not pay homage to the creature. The creature, however, was no mere tiger. He was a wise and powerful spirit ghost that had been trapped inside of the wild cat. His years as the beast had given him a certain affinity for the felids. The spirit, displeased with killing for killing sake, cursed my ancestor and all of his family. Forever would they understand, firsthand, what it was like to be a tiger and the consequences of taking an unnecessary life."

"And what do you think?"

"I think it is a genetic anomaly that happens to reoccur across hereditary lines."

"That's not as narsh" said Thomas.

"No, Scargen. It is not." Loric smiled. "I assure you, from now on, no more secrets."

He put out his hand, and Thomas shook it, agreeing.

"I respect that. I have been guilty of withholding information myself, so I know where you're coming from."

"Are you referring to Merelda Scargen?"

"How did you—?"

"Your mother was a good friend."

"I thought she didn't have any friends in Sirati."

"She had one. Mary never told me, but the second I saw you, I knew you two must be related. The facial similarities are astounding." Mancer Bodes looked at Thomas and smiled. "Perhaps it is time that everyone knew both of our secrets."

"Perhaps it is."

The two began to walk towards the Council's chamber.

"So no secrets, right?" asked Thomas.

"That, Scargen, is what I propose."

"Okay, then how did your clothes transform with you?"

"A technic friend of mine from Lontica designed them shortly after I informed her of my striped alter ego. Adaptable tech, I believe she called it."

"That's pretty narsh."

"Yes. I like to think so," said Loric.

"So you're immortal too?"

"Something like that, Scargen," said Loric as he smiled. "That's enough sharing for one day."

The two walked down into the Council's chamber and took their places at the table. The Mancers had been joined by the rest of the Council, along with some additions. The Eldre and Garron Dar were in attendance along with five gremlins. Ziza stood at the head of the table. Emfalmay stood behind him. Yareli sat next to Garron, and the two were chatting with each other. *I never thought I'd not like Yareli smiling so much*, thought Thomas. Yareli looked over at him and saw him staring. She quickly turned away.

"I have called you here today to inform you that the Ignus has been located. Thomas and a small team have recovered this information from a holomessage delivered by Carl Scargen. Although I am not pleased about the whole Council not being brought into the fold on this mission, I do realize the sensitive nature of the intel that has been recovered."

"High Mancer," said Thomas. "I-I-I don't mean to interrupt, but it seems like a good time. May I speak?"

"You already are, my boy. Please, I think I understand."

"Well, I just wanted to tell everyone that I really appreciate all of you. I appreciate all you've done for me over the course of the last year and a half. Which makes telling you guys this even harder. Some of you already know what I'm about to say." He looked at Yareli, but she was not looking at him. "But it's pertinent information that everyone should know." He paused and cleared his throat. "My mother was Merelda Scargen . . . I mean what I mean to say is, she was Mary—the previous Bearer." He raised the Gauntlet.

Some of the members of the Council began to whisper to each other.

"When did you find this out?" asked Mancer Lolani.

"At the Temple, last year, during first augmentation when I was inside the Gauntlet."

"Wait . . . you did what, Tommy?" asked Malcolm.

"When I fell asleep at the Temple I went inside the Gauntlet and spoke with my mother."

The Council began to murmur.

"When I go inside of the Gauntlet I can talk and train with past Gauntlet Bearers."

"Wait, you can talk with all of the past Bearers?" asked Garron.

"Yes, but I've only talked with a few. Their spirits are sort of downloaded inside of the glove, but we're kind of getting off-topic—"

"It sounds similar to our Ancestor Stones," said the Eldre.

"I too could commune with past Bearers inside the Gauntlet," said Ziza.

"Why didn't either of you share this before?" asked Yareli.

"I did not see the need, my child, and I trusted that Thomas would share what he needed to when he was ready. Which, I believe, he has."

"Look, I never meant to hide this from everyone," said Thomas, looking directly at Yareli. "But a lot happened quickly after that." Thomas scratched his head as he lowered it. "And the next thing I knew, I was running around looking for another stone. The point is, I'm sorry." He looked at Yareli again. "We shouldn't have secrets from each other." He turned to the rest of the Council. "I swear to you guys that I will never keep anything from you again." He paused for a minute and then sat down. He looked at Loric who was barely paying attention. He quickly stood back up. "Oh, and Mancer Bodes is a weretiger."

The Council murmured once more.

"Thanks," said Loric.

"Well, you didn't look like you were going to do it."

"Your powers of deduction are far better than I have previously given you credit for."

"Settle down everyone. Most of the older members here are well versed with the capabilities of the Gauntlet and know full well that Mancer Bodes is a weretiger. I commend Thomas on his honesty. It is not easy to do what he just did, and I ask all of you to first seek to understand how difficult a time it was for him when this all happened—how difficult a time for all of us it was."

Everyone was silent.

"Now, as I was saying: We have learned that Carl Scargen knew more about his son's and his wife's abilities. He had secured the Ignus and had also manufactured a device to help find the other stones. We now know the locations of both objects. We just do not know which is which. There are two Infospheres that Dr. Scargen created before his untimely death. One is located inside Scargen Robotics and the other is being given to the GA tomorrow during halftime of a NRFL game at Sky Field. Inside one of these spheres is the Ignus, the red stone, and the second sphere is the stone-finding device, along with technical files and schematics that Dr. Scargen was working on. It is of the utmost importance that we recover both Infospheres. Mancer Bodes and Mancer Warwick will debrief you on the details of the plan. Mancer Bodes."

"Thank you, High Mancer. The first phase of the plan will involve Malcolm, Mancer Lolani, LINC, and four of the gremlin technics."

The holographic display in the center of the table showed a three dimensional representation of Scargen Tower, the headquarters of Scargen Robotics.

"This team will be charged with infiltrating this building and recovering the sphere located inside the vault which is located on the twenty-sixth floor. The most difficult part of the mission is gaining access to that level. That's where you come in Malcolm."

"Naturally," said the vampire.

"We need your unique vampiric skill set to handle the receptionist and security."

"You mean you want me to sweet-talk duh lady and handle duh security."

"I would prefer if you sweet-talked both of them, but if need be, the ladder will suffice. Your ability to bend people's will should do the trick. Lolani will also be going with you."

"It has been some time since I have done field work," said Lolani.

"You will be posing as Global Alliance agents sent to look at the progress on the new wartifs," said Loric. "Agents always work in pairs. My sources tell me the Global Alliance has had a presence at Scargen Robotics since the merger. You should not be too conspicuous. I have forged and otherwise obtained all the pertinent documentation you will need to properly carry out this ruse."

"Dat sounds pretty easy, all fings considered," said Malcolm

"Yes it does, but remember, you are just mainly a diversion. You will lead the way, and make sure the others have access to the twenty-sixth floor. Your credentials should be enough. All of the classified material is located on this floor. The gremlins are the ones doing the heavy lifting. LINC will be there to ensure retrieval of the Infosphere along with the gremlins, and he, above all of you, should have no trouble blending in."

"I get to work wif duh Tinman again," said Malcolm. "Just like ol' times, innit?"

"I do not wish to replicate the damage that occurred to my internal systems in the course of our last mission together. My preference is that the result of the mission is the exact opposite of 'ol' times' as you so quaintly articulated it, and that I complete this mission with my structural integrity intact," said LINC. "It is easier to follow my prime directive when I am in one piece."

Loric continued. "The gremlins will leave with LINC and make their way to the vault, indicated here on the schematic. Once in, LINC will use the program that Dr. Scargen installed to break the encryption and obtain the Infosphere. Ms. Bugden will be leading the gremlin team of Valv Tinger, Torc Barwin, and Aiken Gloop and will be coordinating with Fargus and Lolani at all times. Once the sphere is secured, they will rendezvous with Lolani and Malcolm, who will communicate with Ms. Talya Grenfald, your teleport dragon, on extraction from the scene. This will have to be timed carefully, because Ms. Grenfald will also be involved in the next phase of our plan." Loric paused. "A word of caution: there is no way of telling which sphere is which, so we need to be prepared for the worst. Anson." Anson stood as Loric sat.

The schematic of the Scargen Robotics Tower was replaced by a schematic of Sky Field. The floating stadium was massive. It could hold upwards of 400,000 people at any given event and was Ricky Nones's prized accomplishment. It was a marvel of modern tech.

"That brings us to the sphere at the football stadium, and the second phase of the plan," said Anson. "We will be leaving with a bigger team than usual because of the circumstances. Thomas, Itsuki, Yareli, Wiyaloo, Garron, Loric, and myself will all be going to the stadium. Bartleby and Talya will be our transport. Fargus will accompany us into the stadium as well. Sky Field will be on lock down. The Three Primes will be on hand to see the transference of the Infosphere along with several high ranking GA officers and military. Security will be on high alert, and I think we all know that the GA is there then so are the Hunters. This is a stealth mission." He looked right at Thomas. "Our jobs are to blend in until the last possible second before recovery of the sphere. We will need everyone's cooperation for this to go off without a hitch. Retrieval of both spheres is key. Our objective is to infiltrate the locker room and seize control of the Scargen sportifs that are to be displayed at halftime. We will impersonate Scargen engineers and escort the artifs onto the field. Fargus, we will need your help to handle the massive artifs. Cooperation between the two campaigns is paramount for this part of the plan. Loric and I have secured as much of the information we could on these new sportifs, but I'm afraid it is not much. I believe once the interface is created inside Scargen Robotics, LINC will be able to locate more detailed schematics. These will be essential if we are to operate the machines. They are meant to perform during half-time. This will give us a built in diversion and access to the field during the presentation. The Infosphere will be heavily guarded. We will have to make our move during the presentation. This way we will be close enough to grab the Infosphere when the opportunity presents itself."

"The tricky part will be infiltrating the locker rooms without being spotted," said Loric.

"No. The tricky part is going to be getting tickets to this game," said Thomas. "It's been sold out for months and it will decide who gets top seed in the division."

"Done. I have already corresponded wif duh agent and duh tickets are downloaded in my wristcom," said Malcolm with a smile. "Don't worry your pretty lit'l 'ed over it no more, Tommy."

"But how did you do—"

"I know a guy," said Malcolm as he winked at Thomas.

"Good to know," said Thomas.

"And as far as getting into the locker room, I can hack the security systems," said Loric. The projection zoomed into the schematic of the floating stadium. "Here is an access point." Loric pointed at the hologram. "If I can get to here, I will have full control of the stadium, including lights, security patrols, and the gravitational stabilizers."

"Hopefully this can be done without tampering with the stabilizers," said Ziza.

"Yes, of course, High Mancer. Worst case scenario perhaps." Loric's eyes shifted from side to side. "I will most likely simply divert some staff at the proper interval. That should buy us enough time to get into the locker room before they realize anything is wrong. Once we're in, we should be able to figure out how to secure the sportifs and hide the real engineers. Fargus I will also need you to reprogram some of the security drones. We will need to look official when we take the field."

"Aw'right."

"I admit, it is not a perfect plan, but it was the best we could do on such short notice," said Anson.

"I have the utmost confidence in your abilities as a team to accomplish this," said Ziza.

"And besides there's always Plan B," said Thomas.

"What's Plan B?" asked Itsuki.

"We just outgun them," said Thomas as he lifted up the gauntleted hand.

"My boy, I hope it does not come to that, but it does remain an option," said the High Mancer. "The Ignus cannot fall into the hands of the GA and neither can the means to find the other Mage stones."

32
the hangar

Marcus approached the massive doors. Gibgot and Fronik were not at their normal post. Marcus's mission had been successful, but he was no closer in figuring out what it meant. He had secured the location of Atlantis and better yet, a means to enter the lost city, but he still did not know why.

" 'ello Capt'n," said Corbin, greeting him before he had knocked on the door. "I'm startin' to get duh 'ang uv dis tech."

"Hello, Corbin," said the Captain. "I believe I'm expected."

The two doors swung open.

"Dis way Capt'n," said Corbin as he walked in front of Marcus, his hands behind his back. "Lord Grimm eagerly awaits your counsel."

Marcus walked forward as he contemplated the information he had just been given, as well as what implications said information would have on the future of the Legions, and more importantly, Evangeline.

"Hello, Captain Slade," said Evangeline as he entered the chamber. "I trust your mission was successful."

"Did you really ever doubt me?" asked the Captain.

"No," said Evangeline as she grabbed his hand and pulled him close. This caught Marcus by surprise. "I'm not sure I ever could." She immediately let go of his hand as the doors to Grimm's chamber slid open. The man slithered into the room, holding the Scythe like a staff.

"Ahh, Marcus. I trust you have good news," said Grimm.

"Yes, my Lord. We have the current location of Atlantis as well as a means to enter the city."

"I asked for one thing, and I receive much more," said Grimm. "I see your trust in this man was well warranted, Evangeline."

She looked at Marcus and quickly turned away.

"Please, elaborate, Captain," ordered Grimm.

"We were able to procure an Atlantean, who . . . with a bit of leaning, gave us the whereabouts and the means to enter Atlantis. He also seems eager to cooperate now."

"Well, that deserves a toast."

Grimm motioned as Corbin ran to them, balancing a tray beneath an artif that poured a liquid out of one of its fingers into three small rocks glasses, made from bone. The concoction was a black liquid that emanated fumes. The imp servant ran them over to Grimm.

"Here you are, my most prestigious of Necromancers and Captain Slade," said Corbin.

The three reached down and picked up the glasses.

"To . . . a successful mission," said Grimm as the other two nodded and then clinked glasses.

Marcus looked into Evangeline's dark eyes as she drank with no hesitation. It was clear to Marcus that Evangeline had slipped further into Lord Grimm's control, and this revelation made Marcus hesitate, which interrupted the toast. Grimm paused before he drank and looked directly into Marcus's eyes as he tilted his head.

"Is something wrong, Captain?"

"No . . . my Lord."

"Good," said Grimm as he finished his cocktail in one gulp, never breaking eye contact with Marcus.

The Captain had done the same. The silence lingered as the two men maintained eye contact. Lord Grimm began to laugh—the kind of laugh that borders on hysterical. The Captain was obligated to join Grimm.

"You are one of a kind, Marcus," said Grimm. "You have never failed me, even when you were the Second."

The words were flattering. The Captain understood this man's way with words. Grimm could push people, using mere suggestion— not unlike a vampire. It was a skill that only well-versed Mages or Necromancers could learn, with much practice. Marcus was aware of this skill, and his awareness was his greatest strength.

"Thank you, my Lord, but there is more."

"I am eager to hear what it is you have to say, Captain, but first, it is time we caught you up to speed on what we have been up to. Like I said before, you are not merely a cog, Marcus." He waved for them to follow.

They moved to the doors that led to Grimm's inner chamber, which slid open as they approached. Grimm moved to the window, staring blankly over the Tower.

"Soon we will be taking our first steps on a long journey." Grimm turned, and looked over to the other two. "Instead of telling you, let's show you what I am babbling about, Marcus."

Lord Grimm moved to the set of smaller sliding doors in the center of his chamber. He waved his hands as the doors opened. It was an elevator car. The three of them entered the car. Corbin jumped in before the door shut. Grimm waved downward and the elevator began to hurtle down the shaft at an extraordinary speed. The elevator was made entirely of glass. Marcus had never seen the Tower from this vantage point. It was oddly beautiful.

The car came to an abrupt halt. The doors slid open to a hall- way. Grimm was first to leave the car, followed by the General and the Captain. Corbin scurried behind. The General's Guard quickly flanked the group as they walked to the opening at the end of the tunnel. The hallway lead to the massive hangar that Taunt had spoken to Marcus about.

"Whoa," said Marcus.

"Captain Slade. I give you the Dred," said Grimm as he raised the Scythe in the direction of the massive airship.

The ship was mainly black. The insignia of the Grimm Legions was painted in red on its side. The tech was impressive, but there was something organic—almost insectoid—about its appearance.

The Captain stared at the ship with his mouth open. He had never seen anything like it. Artifs tended to the exterior of the gigantic ship, preparing the Dred. They too were stamped with the sigil of the Legions.

"Now what was it you wanted to tell me, Marcus?" asked Lord Grimm, waking Marcus from his gaping.

"My Lord, the Atlantean revealed more than the location of Atlantis."

"What could be more important than this information?"

"The location of a unique weapon—an Ancient weapon." Marcus paused and looked at Grimm.

"I believe we have much to discuss then, Captain. Come."

"What of my men?"

"Corbin, summon Marcus's men, and have the Newts load their aringi as well."

"Yes, Your Exaltedness."

Grimm continued towards the ship with Evangeline and Marcus. "Be quick about it, imp. We depart in ten minutes."

"Of course, my Lord. I will have the men and the aringi on board in five." Corbin scurried away.

"Where are we going?" asked the Captain.

"Come now, Marcus. I think it's obvious at this point."

"Atlantis."

"Yes, Marcus. We require its power source."

"Which is?"

"The Medenculus, Captain. The legendary blue Gauntlet stone."

33

scargen tower

Malcolm walked into the lower level of Scargen Tower followed by Lolani, LINC, and four invisible gremlins. Lenore Bugden lead the gremlins. She had never seen a human city so big before. Philadelphia was amazing. The city was as modern as possible, but still retained its quaint history and charm. Talya Grenfald landed on a rooftop a few blocks away. She had been fitted with the same type of new tech that Fargus had developed for Bartleby as a precaution. Talya had delivered them to the coordinates and then took off back through the teleportal as fast as she had arrived. She was also needed in Dallas, but could not waste the amount of energy it would take to form another teleportal.

Malcolm walked up to the receptionist and looked down at her name tag.

"Hello, my dear, Betsy is it?" said the vampire in a completely passable Southern American accent. "I am Agent Myers and this here is Agent Alexander." He smiled from ear to ear. "My associate and I are here to check on the status of a certain top secret project." He winked as he transferred the holodoc from his wristcom. "Here's our credentials, sweetheart."

The receptionist giggled. "Everything seems in order here, Agent Myers. Let me just get you two your clearance badges. I love your artif by the way. He looks like a newer model."

"I assure you I am the finest artif ever produced by Scargen Robot—"

"You'll have to excuse SR58, sweetheart. He can be a bit harsh at times. His programming is still being tweaked. Ain't that right, Agent Alexander?"

"Yeah, he's a tough one that SR58," said Lolani. "But he's the best forensic artif we've ever had, and he makes a fantastic securtif."

"There is nothing wrong with my programming, and my functionality is far greater than mere forensics and security. I would be insulted, had I been programmed to allow it."

"We know, little fellow," said Malcolm as he patted LINC on his shoulder. "He's also great in a skirmish. You should see him in the field. Every agent could use an SR58." He leaned back over the counter and smiled again at the woman behind the desk. "Not that I need the help. Now you were saying you were making us our clearance badges."

"Here they are." She transferred the clearance badges into their respective wristcoms. "Larry here will escort you up to Level 26, after you pass through a quick security screening."

"Oh, security won't be necessary will it L—"

Malcolm turned towards Larry and his words dropped off when Malcolm realized that Larry was not human. LAR-E stood for Linked Armed Robotic Entourage. LAR-E was a securtif.

"Protocol states that all visitors into Scargen Tower must be screened before being allowed entry to the higher floors."

"Then security it is," said Malcolm. "LAR-E's got a great sense of humor."

"Finally someone that understands protocol," said LINC. "It will be my pleasure to follow you to the screening area, LAR-E."

"See you later, sweetheart," said Malcolm to Betsy as he winked once more.

The group followed LAR-E into the screening area. More artifs filled this zone. Sentry drones circled the area.

Fargus's voice erupted over Lenore's earb. "Are you guys in yet?"

Lenore typed her response into her handheld device. NOT YET.

WE'VE JUST BLOODY ARRIVED AND WE'RE STILL VERY MUCH INVISIBLE.

"Oh, okay. We should be landing shortly over 'ere. Call me as soon as the interface is set."

Malcolm and Lolani had been screened already and LINC was the last to go through the scanner. The last of the gremlins had finished sidestepping the scanner.

"Weapon systems have been detected," said the computer.

"Well, that is what he's here for," said Lolani. "We are here to see the newest wartifs."

"Protocol dictates that weapon systems must be deactivated before entering Scargen Tower."

"I'm sure that won't be necessary LAR-E," said the woman as she approached. She was medium height with black hair that was graying. She stopped in front of them almost bumping into Lenore. "I will take them up personally. These agents have been sent from the Global Alliance. I am sure there will be no issue."

"Security override initiated. Security Clearance Vice President Irene Benet."

"Follow me, agents."

"Thank you, ma'am," said Malcolm. "I sure do appreciate the understanding."

They walked to the elevator. Benet moved her wristcom across the controls and the doors opened. Lenore and the gremlins scurried into the elevator. Benet, Malcolm, Lolani, and LINC followed.

"Well, I guess we're all in."

Lenore yanked at his pant leg to indicate yes. The doors slid shut. Benet turned towards Malcolm still smiling.

"So, Agent Myers, what are you actually doing here, and how is it that you have LINC?"

34

kickoff

"I can't believe I'm going to see a game at Sky Field," said Thomas as he bit the last part of his hot dog that he held in the sheathed hand. Goggles rested on the top of his head. "Mmmm, Anson . . . remind me to thank your brother for the tickets."

"I won't forget, Thomas," said Anson.

"You having fun up there, Suke?" asked Thomas.

"It is a spectacle to behold," said Itsuki through Thomas's earb. The Augmentor was located elsewhere in the stadium.

"May I remind you, we are here to perform certain tasks," said Loric. "Tasks that require everyone's cooperation and collaboration. We need everyone to be where they need to be, when we need them to be there. That is going to require your focus when the time comes."

"Is that why we dropped Yareli and Itsuki off on the two tallest parts of the stadium with those personal cloaking devices that Hosselfot gave us?" asked Thomas.

"It never hurts to have the higher ground—even better when they cannot be seen," said Garron.

"Besides it would be rather difficult to pass off an eleven-year-old as an engineer for a multibillion-dollar robotics firm," said Loric.

"And I don't think they'd have let me in with my bow," said Yareli. Hearing her voice made Thomas smile.

"They tend to frown upon weapons at sporting events," said Thomas. Yareli did not respond. Thomas laughed uncomfortably.

"Bartleby and Talya are also at our disposal if need be," said Loric.

"We've found a cozy place on top uv duh stadium to keep an eye out ourselves," said Bartleby across the earbs.

"I'm not sure I'd call perching on floodlights cozy," said Talya. "But the view's pretty spectacular."

"You've got dat bloody right," said Bartleby. "Say duh word and we're in dat stadium in a bloody 'artbeat."

"These people will be in for a treat if it comes to that, Bart," said Thomas. "I imagine the GA would have a tough time covering that up."

"They've handled bigger situations in the past," said Loric. "If the Global Alliance wants to cover something up, they will—even a stadium event with 400,000 people in attendance."

"Speaking of which, we will get to watch some of the game right?"

"Well . . . we cannot actually enact our plan until closer to half-time, so I suppose you can watch for a bit," said Loric. "I am going to do some recon. Fargus, you will come with me. Your invisibility may come in handy."

"Aw'right, Loric. I suppose I don't 'av much uvva choice, now do I?"

"You three be ready to move on my signal," said Loric.

"Thank you so much, Loric," said Thomas.

"It isn't all fun and games. I need eyes on the layout of the field. Look for where the security details are stationed. Between our eyes in the sky and the three of you, we should be able to map out most of the stadium's security. If you can get eyes on the Three Primes, anyone in the GA, or Hunters that will be equally helpful."

"Yeah, yeah, yeah. See you later."

Thomas ran from the concession area and down to the field. Anson followed him and so did Garron. Once they reached the field, Thomas looked up at the game clock. Kickoff was one minute, twenty-two seconds away.

Perfect timing, thought Thomas.

The sportifs were all massive. There were lineman artifs, receiver artifs, running back artifs, and of course the QB12—all engineered specifically for their positions. The average height of the artifs was fifty meters. Some were bigger, some smaller, but they were all gigantic.

Camera drones flitted around the humongous stadium through the crowd and down onto the field. Huge holoscreens floated above the expansive playing field. The field was 500 yards in length not including the end zones. Force-field goals levitated in both end zones. The levitating circular goals were difficult to hit. Only the best-engineered sportif kickers could ever hope to kick the ball through it. Thomas was excited. It had been a long time since he had had the privilege of seeing a live sporting event. *Unless you count lava trolls versus tree samurai*, thought the young man.

Anson leaned over the railing next to Thomas. "I too am going to take a look around. We need as much intel on security as possible."

"Okay, Anson."

Anson moved with grace, slipping into the audience. Thomas was left with Garron and, considering the situation, began to feel awkward.

"So, Itsuki, this is your first game I'd imagine," said Thomas.

"You would be correct."

"How bout you, Garron. You ever been to something like this?"

"Yes. Something like it," said Garron. He looked over at Thomas and smiled. "My father, growing up, was not what you would call a good man, but he took me to a batilloc match when I was six."

"Batilloc?" asked Thomas.

"It's a dragon sport—much like 'ockey and lacrosse combined, but in duh air," said Bartleby. "But we use our tails, not bloody twigs to shoot."

"I have seen my fair share of these matches myself," said Anson through the earbs.

"Dragons 'av been playin' batilloc for centuries," said Bartleby. "I started playin' it when I was a wee dragonling all the way frough into university. I was a fair striker in my day. Almost went pro, but den my folks went missin' didn't dey? Fings changed right quickly after dat. It's a bloody tough game, doh . . . batilloc—especially the pro leagues."

"Sounds pretty narsh."

"My father loved the game and would often watch his beloved Angkora Draks whenever they were on," said Garron.

"Where is Angkora?"

"Not too far from London, Thomas," said Bartleby through Thomas's earb. "Just so 'appens to be free-'undred feet underground. It's one uv duh seven remaining dragon cities—a 'uman-friendly one at dat. It's where the Dragon Council currently sits."

"Wait, there're seven dragon cities?" asked Thomas. "Spells didn't say anything about this."

"Yes, Thomas. You didn't fink we just all knocked about in bloody caves still, did you?"

"I guess I never thought about it." He looked over at Garron. "Sorry. I totally interrupted your story."

"No need for apologies," said Garron. "I remember the first time I realized there was one dragon city, let alone seven."

"Still blowin' my mind actually," said Thomas. "Anyway, batilloc, Angkora Draks, your father . . . go."

"My father had saved up money for quite a while to afford the tickets." Garron looked down. "I was not originally supposed to go to Angkora with him, but my father's friend canceled the day of the match." He looked up and smiled again. "I do not know if it was the fact the Draks scored six goals or that it was the first game he had been to in eight years, but we actually had fun together." Garron looked out across the stadium. "It was the only time he ever told me that he loved me. That day is the one fond memory I have of the man."

"Wow, Garron. I had no idea," said Thomas. "I'm sorry."

"Thank you, Thomas, I appreciate the sentiment, but that was a different lifetime ago." He looked over at Thomas. "I'm going to take a look around. It is always good to familiarize yourself with your surroundings in circumstances like these."

"O-o-okay," said Thomas. He did not know what else to say. Ever since he had found out about Garron and Yareli's relationship, he had found it difficult to even look at Garron let alone hold a conversation, but now it was worse because Thomas felt sorry for the man. Thomas had lost his father, but at least he had been a good father who loved his son.

Garron Dar disappeared into the crowd.

"I guess I'm the only one that wants to watch the game," said Thomas to himself.

He looked down and around the stadium. The place was definitely on high alert. That much was certain by the number of securtifs. Thomas began to chat into the wristcom. He liked to talk when he was nervous.

"It's crazy to think the red stone might be in this very stadium," said Thomas.

"Or it could be at Scargen Tower," said Anson, responding through his earb.

"I know, the suspense is killing me. Good thing I have something to distract me."

Thomas looked down at the field as the ball was kicked off. Green Bay received. The sportif caught the ball and the ball lit a faint orange color. He ran down the center of the field and was stopped by two large, tank-like sportifs. The refbot floated out and the ball levitated to where the marker was set for the next play. QB12 took the field for the Hackers along with the rest of the offense. His hologram appeared on the holoscreens with his stats for the season. QB12 was having his best year in the NRFL. He was made by Scargen Robotics biggest competitor, Lawler Technologies. Lawler Tech was the best in the field of sportifs and wartifs. They had little in the way of competition, but Gideon Upshaw had changed that. Scargen Robotics would instantaneously be a contender in these fields as soon as the new line of sportifs was unveiled. This aggravated Thomas to no end.

I guess I should start poking around too . . . maybe I'll watch a couple of plays first.

The first play was a standard run up the middle. LB54 met RB25 at the line for no gain. But the second play was a bit more successful. QB12 evaded two tacklers behind the line of scrimmage and then rolled to his right and pump faked, causing DB43 to cheat forward on the ball. The quarterback then launched a mammoth throw down the right sideline. WR88 jumped considerably high in the air and nabbed the ball. The ball once again glowed orange as WR88 walked into the end zone. The crowd started booing.

Thomas smiled. *Narsh.*

The Dallas Cowbots were his least favorite team in the NRFL. He was a Philadelphia Fusion fan, and everyone knew there was no love lost between those two organizations, but he still realized how incredible this experience was. He could appreciate the stadium and still hate the team.

"What do you think, Suke?" asked Thomas.

"It's pretty narsh, to borrow a phrase," said Itsuki.

"I was thinking the same thing." *So I'm not the only one watching.*

Thomas's wristcom rang and Anson's voice came across the earb.

"Thomas. Look across from where you are, into the press box."

Thomas lowered his goggles. The display zoomed into the press box. "That's Gideon Upshaw talking with the Three Primes."

"Look closer."

"Thatcher Wikkaden is here."

"He is?" The voice belonged to Yareli. "I mean I guess I knew it was a possibility, but . . ." She trailed off.

"I know your history with this man, Yareli, but this is neither the time or place for any stunts," interrupted the voice of Mancer Bodes. "We have a very specific mission to complete. There is no room for any side jobs. Do I make myself clear?"

"Yes, Mancer Bodes. Loud and clear," said Yareli.

"Scargen."

"Yes, Mancer Bodes?"

"It's time. Meet me and Fargus at the service corridor located behind section C. That goes for you as well, Warwick and Dar. We have found the engineers. They seem to be grabbing a quick bite before work. It is the perfect time to enact our plan." His voice dropped off.

"No more time for games," said Itsuki.

"I'm pretty sure the games are just about to start, Suke."

They met up with Mancer Bodes behind Section C. Loric had quickly filled them in. The team of five engineers had been enjoying some food at the concession stand closest to the Cowbots locker room. The only problem was that the engineers were being escorted by securtifs.

"I need access to the control panel just at the other end of this corridor. Fargus is already on his way to plant the bug that I concocted."

"Remind me what the bug does again," said Thomas.

"It will give me control over the stadium and its security systems and officially make us the new engineering crew."

"That should help."

"To a certain extent. We still have to be extremely careful. The stadium is carefully monitored for these sorts of things, but my work is untraceable."

"Duh bug has been uploaded, Mancer Bodes."

"Stupendous work, Mr. Hexelby. Now . . . we need a diversion."

"I'm on it," said Thomas. He scanned the room, and then he saw the two groups. "Got it."

Two men sporting opposing jerseys stood back to back, speaking to their respective friends who shared their allegiances. The man with the Hackers jersey was eating a hot dog, while the Cowbots fan was enjoying a slice of pizza and drinking a beer.

"Here goes nothing."

"What exactly do you plan to do?" asked Loric.

"You asked for a diversion," said Thomas. "And that's what you're about to get."

Thomas focused on the beer in the Cowbots fan's hand, and when the opportunity came he pushed the cup telekinetically out of the hand of the Cowbots fan and on to the head of the Hackers fan. Before the Cowbots fan could explain he had received a fist across his face. It did not take long for both sets of friends to get into the fray. The two groups began to push each other back and forth.

"Quite effective, Scargen," said Loric as he began to play with the holographic display on his wristcom. "Primitive, mind you, but quite effective nonetheless."

"What are you doing?" asked Thomas.

"Temporarily diverting all local securtifs and drones to break up the impromptu skirmish, and simultaneously disengaging all of the security cameras in this sector. We have to move now."

The group moved quickly towards the table where the engineers had been quietly eating. Their securtifs had left them to fend for themselves. The four men circled around the table of engineers. Loric was the first to speak.

"I need you gentlemen to follow me. We cannot have you caught in this disturbance. You are too valuable to the halftime performance."

The five men stood and followed Loric down the corridor.

"Quickly—into this room. You should be safe here."

The men quickly filed into the dark room. Thomas, Anson, Loric, and Garron followed.

The room was a small storage room. It housed shelves and shelves of processed foods. A lot of supplies were needed to properly run Sky Field.

"Now what?" said one of the men.

Garron closed the door and locked it.

"Well, we can start with your uniforms. We are going to need those," said Loric.

"What is the meaning of this? Who are you people?"

"That is none of your concern. Let's just say either you cooperate or . . ." Loric pointed to Garron who created a fireball above his right hand. "Do you properly understand your dilemma now?"

The engineers began to disrobe. They were not perfectly matched for the group, but the uniforms would do. Anson walked over to the group of half-naked men and began to fasten their hands behind them. Garron stuffed rags into the engineer's mouths and stashed them in a secluded area of the storage room.

"Now if I hear so much as a peep coming out of this room, you know what happens next," said Garron as he again created a fireball and quickly extinguished it.

The engineers shook their heads with compliance.

"Good."

"How do I look?" said Thomas as he put on his new uniform. He looked down at the Scargen logo and immediately thought of his father.

"Like a robotics engineer," said Anson.

"Narsh. That's exactly what I was going for."

The four men finished suiting up as Fargus appeared in front of them.

"We should get goin' before more uv dose securtifs start knockin' about."

"What are we supposed to do if anyone asks where the fifth engineer is?" asked Thomas after doing some obvious math.

"I have planned accordingly," said Loric. "I assure you."

The group entered the warehouse sized room that directly connected to the Dallas Cowbots' locker room. They were accompanied by the securtifs that were assigned to accompany the original engineers. Loric's bug had wiped their memories and had reprogrammed them to escort the group.

It was extremely dark in the room and the air smelled like burnt metal.

"Loric, can we get a little light?" asked Thomas.

Loric waved his hand across his wristcom and the lights turned on, but at only half power. Thomas looked around. Surrounding them were the gigantic forms of football sportifs from past years along with shelves of spare parts. Other levitating artifs were cataloging and moving the serviceable parts. He immediately recognized some of the players from years past.

"It feels like a bloody graveyard in here," said Fargus.

"Because that's precisely what it is," said Loric.

"This is so narsh," said Thomas. "Look at all of these. Some of these players were unbelievable back in the day. This guy here set the record for passing yards in a season. Ooh. This one here, he was the MVP three seasons ago. Now they're just rotting here deactivated."

"What happened to them?"

"Engineers happened," said Anson.

"You know the old story. The moment one of these guys walks on the field it's that much closer to obsolescence," said Loric.

"A few of these guys were the best of the best," said Thomas.

"And now dey're just a bunch uv bleedin' rusted scrap metal," said Fargus.

"Not to me. These guys deserve better. This is one of many reasons my father never wanted to get into sportifs. Most robotics companies use artifs as tools to make them money. My father proved that when you spend the time to treat these artifs with respect, you get better results."

"I hate to interrupt the soliloquy, but we need to keep moving." Loric looked down at the holomap that floated above his wristcom. "The locker room is connected to this warehouse by a long, well guarded corridor. The entrance way is right over there." Loric pointed to a set of double doors across from where they stood. "We will need to proceed with caution. There will most certainly be a security team on the other side of that door. Have your credentials ready. I should be able to control the artifs if something goes wrong, but again, we do not want to set off any alarms—especially before we get on the field."

The doors opened, and the group walked down the corridor towards the security artifs.

"State your business," said the securtif.

"We've been sent here to escort the Scargen sportifs out onto the field," said Anson.

The artif scanned the forged credentials.

"Everything seems to be in order, Dr. Watson."

Anson looked at Loric as he smiled.

A man walked up between the two artifs, wearing a tailored suit. He was obviously a Global Alliance agent. "I was under the impression that you were sent here to do more than escort the sportifs."

"What do you mean?" asked Thomas.

"I was told their programming wasn't quite finished and that you guys were sent to manually operate them. The show must go on, as they say."

"That's what I meant by escort. It's a technical term engineers use," said Thomas.

"Oh," said the man. "The sportifs are stationed down in the Locker Room. These securtifs will *escort* you. A representative from Network will be communicating with you throughout the performance. The scripts have been downloaded into your wristcoms. Enjoy the show."

They began to move down the corridor.

"Wait."

"What is it? We do not have a lot of time here before halftime, and we have a lot to do," snapped Loric.

"Where is the fifth engineer? There are five artifs in the Locker Room and only four of you."

Loric looked back at the group and then forward.

"We have one of the sportif's programming already completed, and we are simply going to upload it once we get there, if we ever get there," said Loric. "Would you please excuse us?"

"My apologies, doctor, please continue. I'm sorry for the delay."

"If this halftime show does not go as planned there will be only you to blame."

Thomas had to stop himself from laughing out loud. The half-time show would definitely not be going as planned.

35

the vault in our stars

"Hello, Dr. Irene Benet," said LINC. "I was certain your knowledge of robotics and the intricacies of advanced artificial intelligence would facilitate your immediate realization of my identity, and, as usual, I was correct."

"Hello, LINC. How could I forget the best artif Scargen Robotics has ever engineered?"

"You are not doin' us any favors by saying dat," said Malcolm.

"Dr. Irene Benet was responsible for implementation and testing of my advanced weapons systems," said LINC.

"Well, I suppose we 'av you to fank for dat," said Malcolm.

"So . . . who are you two?" asked Benet.

"Why should we tell you?" asked Malcolm.

"I'll have you arrested as soon as this elevator door opens otherwise."

"Well, dat might not be as easy as you fink, but in the interest of building a relationship wif each uvver, let's just say we've been sent by Thomas Scargen to recover somefing dat belonged to 'is father."

"Carl? Is he still alive?"

"No, he is not, but Thomas is," said Lolani.

"That's wonderful news. Where is he? Thomas Scargen is the rightful heir to Scargen Robotics. This changes everything."

"How so?" asked Lolani.

"Working here has been dreadful since Dr. Scargen left. Gideon Upshaw is a horrible boss and a worse man. He has single handedly reversed everything Dr. Scargen had been working on for the last twenty years. Upshaw has prostituted Scargen Robotics to the Global Alliance—who we are now working for, apparently. The things we are making now are killing machines or are used solely for entertainment purposes. Carl would've hated to see this. Artifs were more than just mere tools to him: they were living, breathing things."

"I concur that I am a living thing by definition, but I do not have the capability for respiration."

"I was not being literal, LINC," said Benet. "Carl always thought that artifs deserved the same considerations and rights that were afforded to all life. This was never his vision for this company."

"Why don't you just quit den?" asked Malcolm. "Bugger off, as it were."

"Someone has to keep Carl's vision alive. I can make a bigger difference on the inside, but if Thomas came back that could solve the bigger problem."

"I'm afraid dat's not an option, at least not right now," said Lolani.
"Why not?"

"The Global Alliance wants Thomas Scargen dead," said Lolani.

"I guess that makes a lot of sense," said Benet. "If Thomas were to reverse these contracts, that would stand in the way of a lot of powerful people making a lot of credits."

"And trust me when I tell you, he's doing something far more important," said Lolani. "But he needs something that's in the vault."

Benet looked at Lolani with astonishment.

"His father left it there for him," said Lolani.

"Is dat camera recording audio as well?" asked Malcolm.

Lenore tugged on his pants. She had begun jamming the camera's signals the second they stepped into the elevator.

"I don't think so," said Benet. She looked at LINC and then back to Lolani. "I might regret saying this, but what can I do to help?"

"Are you sure about this?" asked Lolani.

"Anything to help Thomas. If he needs something that's in the vault, I'll do my best to help get it, but I have to warn you: it is close to impossible to get in there without proper clearance."

"Leave that to me, Dr. Irene Benet," said LINC. "Dr. Carl Scargen has given me the necessary program to initiate the vault's opening."

"But even getting close to the vault could prove difficult. There are countless securtifs that will act if anything unusual happens. It'll take a small army," said Benet.

"Oddly enough, we got one uv dose too," said Malcolm. "LINC, I think it's time to cloak before dese doors open up."

The artif disappeared in front of them as the elevator dinged.

"He couldn't do that before," said Benet.

"Dr. Carl Scargen downloaded an extensive upgrade directly into my neural processors hours before being terminated."

Benet stared in disbelief.

"We will follow Dr. Benet, LINC," said Lolani. "You will go to the vault and recover the Infosphere according to the plan."

"He can't do it alone," said Benet.

" 'oo said 'ee's alone?" asked Malcolm.

The doors opened and the occupants of the elevator spilled out onto Level 26. Two more securtifs flanked the doors.

"Good evening, Vice President Benet. We are here to escort you and the two agents to the testing facility."

"By all means, lead the way."

"I guess we're going the total opposite direction of the place I was talking about in the elevator, huh?" asked Malcolm.

"Yes," said Benet as they walked in the direction of the testing facility. The securtifs all followed them. The gremlins and LINC stayed just outside of the elevator. Once the others and the securtifs were out of sight, Lenore spoke.

"LINC, are you still wif us?"

"I am in relative proximity to your current position." The artif appeared in front of them. He was interfacing with a terminal that was in the wall. "I am overriding the security systems throughout Level 26. There. We should be free to move about undetected in approximately 7.5 milliseconds."

The four gremlins appeared simultaneously.

"Let's get movin', we don't 'av much time, do we?" asked Lenore.

"We have approximately 10 minutes and 43 seconds before the security override will be noticed," said LINC.

"Like the lady said, LINC. We don't 'av too much time," said Torc Barwin. "The vault is this way."

The four gremlins scurried behind the artif. Aiken Gloop trailed behind waddling down the corridor. Valv Tinger looked back as he ran.

"I told you you shouldn't drink so much uv your own product, Aiken. You've put on quite a few pounds," said Valv. "You're not keeping up wif duh rest uv us."

"I have a glandular problem, fank you very much, and besides, each batch has to be tested. I can't trust just anyone to do dat, now can I?"

"Be quiet you two. We 'av a job to get done and den duh two uv ya can 'av a go at one anuvver," said Lenore.

"We make a right up here," said Torc, looking down at his hand-held device.

As they turned the corner they saw security drones hovering in front of two large doors. There were five in total. The gremlins quickly disappeared. LINC stood there by himself.

"Halt. What is the nature of your presence on Level 26?"

"Lie to them, LINC," whispered Lenore.

"I am here to conduct routine maintenance on the security systems that protect the vault and its surrounding corridors."

"There is no maintenance scheduled for today. What is your clearance?"

LINC raised his two arms as they transformed into canons. Lasers erupted from his forearms incinerating the artifs. Pieces flew in all directions as sparks rained down onto the floor.

"I guess that will have to do."

"Dat was almost funny, LINC," said Valv. "Well done, mate."

"I cannot copulate with you," said LINC. "Mating is not programmed into my complex functionality."

All four gremlins stared at the artif.

"Let's move," said Lenore. The gremlins and the artif moved closer to the vault. LINC wasted no time connecting with the vault's terminal. He uploaded the encryption file.

"How long will this take, LINC?" asked Lenore.

"The upload will be completed in 2.365 minutes."

"Dat's too long. Dose artifs 'av alerted their buddies by now."

"Like I previously elucidated, the security system is currently over-ridden. They could not have communicated with any other artifs."

Torc began to move holographic images above his handheld device. "Then why are there four sentry drones coming our way?"

"The word sentry is the key to your inquiry. Sentries simply patrol. It is just a coincidence that we happen to be in their sentry path."

"Then hurry up."

The drones turned down the corridor before the gremlins could hide and opened fire. The laser blasts bounced off of LINC's newly formed shield.

"Do you still fink dey 'avn't communicated wif dere friends?"

"My prior statement was not entirely accurate." LINC fired a pulse at one of the drones, destroying the artif. "Communication would have to be restricted to this level under the parameters of the override."

"So dey can only call for a certain amount of backup?" asked Lenore.

"Precisely," said LINC.

"How many drones can dere be on one bloody level?" asked Valv.

"Does it matter at dis point?" asked Lenore. "We need to get dis door open as fast as possible."

"It is just as well. The encryption has been uploaded and I have already downloaded the schematics that Fargus Hexelby had pre-viously requested along with several other documents marked TOP SECRET. I have forwarded these files to Thomas Scargen. There are over twenty different sportif models that Scargen Robotics are cur-rently engineering and producing. I have highlighted the pertinent data on the football sportifs that are scheduled to take part in the halftime show. The files marked TOP SECRET seem to be higher-profile projects done for the Global Alliance by Scargen Robotics since the death of my creator, Dr. Carl Scargen—primarily for the Hunters."

Thirty-one sentry drones entered the corridor at once.

"For some reason, I don't think dese guys give a shite," said Valv.

36
the locker room

They entered the Dallas locker room, not knowing what to expect. Thomas could not believe what he saw. There was everything from diagnostic tech to holovisions and tool-bots flitting about. It rivaled anything Thomas had seen at Scargen Robotics. The facility was state of the art. Thomas looked down the expanse of the locker room, and he saw them.

The five sportifs in question were all distinct from one another. There was a quarterback model—tall, sleek. A football rested in his deactivated hand. A running back model—short and stout. There was a linebacker—wide and tall, and there was also an offensive-line-man model—massive and rounded. The last was a tall, thin, pre-sumably fast wide receiver model. All of the sportifs were beautifully engineered and designed. Minus the fact they were wearing Dallas colors, Thomas was in awe. They were definitely Scargens. The S logo on their shoulders confirmed as much. They resembled designs his father had toyed with years ago, before he knew the realities of robotic sports. Thomas struggled with the reality of these artifs. On one hand, something his father had designed before his death had been realized, but they also represented everything that his father hated about the robotics world.

When he had the opportunity, Loric excused the securtifs.

"I pick the QB," said Thomas.

"I'll take the tall one," said Garron.

"The wide receiver?" asked Thomas.

"I suppose," said Garron.

"I didn't know we were drafting," said Loric. "But I'll take the . . . linebacker, is it?"

"I choose the one that is referred to as the running back," said Anson.

"Great, dat means I get stuck wif duh fat one," said Fargus as he appeared. "I suppose dat's about right."

"Wait . . ." said Thomas. "Do any of you actually know how to play football?" All of them shook their heads. "This should be interesting."

"Any word from LINC yet, Thomas—on the schematics?" asked Fargus.

"LINC is transferring the schematics as we speak," said Thomas. "But no further communication. I suppose we can assume they are at the vault."

"Aw'right," said Fargus.

"You should have them. I transferred them to you."

"I've got dem. Give me a second to take a look."

"In the meantime let's get into our respective sportifs," said Loric. "We need to be quite convincing when we get out on the field if this is to work. A bit of practice is in order as well as some contemplation on the task at hand."

"All things are ready, if our minds be so," said Anson.

"Exactly how do we get into them?" asked Garron.

"There should be a release mechanism on the right leg of each artif," said Thomas. They all looked at him astonished. "What? My father did run the most successful robotics company in the world. You tend to pick up a few things here or there."

Thomas reached up and accessed the control panel. The chest of the QB opened up and a ladder extended to the ground. "Not to mention, I've watched robotic sports my whole life." Thomas began scaling the ladder. Once they were fully programmed, these artifs would need no pilots. They were, however, designed with a cockpit for emergency situations and maintenance. The last thing anyone needed was a twelve-meter tall malfunctioning sportif. The cockpits were remnants of the beginnings of robotic sports, when human pilots controlled massive tech suits. Human pilots were deemed too vulnerable after the first fatality. Sportifs soon followed, but the cockpit remained. It was a simplified control system at this point, but it was still quite functional.

Thomas sat down and the artif closed. Holoscreens turned on as the controls initiated. "Hey, fellas. I'm Kyle Gordon. I am the director of today's broadcast," said a voice coming from inside the artif. Thomas looked on the holoscreen for the button to respond. Then something occurred to him.

What about Fargus? thought Thomas. "Why can't I see you?"

"Look at monitor four," said Gordon.

"Oh," said Thomas waving at the pudgy man wearing a cowboy hat. "Why aren't you waving back?"

"I can't see into the artifs. There isn't usually anyone inside these damn things, so there are no internal cameras. Usually it's me talkin' to some damn artif. It's probably for the best. The last thing the Network needs is proof that the Scargen project is behind schedule or that we are putting you boys into harms way. The press would have a field day. That is why you signed that rather lengthy NDA."

"Oh," said Thomas. *That's good. They won't be able to see Fargus.*

The remaining members of the group climbed into and sealed their corresponding sportifs.

Thomas hit the button to talk again. "Hey, guys, meet Kyle Gordon, our director." He turned off the communication with the director and spoke again using the earbs. "We can see him, but he can't see us, so no worries, Fargus."

"Aw'right. Dat will make dis a lot bloody easier if I don't 'av to be invisible duh 'ole bloody time."

Thomas pushed the button to talk to the director again. "Everyone's suited up, Mr. Gordon."

"That's good news. Hello, fellas. I just wanted to touch base before halftime. You are going to go out there, run a very simple play, get the crowd going, and then move on to the ceremony. Sound good?" The companions all responded in turn. "Good. The play is a fake handoff, into a pass across the middle—simple enough. It has been downloaded into your wristcoms and into the artifs as well. This should be easy for engineers with your credentials. I will be here if you need me, but if not, we will connect again right before the half. You boys have a good show."

"Thank you, Mr. Gordon," said Thomas.

"It is no problem, son." The man's picture vanished from the monitor.

"I thought he'd never leave," said Loric. "Now, I want everyone to acquaint themselves with their artifs. We need to be quite convincing once we enter the field of play."

"It can't be that hard," said Thomas as he threw the massive ball into the air and extended his hand to catch it and completely missed.

"You were saying, Scargen?" asked Loric.

"I was saying, we could all use some practice."

"Umm, you guys are gonna want to look at dis," said Fargus. The gremlin had been inspecting the holofiles since entering the offensive lineman model. "Dere seems to be some anomalies in dese schematics. Take a look for yourselves."

A file appeared above Thomas's wristcom. It was a schematic of one of the sportifs—the OL model. The holographic representation zoomed in on the forearm piece.

"Look right dere."

"Why do these artifs have weapon systems?" asked Anson.

"It's cheaper for Scargen Robotics to cross-manufacturer over various platforms. It is vastly more cost-effective to build similar artifs with multiple applications," said Loric.

"You mean these artifs will be playing sports with fully integrated state-of-the-art weapon systems?" asked Thomas.

"Precisely, but they will be offline. There will be no way for them to access the programming required to use the weapons," said Loric.

"It seems the GA are here for more than just some halftime theatrics," said Anson. "They're here to see their newest wartifs as well."

"Well spotted, Warwick," said Loric.

"Are there weapon systems in all of these models?" asked Garron.

"Yep," said Fargus as the schematics for all of the sportifs appeared on Thomas's display inside his artif. "Dey also all 'av fairly sophisticated propulsion systems, an that. It looks like each bloody model 'as its own specialty as well. I'm in a bloody tank buster."

"The GA is here to see their prototypes in action," said Anson.

"It did seem weird that they cared that much about robotic sports," said Thomas. "No wonder Gideon is having his engineers fake their performances. He doesn't want to let on that he's behind schedule."

"And just think, when they are completed, they will have these artifs in place in every major city in the world, and they can be weaponized at a moment's notice," said Loric.

"Are you saying these artifs will be a reserve force for the GA?" asked Thomas.

"I'm saying that from what I learned about Mr. Gideon Upshaw while studying your father, I wouldn't put anything past the man. He is sadistic and a monster. There is no doubt in my mind that these schematics will be used to create wartifs and his domestic reserve force."

"Kind of scary don't ya think?" asked Thomas.

"Unbelievable," said Garron.

"It is quite alarming," said Anson.

"Until that time comes, the sportifs are just here for the show," said Loric.

"Well, then if they're here for a show, then why keep them waiting?" asked Thomas. "Fargus?"

"Yes, Thomas?"

"Can you get these weapon systems online?"

"It should be simple enough. I can do most uv duh work from 'ere. I just might 'av to pinch some parts from that lot back in dat bloody graveyard wif duh 'elp uv some uv dose servicebots."

"Send me a list of essential parts, and I shall put the servicebots to work," said Loric.

"Aw'right," said Fargus as he started to whistle.

"We will show the GA just exactly what they're paying for," said Thomas.

37

the dred

Marcus stared out the window of the Dred's bridge. The ship was moving at an unbelievable pace. He could not believe that this massive airship had been built right under his own nose. It was gigantic, like Taunt had guessed. The interior was dark and sparsely lit. It seemed to be a twisted combination of tech and magic. Marcus had never seen this type of tech before. It seemed ancient, almost otherworldly. Artifs moved here and there, throughout the ship, handling most of the maintenance. These artifs had a dark, simple design and were incredibly advanced.

Evangeline stood across from Marcus. They both overlooked a holographic representation of Atlantis that Grimm had provided. Where he had gotten it was anyone's guess. They had not said a word to each other since Grimm had left. The General's Guard and several artifs manned the controls. The doors to the bridge opened, interrupting the silence. Taunt entered with Vedd Delphin following him in energy shackles. Marcus turned to greet them. Taunt stood at attention.

"I brought the prisoner as you asked, General," said Taunt.

"At ease, Rider," said Evangeline. "I do not think they are needed any longer." She pointed to the shackles. "We have an understanding."

Taunt waved his hand across his wristcom. The shackles disappeared. The Atlantean wrung his wrists.

"Thank you, General," said Delphin.

"I am glad you have decided to cooperate," said Evangeline.

"I only cooperate if you assure me that Atlantis will not be harmed if at all possible, and that I am to be set free when all is said and done."

"I assure you, we do not wish to destroy your city," said Evangeline. "And once our business is done, you will be free to go. Please join us."

Vedd Delphin moved over to the holomap and began to look around. He shook his head in disbelief. "What is it? Is something out of place?"

"This is all wrong. The whole map is incorrect. The city has changed a lot since this holomap was created."

"Yes. I'm afraid our information is rather dated," said Evangeline.

"May I?" asked Delphin.

"By all means," said Evangeline.

"The interface is amazing. It almost seems Atlantean," said Delphin as he moved his hands across the display. "There you go." The holomap began to transform showing the changes he was making.

"You weren't kidding," said Marcus. "It looks like a completely different city."

"After the Medenculus was taken from Atlantis, changes were made to fortify it."

"I'd say so," said Evangeline. "This changes things considerably. I must inform Lord Grimm."

"Where is he?"

"Preparing for the second half of the plan."

"And what half is that?" asked Marcus.

"The demon half."

"We are working with demons?" asked Marcus. He did not like this revelation. Demons could not be trusted.

"You didn't think we were attacking an underwater fortress with just a few squadrons of Riders did you? And besides, they are just a precaution in case we are not able to gain access to the city by other means. Which brings me to my next question Mr. Delphin. Where is our best point of entry?"

"See these Pods on the outskirts of the city? These are where I usually sneak in and out of Atlantis. This is your best bet to enter the city undetected. I can show you the way. You will need me to gain access."

"In what way?" asked Evangeline.

"There are escape tunnels under the city. They were built ages ago, in case of invasion. They provided a way for the Sovereign to exit the city unnoticed. An Atlantean First Guard must unlock these corridors. There is a DNA lock on the entryways."

The irony that these tunnels were to be used for an invasion slowly hit Marcus.

"Once we enter the city we can make our way to the Citadel, here." Delphin pointed to the spire jutting out of the center of Atlantis.

"What is in there?" asked Evangeline.

"This is where the Medenculus is located," said Delphin. "I assumed that is what you are after."

"Your assumption is correct, Mr. Delphin," said Evangeline. "Our mission is to infiltrate Atlantis and secure the Medenculus."

"What do you mean *our mission?*" asked Marcus.

"I will personally lead the first squadron and you will lead the second. Do you have a problem with that, Captain?"

"No, General." Marcus knew there was no point arguing, no matter how dangerous the mission was. She was her own woman. She would do what she wanted.

"The escape corridors will lead you right into the heart of Atlantis. There is one exit inside of the Palace, and another on the north side of the Citadel."

"I will lead the team through the Palace," said Evangeline. "Captain, you will take Mr. Delphin and breach the north side of the Citadel. We will attempt to secure the stone with as little interference as possible. We get in and we get out."

"That will be easier said than done," said Delphin. "There are hundreds of Atlanteans guarding the Citadel and the Palace."

"Then I suppose we will have to try our best, not to be found out," said Evangeline.

"What happens if we are found out?" asked Marcus.

"I hope for Atlantis's sake, it doesn't come to that," said Evangeline.

Evangeline stood at the front of the Dred's hangar as it slowly opened. They would be at the drop zone in seconds. Marcus was with his Riders and the Atlantean. The Captain turned towards Delphin, almost whispering.

"Why are you doing this?" asked Marcus. "Especially after the way we treated you."

"The way I see it, this attack is happening one way or another. With my help maybe some good will come of this, and Atlantean lives will be spared. And besides, the enemy of my enemy is my friend—at least temporarily."

"You do not see eye to eye with the current leaders of Atlantis."

"Our government has become quite corrupt in the last twenty surfacewalker years. Jusip Tad has seen to that."

"You think you can do better?"

"Not me. A friend of mine."

"Leading is not for the faint-hearted."

"Cayde Galeos is anything but faint of heart. He is the true Sovereign of Atlantis."

"I'd like to meet this friend of yours. Maybe he could tell me what I'm doing wrong."

"Your men would follow you into the abyss if you gave the order. I do not think you need help in that department."

"I appreciate that."

"I have a question for you, if you do not mind me asking," said Delphin.

"Don't mind at all. I have a few seconds to kill before diving into certain peril."

"Riders prepare for departure," said the General. "Release the aringi."

Delphin turned towards the Captain.

"What are you doing here?"

"What do you mean?"

"Well, it just seems like this is not in your nature and—"

"How did I get caught up in all of this?"

"Yes."

"Well, Delphin," said Marcus. He paused and thought about the complexity of the simple question. "Sometimes shit happens."

"I guess you have a point there."

"And as far as this not being in my nature . . . you don't know my nature."

Marcus's force field on his helmet engaged as he moved to the jump point and jumped out of the ship. He free-fell for five seconds or so before the aringi caught him. Delphin was in the arms of one of the artifs. Captain Marcus Slade sped through the sky on the underbelly of Teros. The aringi dove down straight towards the churning water. The artif dropped the Atlantean when he got close to the water. He hit the surface in a perfect dive.

Teros continued to fly across the ocean, gaining even more speed with the other aringi. The interlocking circular mechanism on Marcus's back unlocked as he detached from his aringi, and he hit the water with a small splash. The mechanism opened on both sides. Small wings extended from it, the ends of which helped propel the Rider down into the dark waters.

38

a tight spot

"Got anuvva one!" shouted Valv across to Lenore. Valv fired his laser pistol into the mass of tech. One artif exploded as he jumped out of the way of the shrapnel from the drone.

"Please move to behind my shield radius," said LINC as he turned and opened fire.

The gremlin stepped back behind the shield. Aiken and Lenore fought beside LINC, firing into the artifs. Lenore shot twice, incapacitating two drones.

" 'ow much longer, LINC? I don't fink your shield is gonna 'old, is it?" said Lenore.

"The encryption should be initializing in 3.2 milliseconds," said LINC.

The vault door began to unlock. The door opened slowly.

"Proceed into the vault. I will enter immediately after I have eliminated the threat."

"You 'erd 'im," said Lenore.

LINC stepped forward and unloaded on the securtifs and drones. The four gremlins ran to enter the vault. The alarm sounded and the door began to close. Lenore darted at the quickly closing opening, barely crossing into the vault before it closed. The lights flickered and then extinguished. Lenore, Aiken, Valv, and Torc were separated from LINC.

Torc looked down at his handheld device. The glow from the devices was the only light in the room. "LINC, are you there?"

"Yes, I am on the other side of the vault door."

" 'ow you 'olden' up, mate?" asked Lenore.

Two light orbs illuminated the interior of the vault. She had released them from her device. The vault was expansive, and the temperature inside of it was slightly brisk. Hundreds of pieces of machinery and tech were stored inside the vault—housed in several different glass display cases.

"I have destroyed the last of the artifs. My shields are holding at 29 percent."

"Well, den open up duh bloody door again and 'elp us get out uv 'ere."

"That is currently not an option."

"Sure it is, LINC. Just run duh bloody program again," said Valv.

"The encryption program has been eliminated from the Scargen Robotics mainframe. You will have to continue the mission without me."

"But dat wasn't part uv duh plan, LINC!" said Lenore.

"In this instance, the parameters will not allow for the current plan to come to fruition. Therefore a new solution must be found in order for the mission to be successful."

"What do we do now?"

"The Infosphere is in a case located in the center of the vault."

Torc pulled up the holoschematic that LINC had just sent to him.

"Secure the sphere and meet at the extraction site. I am going to relocate to my last position inside Scargen Robotics, and then find, and exit the building with Malcolm Warwick and Mancer Lolani."

"I found it!" yelled Aiken.

The pudgy gremlin was further into the room. One of the light orbs flitted above him. Lenore looked down at the gremlin.

"It's right here." He was pointing at a large case in the center of the room. " 'elp me up."

" 'ow did you find it?" asked Valv.

"I just looked at duh schematic on Torc's 'oloscreen."

"Yeah, dat makes sense."

The three gremlins boosted up Aiken. He stood on the platform that the case rested on and pondered the task at hand.

" 'ow am I supposed to get inside to grab duh bloody sphere?"

Valv took out his laser pistol and shot at the case from the ground. The blast hit the control panel below the glass display. The front side of the glass lowered.

"I guess dat's one way uv doin' it, innit?"

"Your welcome," said Valv.

"Grab duh bloody sphere," said Lenore.

"And den what?" asked Valv.

"We get out uv 'ere," said Lenore.

"But 'ow?" asked Aiken, joining them on the floor with the newly acquired Infosphere. "If LINC can't get in, 'ow are we supposed to get out?"

"I think I know a way," said Torc.

"Out wif it, mate," said Valv.

"Dis place is cool, right?" asked Torc.

"I guess it 'as its charms, yeah," said Valv.

"No, I mean it's cool in 'ere, meaning duh temperature is definitely regulated," said Torc. "Understandable, considering duh tech dat is being 'oused in 'ere."

"Where exactly are you going wif dis?" asked Aiken as he stared at the Infosphere in his hands.

"If duh temperature is regulated, dere 'as to be a vent, right?"

"You are bloody brilliant, Torc," said Lenore.

"Fanks," said Torc, blushing a bit.

"I have reviewed the schematics and have located the closest ventilated corridor," said LINC. "I am sending you the relative location of the ventilation corridor and a full schematic of the ventilation system. I will notify Thomas Scargen that the Infosphere has been secured. There is one more concern: there are regular crawler maintenance patr—" The artif cut off midword.

"What is a crawler?" asked Lenore into her device. There was no answer. LINC's communication had been severed.

"What do we do now?" asked Aiken who continued to examine the sphere.

"Duh vent is dat way," said Torc, pointing upward as he looked down at the holographic display.

"Secure dat sphere," said Lenore.

"Already on dat," said Aiken as he carefully placed the Infosphere into his backpack.

"Excellent," said Lenore. "Now . . . let's get up dere and out uv 'ere."

39

the halftime show

Fargus had been overworking the servicebots. The gremlin had recoded countless lines of data to get the systems up and running. He had learned that his prototype was actually further along than the others. The OL model had most of its programming done, so Fargus just had to finish the job. The Gremlin had become quite capable in artif building and maintenance after having to reconstruct LINC. This model's artificial intelligence was not as advanced as LINC's, so that made the job easier. The OL model was now fully functional. The other sportifs remained manned by humans, but their weapon systems theoretically were also online. There was no time to test them. The Dallas Cowbots were on their way into the locker room. That meant that halftime was about to start.

Kyle Gordon's voice filled the sportifs. "You boys ready?"

They all responded in the affirmative.

"That's good, because it's show time, fellas. Get out there and break a leg."

Thomas's sportif was the last down the tunnel. Everyone had stopped just before entering the field. According to Gordon, they were to wait for their announcement and then enter the field one at a time, perform a task of some sort and then line up for a play. After the play, they were to line up next to one another behind the festivities and wait for the presentation of the Infosphere. Thomas knew one thing was certain: *This halftime show is going to be narsh.*

The latest selection from Domesticated Rats began to play over the PA. A man's voice began to speak loudly over the thunderous beats.

"Hello, and welcome to Sky Field!" The crowd applauded. "Are you ready to see the future of the Dallas Cowbots?" said the public address announcer.

The crowd erupted in the darkened arena. The noise was deafening and shook the floating stadium. Thomas began to feel nervous. He had practiced passing the ball to Garron several times, but not in front of 400,000 people, and besides, this was going to get serious quickly.

"Introducing your newest Dallas Cowbots brought to you by the engineers at Scargen Robotics. Let's hear it for the future of robotic sports."

The crowd somehow got louder as the lights in the stadium began to swirl.

"Get ready, gentlemen. This rodeos about to start," said Gordon.

A refbot came over and handed Fargus's artif a large metallic football. On the side of the football was the Scargen logo in the colors of the Dallas Cowbots.

"Really?" said Thomas. *Dad would hate that.*

"Introducing first: Scargen model, OL74, and the new center for the Dallas Cowbots." Fireworks shot into the night sky as holographic images of OL74 with his accompanying schematic floated above the field.

"You're up, Fargus," said Thomas.

"Aw'right. You ready, Olly?" He had given his sportif a name.

"Affirmative," said OL74. OL74 ran out onto the field, holding the ball. He raised the ball into the air. The crowd responded as Olly assumed the center position, ready to hike the ball.

"That was perfect. Keep up the good work, boys," said Gordon.

"Next up, starting at linebacker, Scargen model LB55."

Loric ran the sportif out onto the field accompanied by even more fireworks and a similar 3D projection.

"Flex those arms a bit," said Gordon. "Let's give them something to cheer about."

Loric flexed the arms of the sportif and the crowd flared. He then assumed his defensive position across from OL74.

"Looking good so far, guys," said Gordon. "Looking good."

"Starting at wide receiver, Scargen model WR82."

Fireworks rocketed upwards. Garron ran as fast as he could onto the field. When he reached the line of scrimmage, he flanked out to his left and assumed the wide receiver stance.

"All right, gentlemen, keep it going. Get me orb 32 and an upshot of that beautiful piece of machinery and then bring it back to orb 12."

"Starting at running back for your Dallas Cowbots, RB27."

Anson lead his artif out of the tunnel.

"Now, Dr. Watson, signal to the crowd to make some noise," said Gordon. "Get orb 22 and pan around him while he does it."

Anson waved his arms upward and the crowd listened. Once the camera orb flitted away, Anson hit the three-point stance behind OL74 who was lined up as center.

"This is looking amazing, fellas," said Gordon.

"What do we think folks? How do they look?" The crowd again spiked. "Now, the moment you've been waiting for. Starting at quarterback for your Dallas Cowbots . . ."

Thomas took a deep breath. *Here we go.*

"I hope you're ready for this, son," said Gordon. "Time to make some magic."

"QB19!" yelled the public address announcer.

Thomas stepped from the tunnel as the music escalated and fireworks rained down in every direction. The sound of the fireworks were muffled inside of the sportif. Thomas ran his artif directly behind OL74. He put his sportif's hands under the center, preparing for the snap of the ball. The place was instantly silent.

"Okay, boys, we're gonna do this just like in the script," said the director.

"Ready, Fargus?" asked Thomas.

"I suppose so. How 'ard could it be? You ready to give dis a go, Olly?"

"Affirmative," said OL74 as he hiked the ball.

Thomas faked the handoff to RB27, rolled out to his right, and then threw the ball to WR82 across the middle of the field. Garron caught the ball, and was immediately met by LB55. The tackle was perfect and thunderous. The crowd rose into a standing ovation. The music and fireworks assumed once more.

"That's what I'm talking about, fellas," said the director. "Amazing, man."

"Nice catch, Garron," said Thomas.

"Thanks," said Garron. "The pass was perfect."

"That was a bit tougher than I thought," said Loric.

"You're telling me," said Garron. "My head is still ringing." His artif still held the football.

"It looked incredible from up here," said Itsuki.

"Bloody brilliant, Thomas," said Bartleby.

"Nice catch, Garron," said Yareli.

Even though he agreed, the compliment annoyed Thomas.

"Thank you," said Garron. "It was exhilarating."

The sportifs all stood and began to wave to the crowd. "Let's hear it for your future Dallas Cowwwwwwbots!" The stadium shook. "Now let me draw your attention to midfield."

"That is your cue, boys. Line up behind the procession—just like we talked about. WR82, please place the football in the center holder. The team would like to keep the souvenir of the momentous occasion."

The sportifs walked over to the center of the festivities and took their places. Garron placed the football in the holder and then joined the others.

"Do not make a move until we see the sphere," said Loric. "Is that clear?"

"Crystal," said Thomas.

The procession was made up of GA agents and officials from the Dallas Cowbots in addition to some higher ranking board members from Scargen Robotics.

"The Dallas Cowbots would first like to welcome all of you to

Sky Field. We are here for a tremendous occasion. One that will change tech as we know it. Mr. Gideon Upshaw is here to present the late Dr. Carl Scargen's finest achievement . . ."

"That is offensive to me and LINC," said Thomas.

". . . the Infosphere, to Andres Nieto, Global Alliance Prime and President of the United Americas, solidifying the relationship between Scargen Robotics and the Global Alliance."

The crowd applauded. "Accompanying Prime Nieto are Prime Mehta from India, and Prime Chang from China.

The levitating platform began to descend from where the Three Primes had been watching the game. Secret servicebots and drones surrounded the platform. A second floating platform hovered down to the field, carrying Gideon Upshaw and Thatcher Wikkaden. They were flanked by two collectorbots. Three four-legged artifs patrolled below them.

"I'm going to kill him," said Yareli into the earbs.

"Another time, Ms. Chula," said Loric. "Focus on the mission."

"Yes, Mancer . . . I'm sorry."

"There is no need to apologize. I too loathe that man and his organization, and if I have the chance, rest assured, I will use everything at my disposal to stop him and the Hunters, but, first and foremost, we need to secure the Infosphere. The field is extremely well guarded by Hunters, GA men, collectorbots, the Prime's secret servicebots, not to mention the HOUNDs. We need to be vigilant."

"I was wondering what those things were," said Thomas. He stared at the dog shaped artifs. They were gigantic and intimidating. "Four-legged tanks?"

"Correct. They are the newest phase of collectorbots. They have been made by Scargen Robotics specifically for the Hunters," said Loric.

"How do you know everything?" asked Thomas.

"I pay attention, for starters, and the files that LINC sent over included their specs. They have incredibly advanced AI and enhanced energy-output detection."

"If we use our powers, they will know?" asked Garron.

"Precisely."

"Then it's almost a fair fight," said Thomas.

"Almost," said Loric.

"I am getting another message from LINC," said Thomas. He played the message into his earb. "He says the Infosphere is secured, but still in the building."

"Do they know which one they have?" asked Garron.

Thomas did not respond right away. He was still listening to the message. "No. There was no indication. The gremlins have it . . . they've been split up. LINC's currently cloaked and . . . meeting up with Lolani and Malcolm. Apparently the little guys are taking the ventilation shafts to the roof. We won't know which Infosphere they have until they get it back to Ziza."

"Not exactly the plan we laid out," said Loric. "But the best-laid plans . . ."

"Did I detect a quote from a famous author?" asked Anson.

"I never said I had an issue with quoting from the works of great writers," said Loric. "I raised an objection to it always being the same one. My point was sometimes one has to improvise, and it seems an extraction is forthcoming from Scargen Tower."

"Talya, you should make your way back to Philadelphia," said Anson. "Meet them at the rendezvous point on the roof."

"See you guys shortly," said Talya. "I'll be back as soon as possible."

I hope they're all all right, thought Thomas.

The two platforms had landed with security flanking the men and women in charge. But something seemed peculiar to Thomas.

"Where's the Infosphere?"

Gideon Upshaw walked over to the Three Primes in front of the football from the demonstration.

"I guess we are about to find out," said Anson.

Upshaw walked up to the podium. "How about the new Scargen sportifs?"

The crowd expressed their praise. Upshaw waited for them to settle back down.

"I want to thank all who have come to Sky Field this evening, in addition to all who are watching at home. Today is a monumental day but also a sad one." He paused like he was holding back tears. "Dr. Carl Scargen would have loved to be here today with his son, Thomas, to see Scargen Robotics take its rightful place as the biggest and best robotics company in the world. I would like everyone to bow their heads in remembrance for a man that was ahead of his time, whose ideas and thinking knew no bounds—a man who has forever changed the world we live in."

"I can't believe he is doing this," said Thomas. "How dare you, Upshaw? You lying piece of sh—"

"And for his son. A flame extinguished before it could truly ignite."

"Something's going to ignite all right."

The crowd became silent.

"Thomas, do I need to remind you about your control issues in the past," said Loric, almost whispering.

"No, Mancer. You do not. We are here because of my father, and I won't let the words of this ass change that."

"Now, the reason we are here today," resumed Upshaw.

Prime Nieto and Gideon Upshaw walked towards one another. The two met in the middle and awkwardly shook hands.

"Prime Nieto, I would like to present to you the amalgamation of decades of work by a true genius. May this gift solidify the bonds between our two organizations and may the Alliance be forever strong."

The ovation shook the stadium as the football, that Garron had placed into the holder, began to transform. The top of the ball folded back to reveal the Infosphere wedged carefully in place. The housing of the sphere slowly raised to reveal the invention.

"You have to be kidding me. It was in the ball the whole time?" asked Thomas.

"It would certainly appear that way," said Anson.

"There is no use beating ourselves up over what is now obvious," said Loric. "We stick to the plan. Anson goes for the sphere. Everyone else arm your weapon systems and be ready to move in five . . . four . . . three . . . two . . ."

40

shafted

"One more should do it," said Valv.

Torc and Valv pulled Aiken up and into the shaft.

"You should strongly consider a different diet, mate. I wasn't sure we 'ad you dere for a second."

"Why you always teasin' me about me weight?" asked Aiken. "I can't 'elp meeself sometimes, can I? Food was meant to be eaten."

"Yeah, just not all uv it by duh same bloke, is alls I'm sayin'." Torc giggled and then caught himself.

"Would you two give it a rest?" said Lenore looking at her hand-held device. She had tried to communicate with LINC, but something was interfering with the signal. "I guess we do what duh artif said and get dis fing to duh roof. 'ow 'ard can dat be? I mean really. The vault was only two floors from duh roof."

"It says 'ere dat we should go dis way," said Torc pointing down the sparsely lit corridor. He was looking at the schematics LINC had sent. The light orbs flitted in that direction.

"Okay, Valv. You take point."

"Aw'right, deary. Dere's no need to worry about anyfing. I'm on it."

They moved down the shaft in a single file. Valv first, followed by Lenore, Aiken, and Torc at the rear, guiding them. The shaft was large and they had no problem standing and walking inside of it. After a few minutes of zigging and zagging their way through the ducts, Valv raised his hand, signaling for everyone to stop.

"What is it?" asked Lenore.

"I fought I 'erd somefing."

"It was probably just an echo of one of us," said Aiken.

"No, it didn't sound like us."

"Maybe a rat den. I 'ear dese skyscrapers 'av loads uv problems wif such fings," said Torc.

"Yeah, maybe," said Valv. "Oh well. I guess I must be 'earin' fings." A rat ran by the group. "Looks like you were right again, Torc. It just sounded more mechanical, dat's all."

As if on cue, the machine turned the corner to appear in front of them. It was as tall as a gremlin but stood on its spider-like legs. An eye was mounted on the top of it. It saw the gremlins instantly. Its optical sensor fluttered.

"I'm gonna go out on a limb and say dat's a crawler."

"Well spotted," said Lenore.

"Do you suppose it's friendly?" asked Aiken.

A laser popped out from each side of its body and the artif opened fire on the gremlins.

"I'm gonna say no," said Valv.

They moved quickly behind a connecting shaft.

"Let's just go dis way," said Aiken.

"I'm afraid roof access is only in dis direction." Torc scanned the crawler.

"So let's just turn invisible and wait for him to pass," said Aiken.

"I don't think dat would 'elp," said Torc. "It seems to work off of infrared heat signatures and sound sensitivity, and I'm pretty sure dere's more den one uv dem."

"What makes you so sure?" asked Valv.

"It is a rather large building, and I fink its safe to assume dat more den one uv dese fings is needed to maintain a building dis size."

"What are dey doing in 'ere?" asked Lenore.

"I would say, dis one in particular is looking for our furry friend dat just scurried in duh opposite direction," said Valv.

"Why's 'ee shootin' at us den?" asked Aiken.

"It probably assumes dat we are more rats," said Torc. "Its job appears to be to clean the shafts of any foreign objects, and I'd say we're pretty bloody foreign."

" 'ow do we shut it off?" asked Lenore.

Torc shot a recon orb out of his handheld device. It went over and scanned the crawler, while avoiding its blasts.

"My scans indicate a weakness just below its optical sensor," said Torc.

The transmission ceased as the crawler had finally hit the orb.

"Okay. I guess dat leaves us no option den," said Lenore.

She rolled out into the shaft with her pistol in hand and unloaded on the crawler. She hit the weak spot with her first and second spread. The laser fire ceased and the crawler's eye sensor shut down. The artif's appendages stopped moving after one final sputter.

Lenore looked back to the others. "See, dat was pretty easy, wasn't it?"

Before she could finish the sentence, the mechanical crawling noise resumed. This time it was amplified and multiplied. Lenore looked down at the lifeless artif. The crawler showed no signs of movement.

"Dat does not sound good," said Valv.

"I concur wif his assessment," said Torc, shooting out a second recon orb from his device.

The orb whizzed past Lenore and the fallen crawler and turned down the roof access shaft. The image that relayed back to Torc's holoscreen was disheartening. The shaft was covered in the spider-like artifs—some on the floor and others crawling on the sides of the shaft.

"So much for a pleasant stroll to duh bleedin' roof," said Aiken. "Are you sure dere's no other way?"

"I'm afraid dis is duh only way," said Torc.

"We'll just 'av to fight our way fru den, won't we?" said Lenore.

"It's never easy, is it?" asked Valv, arming his pistol. " 'ere we go, den. No time for whingin' about it. Let's go boys. We got a job ta finish, don't we?"

The gremlins ran in the direction of the crawlers.

41

forced fumble

"One!" yelled Loric.

Thomas's sportif made a move towards the football. He reached down and shut the ball that still contained the Infosphere.

"That is not necessary," said Gideon Upshaw into the microphone.

The Three Primes' hovercraft backed away as the secret service-bots protected them. Drones and securtifs surrounded the Scargen sportifs. The crowd cheered, unaware that what they were witnessing was not part of the show. Thomas's sportif picked up the ball and raised it above his head. The crowd grew louder.

"What are you doing?" asked Gordon.

"That's a good question," said Loric.

"Put that ball back down," said the director. "This is not in the script."

"We're improvising," said Thomas as he cut communication with Gordon. "Okay, guys. I hope you are ready for this."

He tossed the ball backwards to Anson. The collectorbots moved to engage. Their progress was impeded by a stampede of buffalo that sprung forth from Yareli's spirit arrow. The crowd expressed their approval.

"Let's get out of here before they realize what's actually going on," said Anson.

"Too late," said Itsuki. "The HOUNDs are moving to intercept."

The humans on the field began to disperse. The hovercraft containing Gideon Upshaw and Thatcher Wikkaden had also backed away.

"I guess halftime's over," said Thomas.

"Garron, Fargus, see what you can do about the HOUNDs," said Loric. "Thomas and I will give Anson some cover."

"Got it," said Garron.

"Aw'right," said Fargus.

Olly wasted no time running directly at the HOUNDs from the side, knocking one of them over. The HOUND slid across the field's surface, tearing it apart.

Thomas turned around to see Garron firing at a HOUND as it approached. The artif avoided the blasts and jumped at Garron. Garron's sportif grabbed the HOUND in midair and flung it back towards one of the collectorbots. The collectorbot was destroyed instantly. The HOUND rolled twice and popped back up as if nothing had happened.

Thomas transformed his hands into cannons and began firing at the securtifs. Loric did the same. Anson joined in with his open hand.

"There are far too many innocent people in the stands," said Anson. "We need to move, now."

He did not see the collectorbot coming from behind him. The artif hit Anson's arm that was carrying the ball, knocking over RB24. The ball went flying in the air. One of the HOUNDs jumped and caught it in his teeth.

"Concentrate fire on that HOUND," said Anson as he stood the artif back up.

Loric flew directly at the robotic beast, knocking into it in midair. The ball was jarred loose from the hit and began to fall to the ground. Thomas ran at the ball, reached down to grab it, but before he could, the ball was shot out from underneath his sportif's hands. Thomas looked around to see the source of the blast as more shots rained down at him. He found the origin of the assault. Thatcher Wikkaden's arm cannon was firing down at Thomas from the hovercraft Wikkaden and Upshaw shared. Before Thomas could give chase, another group of HOUNDs entered the fray from the tunnels. Guns emerged from the top and sides of the artifs. They began to fire at the sportifs. A spirit arrow erupted as three large spider spirits landed on the HOUNDs. The arachnids began to spin webs, entangling the robotic dogs.

"I agree with Mancer Warwick," said Garron. "We need to secure the ball and get out of here."

"First , however, we need to even out these odds," said Loric. "I no longer have any control over the stadium or the securtifs."

"Affirmative," said Fargus's artif.

Olly was the first to fly into the sky. He began firing down around the others, destroying artif after artif, but still more entered the battle.

"Bartleby, get down here with Itsuki and Yareli," said Loric. "But do not uncloak. The last thing we need is for this crowd to panic. The longer they think it is part of the halftime show the better."

"On duh way," said Bartleby.

Thomas looked around and there was no sign of Wikkaden or Upshaw. Then he saw the ball. It was sitting in the middle of the field surrounded by collectorbots and securtifs. He moved to engage the artifs when a series of spirit arrows ignited in front of him. Three grizzly bears fell into the circle of artifs and began their attack. Itsuki dropped from above, bisecting one of the collectorbots with his sword.

"Suke," said Thomas. "I'm glad you could join us."

"Behind you!" shouted the boy. He jumped off the artif and over Thomas's sportif.

Thomas turned around in time to see that Itsuki had landed onto the attacking HOUND before the robot could react, stabbing downward into the artifs head. The Augmentor ran down the body of the machine and into the group of securtifs, hacking his way through. Thomas moved into the newly formed breach.

Wiyaloo stood in the middle of the surrounding artifs. The Spirit Ghost Warrior fired pulse after pulse into the mob of robots, incinerating one after another. Thomas joined him as he ran to the ball.

"I'm about to secure the Infosphere," said Thomas. "When I do, we get out of here ASAP."

"We have another problem," said Yareli.

"What now?" asked Thomas as he reached down and plucked the ball from the ground. *Gotch ya.*

"They are closing the roof of the stadium."

The words were still resonating in his head when he was blindsided from the left. Two of the HOUNDs were on him, firing as they advanced. He did all he could to control the ball while fighting off the artifs. His shield was holding but just barely. A third HOUND appeared on his right.

"This isn't good," said Thomas, desperately firing at both sides.

Garron dropped in next to the Bearer. "I'm on it," said Garron as he opened fire on the two on the left, incapacitating both of the artifs.

Thomas was left to deal with the remaining HOUND. He unloaded two missiles from his left forearm. The projectiles found the target, knocking the HOUND backwards.

"T-t-thanks," said Thomas.

"You would have done the same for me," said Garron.

I'm not so sure about that, thought the Bearer. He engaged the propulsion units in his legs and began to hover.

"Protect Thomas," said Anson. "We have overstayed our welcome."

"You heard the wolf," said Loric. "Secure Scargen, and let us make a hasty retreat." The sportifs launched into the sky surrounding their quarterback. Thomas flew straight up towards the closing roof. Thomas's sportif breached the stadium's roof and flew into the night sky. Garron followed him, securing his backside. Thomas could still hear the murmur from the crowd. They had no idea what had actually just transpired.

The others followed, firing down into the stadium. Wiyaloo had grabbed Itsuki and flown up behind them. Thomas looked back down into Sky Field as the roof stopped closing. The remaining HOUNDs transformed into more humanoid shaped artifs and launched after the sportifs.

"Dat was bloody mental," said Bartleby. "Yareli and I are right behind ya."

Thomas saw the dragon decloak. Wiyaloo placed Itsuki on the back of Bartleby. "We finish off dese last few stragglers and high tail it out uv 'ere. We'll all be in Warwick's laughin' in no time."

Thomas began to look around as seven GA battleships decloaked, surrounding them. Hundreds of collectorbots, drones, and the transformed HOUNDs filed out of the airships and filled the sky around Thomas and his companions.

"I think we should hold off the celebration just a little longer," said Thomas.

One of the HOUNDs moved forward. Two of the other HOUNDs fell in behind. These HOUNDs were painted slightly different.

That must designate a higher rank, thought Thomas. *There are people in there.*

It was then he heard the familiar voice fill the inside of his sportif. "This is Thatcher Wikkaden. You are in violation of Section 2452 of the Hunter Code. Return the Infosphere and your lives will be spared." His holographic image was where the director's had been. "If you do not comply, I will have no choice but to destroy every last one of you defects."

He must be in that HOUND in the front. And if I had to bet, I'd say his lackeys, Okland and Pekora, are in the other two. But which one is which? The sniper Okland had almost killed Thomas in London. He had not forgotten him or Pekora who had used her ability to detect his power signature on the roof where the Hosselfot deal had gone wrong. *How could a Mage work for these people?* Thomas reached down to respond to Wikkaden.

"Hey, Thatch. It's been a while. How the heck are ya? I haven't seen you in like a year or so."

"To whom am I speaking?"

"I don't think that really matters at this point, but, if you really must know, the name's Thomas Scargen. You might have heard of me."

Wikkaden's mouth hung open, speechless.

"But you're dead," said Pekora's voice as her hologram appeared on another holoscreen.

"Oh yeah that. Funny thing, turns out, I'm not."

"I remember you now," said Pekora. "You're the kid from London who was with Chula. I never forget a power sig—especially one that high."

"Bingo . . . get the lady a prize. You're not as stupid as Yareli says you are. You're in the HOUND to the right. I'm guessing that strictly based on the sensory equipment rig on your artif—pretty narsh mod, all things considered. My dad's company still does good work. And that would mean Okland's HOUND is on the left. Makes sense that it's littered with an excessive amount of weapons."

"B-b-but how are y—" started Pekora.

"It's been great catching up and all, but I want to talk to the man in charge—not the useless minions," said Thomas, cutting off Pekora's words. Thomas switched off the holoscreen she was on. "So just follow my train of thought for a second, Thatch. Me being who I am, well, that means the Infosphere that you want so badly, technically belongs to me, so I'd suggest you take your freakish cyborg ass, collect up Okland and Pekora, and all your little artif friends here, get in your fancy little battleships, and go back to whatever rock you slithered out from." Thomas paused for a second. "There's no way, while I still draw breath, that you're getting this back. Okay? Comply with that, you asshole." Thomas turned off Wikkaden's holoscreen, ending the transmission.

42

atlantis has fallen

They had entered the city easily. Delphin had been correct about the minimal security in the escape tunnels. The tunnels were a series of swim tubes that lead into the heart of Atlantis. Both teams had made their way to their respective entry points cloaked. The artifs had done the same. Evangeline's team was going into the Palace. Marcus's team was to engage the Citadel to secure the Medenculus.

"I have the RA ready to deploy, Captain," said Taunt.

The recovery artif detached from one of the larger artifs and now rested in Taunt's hand. The Riders had decloaked. They were hidden behind a wall that wound its way around the Citadel. Two menacing Kra guards flanked the entrance, holding energy staffs. Their crustacean-like bodies held up their more humanoid torsos.

"Let it go," said Marcus. "If we do this right, we can obtain the stone without the Atlanteans realizing what is happening."

"Here goes nothing," said Taunt as the small artif took off in the direction of the Citadel.

The RA immediately cloaked. Taunt pulled up his screen so he could track the robots movements and guide it if needed. Marcus did the same in his visor display.

"What do we do now?" asked Jurdik.

"We wait," said Marcus. "And secure this position. We don't need any surprises compromising our location."

"I was afraid you were going to say that," said Jurdik.

"The RA has entered the Citadel," said Taunt. "So far so good."

Jurdik turned towards Vance and Kist. "I need you two protecting our six."

"On it," said Vance as the two moved out.

Jurdik turned to two more of the Riders. "You two move to take positions across the alley. I need eyes on those Kra."

The readings on Marcus's visor indicated the movements were carried out according to Jurdik's orders.

"The Riders are cloaked and in position."

"Good," said Marcus. He looked over at Taunt. "What's the status of that recovery artif?"

"The RA has made its way to the seventh level of the Citadel," said Taunt. "Shouldn't be long now."

"That is good new—"

"We are under attack," said Evangeline into Marcus's helmet, interrupting the Captain's words. "We have been found out. Requesting backup."

"We could make it to your position in a short period of time," responded Marcus.

"You need to stay put and retrieve the stone."

"General, I am coming to personally ensure your safety," said Marcus.

"You are to stay put and complete your mission, Captain. That is a direct order."

"Yes, General." Marcus was not happy, but an order is an order.

"Send as many Riders as you can without compromising the mission," said Evangeline. "It is a small skirmish as of now, but I'd like to squash it before it gets any worse."

"Send ten of the artifs and a squadron to rendezvous at the General's location. Taunt, get me that stone."

"Almost there. We're in the room that houses the Medenculus. I've spotted it, Captain. So far they have not noticed the RA."

The Captain directed his attention to the RA's feed in his visor.

"Nice and easy. We're not going to have a lot of time once the stone is removed. I need everyone to be ready to move on my order."

The recovery artif flew in the direction of the Medenculus. The stone was connected to a series of attachments that fed energy to the city. Marcus could see that the artif was extending its two claws. The claws gripped the stone. "Get ready," said Taunt.

The artif jerked the stone out of its resting place, immediately causing an alarm to sound and the lights to dim in the city. Warnings in Atlantean rang out across the city. The recovery artif secured the stone inside of itself and sped off. Laser blasts fired at the artif. The RA dodged the attacks as it zipped out of the building.

"We have secured the Medenculus," said Marcus.

"Excellent," said Evangeline. "Where is the backup we requested? We are pinned down and need assistance."

"I sent them to rendezvous with you. They must have met some resistance on the way."

"The recovery artif has made its way out of the Citadel," said Taunt.

The artif entered the room they were hiding in and decloaked.

"Good job, Taunt."

"We don't have much time before the city is crawling with Kra, Captain," said Delphin.

Marcus had almost forgotten he was there. He had not said much after they had entered the city. "We meet at the General's location for backup."

The cloaked Riders moved on his orders through the streets of Atlantis. They hopped into the swim tubes and exited on the level closest to the Palace. Marcus could see what had happened to his men. The Riders lay dead around the exit. Their corpses were mixed in with the destroyed shells of the artifs that had accompanied them.

"They must have seen them coming."

"Correct, surfacewalker."

Marcus spun to see who had said this. The Atlantean guard began to surround them on hover vehicles. They all wore armor and helmets with visors. The Mer in the front of the Atlantean guard wore more ornate armor than the others. He appeared to be in charge.

"You can decloak now. We can see you plain as day," said the Mer. "Atlantean tech is unrivaled."

Marcus was the first comply.

"I believe you have something that belongs to me."

"And who might you be?" asked the Captain.

"I am Jusip Tad, the Sovereign of Atlantis."

"Then you're just the man I was looking for," said the Captain as he threw his hand forward. The yellow energy hit the sovereign square in his chest, knocking him off of the vehicle. "Now, Kist."

Rider Kist stepped forward and circled her hands. Her eyes glowed blue as she pulled water from the swim tube, forming a wall in front of the Atlanteans. She pushed her hands outward and the water splashed down onto the Atlantean guard. The Riders attacked at once behind the wave strike. The Atlanteans recovered quickly and engaged the Riders.

The battle waged on for some time at a virtual standstill. Marcus moved out from cover and advanced quickly up to one of the Kra soldiers. He engaged both of his energy weapons and made quick work of the shelled Atlantean. Two more Kra attacked the Captain. He electrocuted the first one and sliced the head off of the second. He looked over to see that Vedd Delphin had engaged Jusip Tad. Delphin had picked up a discarded energy staff. He wielded it like a natural.

"You will pay for your crimes against the people of Atlantis," said Delphin as he rushed at Tad.

Tad blocked the blow. "I know you, don't I? You are one of Galeos's men."

The two traded attacks as the Captain continued to engage the enemy.

"Captain, are you there?" asked Evangeline. "We have secured our position."

"Good. We could use some help getting the stone out of here."

"On our way."

"Taunt, push the men forward."

"What about Delphin?"

"He is fighting his fight."

As Marcus said the words he saw the demons emerge from the swim tubes. Four of them. They were monstrous beasts conjured from the seas of the Dark Realm. They were long creatures with tentacles instead of feet. Their arms sprouted out of their spiked shoulders and ended in massive hands with fingers that were segmented like the legs of a crab. Their faces were covered with a shell mask, similar to the boned mask of a crag.

"Thul," said Marcus. "Lord Grimm isn't taking any chances with his precious cargo." Marcus knew what these creatures were capable of.

Thul entered the city with little pushback from the Atlantean forces. The Kra soldiers who had come out to meet them were quickly handled. The tentacled beasts were fierce opponents. Thul moved effortlessly through the defensive line of the Atlanteans, blazing a trail for the Riders.

The first cannon blast hit one of the demons in his chest, forming a huge hole. The beast screamed in terror and moved towards the cannon. Two more shots and the beast was down.

They must be the Medenculus-powered weapons Delphin spoke of, thought Marcus.

The remaining thul moved towards the guns that lined the walls of the Citadel. The first thul ripped the cannon pilot from his chair and tore him in two. The two cannons to each side of the vacated weapon turned and opened fire on the thul, killing the massive beast where it stood.

Marcus spun around to take in his surroundings. His gaze focused on Vedd Delphin, who now stood above Tad. The sovereign appeared to be dead. Delphin tossed his staff aside and slumped down.

"We have to get out of here," said Marcus.

Instantly the streets were filled with Atlantean soldiers, both Mer in hover vehicles and Kra guards. The Atlantean reinforcements had arrived.

"We're trapped."

"I wouldn't say that," said Evangeline as she emerged next to Marcus. Her eyes were blacked out as she advanced towards the Atlantean troops.

"What are you doing?"

"Getting us out of here, Captain."

She moved back her arms and pushed them forward. Black ooze poured from her hands, enveloping the first line of Atlanteans. Others swiftly took their place, firing down from their hover vehicles, and still more approached on the street level.

"It's not working," said Marcus. "Let's go."

"That is only the beginning." She rushed into the middle of the soldiers in a blur. The Atlanteans turned to deal with her. "Ahhhhhh!" yelled Evangeline.

The dark energy wave started at the center of her curved frame and shot outward at a tremendous rate. The explosion was immense and the power of the blast knocked the Captain backwards. The energy output destroyed the first three floors of the Citadel. The tower crumbled and fell to the ground. Smoke and dust billowed from the downed structure.

When Marcus stood on his feet he looked out to what she had done. *No*, he thought. *How could she be capable of something like this?*

The General returned to her Riders, walking through the corpses of the Atlanteans as smoke swirled around her.

"What have you done?" asked Marcus.

"What was needed, no more," said Evangeline.

"But you nearly destr—"

"I made our escape possible, Captain. And how I run this legion is none of your concern."

"I just can't believe you could—"

"The matter is closed. Now, I have new orders for you from Lord Grimm."

"I want to see if my men are all right and help secure the stone."

"That will be handled. Lord Grimm has hand-picked you for a separate mission—one he needs taking care of as soon as possible."

"Where am I going?"

"It appears you are taking a trip to New Amsterdam. The specifics have been forwarded to you." She hit a button on the Taunter and two small orbs floated over to Marcus. "I was told you will need these."

Marcus opened a compartment on his forearm armor. The two spheres entered it.

"What do they do?"

"I am not certain. Lord Grimm said you would know when they were needed." She walked away from the Captain as if they did not know each other. "Let's get out of this place."

She motioned to the Riders and they all dropped into the swim tubes. Marcus turned and saw Vedd Delphin looking around confused and upset.

"I have made a terrible mistake," said Delphin. "I am the reason they are dead. I did this."

"I am sorry for your loss, Delphin, but sometimes change comes at a cost. Without Tad in power, your city has a chance. I cannot condone what the General has done here, but it might be what was needed for Atlantis."

"What are you going to do with me?" asked Delphin.

"You are going to stay and help your people," said Marcus. "We have no further use for you. You held up your part of the bargain. I will do the same."

"Honor is a quality of an excellent leader."

"After today, I'm not so sure I know what honor is."

"Can you promise me one thing?"

"What is it?"

"Do not kill him. He is the only hope for this city."

"What do you mean?"

"I have been at this for a long time, Marcus. They looked inside of my head. They know about the Axe. It is only a matter of time before you will be sent to collect it."

The Atlantean was right. Marcus's orders were to bring back the Axe, whatever the cost.

"Promise me you will not kill Cayde Galeos."

Marcus looked the Atlantean directly in his eyes.

"You have my word."

43

shutdown

Lenore ran across to the air shaft that was closest to the approaching crawlers. She popped around the corner and fired. One of the crawlers exploded. "Okay, it could be worse. Dere's only about fifteen of dem."

"Only?" asked Aiken. "Dat seems like a bit uv a problem."

"Nonsense," said Valv. "Just a bit uv bloody target practice, right?"

He turned the corner and shot into the advancing crawlers. Two crawlers moved up to the ceiling of the shaft. Valv blasted both of them in a single burst. He returned to the safety of the perpendicular shaft.

"Dey are movin' forward. We need to make a push."

"You heard the gremling. Everyone, get ready to open fire," said Lenore. "We will go two at a time from each side . . . go!"

Aiken popped out and fired. He missed all of the crawlers. Torc had fared no better on the other side. Then Lenore blindly fired out of the side of the shaft, hitting another artif. Valv also had success with his shooting.

"There should only be about ten left."

"What are we gonna do?" asked Aiken.

Lenore did not know what to say.

"I 'av an idea," said Torc as two more recon orbs floated out of his device. "Dey seem to fink duh recon orbs are wurvy targets. So let's give dem some more fings to worry about."

The orbs flew at the crawlers, which began to focus their fire on the orbs. Some of the crawlers began firing at each other in the confusion, destroying each other. The orbs zoomed through the chaos. The crawlers turned to pursue the orbs.

"Let's move," said Lenore. Valv wheeled out into the corridor and fired blindly at the backs of the crawlers.

The gremlins all entered the shaft and advanced their attack, destroying all the crawlers that had filled the space. The four gremlins stood among the mass of ruined tech as it sparked and whirled.

"Dat was fun," said Valv. "But we should probably pop off to duh bloody roof." The words had just left his mouth as he hit by the first blast. Valv spun backward, falling to the ground.

"Valv!" said Lenore, running to his aid. She fired and hit the weak spot on the lone crawler at the end of the shaft.

"Lenore . . ." said Torc.

"What is it, Torc? Me 'ands are kind of full right now, aren't dey?"

"Dere seems to be quite a few more crawlers making dere way to our current location."

"Dat's not good news," said Aiken.

"What do you mean by quite a few more?" asked Lenore.

"Dere are forty-two crawlers on duh way to intercept us."

"What are we gonna do?" asked Aiken.

"It gets worse," said Torc. "Dey are coming from multiple directions."

"Bloody 'ell," said Aiken.

"Don't panic, Aiken. 'elp me move 'im."

Aiken grabbed the one arm of Valv and Lenore grabbed the other and drug him to the perpendicular corridor. This corridor had a fan at the end of it—a dead end.

" 'ow much time do we 'av before dey get 'ere?" asked Lenore.

"None," said Torc as the sound of active crawlers echoed from all directions.

"Okay, you can panic now," said Lenore. "Valv." She shook the gremlin.

He woke from his unconsciousness. "What happened? Oww!" said Valv. "Dose lit'l buggers sting."

"Good, you're alive," said Lenore.

"Not for long, dough," said Aiken.

"What is 'ee whingin' about?"

"See for yourself," said Torc, showing him the view from the recon orbs on his holoscreen. Crawlers began to enter the corridors. They crawled down every inch of the adjacent shafts and soon they would be entering the one the four companions were nestled in.

"Well, I have to say, it's been an absolute pleasure servin' and workin' wif you guys," said Valv.

"Duh pleasure was ours," said Lenore.

The crawlers were getting closer now. It would not be long.

"I never thought I'd die in a ventilation shaft," said Aiken. He pulled the bottle out of his pack. He popped the top off and took a sip of the Gloop. He passed the bottle to Valv. "Dis should 'elp ease duh pain a bit."

Valv took a gulp and then passed it to Torc. Torc drew from the bottle and then passed it to Lenore. She sipped from the green liquid. The mechanized sounds of legs moving echoed all around them now. The end was near.

"I'll tell you one fing, I'm not gonna die just sittin' on me arse," said Lenore.

"Nor I, deary," said Valv.

"I'm in," said Aiken.

"Dat makes four uv us," said Torc. The gremlins all raised their weapons as Valv finished off the bottle of Gloop. He threw the bottle into the shaft and it was immediately destroyed by the blasts from both directions.

"As long as we're breavin', we still 'av a chance," said Lenore.

"Not a good one, mind you, but I know what your gettin' at, deary." The gremlins entered the corridor, pistol's firing.

"Ahhhhhh!" yelled Lenore with her eyes closed. She felt the tap on her shoulder. She opened her eyes and ceased firing.

She could not believe what she saw. The corridor was filled with inactive crawlers—some still dangling from the ceiling. She turned around and saw her companions.

"It appears dey 'av been deactivated," said Torc.

"How?" asked Lenore.

"I have deactivated the maintenance artifs," said the voice of LINC.

"What 'appened to you?"

"I had been hit by one of the securtifs before I could complete my communications with you. The blast resulted in internal damage to my communication tech. The injury sustained was nominal, but took some time for my internal diagnostic program to isolate and correct it."

"I bloody love you, LINC," said Lenore.

"I cannot reciprocate these emotions, but do appreciate the sentiment on face value. Please proceed to the extraction point. I have reconvened with the vampire and Mancer Lolani. We will be at the extraction point in approximately 4 minutes, 21 seconds. We are not alone."

"You 'erd duh bloody artif," said Lenore. "Let's get movin'."

"What did 'ee mean not alone?" asked Torc.

"I suppose we will find out shortly, won't we?" said Valv.

After climbing over the deactivated crawler corpses, the gremlins made their way through the maze of shafts to the roof access point. LINC had no further communication with the group. Valv blasted the grate off. He had had enough of the ventilation shafts.

The four gremlins had made it to the roof in four minutes time and they were the only ones there.

"Where are dey?" asked Aiken. "Dose crawlers won't stay deactivated forever."

Then Lenore saw them.

LINC was carrying Lolani as he flew up and over the side of the building. Malcolm fired red energy blasts down the side of the building—his wings lifting him upward. The artif dropped the Mancer when they reached the top. LINC's arms transformed into cannons. He began to fire alongside Malcolm. Shortly after, Mancer Lolani entered the fray. Hundreds of Scargen securtifs flew up and around the three of them. "LINC, are you aw'right?" asked Lenore. "Do you need 'elp?"

"Negative, Lenore Bugden. We have the current situation under control. Do not show yourselves at this time. The Infosphere must remain out of sight." LINC pivoted at his waist destroying artif after artif—blasts deflecting off of his shield.

"Nice shootin', Tinman," said Malcolm as he flew at one of the artifs, tearing its head off its torso. "You 'av to watch where you're 'eddin', mate."

Lolani remained on the ground, chanting and hurling waves of white energy at the advancing securtifs. Lenore almost felt bad for the artifs. They had bitten off more than they could chew.

Talya's teleportal ripped open above Scargen Tower. The dragon flew straight down into the fight and unleashed a fire attack on the drone systems that had entered the battle. The drones caught fire, exploding above the gremlins. The dragon made her way to Lolani. The Mancer jumped onto the mount. LINC and Malcolm continued to clean up the remaining artifs as Talya landed in front of the gremlins.

"Get on," said Talya. "We don't have much time."

The gremlins crawled onto the Dracavea.

"Aloha. It is good to see you four," said Lolani as the dragon took off into the sky. "Let's go see what we got."

The dragon opened an exit. Malcolm broke off his attack and flew through first. He was followed by LINC and then the dragon.

44

sphere today

The sky above the city of Dallas was lit with laser blasts, fire, and magic. Thomas's diatribe against Thatcher Wikkaden had not been well received. They had successfully defended themselves against the first wave of drones and collectorbots, but successive waves kept attacking. Thomas still had the ball that contained the Infosphere, but the battle had taken its toll on his sportif.

"We can't keep up this pace," said Thomas. "They're every-freakin-where."

"You did say that they would only get the sphere over your dead body," said Itsuki as he slashed into the air, sending a pulse wave at one of the HOUNDs.

"I know, Suke, I know. It seemed like a good idea at the time. I thought we'd just open a teleportal and zoom out of here. How was I supposed to know they were ready for that?"

They had tried several times to retreat, but the artifs just kept surrounding Thomas's sportif, making it impossible for Bartleby to reach him. They split up into two groups. Garron, Anson, and Loric were protecting Thomas, while Fargus, Wiyaloo, Itsuki, and Yareli helped to defend Bartleby. The dragon was the only viable means of escape. Pekora, Okland, and several other HOUNDs had gone out of their way to occupy the dragon, chasing Bartleby across the evening sky. Fargus and Wiyaloo had moved to intercept the dragon's attackers. The gremlin seemed at home in the sportif, and Wiyaloo was more than holding his own. They, assisted by the attacks of Yareli and Itsuki, held the HOUNDs at bay, but the group was still not able to get away.

The battleships were also proving to be an annoyance. Anson and Loric had managed to destroy two of them and incapacitate a third, but four remained. The odds were not in their favor. To make matters worse, Thomas's shields were beginning to fail, and he was pretty sure the others were facing similar situations. They needed to do something, and fast.

"We have successfully extracted the Infosphere from Scargen Tower, Thomas Scargen," said LINC inside Thomas's earb.

Garron destroyed two HOUNDs that had closed in from Thomas's right. Garron had stayed close to Thomas. He was protecting Thomas's right side. Thomas could only use his left arm's weapon systems while holding the ball.

"We have secured the Infosphere and dropped off the gremlings with said Infosphere in Sirati. There, High Mancer Bebami will use the medallions to open the Infosphere and ascertain its contents."

"Well, can the rest of you get your asses here?" A blast bounced off his weakened shield. "We could use some help getting *this* Infosphere secured." Thomas shot another collectorbot out of the sky.

"We'll be dere in a second, Tommy," said Malcolm. "Don't you worry none."

"So we still don't know which one you have?" asked Garron.

"Nope," said Thomas. "We'll know soon enough."

"Anson and I are in a bit of a pickle at the moment," said Loric.

Thomas turned to see the two sportifs surrounded by ten collectorbots.

A teleportal tore open above Thomas. LINC flew through the opening followed by Malcolm, and Talya with Lolani riding on top. They were quick to enter the battle. Malcolm flew downward, landing on one of the collectorbots that circled his brother and Loric. He ripped off the artif's arm, while it was still firing.

"Look what I've found." He turned the weapon on another

collectorbot, destroying it before the weapon had sputtered out. Malcolm tossed aside the arm and punched through the collectorbot's torso. The robot exploded as the vampire leapt from it—wings extended.

"Reinforcements. Splendid," said Anson. "Thank you, Brother," said Anson as he blasted the collectorbot next to the one his brother had just destroyed.

"Who knew I could be so disarming?" said the vampire.

"Better a witty fool, than a foolish wit," replied Anson.

"You two can exude your brotherly love later," said Loric as he rushed at one of the collectorbots, knocking it sideways directly into the fire pouring forth from Talya's open mouth.

"Sod off, Loric," said Malcolm. "You ungrateful git."

"Always the eloquent one," said Loric.

Collectorbots and drones were quick to blanket Talya. She was another perceived means of escape. Lolani moved her hands as a white energy pulse ripped through the oncoming artifs, but still more took their places.

"We need to get Scargen as far away from here as possible," said Loric.

"I'm open to suggestions," said Thomas as he spun and released two missiles at one of the battleships below them.

The starboard side of the ship exploded in flames. Collectorbots and drones poured out of the ship as it began to succumb to gravity.

"Taxpayer's dollars hard at work."

LINC had moved alongside Thomas. The artif began to target and destroy collectorbots. Thomas turned to his right as a blast hit his left arm, spinning him sideways. It was Wikkaden's HOUND. Thomas's sportif began to fall towards the city. Before he could recover, Wikkaden followed with a right cross to Thomas's sportif. Alarms began to sound inside QB19 as the artif hit the side of the skyscraper full force. The sportif landed inside of the building, bouncing a couple times before grinding to a halt.

"What hit me?" asked Thomas as he slowly got up. He did not see the second punch coming.

The hook jarred Thomas's sportif through the floor of the skyscraper and out the side of it. He spun and hit the adjacent building and began to fall towards the street. The sportif crashed into the middle of the intersection.

Thomas shook his head. "Ouch." He stood the sportif back up and shot into the sky. "Where is he?"

The HOUND fell in behind him. Thomas turned to fire at the chasing HOUND.

Once more Wikkaden moved to attack. Thomas was by himself in the middle of Dallas, weaving in and out of buildings. There was no help to be found. Garron was busy with his own HOUND and LINC had engaged several drones and collectorbots that had moved in from one of the battleships above the city. Thomas accelerated and turned upwards, trying to reach his companions, but Wikkaden cut him off, raised the HOUND's weapon system, and took aim. One more direct hit and Thomas's shield would be done for.

The pack of wolves dropped onto the HOUND without warning. They began to gnaw at the exterior of the suit, tearing it apart. Yareli had shot the arrow from quite a distance. Wikkaden accelerated upward, trying to shake the spirit animals, but he could not. The wolves wasted no time. They quickly tore off the HOUND's limbs. Wikkaden was a sitting duck. The middle section of the HOUND's torso opened up and a small compartment jettisoned itself. Wikkaden Thatcher rocketed out of the HOUND and back towards the battleship. Drones moved to protect their leader.

Thomas sighed in relief. "Thanks, Yar."

"He's getting away!" shouted Yareli as she fired another arrow at Pekora who attacked from the right side of Bartleby alongside several drones.

The arrow transformed into a puma. The wildcat latched on to the HOUND as it spun out of control and away from the dragon. Wiyaloo moved to take care of the drones. He unleashed a flurry of energy blasts from his paw. Each blast found its target.

Okland attacked from underneath while the Spirit Ghost Warrior was occupied. The blast hit Bartleby's shield.

"Dat one bloody 'urt," said Bartleby. "I don't know how much more I can take of dis."

Okland opened fire again, but this time Fargus moved in to intercept as Itsuki deflected the blasts.

"Give em 'ell, Olly," said the gremlin as Olly's arm cannons churned out energy blasts.

Okland dodged the first few but the last one hit the Hunter directly in his artif's chest. The HOUND dropped lifeless, seemingly frozen in time as the dragon sped away.

"We're almost clear," said Yareli.

"I wish we could say the same," said Thomas. "I'm one shot away from having no shields and there's a rather large swarm of drones coming this way."

Six squadrons of drones moved in to protect the escaping Wikkaden. Half of them covered the Hunter and the other half advanced on Garron, Thomas, and LINC.

"Get back to back with me," said Garron. "I'll extend my shield to surround you as well."

"But won't that weaken your shield?"

"Yes, but we don't have much of a choice," said Garron. "If you die, this will all be for nothing."

The three companions unleashed their attack on the advancing drones.

The earb in Thomas's right ear chimed, signifying an incoming message. "What do you got for me?" asked Thomas. "We're a bit busy at the moment."

"I know, my boy," said the voice of Ziza. "I have important news."

"Sorry, High Mancer. I didn't realize it was you. Let me put you through to everyone." Thomas continued to engage the enemy back to back with Garron. LINC moved out to meet the advancing hoard.

"I have opened the Infosphere," said the voice of Ziza. "It contains the AIRS unit, or actually, *is* the AIRS unit. Clever contraption actually. It also seems to contain a good number of your father's files," said Ziza. "I just thought you should all know the significance of what it is you are fighting for."

"That's great news," said Thomas as the realization of what he was carrying began to settle in. The Ignus was inside the football he carried, and they seemed to be slowly turning the tide. *Looks like everything's working out just fine. We should be out of here in no time.*

"That means that we definitely have the red st—" Garron's words ended abruptly.

The explosion happened so quickly, Thomas did not know what happened. The blast had knocked Thomas's artif away from Garron's, but he still held onto the ball. Alarms echoed inside the sportif as Thomas's ears rang. His shield had failed. Thomas unsheathed the Gauntlet and pushed his own energy shield out around him. He had to protect the Infosphere no matter what.

"Nooooo!" shouted Yareli.

Thomas turned around to survey the scene. Garron's sportif was engulfed in flames. Smoldering robotic parts fell down into the city below them. The sportif was completely destroyed, and there was no sign of Garron.

"What happened?" asked Anson.

"Garron!" yelled Yareli. "Where . . . where is he?"

Thomas began to search for the attacker when the dark beast flashed in front of him. It was the source of the attack—a wingless black dragon, the one from his dream.

The reality of the situation began to set in. *He's gone,* thought Thomas. The black Aequos had appeared from nowhere and killed Garron Dar. He could not help but think about how Yareli must feel. His thoughts quickly evaporated when the dragon rushed directly at Bartleby. *Man, he's fast,* thought Thomas. There was no way that Thomas would catch him in time with the condition his sportif was in.

"Bartleby, turn around!" Thomas engaged the propulsion systems and raced after the black Aequos, firing at the beast. The dragon dodged the blasts and still gained speed.

Bartleby turned to see the dark beast, but it was too late. He had been engaged with one of the last HOUNDs. The black dragon collided with Bartleby, throwing Yareli off of his back. Itsuki somehow held on to Bartleby. Yareli plummeted towards the ground, her hands flailing at her side.

"Hellllp!"

"Yar!" shouted Thomas, dropping his shield and changing his trajectory.

The dragon had done the same. The black Aequos barreled straight down and caught Yareli with its talons. Thomas accelerated once more as he saw the teleportal rip open in front of the dragon. The beast disappeared through the rift with Yareli.

Thomas bore down, pushing the sportif to its limits. "Come on!"

"No, Thomas, do not go thr—" The words of Anson Warwick were cut off as Thomas entered the teleportal, still holding the ball.

45

axed

Marcus raced through the water below New Amsterdam. He did not like leaving Evangeline and the others, but he had little choice. Lord Grimm had given him a mission— secure the Axe. *I guess I'm going to get to meet Cayde Galeos after all.*

The Captain had turned on his suit's cloaking mechanism as he approached the bottom of Falrin Level. He swam upward, towards the opening. He passed through the force field that held back the ocean waters and landed. Marcus was inside of the Atlantean's lair.

Marcus looked around. The view was breathtaking. The Captain was in awe of the collection of weapons, but these were not the weapons he was sent to collect. The visor's force field displayed the holo-map that Vance had been able to reconstruct from Delphin's mind. The Axe was located on the lower level. Marcus moved to the entry-way that led to this level.

Marcus opened the door, still cloaked, and she was standing in front of him. She was a small Chinese woman—late sixties by the looks of her.

"Show yourself. I don't have all day." The woman sniffed the air. "You know, burgling from an Atlantean sovereign is not wise."

Marcus remained quiet. There was no point in engaging her if he could avoid it.

"Seriously, I can smell you, burglar. I know you're in there, and the sooner you show yourself the sooner we can start this dance." She shuffled into the room Marcus was waiting in. "Suit yourself," said the tiny woman as she transformed into an Aequos.

Marcus looked down at his wristcom and switched on his shield. He was pretty sure what was coming next. She pulled her head back and pushed it forward. The fire poured out onto the level, bending around his shield, divulging his whereabouts.

"Found you."

He barely had time to move. She caught him with the back end of her tail, sending him spinning in the air, but Marcus landed on his feet. His shield had already been drained in Atlantis and now the dragon's fire had all but depleted the suit's reserve power. His cloaking mechanism would be the next to go. If he did not adjust his tactics, his weapon's systems could be next.

"I guess there's no point in hiding anymore," said Marcus as he appeared in front of the dragon. His visor extinguished as the helmet collapsed back down.

"Ah, now that's better," said the dragon. "Now I can see you, burglar." She darted in his direction.

"I'm not so sure you will agree with that statement a minute from now," said Marcus as he pushed his hands forward.

Electricity flowed from the top of his hands and into the approaching Aequos. She stopped in midflight and shook and screamed with pain. Marcus increased his intensity. The dragon stopped moving and Marcus powered down. She hit the ground with a thud, spasming on the ground. The dragon fell unconscious.

"Now *that's* better. Burglar my ass."

"Well, is that not what you are?" asked the man from across the room now leaning in the entryway to the next level.

"I suppose in this circumstance, I am, Sovereign Galeos."

"You know of my name, but I must admit, I do not know of yours."

"I am Captain Marcus Slade of the Grimm Legions."

"I am afraid I have never heard of you. Grimm sounds oddly familiar . . . but I cannot place it."

"Which one will it be?" asked Marcus, changing the subject.

"I do not follow."

"Well, it seems to me that you have a big wall of toys and that we are destined to fight, so I was just wondering which one will it be?"

"Why do you think this is our destiny?"

"In my experience, people don't block doorways, unless they are trying to hide something, and I know what you are hiding." Marcus flew at the man, engaging his energy blade on both Taunters. The red blades illuminated Marcus's face.

Galeos lifted his hand as the staff slapped into it. The staff had blue energy blades on each side. The Atlantean blocked the first attempt and spun the staff in his hands, countering the Captain.

"It seems that this will be more fun than I first anticipated," said Galeos, backing away and setting his feet. "But first, I have to check on something."

Artifs spilled into the room, immediately confronting Marcus as Galeos jumped through the doorway and down the spiraling stairway.

Marcus wasted no time attacking the artifs. Laser fire rained in from all directions as the Captain unleashed his fury on the sentry drones. There were originally fifteen of them, and he had already handled six of them in quick order. Galeos was stalling. Marcus transformed one of his energy weapons into an energy whip. He grabbed one of the artifs in midair and slammed it to the ground. His speed was too much for the drones as he jumped down the stairway.

Galeos met him with an attack of his own halfway down the massive glass stairwell, knocking the Captain backwards. The Atlantean followed it with a blue energy sphere shot from his open hand. The blast caught Marcus squarely in the chest, knocking him into the glass wall. The Captain bounced off as Galeos leapt at him.

Marcus blocked the downward strike at the last second and rolled to his right. He fell down to the next landing. Galeos was quick to join him.

"Giving up so soon, Captain?" asked the Atlantean.

"You should only be so lucky," said Marcus as he pushed forward.

The two men began trading blows as they descended the stairway. Neither one held the advantage for too long. The duel was evenly matched. *What is his weakness?*

When they reached the bottom of the stairway, Marcus was quick to move for the door. The entryway opened up to a long corridor. Galeos again sent an energy attack at Marcus who dove out of the way as he sent his own yellow electricity at the sovereign. Cayde Galeos spun his staff, diffusing the electric current.

"We seem to be getting nowhere," said Galeos.

"I'm not so sure of that," said Marcus. "I have already breached half of your security."

"Ah, but this is where it gets difficult, Captain."

"We'll see about that."

"Sentries, we have a level five alert. Be advised," said Galeos as he moved backwards, towards the set of doors that led to the Axe.

The two securtifs at the doors advanced on Marcus as Galeos himself spun and attacked once more with the staff. Marcus blocked the attack with his energy blade. The two began to exchange blows once more.

I believe this is when I'm supposed to use these, thought Marcus, while blocking the energy attacks from Galeos and the two Sentries.

He lifted the Taunter and a compartment opened. The orbs that Grimm had given him flew from the compartment and straight towards the two securtifs. The orbs whirled around the artif guards and attached themselves to the base of the heads of the securtifs. Seconds later, the artifs ceased their attack. The lights on the robots blinked and changed from blue to red.

"Security override. Clearance granted to Marcus Slade. Proceed."

"Open the doors," said the Captain.

"As you command," said the securtif on his right. The two doors slid to the sides as the interior of the armory revealed itself.

"Thanks for all your help," said Marcus as he raised his hand. "But I'm not sure how long this will last so, you understand." Electricity poured over the two artifs frying them. Their lifeless forms fell to the ground.

"How is this possible?" asked Galeos. "The armory is impenetrable."

"You might want to reassess that last statement," said Marcus.

"You still have to go through me."

"Yeah, I know," said Marcus as he rushed at Galeos.

The Atlantean and the Captain began their dance anew. They continued to fight to a standstill. The Atlantean spun the staff in his right hand and struck down at Marcus, who blocked the blow and pushed Galeos back. *I got it.* The thought jumped into his head. It finally occurred to Marcus what this man's weakness was. Galeos once more moved to engage the Captain.

"It is too bad Vedd isn't here to see this." The expression on Galeos's face changed. "He was right about you making a good leader."

The words froze the man. This was all the time Marcus needed. He made his move, leaping into the air. The Captain's energy blade came down across the forearm of the Atlantean. The staff hit the ground with the left hand of Cayde Galeos still attached. Marcus had sliced it clean off.

Cayde screamed with pain as he fell down, grasping the stub. The energy blade had seemingly cauterized the wound.

"Where is he? What have you done with him?"

"Don't worry, Sovereign. He is safe in Atlantis where he belongs. Delphin made a difficult choice that helped to save your beloved city, but at a price."

"I-I-I don't understand," said Galeos.

"You will soon enough." Marcus walked past the broken Atlantean and directly over to the stasis field that held the Axe. Sentries descended on him. He held out his hand as the Axe flew into it. Energy swirled around his form. The power flowed through Marcus's body. The Captain screamed. The energy shot out from him, destroying all of the remaining sentries. The artifs' bodies crashed to the floor. Marcus had never felt this type of strength before, and he liked it. He could feel his power increasing and not just because he held the weapon. The Axe had awakened his energy level. Marcus turned to walk out and Cayde stood in the doorway—slumped to one side, holding his arm.

"I cannot let you leave here with that," said Galeos. "I made a promise."

"It's like I told your lover. Shit happens." Marcus raised his hand, lifting the Atlantean with the motion. "Lord Grimm awaits."

"I remember now where I heard of this Grimm." Galeos winced with pain. "The demon, Vaw I believe his name was, the one protecting that girl all those years back. The one in China."

Vaw? thought Marcus. *It can't be.* "What was the girl's name?" asked Marcus, pulling the Atlantean closer with telekinesis.

"Evangeline," said Cayde Galeos with no hesitation.

"What?" asked Marcus confused and upset. "T-t-there has to be a mistake."

"No. I will never forget that girl or her name. She said it under fear for her life. She would not lie in this circumstance." The Atlantean stared at Marcus's face. He knew his expression was giving something away. "You know this girl. I can see from your eyes. You and she are close."

"*Were* close . . . don't change the subject. What does *he* have to do with her and the demon?" asked Marcus, dropping the Atlantean.

The Captain powered down. Galeos pulled himself up and leaned himself against the wall.

"Lord Grimm was the beast's summoner. The demon announced this when it rose from the mother's body. Grimm had locked the demon inside of the woman—Evangeline's mother."

"Why would he do such a thing?" asked Marcus.

"That I do not know," said Galeos as he spit out some blood. "Maybe you should ask him."

"I will," said Marcus. *We were there to recover her. But why?*

"What is to happen to the Axe?" asked Galeos.

The question roused Marcus from his pondering. "I will deliver it to Lord Grimm."

"I was afraid you would say that," said Galeos as he made a move towards Marcus, but he fell back down on the ground. Galeos pulled himself up once more, breathing heavily. He slumped down into a sitting position. "What is to happen to me?"

"You will reclaim your place as sovereign."

"You are not going to kill me?"

"No, Your Majesty. I promised Delphin I wouldn't. Regardless of my promise, I would never kill a man of principle and skill like yourself. That kind of death serves no purpose." Marcus looked at the Atlantean's stump. "I think I've done enough."

Marcus walked closer to one of the wells. The helmet reformed itself on his head as the visor shield engaged.

"Don't try following me."

"I don't think I could even if I tried," said Cayde lifting up the stub. "You have it too, by the way."

"What's that?"

"The heart of a leader. You are wasting your energy with this Lord Grimm. You are destined for greater things."

"Aren't we all." Marcus put his boot onto the edge of the well. "Go to Delphin. He awaits you in Atlantis. Things are not the way they were when you left there. Your people need you." He put his other boot up and stood on the well's precipice. "But first, if I were you, Sovereign, I'd get that looked at."

Marcus jumped down the well with Axe in hand.

46

crash and burn

Thomas felt a bit woozy as he tried to exit the cockpit of his sportif. He had gone through the teleportal and almost instantly crashed. He looked down at his wristcom to call Yareli, but it was not functioning. Thomas could not get the cockpit to open. There was a grinding sound but nothing happened. He raised his palm and blew off the chest region of the sportif.

Thomas crawled out of the wreck. He was no longer trapped, but he was a bit confused. Thomas grabbed his head as he looked around. He was inside an ancient temple. There was something oddly familiar about the place. The room he was in was cavernous. He could hear waterfalls around him. *Running water inside . . . or underground?* Smoke swirled around the damaged sportif. The ball was still secured in its hand.

The smoke began to dissipate, and Thomas saw him—the dragon from his dreams. He circled in front of Thomas. Yareli was unconscious in front of the beast.

"I'd step away from her, if I were you," said Thomas.

"I'm not sure you're in a position to be giving orders," said the dragon. "Guards."

Lizards in massive tech suits surrounded Thomas. Their weapons were drawn and pointing at Yareli.

"Who are your friends?"

"They are the Skinx. They do as I say."

"Where are we?"

"Ah, yes. Welcome to Huacas."

"Huacas?" said Thomas. "The Eldre's home?"

"Former home. I'm afraid he has been evicted. We are the new tenants."

"What do you want with her?" asked Thomas.

"Come on, Scargen. Don't be so naive."

"What do you mean?"

"We are not here for Yareli Chula. We are here for you . . . and of course the Ignus."

Two of the Lizards moved over and pried the robotic football out of the sportif's clutches.

"Good luck with that. There's only one way to open that sphere, and I don't have it."

"That is not necessarily my problem."

"How did you know I'd follow you through the teleportal?"

"Your reputation proceeds you. I figured you'd do what any hero would do. Save the damsel in distress."

"I would never call her that to her face, if you know what's good for you, but you got one thing right," said Thomas as he began to form an energy attack. "I am the hero here."

He pushed the energy sphere at the dragon, who flew out of the way and directly at Thomas, spraying fire down on the Bearer. Thomas quickly formed a shield. He could feel the heat as it circled around him. The dragon broke off the attack and landed next to Yareli. Thomas stood there waving his hand in front of his nose.

"Has anyone told you how bad your breath smells?" Thomas drew his hands back once more. His eyes burned hot with power.

"I would reconsider that course of action," said the dragon. "If you attack again, she dies." The dragon moved his hand and Yareli's body rose into the air.

Thomas powered down. The dragon telekinetically moved Yareli over to a glowing circle on the floor. Energy shot up from the floor all around her. A stasis field formed around Yareli, and she floated inside of it.

"There . . . that's better."

The black dragon walked behind a screen that extended across the side of the room. Thomas could see the dragon transform behind the screen. "Sorry for the delay, but this will only take a second."

Thomas could see he had assumed his human form and was changing into clothes.

The man that came out of the end of the screen was slightly above average in height. He had tattoos that stretched up his arms. They reminded Thomas of Arkmalis's markings. The dragon's alter ego also wore a helmet with a distinct mask. An icon adorned the forehead of the mask—an Ancient rune. The inside of the temple was covered in these runes. Thomas recognized it immediately from the story that Cayde Galeos had told him. It was the symbol of the Dragon Council from the city of Drook.

"I must admit, I do find this form repulsive, but it suits its purpose." The dragon's voice sounded slightly amplified. "Where were we . . . Ahh, yes. Why we are all here." He walked closer to the football that the Lizards had pried out of the wreckage.

"What do you want?"

"I'm afraid it's not about what I want." He ripped open the football without touching it, exposing the Infosphere. The sphere floated into his hands. He tossed it up and down in his hand. "It is about what my boss wants."

"And what's that?"

"Well, this . . . and you of course."

"Who exactly is your boss?"

The Aequos looked down on his wristcom and hit a button. "I think it might be best if he just tells you."

The air next to the dragon-man ripped open. Thomas knew what came next. He had seen this before. Two large dark artifs crossed the threshold, weapons drawn. The Grimm Legions' insignia was emblazoned on their bodies. The dark smoke wafted into the chamber from the rift, and then began to solidify. His weapon was the first part of the monster to form. And then Thomas saw him.

He had cleaned up tremendously, dressed in ornately designed black and red robes, but Thomas could never forget this man, who killed his mother and father. Tollin Grimm stood in front of Thomas. He held a dark box in his left hand.

The Gauntlet shocked Thomas. *What was that?*

"Hello, my boy," said Grimm. "How have you been?"

He was stunned, but he moved on instinct. Thomas threw his gauntleted hand forward. "Haaaaaaaaaaaa!"

Grimm swatted the energy attack away.

"Enough!" shouted Grimm. He lifted his hand and Thomas lifted with it. He felt powerless.

"Go ahead and kill me," said Thomas.

Grimm laughed. "I am not here to kill you, Tom. On the contrary." Grimm slithered closer. "I am here because I need your help." He opened the box. A blue glow rose from the container and blanketed Grimm's bandages. "And, Tom, I won't take no for an answer."

The Medenculus floated out of the box. The dragon-man turned towards the blue stone. He seemed mesmerized.

"I got you a little something, Tom, while I was in Atlantis." The Medenculus rocketed at Thomas. He raised his gauntleted hand, and catching the stone, he vanished.

Thomas flashed into existence again and fell to the ground. He sat up with the Medenculus in his hand. He quickly looked around and noticed he was in a cell but something was odd. The architecture and the Ancient tech that controlled the cell were identical to the room he was just in.

"I'm still in Huacas," said Thomas.

He was glad he had not totally abandoned Yareli, but he was still mad at himself for leaving her. Thomas also knew that his best bet for their survival was further augmentation. It was then he saw the Sea Turtle walk out from the shadows. The Turtle was a female, and she was fairly young. She reminded Thomas of the Eldre. She walked over to Thomas and grabbed the Gauntlet. Her eyes glowed the same color as the stone as she looked up and smiled.

"What's your name?" asked Thomas.

"Her name's Yaku," said one of the other two Sea Turtles who showed themselves. "She can't speak . . . well, doesn't speak," said the smaller of the two. "My name's Turu, and this is my brother Kucha. What's your name?"

"That's Thomas Scargen, Turu. He's the reason we're down here I'd guess. He was the one the Eldre went to see."

"That makes a lot of sense. You are the Eldre's disciples."

"I guess you could call us that," said Turu.

"Don't change the subject, Bearer," said Kucha. "Why are you here in Huacas or, better yet, why are these Skinx and the others here?"

"Yeah, about that," said Thomas. "I know why I'm here, I think, and I'm sorry and all about the bad guys, but if I know how this works, and believe me I really still do not, but if it goes the way I think it does . . ."

"Spit it out," said Kucha.

"Which one of you is my Second Augmentor?" asked Thomas.

The three Turtles stood there with strange looks on their faces.

"That would be me, wouldn't it?" said the deep voice from the darkened cell adjacent to them.

Thomas heard the figure move. The ground shook. Whoever it was, he was English and humongous. That much was certain. The figure moved once again.

"I see you have what I need."

The voice seemed somewhat familiar. Thomas turned the glowing rock towards the other cell to see who had made the claim. The dragon's head was extremely close to the bars between the two cells. The four cellmates jumped back startled.

"Do I look that horrid?" It was a massive Dracavea. "It has been quite some time since I have had a proper shower."

"Who exactly are you?" asked Thomas.

"The name's Larson Ragnor, Second Augmentor to the Bearer, Thomas Scargen."

47

which way did he go?

Itsuki clung to Bartleby as the dragon regained his composure and straightened out his flight path. Itsuki had not seen what had happened, but like Yareli, witnessed the aftermath of the dragon's attack. Garron's sportif had been destroyed with him inside of it.

"Thomas, are you there?" asked the Augmentor into his wristcom. No response.

The reality of the situation began to set in. Garron was dead. Thomas and Yareli were missing.

"LINC, scan the debris for any signs of life," said Loric. "After you have completed your scan, see if you can locate Thomas Scargen. And someone get up there and see if you can track the telesignature of the Aequos."

"There are no indications of life inside the remains of the sportif. The only evidence left of Garron Dar are shards of his charred clothing—no organic matter. The beacon in Thomas's wristcom is either deactivated or has been damaged. I have no way of ascertaining the current location of Thomas Scargen." LINC unloaded on a group of drones that attacked in formation.

"I'm gettin' nuffin', Loric," said Bartleby. "Dere's no teleport signature. I didn't see 'im comin'. Dis is all my fault."

"Come on, Bart. Don't be so 'ard on yourself," said Fargus still firing at the remaining collectorbots and drones. " 'ow could any uv us, see dat comin'?"

"Yeah, this is not your fault," said Talya soothingly.

"Talya is right, Bartleby. For all we know that dragon is working with the Hunters. Open up a teleportal and let's get out of here," said Anson.

The number of collectorbots and drones had dwindled. Teleportation was now plausible.

"Where are we going?" asked Bartleby.

"Sirati," said Anson.

"Why?" asked Talya. "What about Thomas and Yareli?"

"We need to regroup and—" said Anson.

"Although LINC was not capable of finding Thomas Scargen, we, in fact, have just acquired the means to locate the Ignus," interrupted Loric.

"And if we find the stone, we should be able to find Thomas and Yareli," said Itsuki.

"And dat damn dragon," said Bartleby.

"You are brilliant sometimes, Anson Warwick," said Loric. "Emphasis on *sometimes*."

"It runs in duh bloody family," said Malcolm.

"The High Mancer will not take this well," said Lolani.

"I can't bloody blame 'im," said Bartleby, opening a teleportal.

Talya went through first with Mancer Lolani. Anson and Loric's sportifs went through next while LINC and Fargus held off the last of the artifs. Fargus and LINC followed. Bartleby was last to go through with Itsuki.

Everyone had gathered around the conference table in the Council's chambers in Maktaba. A few of the chairs remained empty. Onjamba made sure everyone was fed and Fargus and Aiken had supplied everyone with some Gloop. Almost instantly Itsuki could feel his strength coming back.

Ziza had not taken the news well, and after hearing the fate of Garron Dar, the Eldre had not said much. The only words he had uttered since being told the news were, "He was like a son to me."

"We do not have much time," said Anson. "We need to discern the location of the stone, and then we have to depart. Time is not on our side."

"I am in agreement with Mancer Warwick," said Ziza as he floated the AIRS over to Loric's hands "Thomas and Yareli could be in grave danger. I am afraid to know whose hands the Ignus may have fallen into."

"How did the Aequos know where we were?" asked Itsuki. "And why did he single out Garron and Yareli?"

"These are all very good questions. Perhaps there is more to this than meets the eye," said Ziza.

Loric looked at the device. "There is no need to speculate. We will know where Thomas is located shortly." He looked over at LINC. "LINC, would you be so kind?"

"Activating the AIRS unit," said the artif.

"Thank you." Loric hit a button and a holographic interface emerged. "Seems simple enough." He waved his hands across the holographic display. "The red stone's energy signature is the only one programmed into the device."

"I believe that was the only one that had been confirmed," said Itsuki.

Loric chose the signature of the Ignus on the interface. A globe emerged above the device. The signature was found and designated on the globe. The Ignus was in South America. The image zoomed in to the Andes Mountains. The interface pointed to a specific area on the holomap and then vanished just as quickly.

"I don't understand. It was working correctly and then nothing," said Loric.

"B-b-but that cannot be," said the Eldre, finally talking once more.

"What is it, Eldre?" asked Ziza.

"The map was pointing directly to my home, Huacas. That would explain why the signature is unstable. And that dragon must be the dark beast the others have talked about for years. He has finally found a way into my home."

"The stone is in Huacas?" asked Anson. "What is it doing there?"

"I do not know, Mancer Warwick," said the Eldre. "But I plan to find out. I lost one of my family today. I do not plan to lose the rest."

"I will see to it that does not happen," said Ziza.

"It is settled then," said Loric. "We depart in five minutes."

"I will ready myself," said Ziza.

"Are you sure that is wise?" questioned Emfalmay. "You are not at full strength."

"Regardless, I am going, and that is final," said the High Mancer.

"Then I am going with you," said Emfalmay.

"I was sure you would say that," said Ziza. "Lolani and Neficus, you will remain here to protect Sirati. I have a strong feeling that Grimm is behind this, and if Japan is a sample of his capabilities, we have to take every precaution. I cannot risk the future of this city if, somehow, I do not make it back."

48

the tale of larson ragnor

"Wait . . . how are you my Augmentor? Larson Ragnor? I saw you help steal this stone."

"So you got the message."

"You're saying you sent me that message?"

"Well, yes. I created a spiritual connection with you, momentarily. I've had a lot of time to meditate during my incarceration. I was trying to warn you about my son, and give you an idea of where the blue stone was most likely located."

"So you're my Second Augmentor?"

"I know. I do not seem like a likely candidate, but it wasn't my choice, was it? You don't choose these things, Thomas. I like to think it as more of a calling."

"Last time I checked, you killed my friend's parents, and, as if that wasn't enough, you also ripped off his wing."

"You mean Bartleby Draige," said Larson. His face changed. "That poor boy. I must admit, I have done some horrible things in my life. I am not proud of what I did to him, but I assure you that I have changed, and I assure you that I am most certainly your Second Augmentor."

Thomas could tell this was sincere, and he did not want to waste any more time.

"We have to get you out of here," said Larson.

"I'm not going anywhere without Yareli."

"Who is Yareli?"

"She's my friend, and she needs our help."

"And where is this Yareli?"

"With the Aequos and Grimm."

"Brax," said Larson.

"Who is Brax?" asked Thomas.

"My son, the dragon who is responsible for all of this."

"So he *is* your son?"

"If you can call him that. I figured something was amiss when they came for me. I'm not as spry as I once was, but they injected me with this green liquid while I was sleeping. Not much honor in Skinx."

"Rachnid venom?" asked Thomas.

"I'm not sure what it was, but it makes me sleepier than usual, and dulls my powers."

"You have powers too?" asked Thomas.

"Like I said, I'm your next Augmentor. Now answer me one question. How did you end up here?"

"Your son grabbed Yareli and I followed him through the tele-portal, right after he had appeared from nowhere and killed Gar—"

The words had began to leave his mouth, when Thomas realized who he was speaking in front of. Garron had lived with these Turtles for years.

"G-g-garron's dead?" asked Turu.

"I'm afraid so, Turu. He died trying to help us escape."

"I can't believe it," said Kucha. "He always seemed so strong."

Yaku had walked over to Kucha and tugged on his flipper and hugged his side. Turu looked off into the darkness. A tear rolled down his face.

"He was strong," said Thomas. "And now we have to be."

"What can we do?" asked Turu.

"Can you fight?" asked Thomas to the Turtles.

"We are peaceful creatures, but we are practiced Mages and the sole defenders of Huacas," said Kucha.

"Good. I'm going to need your help to get back where they are keeping her."

"That's exactly what they want you to do," said Larson. "It is no coincidence that I am so conveniently locked up in a cell extremely close to where you were lured. It's definitely a trap."

"Trapping me is not that easy," said Thomas. "I'm going up there with or without your help, Ragnor." He turned back to the Turtles. "Are you guys with me or not?"

"What chance do we stand if Garron couldn't defeat the Dark Beast?" asked Turu.

"If no one stands up and takes his place, then Garron's sacrifice will be for nothing," said Thomas.

Turu wiped the tears away from his face. "I'm in," said Turu.

Thomas turned towards Kucha. Yaku was raising her hand, signifying that she too was in.

"I'm not letting these two have all the fun," said Kucha.

Thomas looked back at Larson.

"Fine. Have it your way, but I must augment the Gauntlet first. If we're going to walk into an ambush, we will at least be ready."

"Okay. What do we do next?"

"Open your palm."

Thomas reached out the Gauntlet and the stone floated between the slots of the cell and into the dragon's talons.

"Won't that take hours?"

"Normally, yes, but I owned the Medenculus for almost three years. I have already done the most complicated part of the procedure. Just have to make sure it wasn't tampered with too much."

The stone began to glow as it levitated in front of the dragon. Larson's Light was reddish purple.

"Why would you ever get rid of it?" asked Thomas.

"I did not make that decision. My son did."

"Yeah, what happened there? Why are you locked up?"

"My son knows I am destined to be your Second Augmentor. He also realizes that no matter what, you will have to find me. My son is obsessed with the Medenculus. It happened the night he procured it from Atlantis. I did not see the evil slowly growing in Brax, but Grimm had tainted him long before. Now he is the Necromancer's pawn. The evil inside my son and the power he felt when he touched the stone destroyed what was left of his sanity. He became obsessed." The dragon held up the Medenculus. "This obsession is why I am imprisoned."

"I'm not following. Where did Grimm meet your son?"

"The same place I did. My son and I met in an odd way. You shouldn't meet your son in a prison, especially one that is used for experimenting on dragons. Back then, I was out of control. I had been blinded by rage and vengeance. I lured the Draiges to Grimm to avenge the death of my wife. He was doing experiments on dragons and needed two specific types of dragon bones."

"The Scythe?"

"Yes, he needed the bones to create an indestructible handle for the Ancient weapon. But I assure you, I had no idea what Grimm was doing. I surely did not know at the time that I was destined to be your Augmentor. Everything changed once the Farod woman was killed. She had been the one helping Grimm with his weapon. Delonius had not taken it well when they killed Desdemona. Bartleby's father broke free and impaled the Farod woman. She bled out quickly. It was not pretty what they did to Delonius after that." Larson looked away.

"My anger did not subside with the death of Delonius. I had dreamt of that moment for years, but I felt nothing but pain when my old friend died, and the anger remained. But on the day I met my son, my anger began to subside. After Farod's death, they began to collect more dragon specimens for a different type of experiment—a new species."

"The aringi."

"Precisely. They did not care about prior services. I was brought in and was incarcerated. They began taking DNA samples from us. Two months later, they brought in the black Aequos. I knew he was my son the second I saw him. He looked like the perfect combination of Ilyana and me. One conversation and it began to fall into place. I felt ashamed. I had left in such haste that I did not realize that my wife had laid eggs on that horrible night. That moment changed me forever."

"So how did Grimm get to him?"

"Brax made a deal for our release, but it came with a price. The Daimecron was the price."

"What is that?"

"The tattoo that binds my son to Grimm. Grimm needed someone to perform a task. He must have seen something in my son that was corruptible for his own gains. Brax agreed to the deal, and we were freed—at least, I was. For a time, we were close, but that was short-lived. Unknown to me, my son began to train with Grimm as part of their arrangement. I didn't know it at the time, but he was forever bound to the Necromancer through the Daimecron. That is until Grimm died."

"He never died."

"A fact that I know all too well, Thomas, but when Grimm disappeared the stones were released. The new Bearer was to be found, and I was chosen by the Gauntlet as your Second Augmentor. I had my first vision the day Cairo was attacked. I saw a young man wielding the Gauntlet, the son of the former Bearer, his father a powerful technic. I saw you with your companions, battling against Grimm and his legions."

"Did we win?" asked Thomas.

"It was hard to see the outcome of the battle, but that is how I knew that you were friends with Delonius's son." Larson looked at Thomas. "There is another dragon in these visions as well—a female."

"Talya Grenfald," said Thomas.

"Grenfald . . . I knew a Grenfald once—before the War," said Larson. "Before Ilyana passed."

"Your wife?"

"Yes, Thomas. Seems like a lifetime ago." The dragon looked down. "I did some foolish things back then."

"I've done some stupid things in the past too, Larson, but that's where they're going to stay. The trick seems to be learning from them and not doing the stupid things again."

"Wise words, Bearer."

"That's a first," said Thomas, smiling. "There's something I'm not quite understanding. So you had this vision of me doing my Bearer thing and all, but how did you know you were my Augmentor, and how did you know it was the blue stone that you were meant to augment?"

"It wasn't long before I started to get visions of me augmenting the Gauntlet, and in each of them, I was holding the Medenculus. That is when I knew I was slated as your Second Augmentor, and I was assigned the blue stone."

"And Atlantis?"

"I knew what I needed, I just didn't know where to find it. The Gauntlet spoke to me once more, but this time the visions were different. I saw an underwater city—Atlantis. Through the premonition, I figured out the city was powered by the Medenculus."

"How did you find the place?"

"I often revisited this premonition, so much so that I knew Atlantis and its location like the back of my claw."

"I thought augmenting was a lifelong calling."

"I assure you, just as each Bearer does, each Augmentor has his or her own path. I may have not known my whole life that I was destined to do this, but that doesn't make it any less important to me. I wasted a long period of my life hurting people. I want to start helping."

"How did shifty get involved?" asked Thomas.

"I asked Brax to help because of his chameleon-like abilities. My son can shift his form as you already know. His mother could do the same, but he is especially talented at it. I needed him to pose as an Atlantean, and you know the rest. If I had known my son had worked for Grimm in the past and had become, himself, a Necromancer, I never would have allowed the boy to know the whereabouts of the Medenculus, let alone feel its power, and I most assuredly never would have told him I was to be your Augmentor."

"So you thought you'd grab the Medenculus and wait for me to come around?" asked Thomas.

"Yes. Considering the circumstances, it seemed like the best course of action, and it would have worked if it wasn't for my fool of a son stealing the stone. But no matter. It has come back to me, although not in the best of circumstances." He lifted up the Medenculus as energy surged around the stone. "Enough about old tales, Thomas. It is time to write some new ones. It is time. The stone is ready."

The dragon reached over and slammed the blue stone into the still pool on the back of the Gauntlet. Blue energy rippled around the Gauntlet and Thomas.

"Okay, I know what happens next." Thomas laid down in his cell and yawned. "I'll see you guys in a coup—" Thomas was unconscious.

49

never tell me the odds

They had arrived about a mile outside of the back entrance to Huacas. According to the Eldre, this was the only plausible entrance to the city. There were seven Mages in total—Loric, Anson, Malcolm, Emfalmay, the Eldre, the High Mancer and Itsuki himself. Together with Bartleby and Talya, LINC, and Fargus—who still piloted his rather large sportif, Olly—they made quite a formidable force.

Itsuki was growing impatient. Malcolm had left five minutes earlier to gather intel, and Thomas was inside. It was the First Augmentor's job to protect him, but Itsuki knew that rushing in would not help. He would wait for Malcolm to return—for a plan. Until then, he meditated. The blue wisps circled his still body as he floated above the ground, while the rest of his companions looked down at the lush mountainside.

"So dere are a few fings dat stood out." Malcolm leaned on a tree in front of the group. He had appeared out of nowhere. "Outside of duh city, I counted ten lava trolls, twenty or so Riders, and a small battalion of dose Lizards in tech suits, plus loads more uv duh bloody geckos not in tech suits, but still fairly well armed, and a plethora uv artifs. I also smelled some sort of conjurings done by a fairly advanced Necromancer—pretty strong magic. And dat's just outside, mate. Dere's no tellin' what's on the uvva side uv dat door."

"Grimm," said Ziza.

"I would assume," said Loric. "But, as you are painfully aware, I do not like to do that." He held the AIRS unit in his hand. "There are far too many conflicting energy signatures."

"It is an old, powerful place," said the Eldre.

"It could be that, but one thing is certain: if I am reading this correctly, the Ignus is most assuredly in Huacas, but it is not the only substantial power source inside of the mountain."

"The Gauntlet and the Scythe," said Itsuki.

"Perhaps," said Loric. "It is hard to say. As I said, it is difficult to be sure with all of the interference." Loric handed the AIRS unit to LINC. The artif placed it into the storage compartment on his back.

"We must be cautious," said Ziza. "We have no idea what is going on inside of the city or who is waiting for us."

"There's only one way to find out," said Loric. "We will need to force our way through that door." He pointed down the side of the mountain at the entrance that was flanked by the lava trolls.

"I agree," said Anson. "We do not have time for strategy. We need to take the city by force. Itsuki, Loric, and I will attack from the right. Emfalmay, the Eldre, and the High Mancer will come from the left. Malcolm, Bartleby, Talya, LINC, and Fargus, I need you to light up the sky and give us some coverage on the ground. Do not engage until we are in position."

Itsuki made his way down the side of the mountain behind Anson and Loric. The *hitodama* flew behind him. The groups had split up and were now moving into position. The reality of what they were about to take on hit the First Augmentor. The group stopped. Itsuki looked across the soon-to-be battlefield at the enemy and the environment. The entrance was carved into the side of the mountain. Large stones were laid in an intricate pattern, forming an exterior floor that spread far in every direction. Statues marked the perimeter of the paved area. This place had seen better days. Vegetation had reclaimed the mountain centuries ago. Itsuki was sure of one thing: this place was old. He could sense that much.

Artifs were the first line of defense. Their design was different than most Itsuki had seen. They looked advanced. Then there was a line of Skinx, some in armored tech suits, others with energy weapons. The lava trolls were behind them. Riders filled the sky. Itsuki could also sense the demons nearby. *They are hiding, no doubt.*

Anson moved in front of Itsuki. "From camp to camp, through the foul womb of night, the hum of either army stilly sounds." He looked over at the First Augmentor. "These things are never pleasant. Are you ready, Itsuki?" asked Anson.

"Yes, Mancer."

"We will find Thomas and Yareli," said Anson. "I promise you this."

"That I have never doubted."

"Is everyone in position?" asked Loric.

"We are in position," said Emfalmay.

"Air support is bloody ready as well," said Malcolm. Itsuki drew *Onikira* and held the sword down at his side.

Anson transformed into his werewolf form. He looked over at Loric. "Well?"

"Well what?" asked Loric.

"Are you going to shift?"

"I suppose it is warranted under these circumstances," said Loric. "But I am only doing this for Scargen and Chula." He began to shake as the sweat poured from his face. Fur sprouted out of his skin as he grew in size—his clothes adjusting to the change. Loric stood in front of the Augmentor now as a hulking weretiger. "I'll race you to the door."

"Sound trumpets! let our bloody colours wave! And either victory, or else a grave," said Anson charging down the mountain.

"Attack!" yelled Loric as he growled into the air and leapt down the side of the mountain, catching up to the werewolf.

The werewolf and weretiger were hard to keep up with, but Itsuki did his best. *Onikira* glowed behind him. They hit the artif line before the robots could react.

Anson and Loric cut through the first two. Loric jumped up and grabbed one of the artifs, tearing it in half. He threw one end at an advancing artif and the other at the next one in front of him, destroying both. Loric motioned upward with his hand. The stone below the artifs sprang upward. The jagged rocks ripped through three of the artifs before they could advance.

Itsuki sliced through two of the machines, deflecting laser blasts as he moved forward. He could see flashes of green and purple coming from the center, and other bursts and explosions from the far left. The ground attack had begun. Laser blasts and fire filled the night sky.

Itsuki saw Bartleby rush across the trees. The dragon incinerated three artifs with his fiery breath, while Fargus, inside of Olly, was holding his own versus three Riders.

Itsuki had engaged two of the Skinx in the armored tech suits. He sliced up one soldier, cutting off the machine's arm. On the down slice, he cut off the guard's other arm. The tech suit flailed around. The *hitodama* flitted in the face of the second Skinx, distracting the soldier. Itsuki spun and sent an energy pulse at the second Skinx. The blast blew the Skinx into a third soldier, knocking the Skinx off of his feet.

As he advanced, Itsuki looked ahead. He could make out Anson and Loric taking on four of the armored Skinx. The two beasts moved with great speed. The tiger and the wolf looked like they had performed these maneuvers before. The two worked well together. Anson used his speed while Loric used brute force.

Itsuki blocked another blast and swiped the leg of an armored Skinx. The machine collapsed to the ground. When Itsuki rolled back up he saw them, but it was too late to react. Two lava trolls had moved to intercept the First Augmentor.

The first troll slammed down with his hammer, but before it could hit Itsuki, the troll was tangled up in large winding vines. The vines started to writhe and twist around the weapon and across the lava troll's body. The second troll had tried to advance as well, but he too had been caught in the living vines. They struggled to move as the vines covered them, lifting the lava trolls in the air and smashing them together. The stone monsters shattered.

Behind the dismantled lava trolls stood Ziza. His eyes glowed green as he controlled the vines with his staff. Itsuki's blue wisps spun around the High Mancer. The Eldre moved in beside Ziza, manipulating water he had drawn from the atmosphere and using it to attack the advancing lava trolls. Emfalmay was perched on the back of another one of the trolls wielding his glowing sword.

Itsuki did not hear the demons before they materialized. The four crag appeared behind Ziza. From what Itsuki could sense, they were High Demons, and strong ones at that. *This should be entertaining.*

Ziza spun and raised his staff. The energy hit the first demon and cut him in two. The vines grabbed and began to suffocate the second. Ziza thrust his other hand forward, sending a green blast at the third crag, destroying the demon instantly. Three more materialized on the other side of the High Mancer.

The Eldre battled what remained of the lava trolls. He could not help Ziza. Emfalmay, Anson, and Loric still had their hands full with the Skinx. There seemed to be an endless supply of them pouring out of the entrance to Huacas.

Itsuki made his way to help the High Mancer. His passage was blocked by a falling Rider, who landed on her feet in front of him. The woman had robotic legs, but looked unexpectedly familiar to Itsuki. *The Rider from the Temple*, thought Itsuki. *I can't believe she is still alive.* He looked over at her astonished at what he saw and felt. *Her power is uncanny.*

50

Thomas awoke in what he had dubbed the waiting room, inside of the Gauntlet. But this time Ziza, Alican, and his mother awaited him. Entering the Gauntlet was always disorienting to Thomas, and it always took a few seconds for him to adjust. He looked down his arm to confirm what he already knew. He did not currently bear the Gauntlet.

"This is no time for rest, Scargen," said Alican. "It is time I taught you a thing or two about aquamancy and the Medenculus."

"You never bore the Medenculus."

"That may be true, but I share its Light. Once the augment is complete, you will need to know how to wield its powers."

"Wouldn't be much help otherwise," said Thomas.

"How did you come upon the Medenculus?" asked young Ziza.

"Now that's a funny story."

"Meaning?" asked his mother.

"Well . . . Grimm sort of threw it at me."

"This is most disconcerting," said Ziza. "Did he say anything?"

"He said he needed my help with something."

"He aims to use you in some way," said Alican. "All the better reason to show him the power of the blue Light."

"Or maybe that's precisely what the Necromancer wants," said Merelda.

"We have little choice in the matter," said young Ziza. "The stone is already inside of the Gauntlet. We all felt the shift. It would be unwise not to help Thomas understand the new stone."

"It is settled then," said Alican. "We need to make our way to the Ludus."

They all left the waiting room together and proceeded down into the large hall. They passed several Bearers from various time periods. The former Bearers seemed to be whispering to one another.

"They seem excited," said Thomas.

"They have felt the Medenculus," said Merelda. "It's all anyone can talk about."

"I'd be more excited about it myself if they weren't holding Yareli hostage."

"Who are *they*?" asked Merelda.

"Tollin Grimm and Brax Ragnor."

"Who is this Ragnor?" asked Alican.

"He is an Aequos who is working with Grimm, but he's also a Necromancer."

They stopped once they reached the dark circles. They all stepped into their own circles. The circles glowed as the group began to descend.

"You will need all the firepower you can muster," said Alican. "And by firepower I mean water power."

"I agree, but I need to get back as soon as possible."

"You know how that works here," said Ziza.

"I know, I know. When the Gauntlet's ready."

"Precisely," said Ziza.

"Where are you currently located?" asked Alican.

"I am locked in a cell with three Sea Turtles and a Dracavea, who is the father of the before-mentioned Aequos, who also happens to be my Augmentor."

"That's a lot to take in," said Merelda.

"I know, right?" said Thomas.

"Did you say Sea Turtles?" asked Alican.

"Yes I did. Oh yeah, I forgot to mention. I'm inside of your old stomping grounds, Alican."

"Huacas?"

"That's the place. Turtles and Lizards walking around, loads of water."

"That gives us an advantage," said Alican.

"How?"

"I know that city better than most. Furthermore, the Gauntlet can control Huacas. It is its power source."

"Narsh."

"We best make haste," said Alican.

The four Bearers stopped moving. They were now standing in the Ludus, the training facility inside the Gauntlet. Alican interacted with the interface. The training facility began to transform into the main chamber inside of Huacas.

"This would be the spot," said Thomas.

"There might not be a more perfect place for you to use your new gift," said Alican. "Can you feel all of the water surrounding you?"

"Honestly? No."

"Let us start there."

The massive man sat down on the floor of the large structure. Thomas did the same.

"Now close your eyes."

Thomas followed the instructions.

"Listen to the sound the water is making all around you. There is a calmness about it, but also a power. Can you feel that power?"

Thomas listened, but he could not stop thinking about Yareli. "No, Alican. I'm sorry."

"Clear your mind, Thomas. One thing at a time. The young woman is relying on you."

Thomas shook his head and thought of nothing. Since his training with Lolani, Thomas had meditated daily and had become proficient at it.

Yareli is counting on you. Concentrate on the water.

"Now, Thomas, begin to picture the particles that make up the water. They are working in unison, flowing where gravity takes them for the most part."

Thomas did as Alican said. He had become adept at energy manipulation, but this was different.

"Once you understand the uniqueness of these particles, it becomes easier to ask them to cooperate. You are made up of similar particles. The Earth is as well. I want you to start moving your hands in a circle, while concentrating on the particles."

Thomas could see the particles and their movements. He could feel the water that churned around him.

"Now move your hands like you see the water moving."

Thomas circled his hands, moving them as he saw the water moving in his head.

"Now open your eyes."

Thomas could not believe what he saw in front of him. A ball of water formed and flowed the way his hands were moving.

"The water becomes an extension of your own hands."

"That is completely and utterly narsh," said Thomas as he continued to manipulate the water. "But this is where I messed up last time."

"You do not seem like one who struggles with confidence," said Alican. "Learn from your past mistakes and own them, Thomas. The water is not a separate thing. It flows through everything around us. It *is* everything around us. The water is you. You are the water."

"The water is me," repeated Thomas. "I am the water." The water began to churn faster as Thomas stood. He finally understood the most basic concept of aquamancy. Tuguna the Eldre had tried to explain it, but Thomas could not hear him. Aquamancy is not simply a tool to master. It is a way of thinking—of being. Your spirit must move with the spirits in the water. They must become one. "I *am* the water."

Something inside Thomas had changed. He was not sure if it was the augment or the fact that the woman he loved was in grave danger, but he could now feel the water like it was a part of him. It felt amazing. Thomas stopped his hands and the water stopped too.

"I think you are more of a natural at this than you let on," said Alican. "Attack me."

Thomas nodded while his eyes burned. Thomas methodically moved his arms, pulling more water from the streams that surrounded him. Thomas lifted up the water and then focused his energy forward. The water poured at Alican, but right before it hit him, Alican froze the water by simply moving his hand. He blasted the ice apart and then forced the shards back at Thomas. Without thinking Thomas raised both of his hands and a wall of fire formed in front of him, melting the ice attack.

Thanks, Garron, thought Thomas.

"Very impressive, Thomas," said Alican. "Now it is your turn."

Alican moved his hands as a wave of water formed and lurched at Thomas. Thomas stood his ground and pushed his hands at the water, freezing it.

"Haaaa!" yelled Thomas as the ice splintered. Thomas flipped the shards telekinetically and forced them into the ground in a perfect circle around Alican.

"I don't think you ever had a problem with aquamancy, Thomas. You had a problem with understanding what aquamancy truly is."

"It doesn't hurt to have an incentive to learn faster," said Merelda.

"No. I suppose it doesn't. Speaking of which, I think it's time."

"I am skeptical about what awaits you in Huacas," said young Ziza. "But we have little choice in the matter. Be mindful of your decisions. Grimm seems to have the upper hand, and I know how he thinks. He is always three steps ahead of where you think he is. There is a calculated reason for everything he does. He is truly a formidable adversary, and you need to be mindful of this."

"I will," said Thomas.

"The augment will kick in soon enough," said Merelda. "I wish any of us knew what to tell you about its power, but the truth is none of us has ever wielded it." She hugged Thomas. "I have faith in you, Son. If anyone can handle it, it is you." She kissed him and backed away.

"You are ready. Trust me. I know these things," said Alican, patting him on the back. "I never got the privilege of connecting with my Light's stone. I envy you." The massive man smiled. "Just remember, Thomas: you are the water."

These were the last words Thomas heard as the darkness surrounded him.

51

the not-so-great escape

Thomas woke up to see Yaku staring at him. She smiled. Thomas sat up.

"Okay, I guess nap time is over." He looked down to make sure the Gauntlet was there. It was. "Now how do we get back up there?"

"That part is easy," said Turu. "There are several passageways, but there are guards everywhere, and not just the Skinx. There are artifs and lava trolls as well."

"Yeah, but we have a dragon, and this," said Thomas as he raised the Gauntlet.

"Not to put a damper on your plans, mate, but they've injected me with loads of that bloody rachnid venom," said Larson. "I used what was left in me to finish augmenting the stone. It's probably the only reason they didn't give me a higher dose today. I don't think I am moving anytime soon . . . unless . . ."

"Unless what?" asked Thomas.

"Well, you should be able to heal me, shouldn't you?" said Larson. "I mean, with your power, I'd imagine you could make me right as bloody rain in no time."

"I've never tried that before. Doesn't it take another spirit for that to work?"

"Healing is tricky, Thomas, but unless the person is close to death or has just died, it does not require a sacrifice," said Kucha. "This is only in the extreme cases, and even a sacrifice does not guarantee healing will work then. Normally healing only takes away from your own energy level, like any energy output would. The more severe the injury, the more energy is required. I imagine, in this case, it won't take much for someone as powerful as the Bearer."

"And once the Medenculus finishes augmenting, this power should be amplified," said Larson. "Shall we get going?"

"I was thinking the same thing," said Thomas as he raised the Gauntlet. The bars of the prison bent open, garnering the attention of the artif guards. Thomas pushed his hands forward. "Haaaa!" A blue energy stream incinerated the dark artifs before they could react.

"I am glad that I'm on your side," said Larson.

Thomas bent the bars on the cell holding the dragon and walked up to the beast.

"Just so you know, I've never tried this before," said Thomas.

"I'm sure you'll do fine," said Larson. "Besides, I'm not sure I could feel much worse."

"A big hole in the side of you might change your mind," said Thomas, trying to play off his uncertainties.

The dragon laughed.

"You have a blue Light, Thomas. This means you should be a natural healer," said Kucha. "But I could show you a few pointers."

"That would be great."

"First you want to channel the blue Light into your hands and then focus that energy into Larson, but not like an attack. It is more like you're sharing your energy."

Thomas began to focus the blue Light into his hands, but when he placed them on the dragon, they extinguished.

"Why don't you just do it?"

"I have never attempted healing anything as large as a dragon before. It does not come easily to me. The Eldre is the healer of the group. He is quite good at it."

"I know. I've seen him in action."

"Let's try again," said Kucha.

Thomas focused the Light once more into his hands.

"This time, try to imagine this Light coursing through Ragnor's body, restoring him."

Thomas pressed his hands on the dragon and closed his eyes. He could feel the energy transferring into Larson. He opened his eyes as the energy rippled through the dragon.

"Now that's better," said Larson. The dragon looked at his talons. He formed an energy ball in his hand. "Much better."

"Good, let's get going," said Thomas. "Kucha can you lead the way?"

"Yes, Bearer."

Thomas thought of Garron. *He always called me Bearer.* Thomas felt ashamed for not getting to know the man better.

Kucha made his way to the large doors of the prison. They slid open.

On the other side were two Skinx. Larson was the first to make a move at them. They shot, but the blasts did little. The dragon created an energy sphere and unleashed it on the first guard, while he spun and knocked the second down with his tail.

"On we go," said Larson as the two guards were rendered useless.

Skinx poured into the hallway. The group methodically dealt with the Lizards as they made their way down the long corridor.

At the end of the corridor were two large doors. A stone interface stood to the right of the entryway. Thomas did not know what it would do, but he felt compelled to put his hand onto the top of the interface. He placed the Gauntlet on the sphere and the doors opened up.

"The Gauntlet is the original power source of Huacas," said Kucha. "You can interface with the city at any of these stations."

"Narsh," said Thomas.

"What's *narsh* mean?" asked Turu.

"It's another way of saying something is amazing," said Thomas.

"Narsh," said Turu.

The companions made their way through the set of doors. They walked down the hallway cautiously. They came upon a tunnel that split in two directions at a three-way junction.

Turu poked his head around the corner. He came back around and motioned for them to be quiet. He then instructed Thomas to have a look.

On the other side, there were a group of Skinx corralling other lizard-like creatures.

Thomas rejoined the group. "What's going on there?"

"The Skinx are rounding up the remaining Salamen," said Turu. "We must help them."

"We don't have much of a choice. They are between us and the next set of doors," said Kucha.

"I got this," said Thomas.

He walked out into the hallway and began to move towards the Skinx. There were ten in total. "Excuse me. Hi. How are you fine Lizards doing today?"

The Skinx opened fire. Thomas jumped back around the protective wall.

"I guess they don't want to talk. Okay. Diplomacy has failed. I guess it's time for action." Thomas turned the corner and threw his gauntleted hand forward. "Haaa!"

The blast caught the leader of the group square in the chest, knocking him backwards. The other Skinx moved to intercept. Larson bounded around the corner. He unleashed fire on the advancing Skinx, incinerating three where they stood. The Sea Turtles entered the fray, their eyes glowing purple as they formed energy spheres and launched them at the Skinx. The attacks found targets, dispersing the remaining Skinx. Thomas moved forward with his new team.

Turu ran over to help the Salamen. "How many more are there?" asked the Sea Turtle.

"There are hundreds more of us in holding cells throughout the city," said one of the Salamen.

"We are about to start something, and we have no way to know how it will play out," said Thomas.

"I need you to go and evacuate all of your brothers and sisters from the city," said Kucha. "Use the escape tunnels."

The Salamen nodded in agreement. The group of Amphibians took off down the hallway in the opposite direction.

"The Eldre is here," said Kucha.

"I sense the Eldre's presence too," said Turu.

"How do we find him?" asked Thomas. "My friends are most likely with him. I sense a high level of power close by, but it could be anyone."

"Over here," said Turu.

Yaku was standing next to another connection station.

"Interface with the city. It should show you where the Eldre is as well as your friends."

Thomas moved over and interfaced with the station. It was like the city was alive. He could feel the different parts of the vast network of Huacas. The station could show him what was going on inside of the building, almost like an Ancient security system. He saw images of his friends fighting an army of Skinx outside of one of the entrances—the southern entrance.

"Found them," said Thomas. "They are by the southern entrance. They are under heavy fire, but overall I'd say the odds just got a lot better for us. Larson, I need you to warn the High Mancer of what's happening, and take Yaku with you. She does not need to be a victim of whatever is to transpire."

"Yaku stays with me," said Kucha. "She's not as fragile as she might appear. Turu can go with the dragon. He can show you the way out."

"Are you two sure about this?" asked Thomas.

"We serve the Bearer," said Turu and Kucha simultaneously.

"It's settled then."

Yaku ran over and hugged Turu's leg.

"It will be fine, Yaku. I'm going to find the Eldre." She made a sign with her hand. "I love you too." He turned to Thomas. "Protect her."

"You have my word, Turu," said Thomas.

Turu jumped up onto Larson and the two took off down the corridor. Thomas continued to view the inside of Huacas via the connection the Gauntlet provided him. He found where Yareli was being held and where Grimm and Brax Ragnor awaited them.

"I found our destination. They're holding her in the main chamber."

"I'll lead," said Kucha. "It isn't far from here."

"Let's get going," said Thomas.

The three of them quickly made their way down the corridor. They turned through a series of hallways until they reached the one that connected with the room in which Grimm was holding Yareli. Thomas knew he was walking into a trap, but he had no choice. Yareli was in danger.

The chamber doors where being guarded by two large lava trolls. Water flowed through this level. Streams lined the sides of the hallway that led to the doors.

It was then Thomas felt it. The energy was astounding, forcing him to freeze where he stood. The power of the Medenculus lifted him off of the ground as the energy poured through him. He could feel the water around him. He was uncertain at first, but when the two lava trolls made a move towards him, he knew for certain. The augment had kicked in.

His body burned inside. He shifted the blue stone into place, landing in the crater his energy outpouring had created. The lava trolls had almost reached him. That was as close as they would ever get. Thomas lifted the water that circulated through the streams and focused it on the two trolls.

"Haaaa!" The water pushed the trolls backwards and through the two massive doors that separated him from Yareli.

He rushed into the chamber behind the wave of water he still controlled. The two Turtles followed.

Grimm stood there clapping at Thomas when he turned the corner. "I was starting to worry that you weren't coming."

"Haaaa!" said Thomas, directing the water at Grimm.

Grimm moved his hand and the water deflected back at Thomas. Thomas jumped out of the way, but Kucha and Yaku were not as lucky. They were caught in the wave. The two managed to swim out of it and flipped into the air, landing on opposite sides of the Bearer. The remaining water settled into the pools that circled the chamber.

"Where is Yareli?"

"I'm sure she will be around soon enough. I see you found some friends. And aren't they adorable."

Kucha moved quickly at Grimm, unleashing a torrent of attacks. Grimm batted them away without hesitation.

"Impressive, but can you do this?" Grimm lifted Kucha where he stood and threw him to the right, catching him inside of a stasis field.

Yaku moved in from the other side. She peppered the Necromancer with a volley of energy spheres, making him back up a few steps.

"Aren't you powerful for your size?" He lifted her up and threw her into a similar stasis field across from Kucha.

Thomas pushed the Gauntlet forward. "Haaaa!" Energy poured out directly at Grimm.

In one motion the Necromancer pulled the Scythe from its resting spot and swirled the blade in a circle forming a shield. Thomas's attack bounced off of it and into the ceiling.

"Enough! This has been amusing, Tom, but let us get down to business. Or do I need to start killing your friends to make you to listen to me?"

"What business do we have?"

"I am here for one reason only. I need your help."

"I thought you were this supremely powerful Necromancer," said Thomas. "But I guess not, if you still need me."

"Please, Tom. Spare me the quips. You are better than that. I require a unique power source that only you possess at the moment. With the addition of the Medenculus, I would say you are just about ready now."

"For what?"

"All in due time, Tom. First, I want you to say hello to someone."

Yareli walked out from behind the screen holding hands with Brax. Brax carried the Infosphere that contained the Ignus. Yareli was alive and conscious. This pleased Thomas, but something was wrong. She was not in control. Her pupils glowed red, and she was smiling.

"What have you done to her?"

"Consider it an insurance policy for my investment," said Grimm. "Don't look so troubled, Tom. She is under Brax's control now. She is in good hands. After all, they were a couple once."

"I swear if you so much as scratch her, I will do everything in my pow—"

"To do what?" interrupt Brax.

The dragon-man made a hand gesture, simulating a scratch. Yareli mimicked the movement. She took her right hand and scratched her upper left arm deep enough that she drew blood.

"What were you saying, Tom?" asked Grimm. "I am afraid I could not hear you over the sound of tearing flesh."

"Make her stop." Thomas powered down. "I'll do what you want, just make her stop."

Brax moved his hand, and she ceased.

"Now where were we?" asked Grimm. "Ahh, yes. I believe you owe me a favor."

52

grimm realities

"Let me say, first, my dear Tom, I am so glad you made it back to us unscathed," said Grimm as he sauntered towards Thomas. "And I see Larson was able to augment the Gauntlet even with his venom poisoning."

"It *was* rachnid venom."

"The Captain went back with a team and commandeered whatever they could find from Sangeros and the Hive. Thank you for taking care of that situation, by the way. Amara Scornd was always such a prickly thorn in my side. Vampires can be such vile creatures."

"What do you want from me?"

"Ah, I enjoy our conversations. Alas, it seems you do not. Sad, really. I had such high hopes for us." Grimm smiled. "To the point then. It is simple really, Tom. I need you to recharge Huacas with the Gauntlet, but more specifically using the Medenculus."

"Why?"

"Come now. Do you really think I am going to stand in front of you and divulge all of my secrets. Where is the fun in that, Tom? Let us just say, that I need a power source that only one person on the whole of Earth can provide, and that person happens to be you."

"Even if I did what you ask, how could you contain it," said Thomas.

"For being the son of a genius, I swear sometimes you are short-sighted, and, dare I say, a bit dimwitted." Grimm pointed to the semicircle of Ancestor Stones behind him. "These carvings are, to put it as simply as I can, huge receptacles—batteries if you will. They can store various types of energy. They are just in need of a charge, and you, my dear boy, are my spark." He moved over and touched the Gauntlet with his left hand. "And remember, Tom, your precious girlfriend is under Brax's control. Any false moves, and she will die."

"You have to promise me she will be unharmed. The same goes for Kucha and Yaku." Thomas pointed to the respective stasis fields.

"You have my word," said Grimm as he turned away.

Thomas did not trust the Necromancer, but he had little choice in the situation.

"What do I do?"

"Place the Gauntlet onto this sphere, shift the Medenculus into position, and then exert as much power as possible into the stone."

"Why does it have to be shifted to the Medenculus?"

"That is none of your concern!" shouted Grimm. "Just do as I say."

"I just would like to know all the parameters involv—"

"Do not bother stalling, Tom. Complete the task as I have asked or I will start killing your precious friends."

Thomas could not let anything happen to Yareli or the Turtles. He walked over to the interface. "Here goes nothing," he said as he shifted the Medenculus.

Thomas looked at the Glophitis on his palm as it transitioned from orange to a darker blue. The blue energy started in his palm and extended across the Gauntlet and through his whole body. He could feel the power of the Medenculus course through him. The familiar lighter blue energy soon returned and began to swirl around the Gauntlet.

Thomas placed the Gauntlet onto the sphere. The stone pedestal and the sphere flickered a faint purple color. Thomas concentrated on the Gauntlet and could feel the connection immediately. He could feel the city again. This time it was much stronger. This was the central hub of Huacas—its main control room. Thomas could sense that he was not the first Bearer to charge this city. Alican had done the same centuries before. He concentrated on the sphere and collected his energy into his palm.

"Haaaaa!" Thomas released the accumulated energy into the sphere. The pedestal now glowed blue. The city began to spring to life as energy rippled around the Bearer. Purple lights began to glow throughout the chamber. Thomas continued to push his power into the monolith.

"That's it, my boy. Push your energy level as far as it can go. It is almost complete."

The *tuqi* began to glow bright blue, absorbing the energy that Thomas was expending. Thomas could feel his power draining into the city. He could not hold the connection much longer. When Thomas was drained of energy he could barely stand. The connection ceased, and he was thrown across the room.

Grimm moved to the Ancestor Stones, which were engulfed in blue electricity. He raised his wristcom as it scanned the stones.

"Excellent work, Tom. It is done. They are ready." Grimm touched the markings on one of the Ancestor Stones. The carvings glowed blue as he caressed them. "I am impressed, Tom, and I am not easily impressed. The power in just one of the *tuqi* far exceeds my needs."

He motioned to the artifs. They flew over to the stone Grimm stood in front of. They placed their hands on each side of the Ancient stone and lifted the massive rock.

"What are you gonna do with that?" asked Thomas.

"If you only knew, my boy," said Grimm. "If I were you, I'd consider conserving what little power you have left."

"I did what you asked. Now let her go."

"I'm afraid that was never part of the deal." Thomas attempted to move, but Grimm telekinetically threw him onto the floor. The Necromancer turned to the dragon-man. "You have done well, Brax." He gestured towards Thomas. "I leave you your prize."

"Thank you, my Lord," said Brax.

"The other *tuqi* will remain here in Huacas. As per our

arrangement, I promised the Skinx their new city would have its power source intact." Grimm spun around with the Scythe, tearing a large opening in front of the artifs. The artifs floated through the tear, carrying the massive stone. Grimm moved to follow but stopped.

"I almost forgot." The Infosphere shot out of Brax's hand and into Grimm's. "I do not want to leave this behind."

"Good luck opening that," said Thomas as blood trickled down his lip and onto his chin. He wiped off the crimson liquid. "The Infosphere is no good without the key."

"I agree," said Grimm as he moved his hand across the surface of the sphere. "Good thing I have one."

A holographic screen appeared above it. Grimm moved his hand across the holographic interface and the Infosphere began to open. Grimm let go of the sphere, and it hovered in front of him. The Ignus rose out of the center of the sphere.

"Remarkable, is it not?"

The red stone glowed as it spun in front of the Necromancer. Grimm motioned and the Ignus flew into his wrapped hands. Tollin Grimm now held the red stone Thomas's father had found in Mexico.

"It is only fair, Tom. I gave you the blue one: I should get the red one."

"I don't understand," said Thomas. "The key to open that is thousands of miles away from here. How did y—"

"This revelation, I must admit, puzzled me for quite some time as well. But the easiest way to explain it is that more of your father crossed into me when I absorbed his spirit than I had originally thought. It was a residual effect that I had not accounted for. Not only did your father's abilities transfer to me, but some of his memories did as well. It, however, was not a perfect transfer. Vague details of events and people ran through my head that, at first, seemed foreign yet oddly familiar. I could remember your first day of school, dancing with your mother at the wedding—nothing quite useful at first. It was like staring at a puzzle, but I did not have all of the pieces to complete it.

"As time passed, more of these pieces began to materialize. I realized why your father had started dabbling in archaeology in the first place. It was not a fanciful pursuit of a man that had too much money. No, it was much more than that. It was his quest to find these stones for his son—for you, Tom. A quest which brought him straight to me and my prison. I remembered the Ignus and its location, but I still did not remember anything about the Medenculus or its whereabouts.

"That is when Brax returned to me. He had been an apt pupil before the days of Arkmalis. When he realized that I had returned, he came to me asking for help and rededicated his service. We made a deal. I would get him his precious Medenculus, and he would help me secure the Ignus and lure you here to charge the Ancestor Stones. I thank you for that. We just needed bait and Ms. Chula was kind enough to volunteer."

Grimm turned and smiled at Yareli. "It all worked out exactly as I had conceived it—better actually. I had no recollection of the Axe when Brax returned. Finding that was pure serendipity."

"No," said Thomas. He was beside himself. The Axe had been compromised.

"I remembered the story your father had been told by Galeos, about the Ancient Mages and their Artifacts, but Dr. Scargen had no knowledge of the Axe's whereabouts. Your father had charged Galeos with hiding it. If not for Captain Marcus and his diligent work, I maybe would have missed this opportunity."

"What do you mean?"

"My Captain has secured the Axe, Tom." A holographic scene of the Captain wielding it appeared above Grimm's wristcom. "An astonishing weapon. Is it not?"

"But how did you know where it was?" Thomas was frightened by the prospect.

"Vedd Delphin revealed this to us. He resisted for a while, but in the end you cannot stop a mind tearing once it has begun. It is a bit invasive, but we needed to know the exact location of Atlantis for extraction of the Medenculus. The Axe was a consolation prize, and a marvelous one at that."

"What have you done to Cayde?"

"I have done nothing, but Captain Slade on the other hand . . ."

"What are you going to do with the stone?"

"I'm going to put it back where it belongs—back into the Axe, my boy."

"But how is that possible? Only an Augmentor can do that."

"I guess Ziza never told you the truth of our relationship."

"He said you two were close friends."

"Eventually, yes, but not at first. Our association was forged by the very weapon you wield."

"How?"

"Oh, Tom. I am truly sorry that your High Mancer keeps these things from you. Had you chosen to join me, I would have shared everything with you."

He moved close to Thomas. Thomas could feel the bandages on his face and the hotness of the Necromancer's breath as he whispered the words.

"I was his First Augmentor."

Grimm stepped back and telekinetically lifted Thomas off the ground. He pushed the Ignus into Thomas's face.

"I augmented this very stone for him, and I swore to protect him." Grimm's eyes went dark as he began to breathe heavily. "I was an excellent First Augmentor!" shouted Grimm. His breathing slowed again as he turned away. "He betrayed our bond. Your beloved mentor did this to me." Grimm walked forward and Thomas dropped to the floor.

"The way I look at it, this is mine to give out to whom I see fit. I have earned that much." He looked back at Thomas. "Goodbye, Tom. I am afraid I do not envy what is to happen to you."

Grimm made his way across the tear. The rip sealed behind him.

Thomas was spent. His energy level was the lowest it had ever been. *What am I going to do?*

Brax Ragnor wasted no time.

"Get up," said the dragon-man. Yareli stood at his side.

"I just sat down," said Thomas. "Cut me some slack, Brax. If you haven't noticed, I'm having a pretty shitty day."

"Have it your way."

Brax lifted Thomas and hurtled him across the room. He hit the stone wall and fell to the ground. His body ached as he tried to lift himself up.

Thomas had little energy left, but he had to do something if he was going to survive. He concentrated on the Gauntlet. He collected what little power he could muster into the stone glove. His eyes began to burn as he stood.

"Don't you know when to just stay down?" said Brax.

"Nope," said Thomas. "Kind of my thing."

He pushed the Gauntlet forward and unleashed an energy attack with his reserve power. The blast knocked Brax into the far wall. His armor smoked as he lifted himself back up.

"Impressive, but I imagine you don't have much left in you now," said Brax.

Thomas watched the man walk towards him. Brax's mask had been cracked open by the attack, exposing a small part of his face.

"Let Yareli go," said Thomas. "You've killed enough of my friends for one day."

"I don't think I follow you," said the dragon.

Thomas dug deep and shot another energy blast at Brax, catching him in the shoulder.

"Does that jog your memory?" asked Thomas.

"Can't say it does," said Brax as smoke circled around his body. The blast had little effect on the dragon.

"Don't play stupid with me. You blew up the sportif my friend was piloting over Dallas. You killed Garron Dar, and you will answer for that, Ragnor."

"I think your temper has confused you, Thomas."

Brax reached back on his cracked helmet. The mask depressurized and opened to reveal the dragon-man's face. He was still obscured by the swirling smoke.

"I'm not sure you have your facts straight." The man stepped from the cloud he had been concealed by. His face was partially covered in the tattoos that extended across much of his exposed body, making it hard for Thomas to see the man in the shadows. "I could not have possibly killed Garron Dar." He stepped closer into the light and the purple glow lit his face.

Thomas could not believe his eyes. Even with the markings, there was no mistaking what he saw.

"I *am* Garron Dar."

"No," said Thomas. "You can't be. The tattoos. Garron didn't have tattoos."

"What tattoos?" The dark marks that covered Brax instantly vanished. He smiled as the markings returned as quickly as they had disappeared.

"It *is* you," said Thomas. *Garron's not dead. He's the black Aequos— the dark beast. Garron is Brax Ragnor.*

"And I think you know Wiyaloo."

Thomas did not have time to react as the Spirit Ghost Warrior materialized and attacked. The blast knocked Thomas sideways. When Thomas turned around, he saw the three of them. Wiyaloo was a twisted abomination of his usual form—far darker—more demon than spirit. His eyes glowed the same red color as Yareli's. The young woman nocked a glowing red arrow in her bow and pointed it at Thomas. Wiyaloo did the same with his staff.

"You see, Thomas. You worried for no reason. All of your friends are here and very much alive."

53

fruit of the vine

Before Itsuki could wrap his head around the fact that this Rider from the Temple had survived, she attacked. The dark energy flew at him. He deflected it to the side. Itsuki swung his blade, sending a wave at the Rider. She dodged his attack and pushed back Itsuki telepathically. When he collected himself, he could see that she was running right at Ziza. Itsuki moved to intercept. The female Rider pointed to two of the crags and then back at Itsuki.

"Get him," said the Rider.

The two demons broke off of the fight with Ziza and barreled towards Itsuki. The Rider was the conjurer of the crags.

The first demon moved at Itsuki. With *Onikira* he struck downwards, slicing an arm off. Itsuki ran towards the High Mancer as the chaos continued. He jumped up onto one of the fallen lava trolls that Loric had bested earlier in the battle, running across its downed rock corpse. He pushed off from the back of the troll and higher into the air. Itsuki fell down next to Ziza, bisecting the crag that the High Mancer had squared up against. The crag stumbled backwards. Ziza incinerated it with an energy discharge from his staff.

"Impressive for a child and an old man," said the female Rider.

Ziza turned to see who was speaking. "Take care of the remaining crag, my boy. I will handle this one." His eyes glowed green.

"You seem rather confident considering you don't even know what you're up against," said the Rider.

"I know the type," said Ziza as his hand blurred forward.

The blast knocked the Rider backwards. She landed, digging her robotic legs into the ground.

"*Eerah natusum apacarita, Eerah vipannaka uparatta Narg, vigatta, natusum!*" She moved her hands upward, and *Eerah* pushed up from the Earth, oozing through cracks in the side of the mountain.

The black tar-like beings were all too familiar to Itsuki. The dark ones bubbled and flopped down the mountain, racing straight for Ziza. He did not attempt to fight them or run away. The *Eerah* swarmed the High Mancer, locking him in a cocoon of darkness.

Itsuki could only watch in horror. He was engaged with the crag, and Ziza appeared defenseless. The High Mancer's entire body was covered in *Eerah*. His face was the only thing exposed. The female Necromancer stood in place as the *Eerah* twisted and churned, moving Ziza close to her.

"Introductions are in order. I am Evangeline—General of the Grimm Legions."

"I think you already know who I am," said Ziza, still maintaining a smile.

"You are nothing but a pathetic old man, who clings to antiquated ideals."

"Did Tollin tell you this?" asked Ziza. "He has clouded your thoughts and judgment. Tollin has awakened an anger inside of you."

"Show him the respect he deserves. You will refer to him as Lord Grimm."

"Not while I still draw breath will that title leave my mouth."

"Well, from where I stand, that won't be for long."

"You need to look again, my dear," said Ziza as his energy level jumped. "One's perception can sometimes be quite limited."

The High Mancer's eyes burned green as the energy radiated outwards. The *Eerah* screamed in terror as they were completely eradicated. The force of the shock wave knocked Evangeline backwards. Ziza floated above the crater he had created.

"Your master is the only one who has antiquated ideas."

The High Mancer moved his staff. Vines and roots shot out from the ground and grabbed Evangeline before she landed. They circled around her form, holding her extended over Ziza. A root rose from the ground, lifting Ziza face to face with Evangeline.

"You should learn to respect your elders."

A second Rider fell from the sky without warning. With a downward chop of the large glowing Axe, he severed the vines and roots. They shriveled and died, losing their grip on Evangeline. The female Rider fell to the ground. The weapon glowed red in Captain Marcus Slade's hands.

Ziza turned towards the Captain. "You?"

"A conversation for another day," said Marcus as he swung the Axe unleashing a red wave at the surrounding Mages.

The blast knocked Itsuki off of his feet. The Captain of the Riders grabbed his General. An aringi dropped from the sky and covered the two Riders. The aringi took off into the night sky through the teleportal it had opened. The remaining Riders began to follow their Captain's lead.

"They have the Axe," said Itsuki.

"And I fear that if we do not get to Thomas soon, they may have the Ignus as well," said Ziza.

The High Mancer spun with his staff. A large root tore from the earth and grabbed a charging lava troll. The root tightened, crushing the troll. Magma poured down the vine and onto the stone surroundings.

Itsuki looked around. The odds had quickly changed. With the threat of the Riders diminished, the others had joined the ground assault. Only Bartleby and Talya still battled in the skies with the remaining aringi. Few lava trolls remained. The Skinx had been reduced to a much smaller force. The soldiers that remained who had not retreated had backed themselves against the entrance. Emfalmay, Loric, Anson, and the Eldre had seen to that. A handful of artifs still fought. LINC flew in alongside Fargus and Olly and began to attack the dark machines.

Malcolm landed next to Itsuki. "Now dat's what I call a knock."

A black creature streaked across the sky. Itsuki could tell instantly that it was a dragon, but it was not the black Aequos. It was a Dracavea, and it did not look friendly. Itsuki had thought the fighting was almost over, but this did not bode well. It made a beeline towards the group. Itsuki lifted *Onikira*, expecting the worst.

Bartleby moved, tracking the dark beast. He barreled into the side of the monster before it could reach the group. Its passenger jumped off, flipping into the air. The black dragon was sent flying into the side of the mountain and landed by Loric and Anson. The Eldre and Emfalmay were close by and moved in to address the possible new threat.

The young Sea Turtle landed in front of Itsuki. "Are you looking for Thomas?"

"Yes," said Itsuki. "Where is he?"

"Inside, we can take you to him."

Bartleby landed and walked over to the unknown dragon to see what they were up against. The Dracavea lifted his head and looked at Bartleby.

"Larson Ragnor!" yelled Bartleby. He rushed at the downed dragon.

The Eldre jumped between the two dragons. "Wait a second, Bartleby," said the Eldre. "One of my kind was riding this beast when it arrived. Maybe he's friendly."

" 'ee's anyfing but, Eldre," said Bartleby. "I knew you 'ad somefing to do wif dis and dat dat Aequos was your filfy son."

"Well, hello, Bart. I understand your anger, and I am in complete agreement about the filthiness of my son. I do have something to do with this but not in the way you think." Bartleby snarled and let out a roar. "Before you overreact, let me explain, and if you still want to kill me, I won't stand in your way."

"You've got five seconds."

"Good, good," said Larson. The dragon lifted himself out of the rubble. He was an old dragon, but a strong one too. "I am here to bring you to Thomas."

Malcolm, Ziza, the new Sea Turtle, and Itsuki made their way over to Larson, Bartleby, Loric, Anson, Emfalmay, and the Eldre. This position was well sheltered from the attacks from their few remaining opponents.

"He's telling the truth," said the young Sea Turtle as they approached.

"Turu?"asked the Eldre. "Thank the Ancestors you are still alive. And your siblings?"

"They were both fine last I saw them. They are with Thomas. He promised to protect them."

"And sent us to find you," said Larson.

"'ow do you know Thomas?" asked Bartleby. "Come on, out wif it."

"I am Second Augmentor to the Bearer, Thomas Scargen."

"No bloody way," said Bartleby.

"Look, I know we have loads to discuss later, but your friend, my Bearer is walking into a battle he cannot possibly fight alone."

Itsuki looked at the dragon. It was not out of the question that an Augmentor would be a dragon. If Thomas had a Second Augmentor then he must have recovered the stone.

"My son has gone mad."

"Of course. Ragnor," said Loric as he shifted to his human form. "I cannot believe I didn't see it before. It is so terribly clever."

"What is so terribly clever?" asked Anson as he too transformed back into a human.

"Garron Dar is not dead."

"We saw his bloody sportif explode in front of us," said Malcolm. "What are you goin' on about?"

"It did explode. That much is fact, but how and why did it explode are the real questions. That, up until this very moment, no one was asking."

"I'm not following," said Anson.

"Please, Mancer Bodes, explain yourself," said the Eldre.

"We did a lot of supposing in a time of mourning and confusion, but something did not sit right about the events that took place above Dallas, Texas."

"For instance?" asked the Eldre.

"Let's start at the beginning, shall we? It is safe to say that the Hunters were not in cahoots with the dragon—a practice they have always shied away from. If the black Aequos teleported into the city, why did the Hunters not move to intercept him? They had encircled Talya in no time at all once she reappeared over Sky Field and they also maintained a presence around Bartleby throughout the whole battle. They seemed as surprised as we did by the sudden appearance of the Aequos. Which leads me to believe, that there was no incoming teleportal."

"How is that possible?"

"I will get to that shortly. The blast that destroyed Dar's sportif did not seem to be an attack from a dragon. The blast, from all indications, seemed to originate from the center of the sportif—a very localized attack. Precision is not a dragon's forte, suggesting that it wasn't created by a dragon attack."

"We do tend to go big, don't we?" said Bartleby.

"Which leads me to the most damning of evidence: when LINC scanned the wreckage, he found no sign of organic life—peculiar in a blast of this nature. The sportif had not been completely destroyed. In fact, the odds that charred clothing would remain in the aftermath of this type of an explosion with no organic matter being intact are astronomical—one might say, impossible. Yet when LINC scanned the sportif, he found no such evidence—again peculiar. All of these things when combined point to only one possible solution."

"What are you trying to say, Loric?" asked Anson.

"I am trying to say that Garron Dar did not die in the explosion over Dallas. He, in fact, transformed into the Aequos and tore from the sportif's chest, causing the explosion in an effort to make it seem like he was deceased."

"No bloody way," said Malcolm.

"That would explain why nobody saw the dragon before it destroyed the sportif," said Anson. "What is your proof?"

Loric moved a few holographic keys.

"I didn't look for footage before, because I did not know what we were looking for. If I just hack into the Hunter's database . . . they would have had cameras on every drone and artif that participated in the battle." Loric moved his hand across the holographic display. "Ah, here. The answers are at our fingertips."

The footage played, showing Garron's sportif from several different angles. The dragon ripped out from the center of the sportif in slow motion.

"Garron Dar and the black Aequos are, in fact, one in the same."

"Garron is an anagram of Ragnor," said Anson.

"Precisely," said Loric. "I imagine when he started his training with you, Eldre, he never could have imagined anyone putting the two together. He must have wanted to maintain a connection with the Ragnor name, after he learned his true identity."

"I have no words," said Tuguna.

"He knew about me being his father for quite some time before fate brought us together," said Larson. "He hated his adopted parents. They did terrible things to him. He changed his name to Ragnor soon after we met."

"It stands to reason that he, in an effort to distance himself from his adopted family and reconnect with the Ragnor name, could have changed his name to Garron well before meeting you—his actual father. By the time he got to Sirati, it was far too late to change it again, after answering to the name Garron for a decade under the Eldre's tutelage."

"How did we not see it?" asked Anson.

"How did *I* not see it?" asked the Eldre. "He was with my family for ten years, and I brought him into your city."

"We were all fooled, Eldre," said Ziza. "No one is to blame. But now we must find Thomas."

"So Garron is your son. You two were workin' togevva," said Bartleby. "It makes total sense. Evil must run in duh family. You knew 'ee was playin' us duh 'ole bloody time, didn't ya? Out wif it."

"I know my past might lead you to expect otherwise, but I am a different dragon now, Bartleby. I promise you: I had no idea Brax was impersonating anyone or had a bloody pseudonym. He returned to my life a few months back, begging for me to forgive him, and just when I was about to, those Skinx of his drugged me and took me captive—after a bit of a fight of course. Look, the bottom line is, Thomas needs our help and we can either waste time bickering over the past or we can go help him and deal with our issues later."

"You're right. We will go find Thomas, but we're not finished, not by a long shot. We will continue dis conversation later," said Bartleby.

The lights around the entrance flickered and beamed stronger than ever. A shield formed around the entrance.

"The shield is up," said the Eldre. "He must have awoken the city."

"Who?"

"Well, the only one who could, Thomas Scargen."

"What are you sayin'?"

"He's saying that the Gauntlet gives Thomas the key to the city, or makes him the key to the city," said Larson. "He was able to interface with everything in Huacas."

"It's more than that," said the Eldre. "He has recharged Huacas to full capacity. The Ancestor Stones."

"What about the Ancestor Stones?" asked Loric.

"If the city is charged, that means the Ancestor Stones are as well," said the Eldre. "This is worrisome."

"What's so bad about that?" asked Larson.

"The Ancestor Stones contain vast amounts of knowledge, but they are also the energy storage units for Huacas."

"In the wrong hands that kind of stored energy could prove extremely dangerous," said Loric. "Find these units and you will most certainly find Scargen."

"Lead us to him, Larson," said Ziza.

"Of course. Follow me."

The group made their way to the entrance, blazing their way through the remaining defenders.

"If you are the Second Augmentor, does that mean you will be augmenting the Ignus?" asked Ziza.

"No. I've already augmented the Gauntlet with the Medenculus," said Larson.

"What do you mean?" asked Itsuki.

"I augmented the blue stone. That is why we have to hurry. Brax will do anything to get his hands on the Medenculus—even turn on his own scales and blood."

"And the only way for him to get the stone is to kill the Bearer," said Anson.

"And if I know my son, that is exactly what he plans to do."

What happened? thought Itsuki. "Where is the red stone?"

"I'm guessing Brax has it," said Larson.

"Or someone far worse. We must hurry," said Ziza. His eyes glowed green as roots rose from the ground and pried open the entrance, ripping the doors off in the process and destroying the shield. "Please, Larson. Lead the way."

The companions began to move into Huacas. Several crag materialized in front of the entrance, cutting off Malcolm and Itsuki from the rest of the group. Anson, Loric, and Ziza turned to face the threat from inside the entrance. Itsuki had never seen so many demons together at once.

"Halt!" wailed one of the demons. "We shall not grant you passage."

"Oh dis is just what we needed right bloody now," said Malcolm. "Free dozen bloody crag to deal wif."

"I counted thirty-seven," said Itsuki.

"Maf was never my strong suit," said Malcolm.

Talya rocketed towards their position and landed behind Malcolm and Itsuki.

"Looks like you boys could use a claw," said Talya.

"These crag are, no doubt, a last line of defense as it were," said Loric. "It seems your subtle way of opening doors, High Mancer, triggered this response—a clever bit of Necromancy, I must admit."

Ziza moved to help, but Anson stopped him.

"There is no time," said Anson. "Loric and I can handle this."

Anson shifted once again into his werewolf state and Loric into his tiger form.

"No problem," snarled Loric.

"Go with the others," Anson said to Ziza. "Find Thomas and Yareli. They need you."

"Good luck, Anson," said the High Mancer.

Ziza turned and made his way down the corridor behind the other companions. Itsuki drew *Onikira* as Malcolm crouched, exposing his fangs—ready to attack. Talya roared fire behind them.

"Hell is empty, and all the devils are here!" shouted Anson.

The demons moved to attack.

54

the dragon con

"H-h-how are you doing this?" asked Thomas.

"It's quite simple actually," said Brax. He waved for Yareli and Wiyaloo to stand down. The two backed off and stood at attention behind Brax. "Have you ever heard of a lurchon?"

"Demons that can be controlled through a host by the conjurer," said Thomas, remembering the passage from Spells.

"That is right, Thomas," said Brax. "I am impressed. I guess Spells deserves some credit on that one. There is a small demon attached to your dear friend. It allows me to command her to do as I wish, and as you know, if I can control her, I can control Wiyaloo as well."

"Why are you doing this, Garron?"

"I want my stone back."

"What makes you think it's yours?" asked Thomas.

"I felt its power long ago, and it spoke to me. The Medenculus belongs to me."

"You ever consider psychiatric treatment?" asked Thomas.

"All of the stones belong to the dragons. *We* created them in the forges of Drook. *We* were the original Augmentors."

"Is that what the symbol on the helmet is for?" asked Thomas.

"You learned much from your time with the Atlantean. It is the original seal of the Dragon Council. It is one of the Ancient power runes—like the Glophitis that resides on the palm of your toy. It is called the Dracsulo."

"Thanks for the history lesson and all, but I hate to state the obvious." Thomas wiggled his fingers of the Gauntlet. "The stone belongs to me now."

"*Now* being the key word," said Brax.

"Even if you kill me, you do realize the stones will eject from the Gauntlet and shoot who-knows-where?"

"I know."

"Then what's the point?" asked Thomas.

"Who-knows-where is better than Atlantis. There was no way I would have been capable of getting the stone out of that city a second time. Lord Grimm, on the other hand, is a different story."

"What happened to you? Your father said you were crazy, but you lived with Kucha, Yaku, and Turu for a decade—not to mention the Eldre. Don't they mean anything to you?"

"Yes, of course. I must admit, at first, I was merely using them, but I became accustomed to their presence. For a time, they were the only family I had."

"Some family," said Kucha. "We considered you a brother."

"And I you, but the Medenculus is my new family. Lord Grimm is my new family."

"You have completely lost it, Garron," said Thomas.

"My name is Brax Ragnor!" shouted Brax. "Garron was a pseudonym I assumed after running away from my adoptive parents. I left once I discovered I could shift. I could hide in this new form and no one, not even my parents, would know who I was. I could finally be free. I moved to Angkora. I wanted a fresh start—a new beginning. No one would find me again if I didn't want them to. The first thing I did was try to find my birth parents. It took some time, but, after some digging through the Council's archives, I found who they were—Larson and Ilyana Ragnor. I was a Ragnor. I changed my name that day. I wanted to distance myself from my adoptive name, Brax, so I changed it to Garron. I could be a Ragnor, but no one else had to know. The Ragnor name was not held in high regard in those days, and I was still quite insecure and weak. My father's legacy was anything but. The name gave me strength. Garron Dar."

Garron is Ragnor jumbled up, thought Thomas. "So the story about your father and the batilloc match, that was true?"

"Yes, Thomas, every word of it. My adoptive father was a gambler—a bad one at that. That game was the only time he told me he loved me, but it was because he had made some quick credits on the result. That man had no love for me—for anyone. Like I said before, he was not a good dragon. I have the scars to prove it. They, I am afraid, do not change, even when I shift."

Brax took off the tactical vest and turned, showing Thomas his back. It was covered in the mutilations. They almost blended with the dark tattoos. He turned back to Thomas.

"Once I met my birth father, I took the Ragnor name. I didn't have to hide who I was anymore. I had come to realize that both parts of my life made me who I was, so I used my old name Brax along with my birth name Ragnor."

"I'm sorry, Garron . . . Brax . . . whatever your name is, but that is no excuse for what you are doing now."

"I was always so powerless, but I will not be powerless ever again."

"Did he promise you that?"

"Grimm? No, he *gave* me that. I owe him everything. He taught me that power is the only thing that people respect, and magic is a great way to get power. He showed my father and me mercy and took me under his wing. I spent years thinking that my master was dead."

"But what about your father?"

"I didn't know my father until I was an adult. When we finally escaped and could finally be together, he changed. The strong dragon of history became a peaceful Augmentor. All my father could talk about was his premonitions. But when he asked me to help him retrieve the Medenculus, I finally felt like we were a family. I wanted to help. We spent months perfecting the plan. They were great times. But everything changed when I touched the stone. Everything I ever thought important became secondary. I had finally felt the strength I had been searching for all those years. When the opportunity presented itself, I stole the stone from my father and hid it safely alongside something I had hidden for Lord Grimm years before."

"What did you hide for Lord Grimm?"

"That is no matter, Thomas. When I went back to collect the stone, it was gone. It was not until twelve years later that I would realize that my Lord had returned. He summoned me back into the fold."

"Summoned you?"

"Shortly after his reemergence after the battle at the Augmentor's temple, when you defeated Arkmalis."

"But how?"

Brax pointed to the tattoo on his hand. "It is actually quite simple. He used the Daimicron."

Thomas recalled Larson's explanation of the markings.

"It is my connection to my Lord and his magic. All that have trained with Lord Grimm have them."

Thomas thought of the tattoos on Arkmalis and how they covered his body as well.

"How does it feel being the consolation prize?" asked Thomas.

"Arkmalis? He was a boy when I studied with my Master. I was Lord Grimm's first pupil. The day he was imprisoned, I was the one who attacked Cairo."

"And when he woke up and called you, you came running back like a cowardly dog."

"You have no idea the power that Lord Grimm wields. When he summoned me, I went to him with open arms. I was a good pupil. I told him about this place and its marvels, and why I came here in the first place."

"Why *did* you come here?" asked Kucha.

"A very good question, Kucha," said Thomas.

"My father's vision showed him that he was to augment the stone in Huacas. I figured I would wait for that to happen and again steal the stone for myself. My father, however, had not shared all of the specifics with me. I did not know how long I would have to wait for your arrival, and I had not spoken to my father since I had taken the Medenculus from him. I knew the Atlanteans had resecured the stone, and that I would never find Atlantis on my own. I also knew that, even if I did, that it would matter little. It would take an army to get it a second time. I figured my best bet was to worm my way into Huacas and wait. While I waited, I would learn as much as I could about the Gauntlet and its ways. Here, I could study the only living archive that contained information on the Medenculus. I admit, it took me some time to gain the Eldre's trust, but time is something I had plenty of."

"He loved you like a son," said Kucha.

Brax ignored the Turtle. "I explained all of this to Lord Grimm. He was sympathetic to my need for the Medenculus, and he enlightened me to your situation. Once I told him that my father was slated to be your Second Augmentor, the plan began to evolve. He said he had a mission for me. Just like old times. He knew of the whereabouts of the Ignus and knew that, sooner or later, you would find it. He said it was only a matter of time before you would discover the Infospheres. He was right about that. I would help him obtain the Ignus, and he would help me reclaim the Medenculus. He had the army I needed to take back what was rightfully mine. Lord Grimm had plans for the blue stone as well, but it would be returned to me when he was done with you. I would suggest an audience with you at Huacas and convince you that you needed our help in your training. I must admit, I was beside myself when you did not show."

He smiled and continued. "But as luck would have it, that made it that much easier to coerce the Eldre into going to Sirati. He already had a fantasy of delivering you some silly prophecy from the Ancestors, so I played off of his delusion. The rest was simple. I was to infiltrate Sirati and, when the opportunity presented itself, take the stone and lure you back here. In the meantime, the Skinx would take over Huacas. I had befriended them in my dragon form years ago, when I first arrived here. Getting them on board was easy. Over the years, the Skinx have developed a pretty robust slave trade by kidnapping the Salamen who are imbecilic enough to leave the protection of this city. I promised the Skinx Huacas and all the Newts they could possibly need—a whole city full of new slaves for the taking.

Grimm offered them advanced tech and a power source. In return, they would do whatever I asked of them."

"Like kidnap your own father?" asked Thomas.

"I was just fulfilling my father's precious premonition. I had to make sure Dad was close by for the augmentation. Grimm needed you in possession of the Medenculus and augmented at full strength to charge the *tuqi*. After that, you would be drained of your power and far easier to deal with."

"Is that what he told you?" asked Thomas. "Is that why he left you here to fend for yourself?"

"I am more than capable of taking care of myself, Bearer. Lord Grimm has plans for this world—grand, amazing plans, and I am a key component in them. A war is coming, Thomas—the size and scope of which you could not possibly fathom. Besides, I am not alone."

The demonic Wiyaloo and Yareli stepped forward. Yareli reached into her quiver and pulled out an arrow that glowed red and nocked it into her bow. Wiyaloo twirled his staff and pointed it at Thomas.

"And seeing how I don't like doing the heavy lifting."

"Finally. I thought you were just gonna keep on talking till I died of boredom," said Thomas. He had stalled for as long as he could. He had regained some of his energy, but not much. "Is it me, but do all bad guys feel the need to tell you way more than you asked?"

"I am done talking, Thomas." He motioned to Yareli and Wiyaloo. "Destroy the Bearer."

"Do you really think you can control them forever?" asked Thomas.

"No, but long enough to destroy you and get my stone," said Brax.

"Don't worry, Tommy," said Yareli. "I promise this won't hurt a bit."

"Yareli, wake up! Can't you see what he's doing to you?"

"Oh, I'm wide awake. More awake then I've been for years." Yareli loosed her arrow. The red glowing arrow erupted into a demonic looking grizzly bear. The bear growled and advanced rapidly.

"That's new," said Thomas as Wiyaloo simultaneously attacked.

Thomas flipped backwards and avoided the swipe of the massive demon bear. Wiyaloo spun his staff. Red energy flowed at Thomas. Thomas formed a shield deflecting the attack. *This feels oddly familiar.*

Brax jumped up onto one of the remaining Ancestor Stones and sat down smiling. "This should be amusing."

"Wiyaloo, snap out of it," said Thomas.

"I serve my lady," said Wiyaloo, moving in to attack the Bearer.

He spun his staff and again shot at Thomas, who moved backwards, avoiding the shot. Yareli loosed her second arrow The arrow transformed into a disturbing version of an eagle. Its dark features and glowing red eyes descended upon Thomas. He reacted as fast as he could, rolling to his left to avoid the swooping monster. Thomas tracked the bird as it moved to attack again.

"Haaaaaa!" said Thomas as he flung his energy at the eagle, destroying the dark bird.

The bear barreled at Thomas and caught him in his midsection. The Bearer flew sideways, hitting the stone ground. The bear pressed its advantage and jumped on top of Thomas.

"You need to lose some weight." Thomas increased his energy level, pushing himself as far as he could. Energy emanated from Thomas's body, destroying the dark creature. "There that's better."

Wiyaloo fired several blasts, and in Thomas's weakened state they all found their target. Thomas crawled on the ground, clothes singed and smoking. He flopped down face-first. He could not move. That is when Yareli appeared above him. He looked up at her and smiled.

"You look great in red, Yar."

She put her boot under his chin. "Get up."

He sat up as much as he could.

"Yareli, you have to fight this."

"Why, Tommy? I'm having a great time." She leaned over and kissed him on the lips. He pulled away.

"Yareli stop."

"Isn't that what you wanted, Tommy?"

"Not like this, Yar. This isn't you."

"How would you know? You're just pathetic. That's why I could never be with you."

"What are you saying?"

"You are half the man that Brax Ragnor is."

"Technically he's not a man," said Thomas.

"Always making jokes. Well, this isn't a joke, Tommy."

"Please, Yareli. Stop," said Thomas. "Can't you see. He's making you do these things."

"What's the problem? Can't you handle the truth?" She pulled him up on his feet and lifted up the Gauntlet. "Maybe you don't deserve this after all." She dropped the Gauntlet and moved her hand forward and screamed. "*Ta-tai!*"

Thomas's body flew backwards. The force of the attack caught him off balance. He hit the side wall and fell face first into a pool of water. Thomas gasped in and swallowed water. His instincts told him to get up, but he could not. His power was gone.

The water began to churn around Thomas. He could feel the push and pull of the circulating water. The Gauntlet twinged. Thomas formed a fist at the shock and opened his eyes under the water. He looked down at his fist and opened his hand. The Glophitis glowed blue. The regenerative force began to slowly spread throughout his entire form. *The water's healing me.* His energy level climbed as the restorative power now coursed through him. It felt amazing. He had energized the whole city with the Medenculus. The stone's healing qualities had transferred into the water, and now the water had revitalized him. A fact he would not share with Brax Ragnor. Thomas began to crawl out of the pool, feigning injury. Wiyaloo stood above him and pressed him down into the pool with his staff.

"Wait, Wiyaloo. What are you doing?"

"My lady has commanded me to destroy you."

"When do you ever remember Yareli commanding you to attack friends?"

"I must do what I am told."

"Even if that puts Yareli in jeopardy?"

"I am just protecting my lady."

"Don't you understand, this is not protecting Yareli. This is the exact opposite of that."

"I need to protect her."

"You know I'd never let anything bad happen to her, so why am I the one you are fighting?"

"I am not sure."

"It's because Brax is controlling you and putting Yareli in danger." Wiyaloo turned his head.

"What are you waiting for fox?" yelled Brax. "Finish him."

"If you don't start fighting this, then she will die, Wiyaloo," said Thomas. "I need your help."

The fox stared at him for what felt like hours.

"She has commanded me," said Wiyaloo. "I must do her bidding."

"That doesn't sound like the Yareli I know. She would never want you to do something against your will."

"I am confused," said Wiyaloo.

"Please, Wiyaloo. The only way you can save her is to break your connection, and help me defeat Brax."

Wiyaloo looked at Yareli.

"She is not herself. She is not in control. I need you right now, Wiyaloo." Wiyaloo looked back at Thomas. "She needs you."

The red in his eyes slowly transitioned back to white. The white energy flowed across his body as he returned to his familiar form.

"Agreed," said the spirit ghost. Wiyaloo had broken the connection with Yareli. His love for her had severed the link.

"It is good to have you back, Wiyaloo."

"It is nice to be back, Thomas Scargen."

"Now, concentrate your energy on the stasis field on the left and I will take the one on the right. It's about time we turned the odds to our favor."

"Agreed," said Wiyaloo as he turned and fired at the stasis field that held Yaku.

The field failed and the young Turtle landed on the ground. Thomas had simultaneously did the same to Kucha's field.

Yareli spun and fired another arrow in the direction of Thomas and Wiyaloo. This one erupted into several dark ghoulish monkeys. They moved speedily at Thomas and the fox spirit, but Thomas was renewed. He threw the Gauntlet forward blasting three of them as they moved across the floor. Wiyaloo battled two of them as they flew up at him. He fought them off with his staff as he fired blasts at three others that advanced. Thomas just continued to incinerate the beasts as they loped and jumped at him. One of them grabbed the Gauntlet pulling it backwards. Thomas ripped his arm forward and the demonic monkey went flying in the air. Wiyaloo blasted it out of the sky. They had handled the monkeys.

Yareli nocked yet another arrow into her bow, but this time before she could fire it, Yaku walked up to her and touched her leg. Purple energy poured through Yareli. She looked like she was being shocked, and her eyes went from red to white as a diminutive demon appeared and popped off of her back. The lurchon tried to slink away, but was met with a purple energy sphere from Kucha. Yareli dropped to the floor unconscious, but Wiyaloo did not disappear.

"I guess it worked," said Thomas.

"Our connection was permanently severed when I disobeyed her order to kill you."

"Wow. Thanks again for that."

Brax dropped from his perch and moved forward. "I guess it comes down to this."

He lifted his hand, and dark energy poured out of it, encapsulating Yaku. She fell to the ground in a dark cocoon.

"Yaku!" screamed Kucha as he ran to her, but he was met with the same fate. The two lay there incapacitated next to Yareli.

"I don't always like to get my talons dirty, but in this case . . ." Brax transformed into his dragon form. "I'll make an exception."

"You ready, buddy?" asked Thomas.

"I am."

"You take the left and I'll take the right."

"Agreed," said Wiyaloo.

Brax darted directly at Thomas. Thomas pushed the Gauntlet forward, directing blue energy at the advancing dragon. Brax flew into the air, spun, and dove downwards at Thomas. Wiyaloo appeared in front of the dragon and delivered an attack from his staff. The blast caught the dragon in his side, knocking him out of the air. Brax landed on his feet and slithered at Thomas. Brax stopped short and breathed fire into his talons, gathering it into a massive fireball. The dragon threw the sphere at the Bearer. Thomas lifted his hands. Water from one of the surrounding pools moved through the air, connecting with the fireball. Steam filled the cavernous room.

"Very well done, Bearer. You must be practicing. The Eldre would be so proud." Brax threw his claw forward, shooting dark energy at him.

Thomas moved at the last second to avoid the strike, but the dragon had moved in behind him, swiping his tail under Thomas's feet. Thomas was sent flying into the wall. The dragon advanced once more, but the Spirit Ghost Warrior moved to intercept.

Wiyaloo spun his staff, collecting energy into the weapon. He thrust the staff forward. Energy poured at the dragon. Brax formed a shield that deflected the attack. Brax started chanting behind the force field. Thomas could not hear the words, but he was fairly certain what he was doing. He had seen Neficus do the same in the elephant graveyard. The ground cracked below them as the dark smoke seeped out, forming into two crag.

"What is your bidding, master?" asked the two crag.

"Destroy the fox spirit."

"Yes, my master."

The dragon turned towards Thomas. "I like these odds better," said Brax as the two crag moved at Wiyaloo.

The three began to fight as Thomas attacked the dragon. The blast knocked Brax backwards, destroying his force field shield. The dragon jumped up and off of the adjacent wall and was on Thomas in seconds. Fire rained down on Thomas as he formed another shield of water. Again, the fire steamed as it hit the liquid barrier.

"You're all fired up," said Thomas. "I think you just needed to let off some steam."

"We'll see about that," said Brax as he lunged at Thomas.

The dragon's fist connected with his side, sending him flying backwards. The wall stopped his momentum. He stood up slowly in just enough time to see Wiyaloo defeat the first demon with an impressive flourish from his staff. The dragon moved towards Thomas, connecting again with a blow from his tail. Thomas fell to his knees. The dragon lifted him up with his talons.

"This is where I destroy you and take back what is rightfully mine."

"It's a bit early to start claiming yourself the winner," said Thomas as he raised his hands collecting the surrounding water, forming a fist.

The water hit the dragon square in the side of his head. Brax dropped Thomas. Thomas churned the liquid, encircling the dragon in a watery prison. The Aequos swam through the current and flew out of the side of the water attack.

"Come now, Thomas. I'm a sea dragon. Do you think water is going to stop me?"

"It was worth a try," said Thomas as he jumped back avoiding the dark blast from the beast.

Thomas shot a series of energy spheres back at the dragon. The Aequos danced around the shots as he barreled down at Thomas. The black energy knocked the legs out from underneath Thomas. It formed into a hand of sorts and grabbed Thomas, pinning him against the wall. The dragon advanced, adding more and more dark energy to the prison. Layer upon layer of dark, oozing energy covered Thomas. He looked around for help.

Wiyaloo was trading blows with the second demon. The crag was proving more difficult to destroy than its predecessor. Thomas was on his own and was helpless. It was only a matter of time before Brax would finish what he started. The dragon walked over to Thomas. He lifted his head and was even with Thomas's face.

"Look who fell right into my trap," said Brax. "Thank you for making this easy." The dragon lifted his claw over Thomas's head. "Goodbye, Bearer."

"*Sug-mani-tu!*" shouted Yareli from across the room.

He heard her words before he saw the familiar white spirits. The wolves jumped onto the back of the black Aequos, forcing him to cease his attack. Yareli had awoken and fired her last arrow to save Thomas.

It's now or never, thought Thomas. He reached down deep and raised his energy level. The cocoon that had twisted around him was incinerated in seconds. He was free. Thomas fell to the ground, but landed on his feet. Thomas pointed the Gauntlet at the crag that was still fighting Wiyaloo. "Haaaaa!" The energy output tore the demon apart in seconds.

Brax had been backed into a corner by the attacking wolves. The pack was all over his body. Wiyaloo appeared on the beast's left and Thomas walked towards the right side. He drew his hand back and began to collect energy. His eyes burned with power.

"I guess you were wrong. It's you who's trapped," he said as he moved the Gauntlet forward.

Right before the blast connected with Brax, the dragon opened a teleportal and slithered through it. A second teleportal opened next to Yareli, and Brax slipped out of it. The Aequos grabbed the bow with one claw and crushed it.

"And to think, I was beginning to like you."

His other claw moved so quickly, neither Thomas nor Wiyaloo had time to react. The sharp talons impaled Yareli through the stomach. She let out a cry of pain and fell silent.

"If I cannot have what I want, then neither will you." The beast dropped her to the ground.

"Nooooooooo!" shouted Thomas as he blurred across the room connecting the Gauntlet to the jaw of the black Aequos.

Thomas heard the snap as soon as he made contact. The dragon stumbled backwards and turned to see Wiyaloo. He swirled his staff creating an attack the size of which Thomas had never seen before from the Spirit Ghost Warrior.

"You are done here, dragon," said Wiyaloo as he pushed the staff forward.

The white stream of energy collided with Brax, knocking him backwards into the wall. Brax collapsed onto the ground. Blood speckled his elongated, dark form as he lied there twitching in pain.

Brax's eyes rolled back in his head, and he fell unconscious. The prisons that had surrounded Yaku and Kucha vanished.

"Yareli," said Thomas as he picked her up off the ground. "Talk to me, Yar. Talk to me."

"Thomas. I-I-I can hear you," said Yareli as she spit out blood.

Wiyaloo appeared behind the Bearer. "My lady?"

The two Turtles hung back behind them.

"It's going to be fine, Wiyaloo. I'm returning to the Spirit."

"Yareli, No. You stay with me. You are going to be fine. I promise." Thomas looked down at the wound. *No.* Blood seeped from the lacerations made by the dragon's claw. "It doesn't even look that bad."

"You are a terrible liar, Thomas. You always have been." She looked past him and at the spirit ghost. "Wiyaloo you are finally free. This makes me happier than you will ever know. I love you so much. Thank you for everything you have ever done for me."

"The pleasure was all mine, my lady. But the Bearer is correct. Your time has not come yet."

"I wish I believed either of you, but I know you both too well." She coughed again as blood trickled down her jaw. "There isn't much time now. I can feel my spirit slipping from Earth Realm."

"But Yar—"

"Shhh, Thomas," said Yareli, putting her finger on his lips. "I have something I want to say before it is too late."

Thomas began to cry. He could not control the steady stream that crept from his eyes.

"You came into my life and showed me that there was more than anger and hate in this world—a world that needs you now more than ever. You are amazing, Thomas Scargen, and I love y—" Yareli slumped down in Thomas's arms. Her eyes closed, and she was still.

"I love you too, Yar."

55

a horde of demons

Itsuki wielded *Onikira* through the advancing horde. He sliced the katana diagonally at the first crag, dividing the demon. He spun to his left to deflect the tendril attack of the next, spinning the blade downward and separating the appendage from the crag. The monster yowled and reeled. Itsuki swiftly brandished *Onikira*, sending an energy wave at three more crag. The blast destroyed the three demons instantly. The *hitodama* flitted behind the Augmentor.

Talya flew above the battlefield. Four of the demons followed, flapping their tattered wings. Malcolm moved to intercept the crag that trailed behind the dragon. Three more pursued him. Talya turned around and rained fire into the crag that chased her. Malcolm banked to his right to avoid the firestorm. The vampire turned to face the demons behind him.

Itsuki looked across at the wolf and the tiger. Crag separated his group from theirs. Loric pounced on an attacking demon, ripping through the crag's torso. The dark beast screamed in pain as the weretiger roared.

"Is that all you got!" He bounded up a rock formation and down into the dark army. The demons moved to surround the weretiger.

Anson shot a pulse into the demons, dispersing the crag. Anson ran into the swarm of demons standing back to back with Loric.

"What the dickens have you got yourself into?" growled Anson.

"I'd say the thick of it," said Loric. Both of the men began to systematically attack the crag.

Itsuki continued to cut his way through the crag, annihilating demons as he crept through the scattered artif, Lizard, and troll bodies that littered the battlefield. He used them as cover as he quietly made his way to the wolf and tiger.

Two crag materialized in Itsuki's path. The demon on the right shot dark energy at the Augmentor. Itsuki spun the sword creating a shield, deflecting the dark attack to the side. The second crag joined in, pouring more of the dark energy at Itsuki. He moved his sword in a blur defending himself from the two demons. Since he was occupied with the two crag, he did not see the third sneak in behind him.

A tendril thrashed out at Itsuki, sweeping his legs out from under him. A second tendril wrapped around the Augmentor's left leg and then retracted. Itsuki was pulled across the jungle floor. He stabbed *Onikira* down into the dirt to slow himself. He came to a halt. Before he could react, he was yanked once more. Itsuki lost hold of the weapon. The dark energy poured down on him, squirming its way around his body. Before long, he was trapped inside a dark prison. *Onikira* sat stuck into the ground ten feet away. Itsuki writhed and turned to try and get out, but it seemed the harder he struggled, the tighter the prison became. He ceased moving and began to meditate.

Itsuki could sense the spiritual energy from the jungle and the city. Huacas was built on a nexus just like Sirati. He could see the spirits moving on the outskirts of the battle. The demon activity must have stirred them.

The sound of the scream woke him as the dark cocoon fell from the sky and landed next to Itsuki.

"Dat was bloody mental," said Malcolm as he rolled over to look at Itsuki. The vampire's fate mirrored his own. The two lay amongst the carnage of the battle—trapped. "Dere's just too many of dem." Crag surged towards them. Two more crag landed, retracted their wings, and advanced. "Dose are duh ones dat bloody did dis to me."

Malcolm and Itsuki were surrounded. He hoped Loric and Anson were faring better.

The fire erupted behind the dark creatures, burning through the crag. Talya landed in front of Itsuki and Malcolm. The crag moved with incalculable speed and were on the dragon as soon as she landed. Talya tried to stave off the assault, but the odds were not in her favor. Tendrils wrapped around Talya's legs and then around her front claws.

"You demons have no idea what you're doing," said Talya. "I am going to get out of this and tear each and every one of you apart with my own talons."

"You are in no position to be issuing threats, dragon," said one of the crag. He and several other crag encircled Talya in the dark energy. She collapsed to the ground.

"So much for duh rescue effort," said Malcolm.

"Is this really the time?" said Talya.

The demons began to descend upon them. Itsuki looked over at his sword. The wisps circled around the hilt. The handle was shaped like twisting yodi—forest demons. Itsuki closed his eyes. He concentrated on *Onikira*. The katana rose out of the dirt, flew over to Itsuki, and sliced down the dark cocoon, releasing him. The sword slapped into his hand as he jumped into the air. He sliced downward through the oncoming crag. The beast shrieked and then dissipated. Twelve more rushed towards the Augmentor.

Itsuki concentrated and focused. He closed his eyes. He could now see the spirits. They were flying around him. The spirits flew into the sword. Itsuki opened his eyes. They burned hot as the spiritual energy built inside of him. Itsuki had never felt this kind of power before. As the demons simultaneously attacked, Itsuki planted his feet, electricity crackling around him.

The Augmentor collected the spiritual power into the sword. He twirled *Onikira*, the Demon Killer, in his hand. He leapt and sliced the sword through the air.

"Yahhhhhhh!"

The pulse wave tore through the demons, incinerating the advancing line of crag. The spirit wave disappeared as the spirits separated and made their way back into the jungle.

"Bloody remarkable," said Malcolm.

The dark energy that surrounded the vampire shriveled and wilted. Talya was also freed. Itsuki powered down. The *hitodama* whirled around, surveying the area the demons had been destroyed in.

"Where did you learn dat lit'l trick?"

"I am not sure," said Itsuki. "My power level increased with the help of the spirits, and I just knew what I was supposed to do."

The Augmentor looked out across the battlefield. The tiger and the wolf had held their own against the other half of the horde. Only five crag remained, but Anson was in trouble.

Two of the demons held him in the air, while a third crag stood in front of him. This demon was bigger than the others. Itsuki sensed that this crag was powerful as well. Loric was busy fighting the other two and was quite a distance away from the werewolf. Anson looked exhausted and unable to move. The large crag moved his fist forward and a bone jutted out from the top of his wrist.

"You will die now, dog." The demons hand flashed forward towards the head of Anson Warwick.

Loric blurred in front of the crag, catching the attack in his midsection.

"Ahhhhhh!" shouted Loric. "Wake up, Warwick!"

Loric moved his hands upward. Rocks jutted up from the ground, impaling the two crag who held Anson. Anson hit the ground and rolled to his right. He spun around and blasted the skewered demons, incinerating them.

The crag lifted Loric, piercing the tiger further. Loric raised his paws and smashed down, shattering the demon's boned weapon.

"Yahhhh!" shrieked the demon as it reeled backwards. Loric dropped to the ground. Blood choked from the tiger's mouth and poured from his open wound. He slumped over lifeless. The crag laughed above the fallen tiger as Loric slowly transformed into his human form.

He's dead, thought Itsuki. *Mancer Bodes is dead.*

The two crag that were previously battling Loric moved to engage the werewolf. Anson raised his hands and telekinetically grabbed the two crag. He threw them backwards. Before they could recover,

Anson streamed orange energy towards both of the demons, destroying them. Itsuki and Malcolm moved to help Anson.

Loric sprung to life and gasped for air. He choked as he raised himself to his feet. Anson moved in next to him. The demon lurched forward, looking down at Loric.

"I don't understand," said the crag. "You were dead."

"Do you not know cats have nine lives?" said Loric.

Itsuki and Malcolm moved in behind the crag. They had the beast surrounded.

"No matter. I will destroy all of you as many times as I have to."

Anson moved his paws back, drawing energy into them. Itsuki and Malcolm did the same.

"No," said Loric, putting his hand up. Loric shifted back into his tiger form. "I've got this one."

Anson, Malcolm, and Itsuki powered down.

"By all means," said Anson. He walked away from the demon and the tiger and shifted to his human form.

"You are pathetic," said the crag. "I am not afraid of a mere tig—"

Loric's claw connected with the demon's abdomen before the crag could react, ripping through the dark beast.

"How's that for pathetic?" The demon stuttered backwards. Loric roared as he placed his paw on the injured demon—his eyes glowing. "This is for killing me."

The energy consumed the demon instantaneously. The hulking tiger growled into the sky. Loric powered down and returned to his human form. He dropped to his knees. Black blood covered him.

Malcolm walked over to Itsuki. "And dat's why I'm not a cat person," he said. "Bloody killing machines."

Itsuki smiled. Anson helped Loric to his feet. The two walked over to Itsuki. "No matter how many times I die, it always bloody hurts like the first," said Loric.

"How many is that now?"

"That is the fifth time I have perished, but it is the first time by demon."

"Thank you," said Anson. "I just want to say, Loric, what's past is prologue."

"For once, one of your quotes is applicable," said Loric. "You would have done the same for me, and did do so in the past. I have always been honored to call you colleague." Loric sat down on a rock. "I concur with your assessment. Perhaps we should let sleeping dogs lie, as it were. If not for ourselves, then for Scargen."

"Yes . . . for Thomas," said Anson. He too sat down.

"It's about bloody time you two kissed and made up," said Malcolm. "You need all duh friends you can get, Anson."

"I agree with the vampire," said Talya.

The spiritual disturbance hit Itsuki like a shock wave, freezing the Augmentor where he stood. "Oh no," said Itsuki as he fell to his knees.

"What's duh problem, Suki?" asked Malcolm. "We just kicked a substantial amount uv demon ass."

"Something is wrong," said Itsuki. He could feel overwhelming pain and sorrow coming from inside Huacas. The Augmentor stood and moved towards the entrance with the *hitodama* trailing behind.

"What exactly do you intend to do?" asked Loric.

"To help," said Itsuki. "Something terrible has happened."

"I felt it as well," said Loric. "But there is no way you are in any condition to help."

"I have to try. It is my duty."

The mountain began to rumble and shake. A small avalanche slid down the mountainside, burying the entranceway. Loric sprang to his feet and lifted his hands upward. Some of the rocks that blocked the entrance moved to the side, revealing more boulders. Loric sped over to the entrance and placed his palm against the collapsed earth.

"It is no good," said Loric "I can sense that the whole hallway has collapsed inward, and, I'm afraid that in my current state, I cannot move all the debris. I am sorry, Itsuki."

"What exactly did you feel?" asked Talya.

Itsuki stared at the blocked entry. He sheathed *Onikira*, and turned around.

"The dimming of a spirit," said Itsuki.

56

a girl and her fox

"Yareli . . . Yareli . . . wake up!" yelled Thomas. He could not believe what had just transpired. Wiyaloo had broken his connection to Yareli to save Thomas and to help defeat Brax, but in the fight, Yareli had been mortally wounded by the dragon's final assault.

"You have to act quickly, Thomas," said Kucha. "Remember what we talked about."

"I'm not sure I can."

"You are the only one who can," said Wiyaloo. "The rest of us do not have the required power."

Thomas concentrated the energy to his palms and then pressed them onto the open wound. The energy went through Yareli and dissipated. Blood continued to pour out.

"It's not working."

"Concentrate, Thomas," said Kucha.

Thomas once again tried to fix the injury with little success.

"You need to use the water, Thomas Scargen," said Wiyaloo.

"Wiyaloo's right," said Kucha. "You have already energized it with the power from the Medenculus. The water spirits might be her last hope."

"Okay," said Thomas. "Stand back."

Thomas began to concentrate on the water. He focused his attention on the flowing liquid that ran throughout the city. He asked it to help him. The water flew through the sky and began to slowly twist and curve its way around Yareli as she was lifted into the air. Thomas's eyes burned as the energy coursed through him and into the water. The water spirits rose out of the liquid and swam in the same patterns as the water. But something was wrong. Yareli's status had not changed.

"She is dying," said Wiyaloo.

"It's not working," said Thomas.

"She is too far gone. She needs more energy," said Kucha.

Wiyaloo appeared next to Thomas. He knew right away what the Spirit Ghost Warrior had in mind.

"There is no other way, Thomas Scargen," said Wiyaloo. "She does not have much time."

"She will never forgive me," said Thomas.

"But she will be alive, and I am making this choice—not you."

"Help me to heal her," said Thomas.

"You and I both know that is not how this works."

"You can't do this, Wiyaloo. She needs you to protect her."

"If I do not do this, there will be no her to protect. This is the only way I know to help her." Wiyaloo looked over at Thomas. "She has you now. I am no longer needed in this Realm. Good bye, Thomas Scargen. Take care of her."

"Agreed," said Thomas as Wiyaloo's form collapsed into the Gauntlet.

flash

Thomas could see her running in the woods. She was much younger. She could not have been older than seven. She had her bow and real arrows in her quiver. She seemed to be aiming at random things and hitting them with her arrows. The little girl would laugh every time she hit her imagined target. She stopped in a clearing, nocked the arrow, and fired into the brush. The yelp that came from inside the bush frightened the little girl, but she went to investigate. She dug through the brush and found what she had hit.

It was a fox, a young one at that, and it was bleeding profusely. Yareli reached down and picked up the scared creature. She pulled the arrow from its side.

"What have I done?" She put her hands on the creature to try and stop the bleeding. "No, no, no, don't die."

The fox struggled for a bit, but died in her hands. She began to cry out loud. She had inadvertently shot and killed this poor defenseless creature. Her mourning was abruptly interrupted by the pack of wolves that began to circle around the girl. She stood up, holding the body of the fox.

"You cannot have him. His spirit is his own, and you'll have to kill me if you want it." And with these words, he appeared. Wiyaloo sprang forth from the fox's glowing corpse, which then vanished.

"Yaaaaa!" yelled Wiyaloo, causing the wolves to scatter.

"I-I-I-I don't understand," said Yareli.

"You have freed my spirit, my lady. I am forever in your debt."

"You're a spirit?"

"Yes. I was locked inside the body of that fox by a powerful Necromancer long ago. That is, until you freed me."

"Where did you come from?"

"From the Spirit Realm, my lady."

"Can you take me there?"

"Yes, my lady. I can." The fox spirit held out his hand and the little girl accepted it.

"Why are you here?"

"It seems I am here to protect you."

"How do you know?"

"Because, my lady, things happen for a reason. I am a Spirit Ghost Warrior, and you are my Spirit Summoner. I owe you my spirit, and I am yours until that debt is paid."

"What should I call you?"

"Wiyaloo."

"Whyyyyaaalooo," said Yareli as she smiled. "I like that."

flash

Thomas awoke once more to the present. He had seen the connection between these two at its origin, and he felt Wiyaloo's spirit. It had passed through Thomas's stone palm and into the water. His energy mixed with the healing blue light and water that churned around Yareli. The water flowed vigorously around her body, encapsulating her in a cocoon of water. Thomas pushed his energy level one last time. The cocoon glowed the brightest of blue hues and then ceased. The water fell to the side, and Yareli floated in midair, surrounded by a blue glow. Thomas ran over to her as she fell into his arms. She lay there motionless.

Ziza walked in through the entrance followed by Emfalmay, the Eldre, LINC, Larson, Bartleby, Fargus inside of Olly, and Turu. They stood there in silence.

"Yareli, are you in there?" asked the Bearer. "Please, that had to have worked." Yareli did not stir. She was still, and she was not breathing.

"Come on Yar, come on, come on," said Thomas as he rocked her back and forth. "Come on."

The others looked on. Ziza dropped his head as did Emfalmay. Bartleby began to tear up. Thomas drew her up to look at her face and whispered into her ear. "Please wake up. I love you too."

She jumped upward with her first breath and began to choke. Thomas looked at her stomach. The wound had healed. The only evidence that remained of the incident was the tear in her clothes.

"Yareli . . . oh . . . Yareli," said Thomas as he hugged her. "I thought you were gone. I can't believe it worked." Thomas pulled back to look at her.

"Well . . ." said Yareli, coughing, "apparently it did." She smiled back at him.

"Yeah, I can't take all the credit for that." Thomas paused and put his hand on the back of his head. "There's something you need to know."

"When did you start being so modest?" She smiled. "Where's Wiyaloo? I can't sense him."

"That's what I wanted to talk to you about." As soon as he said the words the smile faded from her face. "He's . . . he's . . .gone, Yareli."

"What do you mean he's gone? He can't be gone. He was just here."

"He sacrificed himself so you would live."

"I-I-I don't understand. He swore to protect me."

"That's exactly what he did."

"How could you let him do this?"

"I'm sorry, Yar. I—" The sound of the rocks falling down from the ceiling stopped Thomas's words. "We got to get out of here."

A big chunk fell from the sky directly above them. It was falling straight down on the two of them. LINC sprang into action, catching the rubble before it could hit Yareli and Thomas.

"My scans have concluded that the current structure can no longer hold its integrity due to Thomas Scargen's energy output. The only viable course of action is retreat." LINC tossed aside the piece of the ceiling out of harm's way.

"I'm with you there, buddy," said Thomas. "Bart, open up a tele-portal and get us freakin' out of here."

"Dat is exactly what I intend to d—"

The dragon fell silent as the second chunk of ceiling fell on him. The dragon appeared to be unconscious and trapped. More of the roof collapsed down as Thomas caught it telekinetically. It took what was left of his power to hold off the avalanche.

Fargus and Olly ran over and immediately tried to pry the stone off of Bartleby.

"What 'av you gone and bloody done now, Bart? Dis is no time for a nap."

The sportif clamped its hands down on the rock and tried its hardest to lift, but could not budge the structure. Larson moved in to help. Small pieces still rained down upon the companions. Larson grabbed the other side of the stone and pulled. The stone began to move upwards as Bartleby came to.

"What is goin' on?" said Bartleby was he looked up to see Larson and Olly pulling the stone off of him. "I fink I can get out now." Bartleby pulled himself from the structure while Larson and Olly held up the piece of the structure. He looked at Olly. "Fanks, mate." He turned to Larson. "Fanks."

"Don't mention it," said Larson.

"Probably won't ever again," said Bartleby. The dragon wasted no time forming a teleportal. "Now, everyone, let's get goin'."

The roof started to completely fall apart and began to collapse. Thomas had no reserves left. He was helpless.

The geysers of water shot up from below and pushed the mass of ceiling back in place. Thomas turned around to see the Eldre holding up the ceiling with the water. Streams of water flowed upwards, staving off the inevitable. Thomas let go of his hold.

"You look like you could use a hand," said Ziza as he joined the old Turtle and lifted his staff. Large roots sprang from underneath and helped hold up the structure.

"Come on," said Bartleby. "I fink we've overstayed a bit." Larson grabbed his son and drug him through the teleportal.

"LINC!" shouted Thomas. "Take Yareli and get her out of here."

"I cannot leave you here in immediate peril," said the artif. "My prime directive states—"

"I don't have time to go through this again. Take her now. I will be through in a minute. I want to make sure everyone gets out."

"Affirmative, Thomas Scargen," said LINC, swooping down and snagging Yareli from Thomas's hands. "It is good to see you again, Yareli Chula."

"You too, LINC," said Yareli as the two crossed the teleportal. The Bearer looked around to see the Eldre and the High Mancer holding up the structure, each with their eyes glowing hot. Water churned around the Eldre as vines and roots worked hard to build supports for the failing ceiling.

"Fargus," said the Eldre. "Grab one of the Ancestor Stones and take it with you."

"Aw'right," said Fargus.

The sportif walked over to the massive carved stones and lifted one. The spirits of the Ancestors flew out from the remaining stones and circled in the air. They shot into the *tuqi* Olly carried. The sportif crossed through the tear. That left Kucha, Turu, Yaku, Emfalmay, Ziza, Bartleby, Thomas, and the Eldre.

"It's now or never, people," said Bartleby.

"Ziza, this way," said Emfalmay.

"I cannot leave Tuguna here alone."

"It is all right, High Mancer. You are needed back home. I can hold it by myself for as long as needed."

The two looked at each other. Ziza bowed his head to the Sea Turtle.

"Goodbye, my friend," said Ziza.

It was then Thomas understood what was happening. Ziza ran towards the teleportal followed by Emfalmay. As soon as he crossed the rift his root supports began to systematically rot and collapse. The Eldre pushed his energy level one last time to compensate.

"Wait, what do you mean *goodbye*?" asked Turu, turning back. Yaku was at his side. Kucha was on the other.

"Come on, Eldre. Let's go," said Kucha.

"It is okay, my son."

"What do you mean it's okay?" asked Kucha.

"Everything is going to be okay, Kucha." The Eldre smiled. "If I let go of the roof, everyone will die. My energy is almost depleted, my boy. You should get going. My fate is written, but yours is not."

"I'll help y—"

"Enough, Kucha. Take your brother and sister and lead the rest out of here. They need you. My time in Earth Realm is at its end. Goodbye, my children."

The wall of water formed in front of them, blocking the view of Tuguna the Eldre from Thomas and the rest of the companions.

"You heard him, Kucha. It's time to go," said Thomas.

"Go where?" asked Kucha.

"Through there," said Thomas.

The three Turtles walked through the tear as the level began to collapse in on itself. Bartleby jumped through as well, leaving only the Bearer and the Eldre. Thomas looked back one last time and the water wall opened, revealing the Eldre.

"I never did get to deliver you that prophecy," said the Eldre.

"No, I guess you didn't."

The two exchanged laughs.

"Take care of them, Thomas. They are all I have left."

"I will, Eldre."

"And Thomas remember, in the darkest of times, you will need to be their light. Be the water, my boy."

"I know. Eldre. I will."

"My time swiftly approaches, Thomas," said Tuguna. "Goodbye, Bearer. It was truly an honor."

"Goodbye, Tuguna."

The Eldre's eyes ceased glowing as his spirit rose out of his body through the churning liquid. Tuguna the Eldre had sacrificed himself to save the others. The water began crashing down as Thomas jumped through the teleportal.

57

broken silence

Thomas splashed through the other end of the teleportal, landing in a puddle of water in front of his friends. He had teleported to what looked like one of the main entrances to Huacas. Yareli ran over to him and hugged him.

"I'm so sorry, Yar." She began to cry in his arms. Thomas looked around at the aftermath of the battle. Artif parts mingled with the still smoldering bodies of fallen lava trolls. Massive tech suits sparked with electricity. Their Skinx pilots lay still in their cockpits. *These guys must have had their hands full*, thought Thomas. *We're not the only ones with casualties today.*

Larson dropped his son's scorched body to the ground. Talya walked towards him.

"Do you need help?" asked Talya. Larson stared at her for what seemed like an eternity.

"Talya Grenfald."

"That's me," said Talya. "Are you okay?"

"I've never been better," said Larson. "You know, you have your mother's eyes, and nose, and actually her entire face."

"I'm not sure I understand," said Talya. "Did you know my mother?"

"As well as anyone ever could know another," said Larson. "My friends, the Grenfalds, must have adopted you when you were still an egg. I imagine they couldn't afford to take you both in, but they were always such good dragons."

"Adopted? I'm not following you."

"I saw you in my visions of Thomas. I was fairly certain you were my daughter. You look just like Ilyana—a shade darker, mind you, but a spitting image, nonetheless."

"But I wasn't adopted."

"I would have to disagree," said Loric. "I can say, without a shadow of a doubt, from facial indicators and markings that you are, in fact, related to Larson Ragnor. And from my extensive research on the Ragnor family and from pictures I have seen of Ilyana Ragnor, I would deduce that you are in fact their biological daughter."

Talya looked puzzled but then tilted her head. "How can you be so sure?"

"You look just like her, my dear," said Larson. "It's the only explanation."

"You're my biological father?"

"It appears so, Talya."

"And he's my brother?" She pointed down at the body of Brax.

"I'm afraid so," said Larson. "Can't win them all, now can we?"

"Wow," said Talya. She fell backwards into a sitting position. "This is going to take a while to get used to. My parents have been dead for some time now, and to hear this, well, it's a lot."

"I understand, my dear," said Larson. "Take all the time you need. I'm not going anywhere."

"Let me get dis straight," said Bartleby. "One Ragnor just betrayed us in 'opes uv recoverin' the Medenculus. Anuvver Ragnor, who had previously maimed me for life, saved my life. And last, but certainly not bloody least, is dat I'm datin' 'is bloody daughter."

"I don't know if I'd say we are dating," said Talya. She smiled at him.

"Don't you start," said Bartleby.

Malcolm looked around the group. "Where is old foxy at anyway?" he asked. "I want to fank him for saving my arse earlier when dose two drones 'ad me dead to rights back in Dallas."

Thomas looked over at the vampire and shook his head. The look on the pale vampire's face meant he understood.

"Oh, no. I-I-I'm sorry, Yar. Really I am. I-I-I-I didn't know. I can't believe . . . what I mean to say is . . . oh bollocks."

Yareli tucked her head under Thomas's shoulder and began to sob. "I am so glad you're still alive, Thomas."

"I was just thinking the same thing about you, Yar."

Thomas looked back towards Huacas, and that is when he saw it.

A purple spirit emerged from the rocks that covered the entrance and merged into the Ancestor Stone. Thomas was convinced that it was the spirit of the Eldre, joining the Ancestors.

Yaku ran over to the stone and touched it. The energy poured into the young Sea Turtle. She appeared to be getting electrocuted by the stones power. Thomas moved to pry her away, but she raised her flipper, signaling to Thomas to stop. Yaku began to levitate as purple energy rippled around her. The Sea Turtle turned and looked Thomas Scargen directly in the eyes. The young Yaku's stare was gone, replaced with a wiser, older set of eyes. Her eyes began to glow. Yaku opened her mouth and spoke for the first time ever:

> *"Spilt blood of thy enemy who once was brethren,*
> *Will usher in darkness, through souls of lost men.*
> *Three keys will be needed to bring forth this end.*
> *The first one is found in the opener's kin.*
> *The second one bound to the broken demon.*
> *The third one resounds in the dragon within.*
> *Lost Gauntlet stone from shadowed waters ascend*
> *To heal mortal wounds thought impossible to mend*
> *Once friend becomes foe, foes once come befriend.*
> *The fate of all Realms on the Bearer depend."*

Everyone was quiet for a few seconds afterward.

"What was that?" asked Thomas.

"If I had to wager, Scargen, I'd say it is the prophecy you were promised," said Loric. "And it appears we just got our new Eldre."

"I got that much, but what does any of it mean?"

"I will have to get back to you on that one, my boy," said Ziza. "We have all been through quite a lot for one day. It is time we got back to Sirati. You three are invited to stay with us." The comment was directed at Turu, Kucha, and Yaku. "We could use the help."

"The Ancestors will it," said Yaku. "We will need to bring the stone as well. Are the Salamen welcome?"

"We have plenty of room, and everyone will be safe if they choose to join us," said Ziza. "We can also help you to rebuild here."

"It is settled then," said Yaku as she moved over to the entrance. She created an energy sphere that moved over to the stone wall and washed across it, leaving markings.

"What is it?" asked Thomas.

"It is a message for the others that we will be back to rebuild and to ferry those we need back and forth from Sirati."

"Will you be joining us Mr. Ragnor?" asked Ziza.

"I will if you will have me, and it's all right with Bartleby. I'd like to get to know my daughter."

"You can do what you like. I'm not your mum, or nuffin'. What do we do wif 'im?" He pointed to Brax's unconscious body.

"He will answer for his crimes," said Larson. "He will go to the Dragon Council and face the Tribunal. And if you so choose, I too will admit to my wrongdoings to the Council."

"I fink you've been frew enough," said Bartleby. "Dere's no need to stir up old wounds, is dere?"

"Thank you, Bart. That means a lot coming from you."

"Please don't go on about it. Once we drop off dese guys back in Sirati, we will take your son to the Council."

"Let's pop off, then," said Larson. He reached down and scooped up his son.

The companions divided up between the different modes of transportation. Bartleby flew into the sky and tore open a teleportal. All crossed through the rift.

58

the demon awakes

Teros appeared outside of the hull of the Dred. Marcus was attached to the aringi's underbelly, holding the General in one arm and the Axe in his other. The bay door opened up. Teros flew in and attached himself upside down as Marcus released himself from the aringi. He placed the Axe on his back as he helped Evangeline to stand.

"Are you okay?" asked Marcus.

"Yes, Captain. I am fine. I did not need you to interrupt back there . . . but thanks. The old guy is a lot more powerful than he looks."

"He's the High Mancer, what did you expect?"

"Point taken."

The imp servant ran up to the two Riders.

"Lord Grimm requests your presence in engineering," said Corbin.

Marcus had heard some things in the last few hours that opened up some questions that he needed answered. They followed Corbin as he waddled across the floor.

They entered engineering. Grimm was on the top platform that overlooked a complex series of tech connected to the tank containing the still-comatose Arkmalis.

They must have moved him here from the infirmary, but why?

thought Marcus. The Captain moved to Lord Grimm, extending the Axe out to him.

"I retrieved the weapon, as per your request, my Lord."

"Good news, Marcus. I imagine the Atlantean was a bit surprised by your arrival. Your skills are advanced if you bested him."

Marcus wondered how he knew any of this.

"If you do not mind holding on to it for a few more minutes," continued Grimm. "I have some good news as well. I too have successfully completed my mission."

Marcus placed the Axe onto his back. Marcus was happy to hold onto the Artifact for more time, even if it was temporary. The Axe had awakened an energy level in him he had not previously known he could achieve.

"But first Marcus, can I have a word?"

"Yes, of course, my Lord."

The two men moved away from Evangeline and Corbin. Marcus noticed Farod and Taunt on the lower level. Taunt was working on the tech, while Farod seemed to be checking Arkmalis's vitals.

"Marcus, two times now, I have asked you to do impossible tasks, and you have completed them with flying colors."

"Thank you, my Lord. I was just following orders." He wanted to ask him about the demon and about Evangeline but something stopped him.

"Difficult orders, to say the least. I have also noticed the level of caring you have for General Evangeline."

"My Lord, I—"

"Hear me out, Captain. I commend your service in the Legions. You have always been one of my finest men, and I am not trying to stifle this caring. Quite the opposite really. I too have taken an interest in Evangeline—a teacher-pupil type of interest, I assure you, but one where I also care greatly about her well-being. I would hate to see anything unfortunate befall her."

"I agree, my Lord."

"We are at war, Marcus. We will no longer hide because we are different." He paused. "She will be tested, and often placed into mortal danger. I cannot always be there to protect her . . . but you could be."

"I suppose I could."

"Good it is settled then. Effective immediately, you are the head of the General's Guard."

"But what about the Riders?"

"They will still answer to you, but the Second will take over everyday duties." He put his hand on Marcus's shoulder. "I can feel what the Axe has done to you. No one else can do this. I need you to help protect her."

"Yes, my Lord." He turned and moved back towards Evangeline and Corbin.

"Great news. Now, back to why I called you down here. Our mission was also successful today."

"Securing the Medenculus?" asked Evangeline.

"No, my dear. We no longer have that stone."

"What do you mean? Where is the blue stone?" asked Evangeline.

"I traded it for something much more valuable." He pointed to the Ancestor Stone that the artifs were maneuvering into place. The Ancestor Stone glowed the blue color of the Medenculus.

"I don't understand. All that planning, all the Riders that gave their lives."

"All necessary, my dear. I assure you. I did not come back empty-handed. This simple carved rock is much more than it seems."

"Yes, my Lord."

Lord Grimm moved in front of the large artifs that carried the Ancestor Stone. "Place the stone here," said Grimm.

Marcus, Evangeline, and Grimm stood on the raised platform above the tank that held Arkmalis. Evangeline followed him over to the edge of the railing.

"Come now, Captain. You need a good seat for the show." Marcus reluctantly moved over next to them. The artifs shifted the massive carved stone where Grimm had instructed. He waved a few keys on the holographic interface, and the base below the Ancestor Stone clamped down around the bottom of the glowing stone. "Everything seems to be in order." Grimm again moved his hands across the holographic interface in front of him. "Is he ready?"

"Taunt and I have done everything according to your specs, but I must admit, I still do not fully understand what this machine does," said Gamil Farod as he stood on the downside of the platform in front of the dark tank.

"That makes two of us," said Taunt. "I can tell its some sort of energy manipulation, but the energy source is unknown to me."

"You are not required to understand my plans, just follow them. Have you done what I have asked?"

"On paper we look good, but we won't know until we start it up, my Lord."

"Begin the transference," said Grimm.

Farod moved his hand across the interface. The power in the room dimmed for a second as sparks flew from the Ancestor Stone, which had been plugged into the machine. Soon the blue energy began to move from the stone and into the tech that traveled in both directions up from the platform and down into the tank. The blue glow hit Arkmalis's body like a bolt of lightning, making him convulse uncontrollably as the breather inside his mouth and the other monitoring devices detached from his shaking form.

The dark liquid slowly began to glow blue as the energy from the stone continued through the circuit that Farod and Taunt had constructed from Grimm's plans. The Ancestor Stone began to lose its brilliant glow and slowly faded to its original white color. The last of the energy rushed into the tank. The room went dark. The lights flickered a few times, but then returned to their normal dim state.

Grimm was no longer between Evangeline and Marcus. He was standing in front of the tank. The blue glow circled the lifeless body of Grayden Arkmalis and then went inside of the hulking man.

The tank shattered without warning as the blue glow erupted outward. A scream penetrated throughout the infirmary—one word could be heard.

"Scargen!" yelled Arkmalis. The General had awakened. His massive form rippled with energy. The blue glow emanated from his eyes and through his tattoos. His energy level once again jumped as he again shouted. "Scargen!" His energy began to internalize once again. He walked out of the tank and towards Grimm. "Where is the Scargen boy?" He stumbled and fell. Grimm caught his body.

"In due time, my child. You have been away for quite some time. A lot has happened. Your body needs time to heal."

"Yes, my Lord. How long have I been gone?"

"Over a year. The Medenculus's energy has revived you, but it will take more than that for you to regain your full strength."

"Scargen," said Arkmalis.

"I understand, my boy, but there will be plenty of time for vengeance."

"Why are my markings blue?"

"It is a temporary effect of the transference. One I will deal with shortly, I assure you. There are other matters to attend to."

Grimm returned to the top tier of the engineering room and approached the Ancestor Stone. Arkmalis accompanied Grimm as medibots attended to him. He swatted the first few away.

"Let them look at you, Grayden. We have to be sure that the Medenculus healed you properly."

"I don't understand," said Evangeline. "You said you traded the Medenculus."

"I did. To the Scargen boy."

"What?" asked Arkmalis.

"If not for him, Grayden, you would still be very much incapacitated."

"You gave him the Medenculus?" asked Evangeline.

"Yes. He needed it to charge this beautiful stone with his healing energy."

"You handed our most powerful enemy the Medenculus and facilitated its augmentation?" asked Evangeline.

"Are you questioning my decisions?"

"No, my Lord. I am just confused."

"It was a necessary evil. It was the only way to revive my fallen son. But as I said before, Evangeline. I did not leave empty-handed."

He pulled the red stone from the folds in his robes. Grimm held the Ignus in his hand.

"I don't understand," said Evangeline.

"An old friend of ours went to great lengths to procure this. Scargen needed to have the Medenculus inside the Gauntlet to provide enough healing energy to revive Arkmalis. I left our friend to deal with the Bearer, and I promised the Medenculus would be his once he destroyed the Scargen boy. An effort, I'm afraid, that was doomed from the start. He, I believe, has bitten off more than he can chew. It might be in our best interests to keep the boy alive anyway."

The red rock flew over and into the Ancestor Stone. The stone began to absorb the power from the Ignus, recharging itself with red energy.

"You see, blue may heal, but red is sheer, unadulterated power."

The ships systems all came back online at once.

"We now have an unlimited power source at our disposal."

"Amazing," said Marcus.

"Oh there's more. If you would be so kind, Marcus."

The Captain lifted the Axe off of his back and held it out. The shaft snapped into Grimm's hands from across the room. The Ignus flew back out of the Ancestor Stone and into Grimm's other hand.

"I believe its time these two reunited."

Lord Grimm slammed the Ignus into the carved hole on the Axe, returning the red stone to the place it had once resided for centuries. The weapon glowed red with ferocious power. Grimm held it as he laughed.

"The power of this weapon is great. There is no denying that, but it is still no match for the dark power that flows through my Scythe. No, this Axe deserves a different wielder than I." He turned towards Evangeline who held out her hand. "This is not for you, my dear. You are not in need of such things. Your power comes from a far darker, more dangerous place. Your mind is your weapon."

He turned around to Arkmalis. The medibots still flitted back and forth around his gigantic form. "This should help speed your recovery."

He sent the Axe flying at Arkmalis, who caught it in his right hand. The energy from the Axe began to circulate from the handle and through Arkmalis's body, changing the blue Light to red.

"The family reunion is almost complete. Now my plan can proceed. But first, there is the matter of a lost dragon."

59

spirited away

"Feel your feet against the ground, my boy," said Ziza.

Thomas stood across from him barefoot. They had picked a spot just outside of Maktaba to train. After the events in Huacas, Ziza had decided it was time for Thomas to learn phytomancy, but it was not going well.

"Imagine your legs are trunks—solid and unwavering."

Thomas moved to solidify his stance.

"Good . . . now, dig your toes into the ground like the roots of a tree."

Thomas did as the High Mancer asked.

"Focus on the roots and talk to the tree, Thomas. Commune with it."

Thomas tried as hard as he could to focus on the baobab and its roots. He had been at it for a few hours with little result.

"Remember, you are not trying to tear the tree apart. You are directing new growth. You are asking the tree to accept your power and help it to adjust itself. Feel the branches and move them."

He concentrated once more and pushed his power. A leaf sprouted from a central branch.

"A good start," said Ziza.

Thomas powered down. "I beg to differ."

"You just have to spread your energy through the tree."

"Is that how you wield the roots and vines?"

"Yes. It is similar. The roots allow me to control them and their growth. There is a mutual trust."

"Okay. Ask the tree to let me help it grow. Simple enough."

"There is nothing simple about phytomancy. Asking the Earth and its children to cooperate is as difficult as it gets. Now let us try one more time."

"Can I ask you a question first?"

"Is this really the time?"

"It's just that you told me you would tell me what happened to create the Fires of Sorrow, and you still haven't, and we still haven't talked about Tollin Grimm being your First Augmentor or the Prophecy."

"I suppose you are right. We do have a lot to discuss."

Now we are getting somewhere, thought Thomas.

"I had been out collecting flowers for Alana when I felt the power surge. I followed my senses to find the origin of the energy, but I could never have been prepared for what I found. She was lying there in the middle of the woods. She was not dead yet, but she was close."

"Who?"

"Alana, Thomas. This was the day that Tollin had found out about us."

"Oh no," said Thomas. "I-I-I didn't know."

"It is okay, my boy. It is about time I trusted my secret with someone. I found her there, and I was scared I would lose her. I did everything I could to heal her, but as you know, I did not have the Medenculus. If I had, it could have been a different story. I harnessed all of my power and tried one last time, but I was foolish. In my haste I disregarded that Sirati borders a nexus of sorts. The most magical places in the world are almost always crossing points of the three Realms. My power not only eradicated all of the trees and vegetation in a kilometer radius, but also awakened the spirits and demons of the woods who resided there. I had accidentally opened a hole to the Depths. That is when the louhi appeared and possessed Alana."

"That demon is Alana?"

"No, Thomas. After a long battle I was able to separate the two, but Alana's spirit was lost in the Dark Realm. I could not close the doorway into the Depths, so I did the next best thing, I sealed it with the louhi's power and posted the warning. Lolani summoned the fire spirits around the seal to further safeguard the doorway, and Neficus helped me to harness the demon's energy. Your energy level must have reawakened the demon."

"I didn't know," said Thomas.

"I know, my boy, I know. How could you know?"

"So Grimm was your First Augmentor."

"Yes, Thomas. He was my best friend for quite some time, and he was the one who started my time as the Bearer."

"I am so sorry, High Mancer."

"There is nothing you need to be sorry about. That is a part of life. We win sometimes, and other times we lose. We love and we lose. You just have to remember that, and never leave any opportunity behind. I do not regret the time I had with Alana, nor my friendship with Tollin. I would be entirely different without both of them, and I am fond of who I am."

"I am too." The two laughed.

"Just remember that love is a thing that is fleeting, and, when you see it, it is your duty to grab on to it, and experience it for as long as you can."

Thomas thought about Ziza's words. He thought about his future.

"And what about the Prophecy?" asked Thomas.

"Anson and Loric have been working on it since the recitation. They have a few theories, but neither of them are certain what it all means."

"What are their theories?" asked Thomas. He was eager to hear some idea of what lay in his future.

"It appears that will have to wait for another time."

"Why, High Mancer?"

"Someone would like to steal you away, it seems."

Thomas turned around. Yareli stood behind him, leaning on a tree.

"It is good to see you out and about, my dear," said Ziza.

"Hello, High Mancer," said Yareli.

"Hello, my child. I trust you are feeling better."

"Much. Thanks for asking."

"Hey, Yar," said Thomas.

"Hey," said Yareli.

She had chopped off most of her hair. It was just above shoulder length. She was not wearing the type of clothing that Thomas had grown accustomed to. Yareli wore a blue tank top with black pants and high black boots. She looked so different, but still quite beautiful. Yareli had taken the death of Wiyaloo hard, and she had not left her apartment in quite some time. For a while, Thomas had visited her daily, but a few days ago she had asked for some time alone. They had still not talked about what transpired in Huacas or about Wiyaloo.

"You want to take a walk with me?"

"Sure, if its okay with him," said Thomas.

"Our lesson has been completed for today," said Ziza.

"I guess that's a yes," said Thomas as he hastily put his boots back on.

"Just remember what I said," said Ziza. "Experience it. You kids have fun."

Thomas looked back at the High Mancer as he smiled.

"Come on," said Yareli. "I want to show you something."

She held his hand as they walked through the jungle. Tiny raindrops fell from the sky, bouncing from one leaf to another. The rhythmic sound was soothing. They were going somewhere special to Yareli. Thomas did not know any more than that. She had shown up unannounced, requesting his company.

"You okay?" asked Thomas.

"Yeah, I guess. I just wanted to go out for a bit. I've been thinking a lot and there's something I need to show you . . . well, I want to show you."

"Looks like someone gave herself a little makeover," said Thomas.

"I thought it was time for a change."

"I suppose." Thomas paused for a second. "It suits you."

"Thank you, Thomas. I appreciate that." She looked him directly in the eyes. "I just wanted to feel in control of something."

"I know the feeling," said Thomas.

"I just wasn't ready to let go of him yet," said Yareli.

"He was pretty narsh," said Thomas.

"Yes, he was completely narsh."

"I'd like to say that it gets easier, but I'd be lying. If you're lucky, you'll get to a point where it doesn't bother you all the time."

"I can't wait for that."

"There's something sad about when it happens. It's like they're actually gone. My mom died seventeen years ago, and every day that goes by I am reminded of the sacrifice she made for me—for all of us. And my dad . . . I haven't really had time to comprehend what happened with my father and Grimm, let alone come to terms with the fact that he knew all about this world and kept it from me."

"He was trying to protect you, Thomas. Like Wiyaloo did for me."

"Wiyaloo paid back his debt."

"I guess you're right, but it doesn't stop the empty feeling."

"That gets slightly better with time . . . slightly." Thomas paused. "But it's always going to hurt, Yar. But that hurt has to count for something. Wiyaloo left this world knowing you could carry on and make a difference. He believed that. I believe that."

She looked away from him at that moment.

"He told me it wasn't your idea."

"What?"

"Wiyaloo told me, right before he left us. I can remember it now." She let go of his hand and moved up through the brush.

"It wasn't my idea, but I don't want to think of what would've happened if Wiyaloo hadn't saved you," said Thomas as he followed her into the clearing.

In the center of the clearing was an old, dead tree. It must have been impressive when it was alive. Branches swirled and twisted off of its sizable trunk. Yareli knelt and sat cross-legged in front of the tree. She motioned for Thomas to join her. He sat across from her, cross-legged, and close enough so they could touch.

"Okay. So, close your eyes. Begin to feel your breath move with the wind."

Thomas could feel the breeze and its currents.

"Feel the Earth's breath . . . inward and outward, and begin to breathe with it. Breathing awakens your spirit and helps to clear your mind of distractions."

"Like the spirit walk?" asked Thomas.

"Exactly like that."

Thomas concentrated on Yareli's words. Seconds melted into minutes—minutes into hours. He felt as though he were floating and that time was standing still. He felt her reach out her hands and touch his, and he opened his eyes.

Thomas looked out across a foreign landscape. Several floating islands stretched out in front of them. Strange, vibrant-colored plants grew on each island, including the one that they stood on. The farthest island in front of them was bigger than the others and covered in abundant vegetation and trees.

"Where are we?" asked Thomas.

"We are in the Spirit Realm."

"Narsh," said Thomas, still taking in the beauty and strangeness of his surroundings. "But how?"

"That is . . . complicated. Let's just say, you used me to travel here." She looked over at him and let go of his hand. She ran to the edge of the island they were standing on and jumped to the next one. "Come on!"

"Okay," said Thomas as he followed Yareli.

She leapt from island to island as Thomas pursued. He knew what her destination was—the final island in the floating archipelago.

Once she reached the lush island Yareli waited for Thomas to catch up. She held out her hand again, and he grabbed it.

"It's close."

"I hope so," said Thomas as he looked down from the island into an abyss.

Yareli ran forward with Thomas's hand in hers, jerking him in her direction. She sped through the jungle along with Thomas until they reached a clearing. In the center of the clearing was the tree they were meditating in front of in Maktaba, but it was different. The tree was full of life and covered in leaves and vines, and it glowed white. Several luminescent creatures walked by and floated around the radiant tree. They seemed familiar yet alien at the same time. *Spirits.*

Yareli ran to the tree and hugged it. "This is what I wanted to show you, Thomas. This is my spirit tree."

"When you say *your* spirit tree, what exactly do you mean by that?"

"It is the tree that allows me to make spirit arrows—the one Wiyaloo found for me."

"Narsh," said Thomas. He did not know what else to say. She had let him see a side to her that he had never known. He felt honored and privileged. Thomas moved next to her by the tree.

"It's amazing, Yar. How do you ever leave?"

"That's a good question."

The two shared a small laugh. Thomas turned towards Yareli.

"You know he's out there," said Thomas.

"How are you so certain?" asked Yareli.

"It's Wiyaloo, that's why. I don't know. I just have a feeling, I guess."

"I cannot feel his spirit anymore. I have tried everything, but he's gone." She started to tear up. "We are no longer connected."

Thomas paused for a second and looked Yareli in the eye.

"That's where you're wrong, Yar. You will always be connected." He pointed to her heart. "His spirit is where it always has been. In there."

She reached over and kissed him on the head. "When did you grow up so much?"

"Since I met you, I suppose." The two laughed. "I guess things do happen for a reason."

Yareli stood up and reached out her hand. "Come on."

Thomas grabbed her hand, and she helped him up. He felt instantly happy, even in this dark moment.

"Where are we going?" asked the Bearer.

"Home."

dramatis personae

the dragon within

general grayden arkmalis	General of the Grimm Legion
captain nevin cox	Captain of the Aringi Riders
dalco jakobsen	an Aringi Rider
richard sumner	an Aringi Rider
vaw the viscerator	a demon
captain marcus slade	Captain of the Aringi Riders
nolan taunt	an Aringi Rider
gamil farod	an Aringi Rider
evangeline the second	an Aringi Rider
corbin	an imp servant
gigbot	a lava troll guard
fronik	a lava troll guard
lord tollin grimm	a Necromancer
malcolm warwick	a vampire Mage
anson warwick	a werewolf Mage
yareli chula	a Spirit Summoner
wiyaloo	a Spirit Ghost Warrior
garron dar	the Eldre Guard
turu	a disciple of the Eldre
yaku	a disciple of the Eldre
kucha	a disciple of the Eldre
tuguna	the Eldre
thomas scargen	the Gauntlet Bearer
itsuki katsuo	the First Augmentor
mason greer	a guide
booker spells	a Repository of Magic
loric bodes	a Mancer

samuel janik	a bar owner
fargus hexelby	a gremlin technic
webster	a dragon's dog
ELAIN	a holographic interface
lenore bugden	a gremlin
ronald hosselfot	a tech dealer
LINC	an artif
sinclair	a bartender
onjamba	a chef and historian
ziza bebami	the High Mancer
kekoa lolani	a Mancer
elgin neficus	a Mancer
emfalmay	a Mage Knight
flora	a librarian
emkoo	a Sentry Mage
stella	a cat
brett jurdik	an Aringi Rider
herman porf	an Aringi Rider
james neal	an Aringi Rider
harl vance	an Aringi Rider
merelda scargen	a former Bearer
alican dod	a former Bearer
katar kist	an Aringi Rider
alan jett	an Aringi Rider
sabul	a sand troll guard
mikus chard	an Incendias
gor yan	a Dracavea
oramus nizam	the Master of Syn
baramus nizam	a Fimus
mukt	a jinn
valv tinger	a gremlin
aiken gloop	a gremlin

torc barwin	a gremlin
talya grenfald	a teleport dragon
snigwig	an Urchin
madame ling	a store owner
cayde galeos	an Atlantean Sovereign
vedd delphin	an Atlantean Guard
og	the first Gauntlet Bearer
oash	an Ancient Mage
gayan	an Ancient Mage
narg	an Ancient Mage
pyre	an Ancient Mage
denk	an Ancient Mage
lyth	an Ancient Mage
kala	an Ancient Mage
astra	an Ancient Mage
tok-ah	the Darkness
skath	a dragon of Drook
kyle gordon	a Network director
dr. irene benet	the VP of Scargen Robotics
gideon upshaw	the CEO of Scargen Robotics
thatcher wikkaden	a Hunter
pekora	a Hunter
okland	a Hunter
jusip tad	an Atlantean
larson ragnor	a teleport dragon

acknowledgments

I would like to thank. . .

My Kickstarter backers—you guys again made this possible

All the fans—you are why we do this

Richard Sumner—the best carnival barker in the business

Mason Caracciolo—for the accommodations and years of geeking out

Joe Hansche—for still being particular

Nella—my little partner in crime; thanks for staying up late with me

Shanna Compton—for saving my ass yet again; your work is phenomenal

Christine—the best editor and wife anyone could ask for, and somehow I got both

about the author

casey caracciolo

photo by Art Gentile

Casey Caracciolo has been creating worlds and characters since he was a child. Casey is a lover of all things geek, and this comes through in his storytelling. In 2007, Caracciolo began developing the concept of the Scargen series. In this series, Caracciolo wanted to create a world that seamlessly blended magic and futuristic technology. This world serves as the backdrop for the coming-of-age adventures of Thomas Scargen. *The Shadow of the Gauntlet* was Caracciolo's first novel and was published in 2013 by Roundstone Publishing. *The Dragon Within* is the second book in the series, and is Caracciolo's second book, published in 2015 by Roundstone Publishing. He is currently working on *The Broken Demon*, the third book in the Scargen series.

When not writing, Casey is a bartender at Triumph Brewery in New Hope, Pennsylvania. He lives in Lambertville, New Jersey, with his wife, Christine, and their cat, Nella.

To learn more about Casey or the Scargen universe, visit:

scargen.com

the adventure continues in

the broken demon

scargen: book 3

Made in the USA
Charleston, SC
11 August 2016